the LOUDNESS

the LOUDNESS

A Novel

Nick Courage

Sky Pony Press
New York

Sky Pony Press books may be purchased in bulk at special discounts for sales
promotion, corporate gifts, fund-raising, or educational purposes. Special edi-
tions can also be created to specifications. For details, contact the Special Sales
Department, Sky Pony Press, 307 West 36th Street, 11th Floor, New York,
NY 10018 or info@skyhorsepublishing.com.

Sky Pony® is a registered trademark of Skyhorse Publishing, Inc.®, a Delaware
corporation.

Visit our website at www.skyponypress.com.

10 9 8 7 6 5 4 3 2 1

Library of Congress Cataloging-in-Publication Data is available on file.

Cover design by Rain Saukas

Print ISBN: 978-1-63220-414-1
Ebook ISBN: 978-1-63220-937-5

Printed in the United States of America

For Rachel

One million very sincere thanks to Rachel Ekstrom Courage, Pamela van Hylckama Vlieg, Lilly Golden, and Sky Pony Press, without whom this book would not exist. Thanks also to Adrienne Petrosini, Rich and Sandy Ekstrom, and the Henrys, for their support. Thanks to Joe Yoga and Coach (the band) for "Big Dumb River." Thank you to Matt and Amy Rose-Perkins for introducing me to the joys of weekly comics. Bat Matthews, Scott Davis, Justin "Big Hugs" Hargett, Thom Merrick, Mark Fullmer, and everyone who prefers their guitars just slightly out of tune, thank you.

*H*enry Long doesn't have a heart.

I remind myself of this while the doctor rearranges the thermometer, poking it into the soft underside of my tongue. You'd think I'd be used to it by now, but I hate the Hospital. Hate it even more now because this isn't one of my scheduled visits. I try not to gag, unsuccessfully, as the slick glass gauge slips back out of my mouth.

"Just one more minute," the doctor sighs, flipping her hair in frustration as she needles it under my tongue for the third time. My parents are sitting opposite me, looking nervous, and I want to tell them to stop acting like someone's died . . . but I *do* feel like death, and the last thing I need is for the doctor to have to rearrange the thermometer again.

The thermometer.

Just thinking about it starts me gagging again. I try to stop, but I can't help myself; before I know it I'm arching my back, convulsing like a cat with a hairball. It's only after I'm able to swallow down the acrid taste of aluminum that I notice my parents whispering worried questions to the doctor, who seems to be just half-listening to them as she raises one skeptical eyebrow at me. I give her a feeble thumbs up, smiling weakly through my locked jaws despite a splitting headache, which is how I ended up here in the first place.

To distract myself, I soundlessly repeat the same phrase over and over again. It helps remind me why I have to put up with all of this; why I can't just take an aspirin and be done with it like a normal kid.

Henry Long doesn't have a heart.

Not a real one, anyway, which is why I have to get a full medical checkup every time I so much as sneeze. But the funny thing about the Hospital—the reason I hate it so much—is that I always feel worse leaving it than I do coming in.

I was born a year after the first of the Tragedies struck. I was a little colicky in those early days, but the doctors assured my parents it would pass, so they brought me home from the Hospital to the old house with a clean bill of health. By month three of constant mewling, my parents were at the ends of their ropes. They say my silent sobbing toward the end was the hardest to bear, that I didn't even have the energy to cry out loud.

When I was finally diagnosed, the muscles that kept my heart pumping had atrophied in my chest. There wasn't much to do in the way of rehabilitation. Unfortunately, the city was even worse off when I was born than it is now—and the Hospital was no exception, so I ended up with a science fair electromagnet humming in my chest. "It pumps the blood," the doctor had told my parents by way of simple explanation, a hint of apology in her voice.

My body's normalized to it now. But it's no normal heart.

"So much *drama*, Shakespeare," the doctor says, finally relieving me of the thermometer. I take a deep breath and stretch my tongue. "Ninety-eight point six."

She turns back to my parents, consulting the chart. "Everything seems to be normal. Temperature is fine, ticker's fine, EKG is normal." She looks at me and adds, "For Henry."

I cough in response, which sets me off gagging again.

"You seem a little nauseous, though. Eating much?"

Mom starts defending my appetite, and I nod in agreement, tuning out. The gyroscope I have whirring in my chest is a pain, but not because it hurts or doesn't work. There are just . . . other complications. "Side effects," my parents call them, trying to make my electrical problems seem less strange.

"Abdominal pain?" The doctor massages my stomach and I squirm, laughing despite myself. The exertion is too much, and everything goes black for a second—with white spots. Temporarily blinded, I hear the doctor efficiently check another box on her chart and turn to my parents. "Is Henry experiencing any stress?"

I blink the darkness from my eyes in time to see Dad cringing at Mom, who's looking sympathetically at me. Maybe it's their reaction, but I can't help myself; even though it's been years, I flash back to the Tragedies, one of the first ones I can remember. Boarded-up windows and streets like rivers with half-submerged cars for cataracts. The rush to escape and then the waiting, the listening past the static of the radio for good news and the bad news that came instead. The drive home to no home. Walls and roofs spray painted with calls for help. The olive-colored army caravans, the guns; my four-year-old heart, cold in my chest.

I remember to breathe, then shake my aching head.

"I, uh . . . I don't have a phone," I say, which is true. One more complication of the whole not-having-a-real-heart thing—what I have instead interferes with the signal, a quote, *minor side effect*, end quote. I know what it sounds like, but the last Tragedy was years ago, and I was complaining about not being able to call Conor just the other week. Which wasn't stressful, really.

Just not fair.

I *have* recently acquired a real-life record collection, though, which would have made up for the whole no-phone thing—except that I'd wanted to call Conor to tell him about it. It started with some boxes I found while I was rooting through our Salvage Bags in the attic a few days ago. At first I thought they were just a bunch of faded old posters and had asked Dad what he was doing with pictures of all those freshly shaved men, red-cheeked and smiling with trumpets or whatever cradled in their arms, half-hoping he was one of them.

"That's a clarinet, son," Dad said when I showed him, absentmindedly tracing one of the pictures with a finger and then suddenly shaking a large black disc from within. He carefully held it up to the light, scrutinizing, and blew phantom dust from its surface. "These were even antiques Before," he'd said, his voice catching on the memory. "Thing of the past now, but I think it'll still play . . ."

Later that night, I'd asked my parents if we should donate them to a museum or something, and that got Dad wondering how much the records were worth, anyway. I didn't have the heart to tell them my punch line: "No, I mean—should we donate *you two* to a museum."

I ended up tacking a few of the cooler-looking records to my wall, incorporating them into the already jumbled ecosystem of my room. After the headaches started, they were the last thing I remember seeing before the darkness descended.

⚡ ⚡ ⚡

The doctor frowns and assures my parents that everything's normal heart-wise, that "not having a phone doesn't typically qualify as a stress-inducer."

"What about the blackout?" Mom asks, not convinced that I'm in the clear.

"Probably a migraine," the doctor says with finality, signing and inserting my most recent chart into my voluminous files. "You'll want to give him these for the pain," she says, handing Dad an envelope of aspirin. "And keep him in a cool, dark place."

She's talking about me like I'm a bottle of milk, and even though it's painful, I laugh. She arches her eyebrow again, and I look quietly down at my lap instead of meeting her sharp gaze.

"Well," says Mom, not sounding very confident, "I guess that's good, then." She hands the doctor a small stack of scrip, and the doctor makes a show of not counting it, tucking it immediately away in the breast pocket of her crisp white jacket. It feels like my stupid plastic heart is pounding in my skull, beating arrhythmically against the back of my eyes, and I hope she's right about me being okay.

Before long I'm back in my bed, medicated and trying to ignore the pulsing in my head long enough to fall asleep. It's still light outside, and the late-afternoon sun is trapped in my suffocating greenhouse of a room. I kick off the sheets, sweaty, and focus on the collage of records on my wall, trying to imagine what they sound like.

But it's no use; all I can hear is my own hot blood pumping impatiently behind my eyes.

The next morning, I wake up to the muffled ringing of my alarm clock, not remembering having fallen asleep. Dad's records are the first things I see as I lift my sleep-heavy but otherwise clear head up from my well-worn pillow. I say a quiet thanks for the clarity, not quite relishing the insistent bleating of the alarm in my closet . . . but not minding it either. I let the alarm ring until I barely even notice it anymore, too comfortable to get out of bed. Dad knocks twice on the door, and without waiting for an answer makes his way over to the closet.

Most of my electrical stuff is in the closet. It's not the best feng shui, which Mom's obsessed with—something about spiritual energy and design—just a pile of cords in an aluminum-lined hole in the wall. We've tried everything, but hiding them like this is the only way they have a chance of surviving my "side effects." It's a pain, because with the closet full of cords, I have to keep all my clothes in a dresser that takes up half my room.

Plus, I have to get up to turn off my alarm.

I turn over instead, stretching the sheet to cover my entire body so I look like King Tut or something.

"So," Dad says, stumbling out of the closet after finally turning off the alarm. "How's the head?"

"Better," I mumble into my pillow, unheard. I can hear *him*, though, wandering around the room; *surveying*. It's something he's been doing ever since I rescued his records from the attic: stalking around my room, reminiscing.

"You know," he says with audible pleasure, and I can tell without looking that his hands are resting thoughtfully on his hips; it's been his favorite pose since I pinned the records up. "Some of these are *real* stinkers."

"I wouldn't know," I sigh, pulling the covers more tautly over my head and rolling to face the wall.

"Huh," he says, as if the thought hadn't occurred to him. The floorboards creak as he shifts his weight, his hands falling to his sides as he paces back out into the hallway. "*I think . . .*" But he's gone before he can finish his thought. I can still hear his hurried footsteps on the stairs when the alarm goes off again. He hadn't managed to turn it off after all; he'd only hit the snooze button.

I'm still in bed listening to the alarm when he comes back carrying a dusty cardboard box.

"Hey," he says, not to me but to the alarm clock, as he sets a dusty box down in front of the closet and yanks the clock's cord from the wall. "Quiet." In its place, he plugs in some sort of contraption from Before. My curiosity piqued, I prop myself up on my elbows as he untacks one of his records from the wall, shaking a black disc free from its faded sleeve and placing it tentatively on the device; pinching the record player's needle clean and then dropping it onto the spinning, crackling vinyl.

We sit on my bed, staring into the closet, and listen with quiet reverence to a few scratchy old jazz songs from, Dad says, "the sixties." Dad's messy strawberry hair is fading to a yellowing white, and I try to picture him younger; as a happier, more carefree version of myself. The kind of kid who could touch the worn red patina of our wooden banisters without tearing up at the thought of everyone who'd come before.

Shivering, I flash back to soaked walls buckling beneath the weight of mostly blown-away roofs; overstuffed Salvage Bags exploding with rotting clothes and forgotten memories; the sad, moldy tundra of the city as we drove through it after the last of the Tragedies—the terrible, soggy stench of it. The shock of the difference. That was a half-dozen years ago, but I feel it as sharply now as I did then.

"These were old when I got them," Dad explains, his face ashen as if suddenly embarrassed by the music's lightheartedness. "I used to really like old stuff, but I kind of can't stand the thought of it anymore."

"Me neither," I say. The more I think about it, the more I realize it's the truth. Like the records on my wall, my entire life is a patchwork of salvage, and I'd give anything for a fresh start.

Sitting next to Dad in my over-stuffed bedroom listening to a band from way Before waxing bittersweet about some girl who's probably twice as old as my mom—it's not depressing, it's something more . . . something too big for me to handle.

The record finally ends and we both exhale. Dad lets it keep spinning mutely while we stare at the records tacked to my walls. More than anything, I feel guilty. Most people lost everything in the Tragedies, and everyone mostly feels nostalgic about Before, so it feels wrong to feel so resentful of something we were lucky enough to save.

We must look pretty pathetic, because when Mom comes in to ask why the song stopped, she intuitively seems to know what's happened. With an exasperated look at the two of us, she says, "You know, guys, it's not like people stopped making music." When neither of us responds, she walks over to feel my forehead with the back of her hand. "Listen," she says, "Since you're feeling better, you should bike over to this place on the other side of downtown. It's called . . ." She pauses for a second and then smiles. "It's called the Other Side."

"It's a real scene," she laughs, making finger quotes around *scene*, "—and it's not like you were going to go to School today, were you?" Mom's enthusiasm is contagious, and Dad looks at me with a crooked smile that's so goofy I can't help but return it.

And that's how we end up biking downtown, Dad and I, through the construction to an old neighborhood behind the Green Zone proper that I never knew existed. It's no surprise that there are parts of the city that I don't know about; it's been built over three or four times already after every new Tragedy, and we typically stay in our neighborhood, where my "School" is and where my parents work. The surprise is that we've been given permission to explore them.

⚡ ⚡ ⚡

Where we live is called the Green Zone because it's the safest place in the city. Not that it's walled-in or anything, it's just the most thickly populated part of town—almost every house has a family living in it, and the ones without families are now general stores or agricultural or hardware suppliers. Places to get sheetrock and shovels. We also call it the Green because, since the Tragedies, everyone decided it was best not to depend on outsiders for food. It's warm most of the year here, so we're able to live mostly on fruits and vegetables grown in the Zone, and if we get tired of our own supplies, we barter them in the green market for other food.

To be honest, it's a little boring, but Mom says that's the trade-off: our first priorities are making sure we're protected and self-sufficient, then we'll work on having fun. Whenever I complain, she always points out that we also live next to the only hospital in the state, which isn't very much fun either, but I feel safer having it nearby. Besides, Mom basically runs the Green, so what she says goes.

Beyond the Green Zone, which is really only a mile or so all the way around, it's a little more touch-and-go, more so the further away you get from city center. We call that the Grey Zone, and it's not like it's super scary or anything, just that it hasn't been rebuilt yet. Even so, everybody in the Green is usually pretty happy just to stay where they are, especially after everything . . .

And the Green Zone gets a little bigger every day, now that we're pushing for an independent charter. Mom says that once we get the Charter, we'll finally have the resources we need to revitalize the Grey entirely; that since there'll be money to be made, more people will move to the city. Anticipating that, a bunch of contractors have descended on the Green with offers to start rebuilding the Grey on spec, which means they know we need a lot of work done and they figure we'll be able to pay them later.

Which is all pretty exciting, except the city's power grid has been down for a longer-than-expected transition to a "Zone-owned electrical solution." It's not like we're making bonfires in our living rooms or anything—the Green is rumbling with generators, but no internet; no phones. Even though Mom keeps saying how nice it is to have an excuse not to be in constant contact with the *federales* and other cities and provinces, it's making everyone else pretty irritable. They can live with being like me for a few months, for all I care. I've never sent a text in my life.

Still, it feels strange, biking through the Green Zone construction with Dad toward the Other Side. The last time I'd been outside of the Green Zone was with my parents, to take stock a few days after the last Tragedy. It wasn't called the Grey Zone then, though. It was just . . . broken.

That day, I'd sat in the backseat of our car and stared at the crumbs stuck in the bottom of the cup holder, trying to imagine the topography of the patchwork road jostling us toward the lake, point zero. My parents talked in hushed voices in the front seat and I tried not to listen to them, not wanting to believe another Tragedy had happened so soon after the last one.

What I remember most about that trip, though, were the shafts of light cutting through the branches overhead and playing across my hands, clenched in my lap. They seemed so wrong, like they knew what had happened and didn't have the grace to leave us alone.

Everything seemed wrong then.

T he sun is shining this time too, but less cruelly, and our bikes whir contentedly as we hug the road by the river. I tilt my head back and squeeze my eyelids so they're just barely open, my eyelashes merging with shaggy treetops in soft coronas of light. Squinting, I can convince myself we're riding through prehistoric grasslands or Jurassic marshes. That the steam shovels and cranes and cement mixers are lumbering dinosaurs. That no Tragedies ever happened, not even the asteroid that wiped out the dinosaurs or whatever.

A major tenet of our proposed city charter is that the "Grey must be Greened," and we're coasting down the first attempts at that greening: smooth black asphalt all the way from the park by my house to past downtown, on the littered outskirts of the Grey Zone. I take a deep breath, filling my lungs and refocusing on the road. The air is halfway between warm and cool, and it smells like caterpillars, which is strangely reassuring. I'm as excited to be out of the Green as I am worried about being in the Grey.

Mom gave us her blessing, though, when she kicked us out the door. Since she's in charge of the Zone, I decide to trust her despite my instincts.

"It's like a baby Green Zone," she'd said excitedly. "With people from *Outside*." Outside, we're told, things are still pretty much the way things were before the Tragedies . . . or, at least, similar enough that you'd expect the Outsiders would want to stay there. That they *don't* strikes me as suspicious, but Mom thinks that people giving up their lives to start again in what's essentially a wasteland is the first sign that we're on the right track with Greening the Grey. I'd nodded blankly, wary of her enthusiasm. "Henry, it's like . . . *The. Next. Step.*"

That's when I told her the Outsiders sounded crazy.

To my surprise, Mom agreed.

"Oh, they're *definitely* crazy," she'd said, like it was something to be happy about. "They're a bunch of musicians and artists." I rolled my eyes, but she just pointed at me with a twirling finger and said, matter-of-factly, "Turn up the music and people'll start dancing." And to feed the construction workers and other people coming in from Outside, a few sandwich shops popped up, and then a bar, and—Mom said, thrilling at the thought of it—a place to get a decent cup of coffee.

"*That?*" I'd said, noting the happy shiver that ran up her neck when she'd mentioned coffee. "*That* was the next step?"

The sun's in our eyes and the wind's in our hair as Dad and I ride, anticipating the new and unknown; the hot sandwich on thick, nutty bread Mom promised we'd be able to get on the Other Side. Something to take our minds off of Before.

Our bicycle baskets are jammed full of as many old records as we could fit, collateral for bargaining in case our Green Zone scrip isn't accepted on the Other Side. The scrip is basically an official

I.O.U. from the city, loose paper rubber-stamped with the city symbol: flowering laurels around a sprouting acorn. Mom has a ton of it because the city pays her in it . . . or more accurately, as acting mayor of the Green Zone, she pays herself in it. It's the same idea as the cash the rest of the country runs on, but even so, it hasn't completely caught on in the Zone. When you do try to barter with scrip, it's hit or miss—some people will take it and some people won't. Since we don't know what to expect with the Other Siders, it's worth a try . . . and we're looking to unload the records anyway, a sort of psychic cleansing after this morning, so they're good backup.

The construction goes on forever—literally, figuratively, forever—and it feels like everything I think I know about the Grey Zone, a ghostly expanse of empty houses and broken hearts, is proven wrong. Men and women in orange vests are everywhere, and they look tough, sure, but a friendly sort of tough, like they have good reasons for doing good work.

And rebuilding the Grey is definitely good work. Just seeing the workers as we coast through the Grey, chipping away at my fears and expectations with their hammers and crowbars, is enough to erase the melancholy of the morning. I'm riding, smiling at the workers and at the back of Dad's head, the handlebars from Mom's bike just barely vibrating in my hands, subtly buzzing with electricity from my mechanical heart.

And then we reach the bend in the river.

Downtown was never much for high-rises, so the skyline from this distance isn't anything to write home about. There are a handful of buildings with marble facades shooting up ten or twelve stories, glinting forlornly in the midday sun, but the most impressive buildings are less than half that tall, built by the Old French and Spanish centuries ago; rows of wrought-iron balconies rimming weather-worn colonial buildings. The kind of creaky places my parents rented in their bohemian post-college years, before they had me. Those fade like memories into the distance, so it's not the view that stops me.

It's just that Downtown, from so far away, looks almost like it did before.

Like nothing's happened.

The Zone was always the heart of the region, and when it went, so did everybody else. Outside of the Other Siders and construction workers, there're no people for hundreds of miles in any direction from the Green. They all migrated west and east and north, and after that, animals took their places. Alligators, black bears, and swamp panthers. With the exception of us, the state became one big nature preserve, red in tooth and claw.

But now . . . there's an aura of activity; a *presence* that's been missing for years. I can see it reflected in Dad's face as he scans the heart of the Grey from the crest of the levee: a long-lost familiarity; a guarded hope. "Race you," Dad idly challenges, already pedaling toward the ghost of the city by the time I snap out of my thoughts and into the saddle.

As we near Downtown, the construction noises get louder and louder, metal scraping on metal, cement foundations getting jack-hammered to bits. We had planned on riding directly through it, thinking we'd be safe enough in the middle of all that city-endorsed industry, but the noise is unbearable, so we impulsively decide to take a chance and skirt the construction on side streets. Before I'm able to get my bearings, we're bouncing on cobblestones beneath a canopy of broad-leafed magnolias, past quiet houses with imagined eyes in every fifth window. Dad seems to know where we're going, which keeps my confidence up—but all the buildings in this neighborhood still have water marks on their flood-rippled walls, and you can smell . . . not *mold*, but something musty and alive. It's almost overpowered by the magnolias above—big white flowers that are almost *too* sweet-smelling, like they have something to prove. And beneath the fading construction sounds, muffled conversations, the hint of a melody.

And just like that, the old road T-bones and we're suddenly clear of Downtown and in the thick of the Other Side: a riot of greens and blues and pinks and reds. Houses in the Zone are mostly white or dirty white—here they're every color you can think of, sometimes all on the same wall. Everywhere I look, murals and flags, vast swathes of painted tarp and canvas, hang from the buildings on the strip. Some are advertisements for shops inside, like one with a ten-foot tall sandwich eating another, smaller sandwich. The lettering on that one says "Food Eats Cafe," and the place it's hanging from smells so toasty and delicious that any misgivings I may have had about the neighborhood melt away like butter in a hot pan as we roll past it.

"Henry," Dad calls out, and then again, louder: "*Hank!*"

I've stopped in front of the restaurant and am staring into the dark interior. I look toward Dad, squinting blankly. He's pointing at the adjacent wall with his chin: it's painted with cartoon monsters having a cookout—a happy Frankenstein at the grill, a vampire drinking a lemonade and shooting the breeze with a black-lipped and laughing Cleopatra in a gold-leafed snake tiara.

I smile and nod in acknowledgment as Dad keeps rolling down the street. Even though I want to go into Food Eats with every salivating fiber of my being, I follow, and am quickly distracted by the bubbling life of the Other Side. Any surfaces that aren't painted are plastered with flyers: show posters, street poetry, and ads for everything from dump truck trash removal to drum lessons. My favorites, though, are flags that are just blocks of color: frayed yellow and turquoise and salmon-pink sheets blowing lackadaisically in the warm summer breeze against a clear blue sky.

Whatever anyone might call this place, I think, *it definitely isn't grey.*

It's only after I've adjusted to the color that I tune back into the melody, that undercurrent of sound that we'd been subconsciously following since our Downtown detour. I can still hear the pounding construction that's been the city's de-facto soundtrack over the past few months, but mixed with that: another, more urgent thumping. Our bikes are pulled toward the noise like divining rods.

It's funny: the Other Side can't be more than five blocks long, and even though there are one million blaring signs that it's lived in, the street is mostly empty except for the occasional orange-vested construction worker. And *they* all seem to be either going to or coming from Food Eats.

As we near the end of the street, it becomes obvious where everyone is. The colorful stretch that is the Other Side ends in a canal or something, previously spanned by a bridge that's now collapsed in the center. At the apex of the bridge, right before the break: The Sound. And, surrounding it, the Other Siders—a dancing mass of people so incongruously grubby that they almost seem to melt into the muddy banks of the river. We hop off our bikes and walk them toward the crowd, not wanting to look too conspicuous. I nervously straighten the records in my bicycle basket just to be doing something, but no one's paying any attention to us.

Everyone's focused on The Sound, which is coming from three people—a dirty-looking girl on bass and two dirtier-looking guys behind her, one thrashing on a mustard-yellow guitar and the other banging on overturned plastic buckets with heavy-looking drumsticks. The beat is unmistakable—if Dad wasn't here, I'd be tempted to start dancing—but everything else is too distorted to really make out. The girl is yelling something into a taped-together microphone, and I can sort of tell that the guy on guitar is basically just playing the same note over and over . . . but that's it. It's more of a roaring, sonic wave than a song—like they're somehow playing three different songs at once, and it doesn't sound good, exactly.

But it doesn't sound bad either . . . just interesting.

After a few minutes I stop trying to make out the specifics and close my eyes, letting myself fully enjoy the experience without distractions. We're at the intersection of the River and the Other Siders' canal, so even though it's the beginning of summer, there's a cool breeze, and I find myself prickling with goosebumps despite the heat. It could be that my heart's picking up the current from their amplifiers, which are huge, or it could be one of those perfect moments; either way, as I turn my face toward the sun, I feel an undeniable premonition . . . like something *really* good is about to happen.

And then, with a pop and some feedback crackle, the girl unplugs her droning bass.

My heart sinks. Just a few minutes after we get there and my first concert echoes out into instant nostalgia. I reluctantly open my eyes, confirming my disappointment: the band's already packing up the stage. Dad's a few feet away, talking to a woman holding a bouquet of pinwheels, and they must've been at it for a while because he's holding a pinwheel himself. Unstuck from the rest, it spins lazily in his hands while I edge next to them and eavesdrop, wanting to be part of the conversation without really being a part of it. The lady's telling Dad that the band is called Big Dumb River, and that we shouldn't feel bad about showing up late because they put on shows pretty regularly, like every other day. She has an irritatingly high-pitched, but kind, voice, and when she offers me a pinwheel, I take it, even though I don't really want one.

"Welcome to the Neighborhood," she squeaks, a one-woman welcoming committee. I shuffle my feet and thank her, feeling weird to be thirteen years old and still hiding behind Dad, who's holding his pinwheel like it's a glass of champagne. I pull on Dad's arm, anxious to break away and do our own thing, but apparently he's feeling magnanimous because he asks the pinwheel lady if she wants to join us for lunch, our treat, that he'd "consider it an honor." Thankfully, she just laughs and says that everybody eats free at Foods, at least for the time being.

"It's the construction," she says, sensing our confusion, her pinwheels spinning blue and green. "City's paying for everything while they're here. Other Side, brought to you by . . ." She curtseys with fluttering hands and laughs. "But I'll see you around, I'm sure!"

She stares expectantly at me, waiting for an unnecessary response, so I mumble that I'm pretty hungry, especially if we're going to be eating at Foods, and the woman smiles and nods, backing into the crowd as we let ourselves be jostled up the street with the rest of the Other Siders, who—judging by our shared destination—also seem to be pretty hungry.

On the inside, Foods is about as spartan as you can get: one long wooden counter snaking around the front and side walls of a medium-sized room that has a window to the kitchen at the back. In the center of the restaurant, it's mainly an eat-standing-up sort of situation, which is what most everyone in there is already doing . . . with varying success. The menu seems to be a cup of coffee and a sandwich, but the sandwiches are so generous and there's so little counter space that most people—unable to manage both food and drink— have placed their steaming mugs on the already coffee-slick floor as they attack their lunch with both hands. The sound of kicked and crashing coffee mugs punctuates the din of the lunch crowd, so Dad and I are very careful as we pick our way to the back window, where, without comment, a man with tattoos on his neck and a super-villain mustache hands us our sandwiches and slopping mugs of black coffee.

"Not just popular—it's mandatory," an Other Sider behind me jokes as he reaches over my shoulder to grab his own dripping cup.

Apparently, the way it works at Foods is that everyone gets the same meal. Today: a buttery grilled-cheese sandwich on warm, crusty bread. An entire halved avocado brings the combined height of the thing up to about four inches tall. I'd never had avocado before—the wax-leaved trees grow in the Zone, but never fruit— and after my first creamy bite, I make a promise to myself to come back as often as possible.

We don't keep coffee in the house, either, so I've never had a chance to try it. From what I understand, it's the biggest vice I'll have a chance at for years, so even though Dad teases me that it's going to taste like egg-water and dirt, I drain it down before I can second-guess myself. It's not like anything I've ever tasted, definitely nothing like the mineral-heavy water in the Zone, sulfurous and rotten-smelling. It's thick and hot and nutty, and it *does* taste a little like dirt—but in a hearty, good kind of way I wasn't expecting.

I can see myself getting to like this, I think, setting my empty mug down on the sticky floor and starting work on the rest of my enormous sandwich.

The best part of Food Eats, after the avocado and the sludgy black coffee, is that I get to see all the Other Siders up close and personal. Even just superficially, there are some obvious differences between them and us—which, when I notice them, make me a little self-conscious, although Dad doesn't seem to mind. For starters, the Other Siders wear all sorts of clothes, but mainly stuff that seems lived in. Like the singer for Dumb River, who bumps into me a few times at Foods: she's wearing a dress made out of an oversized guy's tuxedo shirt—a black, frilly button-down belted thickly in the middle—and army boots that go almost all the way up to her knees (although she only has them laced halfway up). I spot the two other guys in the band, and they're wearing ripped-up, patched-over jeans and variously stained T-shirts that they've scrawled DMBRVR on. The shirts have the sleeves cut off, and the guys are all arms in them. From across the room, it's hard to tell what's a tattoo and what's a grease smudge.

Everyone else at Foods has something going for them fashion-wise, too. Me, on the other hand—I'm wearing pleated khaki shorts and a plain white shirt, both pressed and looking just like they did the day I got them from the Zone's uniform supply store. Dad's wearing the same, which is no accident. It's not a rule or anything, but City Clothes is convenient and they accept scrip, so most everyone in the Zone shops there.

I thought we looked fine this morning, but now, for the first time in my life, I realize that Dad and I look like . . . well, *dorks*. One of the best things about Dad, though, is that he's pretty much clueless. Which seems like it would be a solid check in the con column, but his complete lack of cool usually has this funny side effect of making him kind of cool. For instance, picture me standing silently in the geometric center of Foods, slowly chewing the last of my grilled cheese and contemplating the cuffs on my khaki shorts with the kind of remorse most people save for funerals. My shirts have sleeves, so I feel regretful about them, too. And my shoes—

I look down . . .

My shoes aren't that bad, actually. Plain black canvas sneakers and a neat double knot. I glance around the cafe and see a few Other Siders wearing them, or similar, and start to feel better about my situation. The shoes are a start. I can build my look from the ground up and . . . I feel Dad's hand squeeze the back of my neck.

"This is my son, Henry . . . Hank, this is the band: Tom, Rachel, and over there is—did you say his name was Greg?"

The band. My eyes dilate as their heads look suddenly enormous; terrifying. To my credit, my mouth isn't hanging open. I know because my lips are dry and sticking together.

"Henry?"

Tom, the spastic guitarist, is holding his hand out like he wants to shake and—startled—I grab it with the wrong hand. Wincing at my own awkwardness, I commit to my very dumb handshake anyway, gripping the outside of his right hand with my stupid left hand. I wonder if I should make up for the misstep by adding my right hand to the mix and double shaking, but by the time that plan of action occurs to me it already feels too late. And my heart must be beating double-time, because Tom twitches strangely and, after a shocked moment, pulls away.

In addition to being a total idiot, I'd forgotten about my "side effects" . . . but thankfully, he regains composure pretty quickly.

"Heck of a handshake, Hank—nice to meetcha."

Dad smiles down at me. "I was just telling Tom here about our old records—he's running a sort of studio down the strip and wants to start a station as soon as he can get wavelength going."

"Radio," Tom chimes in proudly, rubbing the hand I buzzed on his dirt-worn jeans. "Once the power's back up and everything."

"Oh . . . cool," I say, noticing that Dad and Rachel and Tom are all smiling at me encouragingly. It's strange, but a relief to see that everyone's head is back to normal. Greg is behind them, beating a rhythm with his bare hands on the wall by kitchen window. The cook starts to yell at him to quit it, so I have to raise my voice.

"You guys were . . . really good today," I say, just hanging out with the band.

And end scene, clueless Dad for the win.

3

The scene doesn't really end there, though.

Tom's curious to see the attic records we've lugged from home, and Dad makes it dorkily clear that we're curious to see his set-up, so—stuffed—we all leave Foods together and walk our bikes over to Tom's studio-slash-store, which is in a mostly-restored building about a block off the strip. *Mostly* restored, because it's sort of a dump, but livable.

Or, at least, Tom lives there with Rachel.

Their house is a squat, single-story shotgun, a kind of building that's pretty common in the Grey Zone. They're called "shotguns" because they're long and skinny, about five rooms deep and one room wide. All the doors are typically aligned so, if you wanted to, you could shoot a bullet straight through the house from the front yard to the backyard without hitting anything. Of course, no one's actually recommending that you try that—it's just a turn of phrase from Before, when people had time for that kind of thing.

On the outside it looks like most of the other houses on the Other Side, which is to say it's less a house than a carnival. In fact, it makes the rest of the Other Side look like the Green Zone. The entire facade is spray-painted a metallic gold, and it reflects the noonday sun so effectively that I have to shield my eyes. On the porch, a line of department store mannequins (also metallic gold) vogue in various states of disrepair.

And that isn't the extent of their renovation; the inside is a carefully choreographed explosion.

Unlike a traditional shotgun, Tom and Rachel's place is completely gutted—there are no doors, no interior walls, no rooms. Just stacks of records and piles of salvage. And in the far corner, a worn mattress on the floor, a few rugged amplifiers, and a record player. Knotted next to the mattress is a fire hazard of electrical cords, the largest of which feeds through a back door that doesn't shut all the way to a rusted generator abutting the rear of the house. Looking around, I notice there isn't a kitchen or a bathroom in sight.

It's not exactly the most comfortable space, but what it lacks in utilitarianism it makes up for in design. The walls are plastered with the same flyers that are up in the strip, but coated with a thin layer of white paint so they act as a subtle, slightly crinkly wallpaper. Which would be interesting enough in itself, but lining the makeshift wallpapered walls are at least fifty portraits, all of people pictured from the shoulders up, all clearly by the same hand—I recognize the style from the monster cookout mural next to Foods.

The portraits circle the entire interior of the house, making it more art gallery than living room. They're all roughly the same size, but variously framed: some have heavily ornamented, silver-leafed arabesques holding them up, others just simple wooden squares. But the frames hardly matter—it's the faces staring out at me that really make an impression. They're all glossy, brightly painted with the same colors that make the rest of the Other Side so interesting: neon pink hair and tangerine faces, blue pupils and copper lips.

And then I realize, with a start, that I recognize some of them. "This is . . . amazing," I whisper, out loud but to no one in particular, as I place Tom with his skinny turkey neck, and werewolf Greg, and the Food Eats cook (his black waxed mustache turned lilac purple). Looking for more familiar faces draws my gaze around the interior, which slowly comes into focus as the kind of treasure trove you can lose days in: a wooden crate of old photographs, some *really* old; more mannequins, mostly torsos and heads without bodies (one has a scuffed-up old guitar hanging around its neck); a sewing machine; piles and piles of clothes; boxes of books . . .

Tom and Rachel must be used to first-timer gawking, because they just stand near the front door smiling while we take everything in.

"Paintings by Rachel, clutter's all mine," Tom says, jolting us back into the moment.

While Dad claps Tom on the back and says some stuff about how he "likes to see a place that looks lived in," that the Other Side is "really something," I keep looking around at the paintings, wondering what color face I'd have if I was up on the wall. I think probably a light green, since I'm so obviously from the Zone, but there are already a few green faces up on the wall that wouldn't fit in at all in our neighborhood.

Rachel falls in step with me while I pace the room, which has to be done very carefully because of all the clutter—it's less a pace than a hopscotch, really. "So, your dad's pretty friendly," she says, smiling. She looks so nice that I instinctively copy her smile, then frown when I realize what I'm doing. She laughs, silently, like a cat yawning.

"He's not *that* bad, is he?"

"Oh, no—my dad's great," I say. "I just . . . I dunno."

She nods, sympathizing so sincerely that it has me genuinely smiling again.

We both turn around to look at Dad, who is very obviously friendly in the best possible way. He's still talking to Tom, who's nodding in quick, vigorous bursts, agreeing with Dad about "the importance of self-portraiture in urban planning." You wouldn't think a scuzz punk squatter and a guy in orthopedic shoes and cuffed shorts would get along so famously, but maybe that's just the magic of what's happening on the Other Side.

"Get a load of these guys," Rachel stage-whispers out of the side of her mouth, finger pistols waggling at Tom and Dad like she's some corny comedian from way Before. I laugh a little too loudly and both of them look up, startled, remembering that maybe not everyone in the room is so totally absorbed in their conversation.

"Oh hey, before I forget," Rachel says in a normal voice, plucking a record off the top of a precarious stack and flipping it at me. "Our thing."

It doesn't have a cover so much as a blank paper sleeve, and the vinyl feels thicker than the ones I pinned to my wall—more rustic, if that makes sense, with rough edges. "We actually press those ourselves," she says proudly, watching me rub my thumb across its ragged edges. "Tom learned from our friend in Baltimore."

I don't know where Baltimore is, and it seems crazy to be able to imply intimacy with other cities, like it's no big deal to *make records* in *Baltimore*. I look at Rachel to see if she's putting me on, but she just wipes her face with the back of her hand, leaving a streak of sweaty dirt on her forehead. She's definitely—I decide, slipping the record back into its sleeve—the coolest person I've ever met.

Meanwhile, Tom yelps.

He and Dad have moved on to looking over the records we brought, and a quick glance confirms that he's okay . . . he's just seen something he likes. Dad is still feeling magnanimous, maybe even more so than before, and tells him to take it, to take the whole stack of them, that the whole reason we were over here in the Other Side was to get rid of the stuff.

"Oh but no, no. No, *no*. I can't—I don't even have . . ." Tom balks, wanting to take Dad up on his generosity but also stuck. "We're trying to build our record library for the station—I just don't . . . I just don't think I can trade right now."

Dad holds up the record that inspired the swallowed yell. On the cover is a photo of a guy with crossed eyes and a clarinet or something surrounded by girls in tassled vests. It isn't even one of the ones I'd chosen to hang up on my wall—a loser through and through. "I didn't even like this when I bought it thirty years ago," Dad says. "Just thought it was funny . . ."

Tom looks at me for affirmation, which he doesn't have to do—it's Dad's music collection—but I'm flattered to be considered part of the deal.

I nod encouragingly.

"Listen, really . . . just take them all," Dad says, wedging a few records into a precarious mountain of books next to him to prove his conviction. "For the station. We'd consider it an honor to be your first sponsors." A thick textbook of Mesoamerican culture through the ages clatters to the knotty hardwood floor, setting off a dusty avalanche.

"Well, all right then," Tom says, tentatively—but resolutely—shaking Dad's hand and looking relieved when he doesn't get shocked. "But let's still make this thing a *thing*."

He spins around, knocking into the remaining book pile and dislodging a few more dusty volumes. Rubbing his knees, he makes his way toward the mannequins at the back of the room, and I wonder what Mom would say about having one of them, gleaming gold, on our porch swing.

If we'd use some scrip to at least get some shorts on it.

But Tom isn't heading for a mannequin. He's heading for the electric guitar hanging on a headless mannequin by a tatty leather strap. I hold my breath and snap my neck around to catch Dad's reaction, but he's picked up one of the books that had fallen and is flipping through it, totally and immediately immersed. Rachel just smiles.

"It's an old beater, found it down the block when we moved in," Tom says. "The screws are a little loose, and it's a junior model, but if you're looking for some rock and roll, you might as well try to be the band you want to hear."

His voice gets sort of reverent for that last part, like he's quoting something.

"Anyway," he says, handing it over to me. "Here ya go."

I take it from him with a sinking feeling. For him to be giving me a guitar feels like too much—a gesture too big for the circumstances. I try to keep my face stiff so Tom won't realize what a raw deal he's getting, trading a few crummy records for a genuine guitar, but he looks so happy to be handing the thing off that I can't stop myself from breaking out into a big, lopsided grin.

We stay on the Other Side for a few more hours after saying our goodbyes, walking up and down the strip and then, when our eyes can't take it any more—Dad calls it "color fatigue"—sitting on the levee watching the river go by. It doesn't look particularly *dumb*, I think, fingering the Dumb River record Rachel gifted me. Just slow. Which it isn't. One of the first things you learn in the city is not to trust the river. It's unreliable; it tries to jump its banks every rainy season and has a current that'll pull you under before you even have a chance to yell out for a rope.

Which is pretty dumb, I guess . . .

More dumb is that we have to get home before sunset. The Grey is as dangerous as the river after dark. Dad offers to carry my "new" old guitar on his back for the return trip, and even though that sounds like a good idea, I find myself double-checking its braided strap and slinging it over my own shoulder, its finger-worn neck jutting out diagonally and downward. I feel a little silly because it doesn't feel like it's mine yet, but its heft and pull feels just right.

Like it's a part of me.

And then, after only a few minutes of standing-in-the-stirrups pedaling, we aren't on the Other Side anymore.

It may just be the caffeine from Foods finally wearing off, but the instant we roll into the Grey Zone everything starts to feel heavy again, like we'd spent the morning high-stepping on the moon and now, back on Earth, the increased gravity is too much to bear. I sit in my saddle, suddenly tired, and try to gauge if Dad's feeling the same way . . . but his eyes are determined slits, impossible to read.

The sun is still pretty high in the sky, but our ride back through the Grey Zone feels like a midnight retreat. The air is thick with magnolias and something dark beneath, like rotting leaves—a sinister bouquet that was replaced on the Other Side with the happily overwhelming smell of baking bread and brewing coffee.

I'd been too distracted with excitement on the way to the Other Side to really take the Grey Zone in—my attention had been focused almost completely on the resonant thumping of cement mixers and the shouts of the orange vests, the promise of short-distance horizons. On reflection, I realize that I'd actually tried *not* to look at the Grey too closely—the Grey Zone as it is, not the Greened-over Grey.

And I still don't want to look too closely, but—once I realize I've been avoiding it—I find I can't tear my eyes away. Even so, the damage is so random, so *chaotic*, that my impulse is to lose myself in the horizon or the ever-changing canopy of the oak trees overhead, like usual.

Instead, I force myself to I focus on doors.

A peeling light pink one, half-open and bleached by the sun. A glossy red one, somehow freed of its frame, resting against a rusty wrought-iron fence. A bent metal garage door.

And after doors, windows: the mostly-intact stained glass of a church on the corner with tall arched doors, wooden and starred with iron bolts. A bay window with an enormous dead branch sticking out of it, weather-damaged curtains rustling in the wind behind it. A propped-up facade, just the front of a skeleton house with nothing but windows and the blue sky beyond.

Before long I'm considering houses as wholes, not just doors and windows.

The shotgun without any visible damage in the middle of one block, skinny but standing brave despite its neighbors. The fallen friends: roofless, half-demolished with overturned cars in the front yards and only three standing walls. Refrigerators spilling long composted insides onto overgrown lawns. A calico cat with a nice face licking its white paws on a front porch.

I start to feel less heavy, like I could float away at any second if it wasn't for the guitar on my back weighing me down. Even *with* the guitar, I feel as if I'm floating away: as soon as I've started to get a handle on the Grey Zone, it's gone, melted away into the fast-approaching night.

I blink.

We're back in the Green Zone, coasting comfortably up the Avenue; the street lights overhead remain dead despite the darkness. The only light is from the windows of houses with generators and a harvest moon hanging low in the sky. Compared with the out-loud life of the Other Side, everything feels a little less familiar than I expected it would, a little more strange.

Our house is dark, which means Mom isn't home—a suspicion confirmed by a note on the door telling us she's staying late at Grammy's for a Zoning meeting. It's not a surprise: if she isn't at work, she's at Grammy's, which is work, but with finger sandwiches. I drop my bike in the hallway and run upstairs, clicking the unpowered light switch to "on" and waiting for Dad's "All clear?"

"Clear," I yell, sticking my head out the window.

It's best for me to be in my room on the third floor when Dad cranks the generator, so I keep my head hanging out the window until I hear the motor turn over and the snap of my bedroom lights jolting back to life. And then I keep it there a little longer, watching Dad wipe the grease from his hands on the sides of his shorts. He inhales deeply, looking critically around our pitch-black lawn, and seems reluctant to come inside. When he finally does—letting the door slam shut behind him—I hang out of the window for a little longer still, hypnotized by the big yellow moon nearly kissing its reflection in the not-so distant river.

Back inside my room, nothing's changed.

And everything has changed.

Like the Green Zone on our way home, something is off—like we've biked back to a parallel dimension. The only thing that feels really right is Tom's old guitar, resting heavily on my bed like it's always been there. I pick it up by the neck, strum it once, and lean it behind the closet door—hiding it to see if that will somehow switch everything back to normal. The feeling doesn't go away, though, so I pick it up again, pull the strap over my head, and try to get the weight of the thing. It's smooth black, glossy, and just a little chipped on the head and where the body meets the neck. The frets are dusty and one of the volume knobs is missing, but it still turns. It easily trumps Mom's old bike as the nicest thing I own.

Remembering the concert earlier in the day—how Rachel had held the microphone like it was a snake she wasn't afraid of—I pick up the Dumb River record and, holding it by its rough edges with the tips of my fingers to keep from getting shocked, drop it smoothly onto the spindle of the record player Dad set up . . . it feels like a hundred years ago.

After a few seconds of scratchy buzz, Greg counts in ("One! Two! Three! Four!") and the first track starts all at once, the drums and the screaming and the high-wire guitar, a barely contained frenzy of fuzz punk and roll. It's rough, but on record I can actually hear some of what Rachel is yelling about. *Something something*, "Do it! Do it! Do it," *something*, "Yeah!"

And *that's* when I make my big mistake.

It feels like the most natural thing in the world, too. I barely even notice that I've set the guitar down—that I'm pulling the drawers out of my fat wooden dresser—until I'm standing in a pile of neatly pressed shirts and shorts from City Clothes that I've dumped unceremoniously on the floor. I don't know that I'm going to cut all the cuffs from my shorts until after I start scissoring through them—it's pure impulse. And then, gathering momentum, a goal taking form, I vanquish the tyranny of shirt sleeves. The record blasts out fuzz-pulses of inspiration, and I time my cuts to match them:

One! Two! Three! Four!

Cut! Cut! Cut! Cut!

I tend to keep things—you never knew when you'll need a paint-stained work shirt smock, if you'll get big enough to grow into that windbreaker from your well-meaning Grammy—so I have a lot of clothes, and it takes me the first side of Dumb River plus a couple of extra minutes to get through them all (and the one on my back). Finally, shirtless and sitting on the floor—the room silent except for my thrumming pulse—I realize what I've done.

I take a deep breath, surveying. It occurs to me, sitting in the middle of a pile of sleeves on my bedroom floor, big orange-handled scissors in my suddenly shaking hands, that what I have is a problem. Skinny arms. Skinny arms and, after an impulsive, neurotic, totally frantic ten minutes: no way to hide them. With the exception of a nervous breeze from a small plastic fan, the room is hot, but I don't feel it. I don't feel anything. I'm above it all, looking down on myself from the peak of the ceiling. My arms look even skinnier from a distance, and the air around me-on-the-floor is wavering like a mirage, my version of overheating: electrified sweat radiating outwards.

I consider myself for a moment: the heartless boy, electrified and steaming. It's strange—*I'm* strange—but not as strange as me-in-the-air.

That's a new me, one I hadn't met before now.

The morning after our trip to the Other Side, I stretch languidly awake as if yesterday's adventure had all been a dream. The sun is hot on my face, and—yawning contentedly—I consider pulling the sheets up over my head and going back to sleep . . . but just as I'm curling back into the coolness of my pillow, I see it. Catching the light in the corner of my ravaged bedroom, leaning precariously against the emptied frame of my dresser, is Tom's guitar.

Still dreaming, I think, rolling back toward the wall. But now that I've seen it, I can't sleep. Instead, I sit up, rubbing my eyes into focus, and assess the situation. Liberated dresser drawers are littered around a pile of roughly cut sleeves on the floor. I shake my head clear, flipping back and forth between regret and relief, and decide not to stress out about it. Yes, I mutilated my wardrobe and trashed my room . . .

But I also went to the Other Side and brought part of it back with me, I reassure myself, smiling at the thought of Tom and Rachel and Food Eats.

And the guitar.

Besides, the smashers might not look so bad. I pull one over my head and turn immediately to the mirror mounted on my door. When I jut my chin upwards half an inch and square my shoulders, I can almost pull it off . . .

A knock and, simultaneously, the door opens. I drop the pose, but it's impossible to tell whether or not Mom's seen it. She looks at me for a microsecond and jerks her head like she suddenly remembers something she's forgotten in another room.

"School," she says sideways.

"I know."

"Looking good," she mumbles, closing the door, her hand covering her mouth.

I flop onto the bed, naked arms spread out in a T. I consider being embarrassed, but it just doesn't fit. The sun's coming in hot and hard, rays refracting off white walls and vibrating around my room. I might have started the morning off mortified, but another emotion is quickly taking over: excitement, like my electric heart's beating triple time.

Dad has the restraint to not raise his eyebrows when I walk into the kitchen, but I can see him holding back, so he might as well have waggled away. Instead, he's straining to maintain a serious squint, and the corners of his lips are turned slightly downward like he's trying not to smile—not a good sign for me, fashion-wise, but at least he doesn't *say* anything about the smasher. Before his sense of humor has a chance to overwhelm his self-control, though, I decide to spare us both from any further awkwardness and rip the Band-Aid right off.

"These guys have such good personalities," I say, curling my arms up and down like I'm lifting weights. "It'd be a pity not to share 'em with the world."

Dad guffaws, his whole face laughing; eyebrows springing upward and his eyes creased at the corners. Mom looks up from the file folder she has spread out in front of her and—even though I know eyes don't really twinkle—I swear her eyes are twinkling at him.

"Good man," Dad says, after he's finished laughing. "Good man."

Problem solved, I grip Dad's shoulder to let him know we're okay, me and him, and grab two apples from a bowl on the table.

"No loaf?" Mom asks, arching her brow.

I can't handle loaf most days, and definitely not today. It's short for Non-Meat Loaf (NML), a hyper-nutritional brick of a meal made from vegetable scraps and a nutty dough. It's an old Zone recipe, adapted from the emergency rations we all had to live off of after the Tragedies. Healthy, but slimy in all the wrong places and hard to get down. I set my jaws, and Mom knows not to push the issue.

"Meet us at Grammy's after School, we might have news."

I nod over my shoulder, already halfway out the door with a mouth full of Red Delicious, and wonder what they could possibly have to tell me at Grammy's. City business, probably.

It's a beautiful day, maybe the *most* beautiful day. The sky is such a crisp and impossible blue that the trees and houses beneath it seem to be glowing in its reflected glory. It's only five blocks to School, and since the streetcars aren't running, I walk in the center of the tracks bisecting the Avenue. I'm not alone. Since the Powerdown, the tracks have become a hub of foot traffic—everyone gravitating toward the previously forbidden. Not that it's crowded, but there are probably fifteen or so people walking up the tracks in front of me, and I pass four or five walking in the other direction, nodding affably at our shared transgression; wishing me a good morning as I balance along a hot steel rail.

Even though it's summer, it's early enough that it's not too hot, and there's a light breeze. Soon enough I'm standing in front of the chipped sign: a concrete book, open and propped on mossy concrete feet. "Memorial Public Library," a grimy engraving proclaims. Beyond the sign, there are a handful of kids milling around the garden, but the majority will show up later. There's no set hour you need to be at School in the Zone—it's not like anyone's keeping track. Since the Powerdown, everyone's just been guessing at what time it is, anyway.

The Library is in the middle of the Zone, squarely between our house and the park. It's a funny old mansion from way before, and I spend a lot of time there because it's also the School . . . at least until we get our Charter.

For the most part, no one cares what we do at School, so long as we're here. I guess everyone figures it's enough for now just for us to be out of our parents' hair and around all these books, so most kids either play in the garden all day or hole up and read. I do a little bit of both, but ever since I found a way into the attic, I've been spending most of my time up there.

The trick to getting into the attic is that you can't get to it from the inside—at least, not entirely. Which can drive kids crazy when they realize that the windows built into the roof don't correspond to the top floor reading rooms. I don't think anyone consciously blocked off the attic, though, it's just that the interior of the Library has been plastered over so many times through the years that whatever entrances may have existed have long since been sealed.

Most kids—if they get the itch—look for secret doors behind revolving bookcases, as if the Library's a pirate ship or something. But I figured the Library was probably like my house, and if there was any attic access, it would be through a door with a pull-chain somewhere in the ceiling, a retractable ladder that popped down when the chain was pulled. I looked for something like that for a while, and when I didn't find it, I took extreme measures.

I went outside.

Unlike the rest of the Zone, which is almost completely flat, the Library's lawn has a roll to it—two stepped little hills that flare downward from the base of the building into the School's vegetable gardens. It was while walking through these gardens with my neck craned upward that I noticed it: the key. Barely visible in the perpetual shade of a rear-facing overhang: the top few feet of a wide-mouthed drainpipe bolted into the corner of an ornamental third-floor balcony. It was easy enough to get to once I figured out which window I had to force open, surreptitiously leveraging a butter knife against years of disuse, and the brackets holding the pipe against the outside wall turned out to be more ladder-like than I would've dared to hope.

Looking back, the first time was the easiest.

Once I decided to go for it, wedging my body into the corner and climbing resolutely skyward, the ascent was over in seconds. Peering over my shoulder as I scrambled onto the flat, tar-black roof, adrenaline pumping, I expected to see a crowd forming. But the garden was quiet, save for a few kids, hunched over, sneaking tomatoes or squishing caterpillars, too preoccupied to have noticed me.

With a parting look at the world below, I turned my attention back to the task at hand. In the middle of the roof, visible only to a few curious sparrows, was a square service hatch leading down into what I hoped would be the attic. Like the window to the balcony, it was painted shut—but, shielded from view, I was able to take my time prying it open. When it finally popped, instead of the stale breath of centuries I had steeled myself for, I was enveloped with a comforting smell, almost like dust and almonds.

The hardest part about getting to the attic now doesn't actually have anything to do with getting to the attic; it's lying to my friends. After that first day, I'd told them I had to start helping Grammy most afternoons, that she was getting older. I feel bad when I slip away, looping back into the Library and my secret window, and I feel worse about using Grammy . . . but it's worth it, to have something that's just for me; an escape from the relentless boredom of the Green Zone.

Once the new School is built, we'll have to go there instead of the Library, and we'll have to take actual classes like Before, which will be a welcome change, even if it means homework . . . but I'll miss the attic. It's mostly stained glass windows and broken chairs, and I like to go up there after lunch to crack open one of the books from the towering stacks lining the walls, something weird like *When Ladies Go-A-Thieving: Middle-Class Shoplifters in the Victorian Department Store*, and feel lucky not to be outside in the heat, biding time.

At School, I slip into my usual morning ritual, which is to sit on a weather-worn root knotting up beneath the big oak tree in the front yard and eat my breakfast—apples when I can snag them, loaf when I can't—watching for my friends as they trickle in. We'll all fool around for a while under the tree, telling jokes and—if Conor's brought his skateboard—practicing ollies in the soft dirt beneath the tree. There's a curved driveway leading up to the old book drop bin, and if it's not too crowded, we'll try to shoot that, too, slaloming around dirt clods from the garden and trying not to fall.

In the afternoon I'll either try to break away to the attic, or—if I can't slip up to the third-floor balcony unnoticed—dig around in the garden. During planting and harvesting season I always help out, but there are months and months between when there's nothing to do except slop buckets of fishy chum up and down the rows of plants, fertilizing. Or pick bugs off fresh growth, either squishing them between your fingers or running them over to the grass lining the tracks on the Avenue, hoping they'll be able to start a happy new life away from our crop of okra and carrots.

Neither of those options are a lot of fun, so I usually just try to sneak away to the roof. Not that I have to sneak, really. School isn't really "school" anymore—I do my learning at home in the evening, usually with Dad. Since most adults are busy with reconstruction and the Charter, there's only one grown-up in charge of the Library, Mr. Moonie, and he's spread pretty thin. If I get to School early enough, though, he'll join me by the tree for a minute to swap news about the Zone, which is why I try and make it in before the other kids.

"Morning, Mr. Moonie," I call out, seeing him poking down the steps of the Library, one hand clutching the rail and the other waving hello with a rubber-bottomed cane.

Mr. Moonie is a slow walker, so I usually wait until he's right on top of me before I say hello, but I'm on edge today. Rather than wait for him to make his way over to the oak, I jump up and slow-jog over to where he's catching his breath at the bottom of the stairs.

"Hey, Mr. Moonie," I say. "How's the Queen?"

Mr. Moonie purses his lips and pushes his chin into his neck, like usual. You'd think he was a prude if you didn't know that he did that instead of laughing. A lot of people, and not just kids, make that mistake. He always wears a seersucker suit, baggy but freshly pressed, and a dull, rust-red tie. His formality, coupled with his age—and he *is* old—gives him a serious bearing, even if he really is mostly a jokester.

The story with Mr. Moonie, as he tells it, is that the Library was privatized before—still a library, but not technically owned by the Zone. It was also Moonie's home. After the Tragedies, though, he couldn't afford to restore it, so the Zone stepped in . . . under the condition that the Library continue on as before, but as public property. Since the Library had been that way to start with—public—this seemed like a good deal to Mr. Moonie, who didn't have any other options. He'd side-stepped the question when I'd asked him how the Library became his in the first place, but the long and the short of it was that now it was doubling as the School.

Moonie doesn't really care about the School, even though he's supposed to be in charge of it as de facto headmaster-slash-librarian. He likes us kids, but is more concerned with his life's work, a history of the world from the perspective of the city, from primordial ooze through the present. So whenever I see him, I make a point of asking after some random historical personage—like the Queen of England—and he makes a point of answering. like it was the most natural question in the world for me to ask.

"Well, I'll tell ya, Hank," Moonie says, looking contemplative. "She's just having a heck of a time with the young Prince of Wales, a heck of a time." He hitches up his trousers, looking me seriously in the eye, and lets them slip back down to where they originally hung. "Or were you asking about the cruise ship, son?"

We get along so well, Moonie and I, for three reasons.

The first is that he doesn't care that I'm a kid, and I don't care that he's old.

The second is that he'd found out that I'm circuitously related to a way-former governor of the state, one who'd been shot. Old Moonie had been tracing the genealogy of former Governor Long for his book and realized that the Longs from the Zone are a distant root of the late Governor's tree. Apparently Governor Long was working toward something like our Charter when he'd been assassinated, so we'd had a few good talks about that.

And the third reason we get along so well is that I like the Library almost as much as he does, had been going there for years before it had even become the School. Which is another joke of ours, the School thing. We both pretend that Mr. Moonie's actually a teacher and that I'm actually learning something, knowing full well that I haven't been to a real school in years and that Mr. Moonie is as much a principal as he is a caterpillar.

"Okay, Hank, I got some *scholastical* issues on the old agenda today," Moonie says, pulling another long face as he absentmindedly pats his pockets. "You have a good day in class, now, you hear?"

"I'll try, Mr. Moonie," I reply, but he's already turned back to the Library, in search of whatever it is he's forgotten. It's not that School is a joke for either of us—we both know all us kids are getting a raw deal just sitting around the Library all day without teachers or anything, but the Charter is going to change all that, and in the meantime, as Mom says: "Everyone just has to make do."

Conor and Scott roll up to the stairs in time to watch the second half of Mr. Moonie's slow ascent. Or, rather, Conor rolls up on his well-worn skateboard while Scott jogs next to him, jumping to an exaggerated stop an inch from my face so we're standing nose to nose.

"And a good day to you two gentlemen, too," Moonie calls over his shoulder, tipping an invisible cap as he works his way up the last of the Library stairs. We three all watch him go, his cane tapping jauntily on the steps. When he makes it all the way inside, Scott whispers, "*Tri* . . . pod!"

I know better than to put up a fight for Mr. Moonie. We've been through all that before, and they just don't understand how I can be friends with someone so old. It's not worth arguing about, so I do the next best thing and punch him in the shoulder, hard.

"*Hey!*" Scott shouts, incredulous and rubbing his arm. "That hurt!"

Conor laughs, flipping up his skateboard so he's holding it by the tail. "Nice guns, Hinky," he says, squeezing my bicep and smirking.

I'd stopped caring about my skinny arms on the way to School, but now I *know* not to worry about them. If I looked really stupid, I'd have been able to count on Scott to let me know—he's not mean or anything, he just lacks a censor. And Conor wouldn't have said anything at all.

As far as my friends go, Conor's the cool one.

He was the first to shoot down the Library's driveway on his skateboard without falling, the first and only one of us to successfully drop down the back steps on the same skateboard and land it. And he'd probably look the part even if he didn't wear the shiny mesh jerseys that he gets as presents from his older brother Ben, who lives outside the Zone. We can't really follow sports here, but Conor acts like we're from outer space for not recognizing the names on his back, which I guess makes him seem that much cooler—even though I'm pretty sure he doesn't know who those guys are either.

Compared to Scott, it's even more obvious that Conor's the cool one. I hadn't noticed before, but Scott's white shirt is inexplicably wet and tucked into his also-wet khaki shorts. It doesn't help that he's absentmindedly cradling and stroking the top half of his arm like it's a half-drowned kitten.

"Sorry," I say, feeling suddenly sorry for having punched him so hard. "Don't know my own . . ." I laugh, remembering how

I'd flexed my skinny arms for Dad earlier this morning, and then compose myself. "Don't know my own strength anymore."

"Ha," Scott says without inflection, not really laughing, but startled into it by my sort-of apology. "Don't know why you care about weird old Moonie any . . ."

"*That's* settled, then," Conor says too loudly, cutting Scott off as he claps his hands on both of our backs. He double taps mine, a non-vocal appeal to reason, as he wipes his Scott hand dry on his shorts. "No fights today!"

In that moment, I realize that it's not just the jerseys. After Tom and Rachel, Conor is definitely the coolest person I know. Still, a lot of that coolness is trickle-down from Ben, who vanished five or so years ago, leaving the Zone and never coming back. Although "vanished" is a little dramatic: Ben got a job with the federale government. No one really knows what he does, but he lives up north now and seems to be doing well for himself. Conor gets a care package in the mail about twice a year filled with stuff you can't get in the city: the skateboard and jerseys, sour gummies that hurt to eat, comic books . . .

Since there's no regular postal service in the Zone, the packages are a really big deal. They have to be flown into the nearest airport a few hours away and then driven in by a courier service. Which is all very thoughtful and nice and everything, but everyone agrees that of course Conor would be happier with his brother back in the Zone. He's told me as much before, when Scott wasn't around making everything into a joke.

Wet-shirted, goofball Scott.

In the five seconds since I said I was sorry, he's decided he's a gymnast: gripping the handrail as tightly as possible, he's inched his feet out from beneath himself until, arms taut, he's almost parallel to the ground.

Kids have started grouping in the front lawn now, clumps of tittering khaki and white. We're the odd men out: Conor's wearing a bright red soccer jersey, Scott's acting like the village idiot, I'm showing a lot of skin, and everyone's looking at us. Despite attempts at subtlety, most are obvious gawkers—and I feel a little embarrassed at how the attention makes my chest swell. Outside of Conor and Scott, I don't have many friends. I never felt much like putting in the effort . . . my condition is easier to deal with as a secret, and life is hard enough without everyone thinking I'm some sort of freak.

Still, one group in particular has me staring back: a girl with white-blonde hair pulled tightly into a glossy ponytail and her three brunette friends. They're all sporting cuffed shorts and rolled-up sleeves, which I'd forgotten was a "thing" with the more popular girls in the Zone. It's only because I'm staring at their clothes, trying to decide whether or not I look like I'm wearing a girl shirt, that I notice blondie covertly glancing at us.

At first I look quickly down, trying not to make eye contact— but after a few agonizing seconds I sneak a peek. She's mousey, but in a nice way; it's more a furtive smallness than a physical similarity. The brown-haired girls are all laughing around her, brassy and loud, but she holds back, her cheeks pinched in concentration. She's cute, in a weird, quiet way, and my electric heart thrills at the thought of her looking at *me*.

Except . . . I realize, deflating as I follow her gaze, she wasn't looking at me. Connecting the dots, I'm a little disappointed but not at all surprised to see Conor making eyes back at her across the gardens. They're good eyes, too, like . . . *heartthrob* eyes. I can't imagine even thinking about trying to look at someone like that.

It's no wonder he's got the mouse girl hooked.

When Conor finally notices that he's been caught in the act, he winks, totally without embarrassment, and—not missing a beat—twitches his head toward our buddy Scott, who's still stretching himself out from the handrail. It's obvious what he has in mind. I shake my head *no*, but it's too late. Before good sense gets the better of me, we're both on Scott, pinching his mysteriously wet back and sides.

"No," Scott yells, drawing it out from his diaphragm like he's being tortured on a rack, cursing a too-cruel world before he draws his final black breath. A few more pinches and he finally lets go of the rail, catching himself in an uneventful squat. I offer him a hand, and he bounces up with it, landing an inch from my nose again, which gets a laugh out of Conor and me. Some kids are staring, but the mouse and her friends, who've formed a whisper-tight circle, have deliberately turned their backs to us.

"Nothing to see here!" Conor yells as Scott waves, but by then everyone's lost interest. Still, I think, noticing that Conor has untied his rucksack and is holding it open while Scott stands behind him with his trademark lopsided grin, it's looking like today might turn out to be more interesting than most. "Hank, we know where you go in the afternoons," Conor says, his voice low, but playful. I try to keep my expression as blank as possible, mentally retracing my last week of ascents, wondering which one I slipped up on, and when they stopped believing me about Grammy. I knew this was going to happen, that someone was going to find me out sooner or later. That it's Conor and Scott makes me feel slightly less unhappy about it, but still . . .

The attic's *mine*.

"We wanna come with you, Hank," Conor whispers, wrapping an arm around my bare shoulders; piquing my interest despite my reservations.

I guess it wouldn't be so terrible, I admit to myself, mourning and quickly moving on from the loss of my quiet afternoons. We could all go up there and hang out together; it could be . . . *fun*. But, as much as I want to give in to Conor and Scott, something feels off.

"What's in the bag, Con?" I ask, nosing in for a closer look.

Scott's hands flutter excitedly at his sides as Conor tilts the opening of his rucksack toward me. Swaddled loosely in white undershirts is a big plastic bottle of soda, something I haven't seen—much less *tasted*—in years. Ever since the Embargos, the Zone hasn't been a very sweet place to live. Before I lucked into Foods, I'd probably eaten either vegetables or loaf every meal, a regretful side effect of our larger shift toward self-sufficiency.

I lick my lips, which are suddenly dry and expectant.

"From Ben?" I whisper hoarsely.

Conor nods, a mischievous glint in his eyes. "I've been saving it for something special."

"I mean, it's just broken chairs," I say, licking my lips. "Dust."

"Not the attic, stupid. The *girls*," he says, pulling his rucksack closed. "Julia and Alice want to drink it with us up there."

Conor waits for me to be impressed, but I must look as confused as I feel, because after an awkward silence he continues, exasperated: "Only *you* could live in a place as small as the Zone, come to the Library almost every day, and not know any of the kids here." The same group of tittering girls from before—with Mouse still silent in their midst—waves noisily from the far side of the garden, more at Conor and Scott than at me, driving the point home:

I'm clueless.

Still, we all wave back, returning their sly smiles.

"As if you don't already know, Hank," Conor says out of the side of his mouth. "Julia's the girl whose butt you were staring at earlier, the blonde one, and Alice is her friend who lives literally two doors down from you."

"I was—" I start, flustered, bare arms flapping. "I was looking at her *shirt*!"

"Sure you were, Hinkles."

"I . . . she . . . " But it's not worth explaining. Conor doesn't care whether or not I was really looking at Julia's butt, so I decide to switch tactics.

"You want me to bring you chuckleheads and those girls up to the attic to drink some soda?" I ask, and Conor nods, smiling. It strikes me that I can probably convince them to do this somewhere else; that I can keep the secret of the attic safe, at least for now. "Even though it's just broken stuff up there?"

Conor nods, and I realize with a sinking feeling that it's probably the attic or nothing. That this was all planned before I knew anything about it. "We need to do it in *private*," Scott says too loudly, drawing everyone in the front yard's attention again. He flinches, then repeats himself in a conspiratorial whisper. "*We need to do it in private.*"

"All right, all right, everyone heard you the first time," I say. "Emphasis on *everyone*."

Knowing what I know about the soda and the girls, the morning drags on. And it's not because I'm worried—getting everyone into the attic without anyone else noticing shouldn't be much harder than just sneaking in myself; it's just a matter of timing. And I'm not nervous, either—at least not the way Conor and Scott are nervous. Although, I do have to admit that every time I think about the cola buried in Conor's bag, I feel my mouth go wet.

I'm just distracted by the Other Side.

I keep thinking back to Rachel and Tom, remembering Foods and flaking gold mannequins and river mud coffee and the dusty guitar laying on my bed, the one I wish I was back home learning how to play. In comparison, the attic seems so small now. So insignificant in the grand scheme of things. I almost can't believe I ever cared about keeping it secret. My world is bigger now, bigger than the Library and bigger than the Green Zone.

Leaning back against the old oak tree, I try to make myself think about what the Other Side means, Zone-wise—if it really changes everything like I think it might. But I can't focus. Conor and Scott are running around making more plans than our afternoon sneak necessitates, stalking by Mouse and Alice's group of friends, motioning them over to look in Conor's rucksack. *Colluding.* They make whispered arrangements to meet on the third-floor balcony at the back of the Library when the noon bell rings, everyone arriving separately, climbing through my secret window one at a time so as not to draw too much attention to ourselves. But of course what happens is that Conor, Scott, and I show up together and then, shortly after, the girls arrive *en masse.* The girls from before, plus two more girls, which is *not* according to plan.

Neither Scott nor Conor seem as put out as I am about that.

Mouse pats her glossy blonde hair with the tips of her fingers, checking for strays, and explains the extra girls in an appropriately squeaky voice: "They wanted to come, too." It's enough for Scott, who's biting his cheeks to hold back a grin.

"More than enough to go around," Conor says, clutching the rucksack with the precious soda to his chest. "Shall we?"

I consider my friends for a few seconds, taking stock of the moment. Conor and Scott . . . and the girls—a wash of coy smiles and flushed pink cheeks that I try not to stare at; the trees reaching out behind them and the unusual quiet blanketing us all—no rumble of the street cars on the Avenue, no white noise. Just a warm breeze rustling leaves and all the kids in the garden squishing crawlies or soundlessly saving them; some muffled hammering from the Grey Zone.

And then, all of a sudden: an explosive loudness, like I'd been underwater and have finally come up for air—shouts and laughter from the yard, shovels scraping rocky dirt. The beep and squeal of oversized trucks parking on the Avenue. I shake my head clear and start for the drainpipe, quickly scanning the School to make sure the coast is clear.

"C'mon," I say, hoisting myself up, bracket by bracket, until I'm perched—squatting—on the Library's black tar roof. I look down to make sure I'm being followed up the pipe and then quickly prop open the hatch to the attic. Through the hatch is an actual ladder, made of wood shined glossy through over a hundred years of use.

I usher the first girl, whose name I didn't catch before our ascent to the roof, through the hatch. One on one, I feel less self-conscious, and notice that she has a nice face that's screwed up with determination, and honey-colored skin, her arms dusted with almost-white hairs, even though the hair on her head is a dark walnut brown. At first her eyes focus on the horizon behind me, the view of the city sprawling out from the top of the Library, and then, when she sees the hole and the second ladder, she hesitates.

"Quickly," I remind her. "It'll hold."

It's the same with the other girls, and then Mouse, and then Scott, and finally Conor, who claps me on the back one last time before he descends into the attic. I scan the yard again, surreptitiously, making sure no one's seen us. Not that I'll be able to do anything if they have. The realization stretches unpleasantly in the pit of my stomach, but we seem to be clear, so I jump down behind them, letting the smooth wooden sides of the ladder glide through my hands as I fall.

I land on the tips of my toes, knees bent, barely making a sound.

The light, as usual, is something else. The early afternoon sun refracts around the room in the borrowed blues and oranges and reds of the stained glass windows lining the walls, the dust-heavy air slowly dancing its way through the rays.

"Nice place," Conor says, arm propped on one of the stacks of the broken chairs. Everyone else stands in a semicircle, faces mottled with the rainbow colors from the windows. They're all strangely still, except for Mouse, who walks over to a jumble of crystals propped against cracked wainscoting; once upon a time, a chandelier. "I always wondered what it was like in here," she says in a hushed voice, picking up a loose crystal and rubbing it clean. She's acting like she's in church or something, which is so much how I've always felt here that I want to reach out and squeeze her hand.

I don't, though.

Meanwhile, Scott picks at some disintegrating pink insulation peeking out from beneath the beadboard walls, then runs his finger across the top of a wobble-legged bookshelf and inspects the resulting streak.

"Kinda crummy, though, right?"

"It's perfect," Conor says with happy finality, unveiling the soda bottle and unscrewing the cap with a half-hearted fizz. "To Hank," he proclaims, squaring his shoulders and taking the first theatrical swig.

He passes it to Scott, who does the same and passes it to Mouse, who does the same and passes it to me. I can't tell if it's because the soda has been sitting for too long or because I'm just not used to it anymore, but it tastes so sharp and acidic on my tongue that I barely notice the bubbles. The sweetness is there too, though, and I help myself to a deep swallow before passing it on to the tanned girl whose name I didn't catch, who does the same and passes it on to her friend, the girl with translucent-looking freckles, who passes it to Alice, who—now that I think about it—does look vaguely familiar.

We pass the bottle until it's mostly gone, which doesn't take too long—after a few rounds Scott takes a triple gulp, causing the last of the soda to bubble and dribble down his chin and onto his shirt, which had finally dried in the heat of the attic. Alice and Freckles and the girl with the honey skin think this is hilarious, and it is, but I'm suddenly feeling too wired to laugh. The coffee at Foods was strong, but it made me feel like I could take on the world. Conor's soda just makes me nervous, like I can feel it bubbling through my veins and giving me the shakes.

Everybody else seems fine, if a little goofy. Mouse stands on one leg like a flamingo while Freckles and Honey crack up about Scott, who's trying to suck the soda out of his shirt. Meanwhile, Conor has capped the bottle and is sitting on the dusty floor in a ray of orange sunlight, flicking it so it spins lackadaisically, like a tired top.

"You know what might be fun," he ventures, trailing off with a wistful look in his eyes. We all immediately, instinctively stare at the wearily spinning bottle while Conor gives it another lazy flick.

I would be lying if I didn't have a suspicion that this might happen when I first heard about the attic plan, and—from the hesitantly expectant looks on everyone else's faces—they all knew, too. I must've decided, subconsciously, not to acknowledge this possibility . . . but it was always there. That's why they all came, I realize. Why it had to be in secret. Even little Mouse, who's still balancing on one leg, although she's started to wobble a little bit.

"Okay," she says gamely, looking directly at me with wild eyes.

Scott stops sucking on his shirt long enough to shout, "Me, too!" momentarily breaking the spell. But Conor flicks the bottle again, and it has a hypnotizing effect on the room, drawing everyone into a tight, cross-legged circle in the center of the floor.

Except for me.

The soda has intensified the anxious feeling I had just before I jumped down into the attic, and I feel shaky, like my skeleton's moving at a different speed than the rest of my body. Which sounds terrible, but it's not; just different. Despite my trembling bones, everything seems to slow down: I feel every pump of my artificial heart, and I'm strangely aware of parts of my body I never knew existed. Like the things in my lungs filtering the dusty attic air, letting me breathe freely and deeply, which I'm trying to do now. My suddenly sensitive skin is also breathing, exchanging atoms with the books and the broken chairs and the kaleidoscope sunlight.

I'm quietly freaking out, is what's happening.

"C'mon, Hank," Conor says, casually patting the scuffed and dented floor beside him.

Turning to face him seems to take forever, but finally I feel myself slowly shake my head no. "You still have to do it if it lands on you," he says with finality, his attention already back on the spinning bottle.

That's okay, I think, willing the bottle not to land on me. *It'll never land on me.*

And it doesn't. First it lands on the honey-skinned girl. The room makes a collective hushing noise and then quietly chants, "Mary, Mary, Mary."

Conor leans across the circle and gives her a quick peck on her flushing cheek, the only sign she gives that she's just been kissed. And then it's Mary's turn. And then, because Mary refuses to re-spin the bottle when it lands on Alice, it's Alice's turn. And then it's Scott's turn. The circle has fallen into a kind of unquestioning rhythm: spin and peck, like we're enchanted.

Without any conscious effort on my part, my intense bodily awareness turns into a hyper-focus on the game, on its physical dynamics. I tell myself that if the bottle just spins for longer than ten seconds, it won't land on me; that no one will have to know about my flaring *side effects*. Scott spins the bottle and, after a count of thirteen long seconds, it lands on Freckles; he jumps to his feet and gives her a wet, smacking peck before any chanting can commence. She takes the kiss in stride—with barely a flicker of acknowledgement on her face—and gets down to the business at hand without wasting any time, giving the bottle a solid turn.

I count softly to myself as it spins, slows, wavers, and—after sixteen taut seconds—stops. I breathe a sigh of relief, confident in my system; the bottle is pointing at nobody.

Or, almost nobody.

It only dawns on me that its red plastic barrel is pointing squarely at me when everyone starts whispering my name, "Hank, Hank, Hank," over and over again.

"But—" I start, collecting myself in the face of a sudden panic. The bottle spun past ten, I want to say. *It spun past ten.* "I'm not playing," I manage to say, my voice strangely confident. I notice that Mouse, who hasn't kissed or been kissed yet, smiles, and then frowns when Freckles stands up anyway, disregarding my protest.

"Rules are rules," Freckles announces to the room. "Mary kissed Alice."

"No, no," I say, backing hazily against the wall. I'm not freaking out anymore, but I'm still wired, and can feel my heart working overtime. "You don't have to if you don't want to."

But she's determined. Spin the bottle only works when the bottle is king, and we're all living, for the time being, under its random attic rule. I close my eyes and will my heart to slow down; to overpower the soda and the sugar high.

It's no use, though.

Thinking about the kiss just makes it worse, and I can feel my pulse quickening as Freckles steps toward me across the circle, unsmiling in her determination. I try to beg off one last time, a last-ditch effort at keeping my condition a secret . . . but I'm moving so slowly, and by the time I open my mouth to protest, it's too late—I'm backed against a broken bookshelf, my eyes squeezed shut in apprehension as Freckles's soft lips press firmly against my quavering cheek.

Time seems to right itself when she steps backward, shocked, as I try to work up the nerve to open my eyes again and face the aftermath. When I do finally open them, I do it slowly, hoping against hope that she didn't feel it; that the game and our lives can just go on, uneventfully, as before. But of course she felt it— I can tell as soon as I see her. She's staring at me with two fingers resting on her buzzing lips, green cat eyes wider than I would've thought possible.

"*You . . .*" she whispers.

Her brow is furrowed, like she already doesn't trust her memory of what we both know just happened. Cheering, Conor and Scott call for me to spin, not realizing that I've just electro-cuted Freckles, who's looking at me as if she's seen a ghost. I stare back, really noticing her for the first time. She's tall—taller than me—with a tiny, upturned nose and a thin but expressive mouth. And, of course, a thousand constellations of almost invisible freck-les. She's pretty, I realize, smiling, as the attic resounds with calls for me to "spin, spin, spin!"

It's too late to hide what happened, so I try to play it cool instead.

"*Sorry for the buzz,*" I whisper offhandedly, confident that no one else will hear me above the post-kiss chanting. "I have a . . . *thing.*"

I twist around her, making sure we don't touch again, and reach for the bottle, which I spin resolutely. While it's spinning, I try to compose myself. It doesn't help that I can feel Freckles

57

staring at the back of my head, or that Mouse is giving me a sort of inquisitive stink-eye. Everyone else seems oblivious, which is for the best. Just because I'm electric doesn't mean everyone has to know about it. It also dawns on me that spinning the bottle was only a temporary way out of the awkward kiss, one that would lead inevitably to another.

Whatever happens, I tell myself, I'm not kissing anyone else.

I'll think of something.

I take a deep breath, finally centered, while the bottle slows down. It lands on Scott, who puckers up with exaggerated delight.

"Not on your life, friendo," I say, grateful that it landed on him and not Mouse, whose narrowed eyes are shooting rusty daggers at Scott. And then, it hits me: a way out. "Anyone else need to pee?"

Scott raises his hand; Conor raises his eyebrow. Mouse stands up, but only so she can push Alice and Honey back down into the circle. "We got here, like, two minutes ago," she says, pouting. "I haven't even had a turn yet!"

But I'm already halfway up the ladder, reaching for the worn latch and the hot breeze beyond it. I know, as I climb, that it'll be my last time up here. And not because of the kiss, or because everyone knows about it now. The attic just suddenly . . . feels too small, like there'll never be enough air in there again. As I reach the top of the ladder, I look back over my shoulder for one last look around. Conor has his arm loosely draped around Mouse's neck and is telling her that we'll be back, that he has another bottle at home—"orange soda"—and I feel a little guilty.

I really do have to pee, though, so there's no time to get sentimental.

Back on the roof, I hold the hatch open for Conor, Scott, and the girls, who are joking and laughing and taking their sweet time.

With a growing panic, I realize that the claustrophobia that wrapped itself around me so tightly in the attic hasn't dissipated. It's a sickly sweetness, a thickness to the air that sticks to my dusty skin and coats the inside of my mouth, suffocating.

Through it, I hear Scott showing off on the ladder, trying to climb up with just his arms—holding things up.

"Come on," I call down, as quietly but as emphatically as I can. I don't like the way my voice sounds. It's sharper than I want it to be, higher pitched. Walking to the edge of the roof, away from the hatch and everything it holds, I try to will my head clear. The Green Zone sprawls out around the school in a ragged circle, not that I can see its boundaries so much as I know they're there. By eye, it's all trees and roofs and river—and beyond that, the world beyond the Zones. I know there's more to life than this. Conor's brother Ben is proof of that; he went Outside and is doing whatever it is he's doing beyond our borders—teasing us with soda and shirts and artifacts from a world we're not a part of anymore.

And I've read enough books in that old attic to know what I'm missing out on.

After the Tragedies, it felt exciting enough just to hide out, alone, and read about Lewis and Clark and Manifest Destiny and kids who snuck out in the middle of the night to go to the movies. Now that I have a taste of life outside the Green, I'm not so sure.

"Hey-uh there, Henry!" I flinch momentarily before I realize it's just Mr. Moonie. I squint past the sunshine, trying to make out his silhouette in the garden. Scott is still hanging from the ladder below, oblivious and goofing for Alice and Mouse and Mary and Freckles, who are in various states of laughter. Everyone else at School is quietly working among the vegetables, so of course Moonie heard us.

"Oh, hey again, Mr. Moonie," I call down, trying to sound casual, as if I haven't just been caught. He's finally in focus, but it's no use—I can't make out his expression from this far up.

"Y'all gettin' some air up there," he shouts jovially.

"Yessir, Mr. Moonie."

Conor yells, "My turn!" from the attic, and I notice for the first time that with the hatch open the voices actually magnify, trumpeting out across the garden. Moonie adjusts his pants with one hand and shades his eyes with the other, cane hooked over his forearm.

"Nice day for it, too."

Mortified, I just shrug.

"Well, listen, Hank. Reason I come lookin' for ya is you got a message from your Gra'mama," Mr. Moonie shouts.

There's more laughter from the attic, and Moonie waits for it to die down before he tells me that I'm to run to Gram's house at my "earliest convenience," because apparently she has news that can't wait. Message delivered, he tips his invisible cap, says, "Y'all be safe up there, now, y'hear," and shuffles off to inspect the gardens.

The hatch slams, and I turn around to see Conor and the sugar-high gang. Judging from Mr. Moonie's goodbye, they'd probably popped up behind me in time to be seen. Not that it mattered; Mr. Moonie's a quarter deaf and we'd been loud enough for him to think to check the roof.

"All right?" Conor asks, patting my back reassuringly.

"All right," I say, although I feel doubly guilty. Like I've let Conor *and* Moonie down. "Let's get off this stupid roof already."

We're quiet on the way down, even though I guess we don't have to be anymore, tip-toeing down the ladder to the second floor balcony. I go first so I can help people if they need it. Freckles goes next. Alice comes after her, but has some trouble.

Looking up at me, Freckles whispers, "I've been calling you 'Girl Shirt' in my head."

Her voice sounds like cool watermelon, thinly sliced, and despite the heat, a chill spreads across my bare arms. Goosebumps.

"I call you Freckles," I say, "in my head."

She pinches my side, through my shirt, hard enough that it actually hurts.

6

I t's too hot to run, but I'm running. Slowly. Jogging, really. *Trudging.*

Grammy's house is about fifteen blocks from the Library, toward the new city center: university campuses repurposed after the Tragedies. If I'd started from home, I'd have been there by now, but from the Library, with all the construction, I have to zig-zag through most of the sign-less streets of the Green Zone and through the sprawling campus.

It's going slower than I hoped it would, and the mid-afternoon air is so heavy that I'm not breathing so much as gulping.

Conor lent me his skateboard. He insisted I take it when we realized something had to be wrong for Moonie to tell me to get to Grammy's as soon as possible. She's big on social calls, but with civic leaders and local celebrities and cheese plates . . . not with her grandson, urgently, in the middle of the day. In the rush of the moment, I took the board, not remembering that I don't ride too well. Now it's just extra weight slowing me down, its sandpapery grip rubbing the inside of my arm red.

Grammy.

I've covered about six blocks when the real worry hits. Grammy is young for an older lady, but I have a humming in my chest that says any number of things can go wrong.

Or it could be my parents.

A bike accident: Dad—distracted by the gingerbread woodwork on the porch of a house he'd never noticed before—riding right into a ditch. Or Mom could've been hijaacked on one of her routine tours of the Grey Zone. They're careful—we all are—but anything can happen in the Grey.

It's terrible, and I hate myself for it as I jog slowly through the Green, sweat running down my neck, imagining the worst . . . but my next thought is for myself. What if I get to Grammy's and everyone's gone, a freak accident leaving me alone in our big, crumbling house? *I'd have to leave the Green*, I think with a detachment that sends chills down my spine. I'd start off in the Other Side, letting Rachel and Tom comfort me with sludgy coffee at Foods, and then I'd—

It's unthinkable, though.

Literally. I can't make myself think about anything past that . . . my brain just shuts down. I've reached the edge of campus, anyway. It's only a few more blocks to Grammy's and whatever news awaits me there—no need to get carried away with worst-case scenarios when I'll be dealing with facts in just a few minutes. I scrunch up my face, squeezing out tears I didn't realize were collecting in my eyes. I know I'm being stupid, it's just been a strange couple of days . . . the out-of-body experience, the hypersensitivity and electrifications, that thing with Freckles.

I laugh, wiping my eyes and hoping no one saw.

I don't even know her real name.

The campus is maybe my favorite part of the Zone. It's all garden paths and grey stone buildings like forts. If the Green ever condensed even further, it would probably be around the campus, like a walled-off medieval hamlet or something. Which is why the city took it over, probably. The First Exodus occurred after the first Tragedy, when the floods are said to have been Biblical. Only about a quarter of the students came back. And after the Second, only a handful, leaving the campus completely abandoned, save for five or ten graduate students and professors. Urban planners and activists. "Babysitters," Mom called them. "Which one do you want for tonight?" Over time, they were the ones who rallied the shocked local government and moved them into the collegial embrace of the campus. From there, the history of the Green Zone really began: clearing the streets, raising funds for the Hospital, working toward self-sufficiency and some sliver of what existed Before.

Dad was one of them, a professor who stayed. Unlike the rest, though, he was in the humanities—an English teacher. He was radical, sure, but outside of his alternative interpretations of *Moby Dick*, the most forward-thinking thing about him was his wife, my mom. If it wasn't for her, we'd probably have packed up and moved somewhere more normal. He *did* get job offers from sympathetic colleagues in places out west. But there was Gram, who wasn't leaving no matter what, and Mom, who felt the same way.

I squeeze my eyes shut again, hoping they're okay.

And then, *finally*, I'm jumping up the stairs to Grammy's house, taking them three at a time, then holding down on the doorbell. "Grammy!" I yell, not hearing the buzz. Remembering the Powerdown. I bang on the door with the heel of my hand.

"*Grammy!*"

The door creaks open, Grammy's heavily powdered face peeking out past the chain. Before I can say anything, she closes the door again so she can unlatch it and then opens it wide. I'm red-faced and dirt-streaked with attic dust, and still, when I see Gram standing in front of me, healthy as ever, I drop Conor's skateboard and hug her, burying my face in her neck.

"Henry," she says, surprised at first and then, stroking my sweaty hair out of my eyes: "Henry, it's okay."

I take a deep breath and pull out of the hug. "Mom and Dad?"

She looks at me reassuringly. "We just had some lunch, on the back porch."

The worry lifts, as easily as that. All the muscles in my body instantly relax and I slump, not having realized how wound up I was. "It's okay, Henry," my grandmother says, pulling me back into a hug and stroking my head, talking in a low, soothing voice. "It's *okay*."

"Why . . ." My voice cracks.

"Oh, Henry!" she says, pulling momentarily away again so she can see my face. "You didn't think . . ." I try to compose my face, but I can feel my cheeks radiating heat. I must really look like I've been through it, because she trails off. "Poor baby. Poor, poor baby."

She says "poor" like it's two words, drawing it out and wrapping it around me like a security blanket. She's beautiful, Grammy. Her eyes are sharp, like a hawk's, and she still has some black in her hair, even though it's turned mostly grey; her skin still glows like a baby, like Mom's. Behind her is a flowering hydrangea, spheres of blue flowers bursting out from a thick leafed vine working its way around the porch.

"So," I start, unable to contain my curiosity. "Why'd Mr. Moonie tell me . . . ?"

She squeezes my wrist. "That's for your parents to say." And then she smiles, her eyes crinkling up so they look almost soft. "You look hungry."

Gram doesn't really know how *not* to entertain—she's so used to being the perfect hostess that she pulls out all the stops for every occasion. So even though I'm crashing a casual back porch lunch, it's no surprise when I see Mom and Dad sitting around a flotilla of plates piled high with Zone-made cheese wedges, salt-and-peppered tomato slices, and various *"crew-day-tay"*—what less fancy people might call "vegetables from the garden." Dad is sipping a tall glass of cucumber juice, which tastes a lot better than it sounds.

"Hey," Mom says. "Is for horses," she self-corrects, looking at Dad, who snorts some cucumber juice down the wrong pipe and starts coughing. "What's up?"

"Um," I say, pulling myself together. "What's up with *you* weirdos?"

"First," says Mom, "a toast." She holds up her glass, which is mostly empty, and slaps Dad playfully on the back. "Stop coughing!"

He answers with a coughy laugh and then coughs a few more times. Finally finished, he holds up his glass and says, "To your mother!"

Grammy hands me a glass of cucumber juice, rolls her eyes, and murmurs, "To her mother, more like."

It's all so funny, everyone here together, happy—so different from what I was expecting. I break into a smile and finish my juice in one long gulp. Grammy, consummate hostess, refills my glass almost as soon as it's emptied and I take another drink, smaller this time.

"So," I ask, looking from Dad to Mom to Grammy, who's standing proudly to the side—prettily framed by a blush of hydrangeas again. "What's the news?"

"Well," Dad says, "I tried to tell you earlier, but Moonie couldn't find you. Said you were probably lost in a book somewhere." I feel my face turning red again as I remember the girls' rolled up sleeves and the bottle; Freckles' lips for a half second on my low-voltage cheek.

"Must've been a good one," Mom says, and I shoot her a look.

"So," I prompt again, straight business. "The news?"

"Your mother and I—" Dad answers with Shakespearean pomp, "—are flying—in an *aeroplane*!" He gestures outward and pauses. "To the City." Another dramatic pause. "To *finalize* . . ."

"To finalize the Charter!" I shout, sloshing cucumber juice onto the table in my excitement. It's the best news—the culmination of what we've all been working toward for the last eight years: financial reparations and independence from the federale government. The pressure's been on recently because of all the construction— contractors working on spec, expecting to be paid once we get the Charter. Without a big paycheck to start fresh, we'd have a lot of unhappy construction workers on our hands. A few days ago I even walked in on Mom worrying out loud about riots.

Riots.

In the Green Zone.

It would have been completely unimaginable if I hadn't seen it happen before, after the Tragedies. With a Charter, though, we won't have to worry about that anymore. The Grey will be Greened, the Library will be more like a real school, and everything will eventually get back to better than normal. It's—

"It's . . . that's amazing," I say, with a smile so big it forces my eyes shut.

And then I pass out.

No out-of-body experience, no slow motion; just extreme happiness followed by the crash of silverware and china . . . and a profound delight, before I completely shut down, at the sound of soft cheese hitting the ground. And darkness.

Darkness, but not nothingness.

Instead, a pulsing, indistinct and unplaceable, except for its fuzzy volume. It's all-encompassing, and I don't seem to have a choice but to submit to it. And it's not submission, really, because I don't even enter into the equation. It's just . . . it's just the *loudness*.

And then, behind that loudness, a determined beeping. The beeping and the loudness aren't in sync, which becomes more insufferable as the beeping gets louder, competing with the loudness. When it's finally too much to bear, I open my eyes . . . and am instantly blinded by a bright white light tracking between them.

"He's awake," someone yells.

"Oh, thank God," I hear Mom say.

It strikes me, then, that for all my worrying about Mom and Dad and Grammy, I'm the one stretched out on a hospital cot with a doctor checking my wrists for a pulse. I laugh, weakly.

"He's saying something," Dad says. "What's that, Hank?"

The loudness is receding, but it's still there, beneath, and a fifty-pound headache is building itself on top of it, encouraged by the continued beeping from the machine next to my bed. I roll my eyes, close them, and take a thick, deep breath.

"This has been . . ." I say, my voice cracking dryly. "A strange couple of days."

I pass out for real this time, with no beeps and no loudness.

When I wake up, I'm back at home, in my bed.

It's mostly dark in my room, except for the hall light peeking softly in through my open door. A fan is angled at my bare feet, and as I readjust the bunched-up sheet to cover them, I notice Tom's guitar. My guitar. It's reflecting the moon, which is still looming, and even some stars. Powerdown isn't so bad after all, I think, suddenly content despite everything.

"Look who's awake," Mom says. I turn my head to see her. She's perched on my dresser, and there's no telling how long she's been watching me sleep. I raise my arms straight into the air, our old babyish shorthand for *hug me*, and she moves to the edge of the bed and obliges.

"So what's wrong?" I ask, and she smiles bravely.

"Nothing's wrong with you, Panky."

My nickname from when I was a flirty three-year-old shocking all the little girls with my two-volt kisses. I was at a real-life school then. Or almost real—that was when it was just the one Tragedy, not the Tragedies . . . I can barely remember it. Mom used to pick me up after work, and she'd always get an earful from the afternoon teacher. *Too much Hanky Panky,* they'd say. Mom would try to keep a straight face, only to explode into hysterical laughter later, telling Dad about it over dinner.

"So why'd I pass out, then?"

She furrows her brow. "That's not *you*, Hank . . ."

"My heart?" I ask, knowing the answer beforehand.

"The doctors thought so at first, but . . ."

I must look as surprised as I am, because Dad, now propped in the doorway, says, "Don't look so shocked, you know you have a good heart."

"But . . ."

"It's not your heart, son . . ." he says, gesturing to the moon outside my window. "It's something out there, some"—He makes finger quotes—"*resonant electricity* messing with it."

We all think this over for a minute. Or, they think it over. I'm having trouble doing anything except staring blankly at the midnight glow of the guitar. I don't need to think, anyway. With everything that's happened, there's really only one gloomy thing on my mind. I give my parents time to compose themselves before I spring it on them, the question they must know is coming.

"The thing is . . ." I say, baby-stepping into my dark question, but Mom cuts me off.

"Hanky, listen. Your heart's going to keep on pumping, no matter what. It's just that . . ." She breaks off into a heavy silence. Dad, always eager to help, jumps in. Unlike Mom, who's overwhelmed with emotion, he takes a more factual approach.

"You know the Powerdown?" he says brightly. I give him a look. Of course I know the Powerdown. "Well," he continues, ignoring my reproach, "We're powering down because we plan to power *up* with our own stuff soon, after we finally sign this *damn* Charter."

He looks at Mom, who nods for him to continue. "We have our own power source now and everything, but, *ehm* . . ." He stops, deciding on the best way to put it. "Henry, it takes a lot of juice to power a city this size."

I must look confused because Mom cuts in again. "They've been trying to get the right levels and there've been some spikes. You're . . . you're sensitive to them, to the bursts, but we're working on it now. It's not anything you need to worry about anymore."

"You just need to take it easy, Hank, these next few days. We'll have it all figured out in no time."

I'm relieved to hear that it's not my heart. I can't even bring myself to think about the *possibility* of another surgery, which is what I'd been both expecting and dreading. Neither, I can tell, can Mom, who's started to cry on the bed. Even though it's *not anything to worry about.*

"Hey," I croak, not wanting to see Mom like this. "I actually feel really great."

This makes them both smile, Mom through tears. "No, seriously," I continue, sitting up in the bed. Mom puts her hand on my shoulder, pushing me gently back into bed.

"Hank," she says, her voice catching. "We still have to fly to the City tomorrow, me and dad—we may not get this chance again."

"Okay," I say, resting my head back into the coolness of my pillow. For some reason, it doesn't seem like that big of a deal to me, their having to go to the City. If it's just the Powerdown and there's nothing wrong with my heart, then there really isn't much to worry about. I know they have to go, and I'll be fine here.

I start to tell them that, but Mom interrupts again. "When you were at the Hospital . . ." she begins, then pauses. "As soon as Doctor Singh figured out what had happened, I . . . I drove out to the dam. I went out there to tell them to shut that . . . that *thing* down."

I reach out and hold her hand—it feels thinner than I remember, and hot to my touch.

"Hank, they're working on it. They can't stop the river, but they're going to figure out how to manage it." She bursts into tears again, and Dad joins us on the bed, comforting Mom with a one-armed hug and squeezing my knee until we're all three of us a little drained. After a few minutes, he gets up, announcing that we have a big day tomorrow and everyone will be fine if we just get a little shut-eye. Mom stays with me for while longer, though, stroking my hair until I fall into a dreamless sleep.

7

The next morning, I wake up early to a hot pillow and bird-song. There's music playing downstairs, a folksy band I haven't heard before, and laughter. Yesterday seems unreal, and I wonder for a moment if I dreamt it. It would make sense—if last night really happened, I never would have expected to wake up to such a light and happy house. Not when the forecast called for thunderstorms and heart-wrenching goodbyes.

I roll out of bed, still dressed, and hesitantly make my way to the top landing, trying to make out what's going on downstairs without announcing my presence. I'm on my toes, splaying them out on cool wooden floorboards. Creeping. I don't know why, either, it just seems like the thing to do.

But it's hard to make out anything specific from the third-floor landing; I'm too far up, and my parents are in the kitchen.

I grip my fingers around the paint-chipped banister and stretch my arms, Scott-like, leaning over and looking down. Our house is too big, only a little smaller than the Library, which is an end-less source of amusement for my parents (who never expected to live on the Avenue). But I don't see what the big deal is. It's just a big crumbly house, and all the rooms are tiny with too-tall, drafty ceilings. And we're only here because of the Tragedies.

Also, it's impossible to hear anything from up here.

I blow my cover and jump down the stairs, leap-frogging from landing to landing without touching any steps.

"Stompy Hans," my grandmother declares from her post at the kitchen table, stretching out every syllable like they're saltwater taffy, "is awake."

I shuffle in, reprimanded, and the music fuzzes out. On the table is yesterday's spread, starred cucumbers and fingerloaf wrapped and transported to our house by Grammy, who's futzing with the tuning on our solar radio. I don't have the heart to tell her that she doesn't have a chance of making it work, not with me in the room.

"So," Dad says, clapping his hands together. "Glad you're up!"

I cut a slice from a bruised wedge of cheese while the radio whines and pings, then levels out, finally settling on an only slightly static-y country music station from Outside: some lady singing a love song to her accordion, its generous bellows and understanding valves. She's singing in French and English, and it's hard to make everything out above the white noise and her overenthusias-tic washboard player. Mom's two-stepping, prancing like a pony on its hind legs. She reaches for my hand and guides me into an awkward spin. I have to duck to fit under her arm and end up almost swallowing my cheese whole.

"Morning, Panky!" she sings, looking happier than I've seen her in a long time.

"Not that I'm complaining," I address the room, "but is there a reason . . ."

Dad and Grammy look at me expectantly while Mom clip-clops over to the plate of crudités, helping herself to a fingerloaf sandwich.

The accordion song ends, and she keeps dancing as another, slower song starts, a bittersweet-sounding waltz.

"I mean, last night . . ."

"We got word from the dam this morning," Dad says, slathering a layer of jam on a thick slice of toasted loaf. "They checked with engineering last night after your mom went down there and found a problem they didn't even know they had. Which means you should start feeling better pretty soon!"

"Mom wants to head down there after breakfast and check it out again before we catch our flight to the City," he continues, taking a big, messy bite out of his toast. "Make sure everything's good to go."

"Well, okay," I say. "But still, why—why so happy?"

"We'll tell you on the way," Mom, still dancing, sings. Grammy starts clearing the table, snatching Dad's plate just as he's about to put his loaf-toast back down on it. He shrugs and stuffs the rest in his mouth, full-cheeked and finished with breakfast.

"Mwhemeber you're ready!" he says through the toast, jumping up and wiping his hands on his pleated khaki shorts.

In the car on the way to the dam, Mom points out improvements to the Zone in an informational tour guide voice, even though we're intimately familiar with every little thing that happens here. "And of course," she says, tapping on the driver's-side window, "we gave the contractors that little shotgun on the corner as the model for renovations in the Grey. Floating foundation, raised eight feet above the water level on reinforced concrete stilts . . ."

"Mom," I say. "We know."

"And you should see the inside!"

"What's, um . . ." I start. "What's the deal?"

Dad's in the backseat with Grammy. They both have their windows down and are looking out, nodding along to Mom's spiel like they're hearing it for the first time. Mom speeds up, driving a little too fast for the Zone, and I put my hand gently on her knee to try to snap her out of it. She looks over quickly, jerking, a manic look on her face that softens when she sees me.

"Sorry Hank, just . . . it's just nervous energy." She turns back to the road.

We have a long drive ahead of us.

Our new power station is near the base of the river in the ghost of a neighborhood that hadn't been obliterated in the Tragedies so much as just vacated. Ten years later, there are cars parked with open doors and bikes strewn in front yards as if everyone had simply disappeared, vanished in the middle of an otherwise normal day. Which is basically what happened. You'd think they were coming back, too, except everything is worse for the wear after a decade of neglect. A normal scene, except for moldy curtains flapping from open windows, a raccoon peeking out from the open trunk of rusted car.

"So," Mom continues after a minute or two of silence. "The reason I'm so happy is because we're going to be able to fix all this after all."

"After all?" I ask.

"We try to stay optimistic, Hank," she says. "We have to stay optimistic. There's no other choice . . ."

"But?"

"But for a while there, it looked like we weren't going to pull it off—*any* of it: the Zone, your heart, the Charter . . ."

She shakes her head, incredulous, and then smiles. We're passing the old airport, which doesn't have any planes sitting around; *those*, at least, made it out okay and never came back. Past the airport, there are no ruins or anything from Before, just a thin strip of marshy grassland, the river winking white on the left and the lake on the right, waving back.

"What changed?" I ask, and she gestures with her chin toward the vista stretching out in front of us. A group of white egrets standing, statuesque, on the side of the road take off as we approach and pass them. They're slow flyers, like they have all the time in the world. Beyond them, the river and the lake finally seem to meet.

"Oh," I say, under my breath, feeling like I'm on the ragged cusp of realization. "We just had to . . . *go with the flow*?"

Mom looks at me like maybe I'm not her son. Dad laughingly pipes up from the back, "Hardly!" And even though she still looks incredulous, Mom turns around to defend me.

"Well, no, Hank sort of has a point. . . . If we went with the flow, we'd all be underwater, but I can see what he's getting at," she says, stopping the car in the middle of the empty highway and pointing outward.

"Henry, look."

I follow her finger and, past the glare of the sun on the water, make out a thick black line: a wall between the river and lake, its top fifteen feet above the lake on one side and only an arm's length above the river on the other. Grammy yawns, waking up. "The spillway," she says matter-of-factly, blinking at the lake. "I don't think I've ever seen it filled up all the way before."

"The *spillway* changed everything?" I ask, skeptical.

"We used to picnic here on weekends," Grammy continues, fully awake and caught up in nostalgia. "Do you remember that, Sarah?"

Mom—Sarah—doesn't answer. She's still staring at the wall in the water, squinting. The egrets, after flying around in rough circles for a few minutes, have resituated about a hundred yards in front of us. Slow flyers going nowhere fast.

But beautiful.

"It's closed," Mom finally says, looking back at Dad. "It definitely looks closed."

Dad's squints too. "If it was open, we'd see it from here," he agrees. "Definitely closed."

Mom exhales, then switches her attention to Grammy. "How could I possibly remember you coming here as a girl?"

Grammy shakes her head, not doing a good job of hiding her exasperation. "I thought you'd remember me telling you about it," she answers, a little sharply. And then, instantly relaxed, "Parties, potato salad, *fishing*—but that was just sticking a rod in the ground and catching a nap." She laughs to herself and rolls her wrist outside the window, as if stirring dormant memories in the heavy summer air.

"Well," says Mom, abruptly turning the car back on. "Now it's our power plant."

Grammy sighs, folds her hands in her lap, and very quietly agrees: "Now it's our power plant."

"All right," says Dad, compensating for the dip in mood with too much cheer. "Onward!"

We drive for a few more minutes, heading first toward the egrets, and then, when they flock again, toward where the river meets the lake. As we get closer, it becomes more obvious that the meeting is forced, channeled into being by an enormous concrete wall—a monument to human engineering and rusted metal. And standing on top of it, the silhouettes of two people in hardhats, hands on their hips and looking out at the horizon beyond the lake. To the side, there's a corrugated steel warehouse with a few dirty trucks parked on the crushed shell gravel that paves most of the facility.

We pull onto a service road created haphazardly with the same, announcing our arrival with the crunch of wheels on shell, and Grammy's out of the car before Mom even turns it off, leaving her door open and heading for the concrete waterfront. Dad squeezes

Mom's shoulder from the backseat while she takes a deep breath and then follows Grammy's lead.

"Ready," Mom says, not asking so much as stating.

"Ready," I say, half-waving at the hard-hatted man walking briskly toward us. He calls her name when he's still too far away for conversation and then breaks into a jog.

"Sarah," he says again when he makes it to the car door, opening it for her. "It's good to get to thank you in person. You know, you saved us, comin' down here last night!"

She gets out of the car, shoes crunching on the oyster gravel. "And where were *you?*" Her voice is shaking and accusatory. The man steps backward, raising his hands up to show that whatever she's angry about, he's not to blame. "It was out for *days,*" she continues. "*Days.*"

I stay in the car, looking out at the water, not wanting to see their faces.

"It wasn't," he says, and then backpedals. "We were in the floodway, checking the levels, making sure the pressure . . ."

"Show me," she says, and they walk together toward the warehouse, the engineer animated, explaining something with exaggerated gesticulations that Mom doesn't see because she's looking straight ahead. Given the choice of following them or joining Dad and Grammy on the concrete promenade, I decide on the latter and jog out to where they're standing on the water, next to the wall. When I reach them, they're in the middle of another conversation about the wall "definitely being closed."

"Water level's down, nothing going through it, all right," Dad says, verifying the assessment he made in the car.

"*So,*" I ask, "what's this whole thing about?" Both Dad and Gram start talking at the same time, then stumble over themselves to defer to each other.

"The spillway's been here for over a hundred years now—and this is only second or third time I've seen it full," Grammy finally says, gesturing toward the middle of the lake. "That out there, that was just marsh. Called the spillway 'cause when the river got too high and was gonna flood, we'd just spill the water out into here. . . . But it was never *always* full."

Only a few times, in emergency situations, Dad explains; keeping the spillway open for more than a day or so was always a big decision—even during the first Tragedy, when the Zone was mostly drowning. Not that it helped much then. People worried that if we kept it open for too long, the river would slow down enough to get stolen by another river further north, which would just compound the disaster. The smaller river, swelling with our river's deadly current, would overflow its banks and writhe across our neighbors like an angry snake—saving the city at everyone else's expense.

"It's a bad idea to mess with the flow of big old rivers," Dad says. "They're powerful. Took us *centuries* to get ours under control, with levees and dams and weirs." Of course, those neighbors aren't really there anymore, so Dad says it doesn't matter if we open the spillway full-time and divert the river for power; if that changes where the river meets the sea. It's all marshy wetlands anyway, and better marshy wetlands that power street lights and radios than marshy wetlands that just sit there marinating mosquito eggs and alligators.

"Anyway," Grammy says, cutting Dad off. "Since there's no one to worry about but ourselves, we're opening the weird."

"*Weir*," says Dad. "But this is more of a dam, really."

"Whatever."

Dad points toward the dam in question. It's not your typical wall—the bottom ten or so feet are solid concrete, and the top ten are lined with massive sheets of rust-red metal. Even though they're technically closed, water from the river sluices through the seams in choked intervals. "See that, where the water's getting through," he says. "That's where the dam funnels the river to the spillway— inside of those gates, that's where we built the turbines that're gonna power us back up . . ."

He says this with confidence, in full teacher mode. I can feel my headache coming on again, but when he gets this way, you just have to wait it out. Mom and the engineer, done arguing, are standing by the warehouse staring out at the wall. Seeing me, she waves. Dad's still talking, but I figure this is as good a chance as any and jog over to her.

"Hey," I say, and the engineer holds out his hand like he wants to shake. I look at Mom, who smiles and nods, and I take him by the hand. I must be pretty normal, charge-wise, because he barely feels it, not like Tom on the Other Side. It's a good sign.

"Hey," he says, his voice half gruff and half sweet, like a grown up kid who isn't really a grown-up.

"Nice to see ya, Guv," says Dad, who crunches up behind me, holding out his hand to the engineer.

"Tellin' your son all about our evil plot to save the city?"

"Yeah," I say. "I know all about the weird."

Dad starts to correct me, and then notices me holding back a smile.

"And the water wheelers?" Guv asks.

Dad hadn't told me about the water wheelers, but Guv likes to talk almost as much as Dad and is happy to pick up the slack. The whole point of channeling the river through the dam is to catch its current and funnel it through the warehouse, where it's supposed to be translated into electricity. Guv and the rest of the engineers had set turbines—"water wheelers," like the Other Side's pinwheels— into the dam and connected them to an industrial-sized generator occupying three-quarters of the warehouse.

"Anyway, that was the plan . . . but turns out we can't really store the energy after all." Guv shakes his head and looks apologetically at Mom, who's looking apologetically at me. "Not even if we just open the spillway a little bit. It's just too much."

He pats the corrugated tin wall of the warehouse, which makes a warped booming noise, and breaks out into a smile. "You wanna see its guts?"

The inside of the warehouse is like the stomach of an enormous mechanical beast. The structure itself is huge—three stories high with vaulted cathedral ceilings. But the space is dwarfed by the generator, a massive tangle of dripping brown pipes and cement vats, levers and counter levers, and—in the far corner of the room—nothing except cracked floors and broken windows, black blast marks on the wall behind.

I stare for a moment at the empty space, not realizing how much it's affecting me until I notice that I'm clenching my teeth. The air in the warehouse is thick and wet; I can feel it settling on my hands and face, working its way into my pores. I'm hesitant to take a gulp of it, but I can't help myself.

That empty space almost killed me.

"That's where we were trying to store the electricity," Guv says, following my gaze. "We scrapped it after your mom made us close up shop last night." He wipes his nose with the back of his hand, then scratches his head. "Didn't even think to look back here with all the excitement of opening up the spillway."

Mom looks at him with slit eyes, then pats him on the back, joking: "Water under the bridge, Guv." Guv looks like he doesn't know whether or not he's supposed to laugh, so I try to break the awkwardness of the moment by doing it for him, but it feels wrong and falls flat, echoing sharply against the sweating metal walls of the warehouse.

I suddenly wish I was anywhere but here.

Freckles and Conor and Scott are probably already back in the attic, bubbly off the bottle of orange soda they're spinning again. Mouse may finally be getting her turn. They might all be frenching.

It doesn't really bother me, though. So much has happened since yesterday that I can barely remember it. I look back to the scorched corner and try to hold my breath, listening to Dad quiz Guv about the dam ("Can't store that much power," Guv says. "Gonna have to route it straight to the Zone's grid when it's all hooked up.") until I can't take it anymore. Too much talking and standing around. Too much almost dying.

Even the generator's just sitting there, dripping.

Still holding my breath, I run outside, back into the sunlight. But it's raining, a sunshower. They're not that uncommon here during the summer, but even so, it feels unnatural. The sky over the spillway is blue, but both sides of the dam are wavy, the gaps leaking more aggressively than before. The hard-hatted men still on it walk briskly to shore, not bothering to cover their rain-streaked faces.

I jog to the car, where Grammy's resting, and fall into the backseat next to her. "The devil's beating his wife," she says, staring at the spillway.

"What's that even mean?" I ask.

"You know?" she answers, holding her gaze and then looking slowly over at me. "I don't even know. Just something *my* Grammy used to say."

8

The sun is gone by the time my parents are done in the warehouse. The bruised green sky gives the swelling impression that it'll never shine again, and just as they walk outside, it starts storming in earnest. Black clouds churn overhead and the rain comes down in hot, hard sheets that break against the windshield like they're trying to crack it. I don't think they can do that, but I get goosebumps thinking about it regardless. Only, it's not goosebumps from the thought per se.

It's goosebumps from my heart, which buzzes at the thought.

"Who's the devil beating now?" I ask, but Grammy's back to looking at the spillway and doesn't seem to hear me. I sense something out of the corner of my eye and jerk my attention back to my parents, who are running through the rain . . . not to the car, but after Guv, who's running to the walkway.

The dam—my mouth drops open, literally slack. The river is slamming up against it while the two hard-hatted engineers scramble to batten down the hatches. Through the roar of the storm I hear

Guv yelling, "Come in, Come in!" but they don't seem to hear him and aren't making for the shore.

Then: a thunderous rumbling, lightning touching every corner of the sky, and . . . something different. Something I can't put my finger on. The whole scene reminds me of a German painting I saw in an art book in the attic, black and blue skies and a tiny man dwarfed in the foreground, easy to miss. *One* man.

The other must have fallen over.

I grip Grammy's hand and she squeezes back, white-knuckled. My heart's beating double-time again—I can hear it over the rain, pulsing in my ears. I know I'm buzzing Grammy, can feel the current coursing from me to her, so I try to pull away . . . but she holds on tight. Guv is on the walkway now, hot-footing through heavy machinery toward the remaining engineer, who's on his hands and knees in the center of the dam.

Mom and Dad are stopped at the foot of the walkway, drenched, calling out to Guv, their shouts drowned in the wind and the rain and the adrenaline of the moment.

I try to make out what Guv and the other engineer are doing still out on the walkway, buffeted by the elements. It looks like Guv is laying down, the other man kneeling, holding his ankles, and then—after a few eternity-spanning seconds—helping Guv back up, lifting him by the shoulders, helping him pull the dead weight of the third engineer out of the river.

A small flock of egrets flies over them, headed toward the north shore of the lake, while the nearly drowned third engineer, on all fours, vomits water back into the river. I exhale, and Grammy does the same.

"Lucky," she whispers to herself. "Lucky, lucky, lucky."

It doesn't seem so lucky to me, though. That guy almost died. I say as much, and Grammy looks at me seriously, her eyes casting around my face as if trying to memorize it, and says: "He *almost* died. . . ." She pauses, deciding whether to elaborate. "I call that lucky."

Once Guv and the engineers are back on land—the one who got pulled out of the water walking shakily, propped up between the other two—my parents head back to the car. The rain is still coming down, but they walk slowly, and when they finally make it over to us, they slump wetly down in the front seat, leaving their front doors open.

"Poor guy," Dad says. "*Idiot.* River coulda taken him under in a second if he hadn't gotten tangled in that wheel." Mom doesn't say anything, just sits there for a second looking out over the warehouse and the dam, the spillway and the swollen river. Grammy breaks the silence by saying *lucky* again. Everyone nods in agreement, including me.

"Gotta catch that flight," Mom says in a monotone, turning the key in the ignition. The engine flips over and hums, and Dad closes his door. After another long minute listening to the beat of raindrops on the roof of the car, in shock, Mom shakes her head and says "*lucky idiot*" under her breath, then shuts her door as we crunch back onto the slick black highway.

Everyone is completely quiet on the drive back, which seems to take a quarter of the time it took to get out to the spillway. It's a rush of grey and green, trees and rain, until we're back in the Zone, where it's barely drizzling. Mom and Dad couldn't be any more wet. Their hair is matted to their necks and their clothes are heavy on their backs, but they don't complain. Even though it's probably eighty degrees, I'm cold and uncomfortable for them.

Mom breaks the silence by saying, "We'll get there." Everyone nods again, me because I think she's talking about getting home—and then she repeats herself, "We have work to do, but we'll get there." Her voice is confident, and I believe her. The dam almost killed me, but we're lucky like that engineer, and we'll get there.

Meanwhile, we pull into the driveway and head toward the house, dripping and mopey but grudgingly hopeful. Before we go inside, Mom gives me a tight and soggy hug and whispers something into the crown of my head. "I love you too, Mom," I say.

"You know we'd take you with us," she answers in a low and reedy voice.

She looks smaller wet. It's the first time I can remember seeing her look vulnerable, and it scares me. She rests her hand on my chest, feeling for a beat, and smiles. "But you'd probably crash the plane." I laugh, but want to cry. She squeezes my shoulders with cold hands and heads inside.

I wait in the kitchen with Grammy, knowing it won't take long for Mom and Dad to change clothes and grab their travel bags. Grammy's absentmindedly opening and closing drawers, checking the cupboard, like she's looking for something in a daze. "Can I get you anything?" I ask.

"Growing pains," she says, inspecting a pile of freshly picked squash on the kitchen counter. One of them is still home to a stray inchworm, fingernail-length and baby green. She picks it up, placing it gently on the back of her hand.

"Pardon?"

"When you're laying in bed at night and you get that shot of restlessness, taut ankles and pins and needle knees, you know? And you just want to kick 'em around, do anything to make it stop?"

The inchworm makes its way to her wrist and is making a break for her elbow when she turns it around. I can hear Dad jumping upstairs, probably pulling on a fresh pair of khakis.

"There's nothing you can do, though, it's just growing pains. Your bones getting bigger in your body. Terrible feeling, but it goes away. Everybody needs to grow."

I know what she's talking about, remember the need to stretch in the middle of the night, unsatisfied despite desperate contortions. My legs aching, keeping me up until morning. And as terrible as that feeling was, I wish it would happen more—Conor and Scott are both a head taller than me.

Dad's on the stairs now; I can tell because he takes them three at a time like me. It'll be time to go to the airport soon, and for the first time I'm starting to feel a little uneasy about them not being home. Two almost-deaths in two days doesn't bode well. Grammy walks over to the sink and rinses her hands, washing the inchworm down the drain.

"Growing pains," she says again, just as Dad bursts into the kitchen.

"What's that?" Dad asks, and then, not waiting for an answer: "Mom's going to be down in a minute, we should probably go wait in the car." I make to help him with his bags, but he's just bringing the backpack on his shoulder, which puts me at ease—it's going to be a short trip.

⚡⚡⚡

The car smells musty from all the wet, so we crank the windows down to let it breathe. Even though it's still early, probably only three in the afternoon, it feels like night's coming on. The sky's a burnt orange, and the air is unusually cool and refreshing. A consolation prize, courtesy of this morning's storm.

The trip to the airstrip goes quickly enough. Their plane to the City is a four-person puddle jumper that the Zone has on permanent Charter, one of those tiny planes with a propeller in the front. Since we're not much of a travel destination anymore, the old airport—the one we passed on our way to the spillway—hasn't been used in a while. Instead, the four-seater lives in a warehouse off the river and takes off and lands on what's now an access road bordering the Grey.

It would've taken us ten minutes to bike there, but Mom and Dad say they want to go over some last-minute odds and ends. Really, though, I get the feeling they want to reassure me about my heart. Or reassure themselves.

"Because, really," Dad says. "You saw at the dam. Everything's down, totally blasted. And you're feeling *fine.*" He takes a hand off the steering wheel, reaching back to feel my forehead. "You're feeling fine, right? No more headaches or buzzes?"

"No headaches or buzzes," I say. "Not anything more than normal, anyway."

"And the thing is, that would never happen again anyway. Everything blew because they'd been leaking for a few days . . ."

"The capacitors blew because the generator was hooked up to them instead of to the grid," Mom jumps in, explaining it as if she had Guv go over it with her a hundred times. "And they couldn't handle it. When we get back, we'll make sure the spillway power goes directly to the Green, and it'll be just like before—just power for the Green, with none left over to interfere with your heart."

"It's a *science*," says Dad, about to start off on another mini-lecture. Mom gives him a warning look, nipping any impromptu theorizing off at the bud.

"Listen," she says. "You're thirteen years old. You've been okay up to now, and I want you to know that you're going to be okay for another three hundred years." Dad laughs. "Okay, maybe not three hundred. But more than thirty."

"You're going to be fine, is what your mom's saying," says Dad. "And so are we. Everyone's going to be fine. Better than fine."

"We just have some . . ."

Grammy ominously cuts in: "Growing pains."

"Exactly."

We park outside the warehouse, in view of the plane, which is already idling a little further down the block. It's probably about the size of our car, and Mom's right: if I got worked up about anything on one of those things, I'd probably take out its engine or radar for sure. And I can't see myself not getting nervous in a tin can like that. It's so small it can only make it about halfway to the City under average conditions, so they usually stop and refuel in a federale weigh station along the way.

We all get out of the car to hug goodbye. Mom makes Grammy—who thinks I'm old enough to take care of myself—promise to look in on me every day, then Dad hands me a wad of scrip and makes me promise to look in on Grammy. Before I even have a chance to answer, they're ducking their heads to fit through the door of the little plane. Mom blows a kiss. Dad calls out, "Easy on the ladies!"

And they're gone.

Grammy and I stand watching while the pilot spins the propeller and hops into the plane. In under five minutes, they're airborne and we're back in the car, heading home through the clanging construction of the Green. We don't say anything to each other until Grammy drops me off. She still seems distracted, and I'm trying not to think of my parents hurtling through the night with only a thin layer of metal between them and . . .

"All right, Henry," says Grammy. "I have some people coming over tonight, and I have to get everything ready, so I'll see you tomorrow. Okay, baby?"

"Okay, Gram," I say, shaking myself back into the moment. *Why do I even think stuff like that?* I wonder. And then I realize that I'm thinking about thinking and have to shake my head clear again. "Love you."

Her eyes focus on me with a clarity she hasn't had since the accident at the dam earlier in the day. "I love you too, Henry," she says. "Sweet dreams."

I smile and hop out of the car, waving goodnight. It's darker now than it was when we left to drop my parents off, and I watch the rear lights of the car disappear as she turns down the block. Of course Grammy's having people over. If she wasn't . . . now *that* would be a reason to worry.

The house is dark now, too, darker than outside, where some ambient light is still bouncing around the clouds. I reach to turn on a lamp, only to remember again that we're still in Powerdown and—with Dad and Grammy gone—there's no one to crank up the generator. I can't believe we didn't realize this would be a problem beforehand. All that talk about electricity, about my heart . . . you'd think someone would've made the connection.

I throw myself down in a kitchen chair and grab a cucumber from a basket on the table. Biting into it, I consider my options. The easiest thing to do would be to go upstairs and lay down in bed, but I know I wouldn't be able to get to sleep. The cool from the rain wouldn't last long, and I'd be stuck in the dark without a fan, suffocating in the stagnant summer air.

But what else could I do?

In theory, I know how to start the generator. It's like a lawn mower—just pull the cord a few times, and with any luck, the engine takes over. But, with *my* heart, I probably shouldn't chance it. Especially considering how things have been going lately. It's too easy to imagine myself silently splayed in the soggy grass, my chest covered in black scorch marks like the conductors at the dam. So: no music, no fans. No light.

I could always ride over to Conor's or Scott's and get them to crank the generator for me, but then there'd be the inevitable questions, and they might want to hang out in my house. They'd eat everything and touch everything and it'd be just like in the attic. They might even try to get another game of spin the bottle going . . .

Or I could get Alice, who apparently lives next door. But I don't even know which house. I walk outside to check the weather and take another bite of cucumber. It's spongy and light, except for the rind, which is rubbery and still a little dirty. I spit it out into the garden and then toss the rest of the cucumber after it. The worms will enjoy the cucumber more than me.

It hits the far side of the garden with a soft bounce and I make up my mind. I can't lock myself up on a night like this, not after everything that's happened, and definitely not when there's such a weird chill to the air. That doesn't happen much in the middle of summer, not in the Zone, and it feels like a sign.

The bikes are still in a tangle in the hallway from our trip to the Other Side, and while I'm pulling them apart, I get an idea. Not a smart idea or an idea my parents would approve of, but an idea I can't seem to shake. It's spreading from the base of my neck to the rest of my head until my mouth waters and I'm smiling stupidly, just like when I cut off all my sleeves.

It's the perfect weather for hot coffee, and I know a place that makes a great cup.

9

The whir of spokes while I ride makes a sort of crooked beat when it mixes with the post-storm birdsong and the sound of waterlogged construction workers loading up their trucks for the day, and I ride to it, splashing through puddles whenever I can. It's dark, but not scary dark. The moon is bright, and its light refracts off the still-looming storm clouds.

I take a deep breath, filling my chest with the cool evening air and letting a calm wash over me. There's a breeze laced with the sickly sweet scent of magnolias and the river, a comforting smell that I can't quite put my finger on. It's more an energy, or a movement—like the spirit of the Zone. Even though it's night and I'm about to ride solo through the Grey, it's the first time I haven't been buzzing with nervous energy in days.

Spanish moss is waving from the boughs of the oak trees lining the Avenue, silhouetted against the still low-hanging moon, and everything seems to be going right: Mom and Dad are signing the Charter, my heart seems to be fine, Grammy's having a party (like usual), and—for once in my life—I have plans.

Night plans.

The only thing that could make them better is some company.

I must have been subconsciously thinking that since I left the house, because I find myself squealing to a stop in front of Conor's house as soon as the thought occurs to me, my wet brakes not quite doing their job. Unlike my place, the generators at Conor's house are humming and the lights are on and shining orange through drawn white curtains. I drop my bike on the soggy front lawn and knock twice, sharply, on the heavy wooden door. Muffled behind it, Conor's mom calls for him to answer. "Just a minute," he yells, followed by a few resounding thumps and a smack—Conor jumping down the stairs and, unable to stop his forward momentum, smashing into the door. I step instinctively backward as he opens it, letting out the no-longer-muffled "Con-*or!*" of his exasperated mother. He smiles lopsidedly and yells back over his shoulder, "It's Henry, Mom," as if me being at the door explained his hurry to get there.

"So," he says. "What's up?"

"Wanna ride?" I ask flatly, trying to hide my excitement. It occurs to me that riding through the Grey Zone at night might be a hard sell, and maybe I shouldn't have come. My parents are out of town, but Conor's mom is gingerly descending the stairs in a billowing pink nightgown, and I know better than to give everything away in front of her.

"Henry!" she says, smiling genuinely. "Come in!"

"Actually, Mrs. Wallace, I . . ."

"C'mon, man," Conor says, hooking his elbow around my neck. "*Brownies.*"

You wouldn't guess it by looking at Conor, who's such a jock, but his house is probably the prettiest in the Zone. The outside is all swirly gingerbread woodwork, like a dollhouse—and they even grow flowers in their garden, hibiscus and foxglove and azaleas.

The inside is like something you'd see in a magazine: matching couches and curtains, a lace tablecloth, and everything in its place.

Mrs. Wallace jokes that she's able to keep everything "just so" because Mr. Wallace isn't around to make a mess, and even though I usually like going to Conor's house—Mrs. Wallace is always cooking treats from Before, made with northern supplies courtesy of Ben—those conversations are usually uncomfortable enough to keep me from coming around too often. Mrs. Wallace lost Mr. Wallace in the Tragedies. Not that he died or anything . . . he just didn't come back. They're still married, but I've never personally met him, and I've noticed that Conor looks absentmindedly at the floor every time Mrs. Wallace jokes about "how lucky we are that *he's* not here to eat all the cupcakes."

Tonight, though, Mrs. Wallace has something else to talk about.

"So, Henry," she says conspiratorially, "A little bird told me that you . . ." She pauses, looking at Conor mischievously. I look at him, too, wondering what she could possibly be leading up to. "Have," she says, pausing for emphasis. And then, high-pitched and hugging me: "A girlfriend!"

I look over her shoulder at Conor, trying to raise one eyebrow, but raising both of them instead. He's too preoccupied with cutting the brownies to see me. "Who"—I gasp, still getting squeezed— "did the bird say who it was?"

She pulls back and pinches my cheeks. "You! Little *charmer*!"

Conor, typically unruffled, holds out a plate of thick, gooey squares to both of us. Mrs. Wallace looks over at him, still pinching my cheeks. "If only Conor-baby could've gotten to her first."

"Brownie?" Conor offers, turning slightly red around the edges. Mrs. Wallace picks one up with two fingers and bites carefully into it, closing her eyes and cooing softly to herself.

"Okay, Mom," Conor says, pulling me quickly toward the door. "We're gonna go outside for a minute."

Back on the front lawn, Conor starts talking—and fast—before I have a chance to give him the third degree. "So-where-do-you-want-to-ride?" he blurts out, slurring the question into one long, foreign-sounding word.

"Um," I say, caught off guard. Finally, understanding the question and remembering the delicacy with which I'd decided to approach my night ride proposal, I answer: "There's this place on . . . on the Other Side."

"The Other Side?" says Conor, suddenly excited. "Wait . . . *you've been?*"

I guess with everything we had going on at School the other day, I'd forgotten to say anything about my ride with Dad—Food Eats, Tom and Rachel, the concert and the guitar. Conor probably didn't even know about my slightly less fun adventure at the Hospital. I take a deep breath, trying to figure out where to start.

"Conor," I say, preparing—and then realizing that I have a few questions of my own.

"Yes, Henry?"

"Why does your Mom think I have a girlfriend?"

Conor rubs his eyes with the heels of his palms and scratches his shaved head. "Okay," he says. "Julia's mom and my mom are best friends."

"Okay," I say, nodding him along. "Mouse."

"Yeah, Mouse," Conor says. "Well, she's been on a kick about how nice Mouse is and . . ."

"And?"

"And how I should ask her out."

"Oh," I say, starting to get it. "So you told her that I was already dating her." Conor shrugs. "Okay," I say, "I guess that's cool." Conor starts to smile, a big toothy grin. "But," I say, "I don't like Mouse like that. And—*and*—you have to go back in and get me a brownie."

"Okay, Hank, but first . . ."

"Yeah?"

"Lemme get my bike ready."

Conor doesn't even have to sneak out, he just tells his mom that he's spending the night at my place—he's done it loads of times, so she doesn't question it. He does come back outside blushing, though, and I don't have the heart to ask him why.

At first we ride silently, taking in the quiet—unusual after weeks of construction—and the promise of the night. We pass Scott's house and look at each other, silently agreeing not to stop. Tonight isn't for goofing off; it feels too serious for that. Too grown up. My skin is tingling, and I can't tell if it's because I'm scared or if it's my heart.

Or if it's an increased current from my heart *because* I'm scared.

I don't feel scared, though.

Like the Green Zone, the Grey Zone feels empty. If there are any ghosts or thieves or weirdos out here, they seem to be tucked in for the night, too. Regardless, Conor and I pedal hard, and in twenty minutes we're through the worst of the Grey. It took me and Dad almost an hour to get this far the other day, but we'd been stopping to assess the construction along the way. Now that I know how quickly I can make it here, any doubts I may have harbored about biking to the Other Side dissipate.

Our speed makes the Zone feel even smaller, like the Grey Zone's just a harmless, dirty ribbon separating the Green and the Other Side, which is glowing like a string of pulsing Christmas lights on the otherwise black horizon. We're drawn to them as they gently swell and shrink with the power of makeshift generators—it's hypnotic, and I'm so focused on the light that the darkness around us feels like it's intensifying in contrast.

My parents didn't really come here before the Tragedies— Downtown was about as far as they got, and then only on special occasions—but from what I've heard it was a place where people had good reason to lock their doors. Now it looks bad even by Grey standards. A single sign, reflecting the glow of the moon, reads "Royal Street," and it seems like a stupid joke. The houses that are still standing are looming shadows in the night, ruins covered in a thick layer of silt from the flooding.

And yet, I'm not scared.

Conor, on the other hand, is gripping his handlebars tightly and keeping close. I'm glad he's here, and also a little glad that he seems spooked. He deserves it for what he told his mom about me and Mouse, and for tricking me into spin the bottle earlier. Still, the stretch between Downtown and the Other Side *would* be legitimately scary if it wasn't for the closeness of the light beckoning us from the end of the street.

"Do you hear that?" It's the first time I've spoken since we left Conor's house, and it comes out crackly. Conor swerves, almost knocking into me.

"What?"

He says it too loudly, jerkily scanning the shadows, but his voice isn't shaky. If a ghost or something did hop out, he'd probably jump off his bike and try to tackle it. For this, I think, I'll forgive him for the Mouse thing . . . and for forgetting the brownie. With a bittersweet lick of my lips, I wonder if the Embargo extends all the way to the Other Side.

"The music," I say, a distant movement bringing me back into the present. Conor stops peering into the shadows and leans forward. Behind the clatter of our spokes and chains, of the cobblestones under our tires, is a lonely melody. A walking bass line and a trumpet—or whatever. Something brassy and alive, vibrating out across the blanketed wasteland.

Calling to us.

We pedal faster, toward the light and the sound.

And then, like before, after a sharp T-bone off the old road, we're skidding to a stop in the thick of the Other Side, a riot of light and color and music; people milling around, laughing and eating like it's a street fair. Which it seems to be. Lights have been strung from building to building, crisscrossing the Other Side's main thoroughfare.

We stand in the middle of the street, staring. The Other Side is amazing enough during the day, but at night—it stops you in your tracks, especially the thousand points of rainbow light shining against billowing flags, color on color in the middle of the Grey on an ink black night. And the smell . . . spicy and buttery, warm like baking bread. Conor lists toward Food Eats like he's been here before, and I smile to myself and follow him.

We lean our bikes against the wall with the mural of the sandwich eating another, smaller sandwich, and Conor hesitates, unsure of whether or not we should go inside.

"I, um, I don't have any scrip or anything," Conor says.

I put my hand on his shoulder and squeeze, then walk past him into Foods. "I gotcha, buddy," I say, radiating happiness and loving the dazed look he's not even bothering to hide.

"I can't believe you've been here before," he says, awestruck, following me in through the propped-open screen door. Inside, Foods is empty except for a handful of Other Siders scattered around the room—it's late, and we've clearly missed the rush. We walk up to the window at the back of the room and I'm about to order when the guy with the super-villain mustache and the tattoos on his neck hands us two mugs of coffee.

"Buh-scuits in minute," he says with a heavy accent. "Syit."

"Okay," I say, taking the mugs off of his hands and brushing up against a thick, hairy knuckle as Conor looks around the restaurant, realizing that there aren't any chairs, only counters lining the walls. "Thanks, man."

"Yis, syit."

I bring the coffee over to where Conor's leaning and hand him one.

"Cheers!"

"This place, Hank. This place is *wild*."

"I know," I say, smiling and eyeing the rest of the clientele. Most of them are clearly off-duty construction workers, like when I came here with Dad, but there are a few other people who are definitely here for the scene: the pinwheel woman, talking animatedly with two of the workers; a guy with green paint all over his face, eating a biscuit and crumbing up the book he's reading; and, in the corner, brooding over a cup of coffee, a guy that looks like a werewolf mid-transformation.

"Greg!" I call out, already walking toward him. He looks up with a stern expression on his face. I start to second-guess myself, and then he recognizes me and his face relaxes.

"Oh, hey," he says. "Kid from the other day. Cool dad. Hi."

"Hey," I say.

"So howya doin'?" he asks, looking back toward his coffee cup. It's obvious that he's anxious to get back to whatever he was up to before I interrupted, but now we're stuck in a conversation. I kind of wish I hadn't said anything, but there's no helping that now that we're in the thick of it.

"Oh, good. Really good."

The mustachioed chef slaps the aluminum counter at the back of the room. "Buh-scuits," he calls out, and then he disappears into the depths of the kitchen. I try not to let out an audible sigh of relief.

"That's us," I say, heading toward the back of the room and a plate of steaming, golden biscuits.

"Oh, hey," Greg says, looking up from his coffee again. "If you were looking, everyone's at The Corner." I thank him for the heads up, but he's already back to staring into his mug. Conor, on the other hand, is all talk.

"Who's *that*?" he whispers. "I can't believe you know people here. What's The Corner? These look *amazing*!" He delicately picks up one of the biscuits with two fingers, like Mrs. Wallace might, and takes a bite. Unlike Mrs. Wallace, he allows a thick dollop of butter to drip from the biscuit onto his shirt.

I take a bite as well, and immediately decide that I only ever want to eat biscuits for the rest of my life. They're warm and taste like they're made from cornmeal and something like chunks of hot broccoli. The tops are dusted with a red pepper concoction, which makes me sneeze on my first bite, but after the initial burn, the soft interior melts in a soothing pool of butter in my mouth. Even though it's steaming, the coffee helps cut the spice, and our lips leave rainbow oil slicks in our mugs. We finish off the plate, and I go back for a second round.

"I feel so stupid for not knowing this place existed," Conor says, licking grease from his fingers.

"I didn't know either," I say, feeling like I've always been here in Foods, drinking oily coffee and shooting the breeze. "It was my mom who told me. It's all tied into the construction."

"Yeah, but . . ."

"I know, *construction's* one thing. This . . ." I gesture out at the room and the Other Side beyond. "Something else."

"I don't ever want to leave," Conor says, picking up another biscuit.

"Me neither."

When we finish our second cups of coffee, we decide to check out The Corner. Conor, emboldened by the night ride and buzzing from the coffee and "buh-scuits," asks the pinwheel lady where we might find it, and she tells him to follow the sound. She also offers him a pinwheel, and he takes it with a smile.

Bellies full, we kick off into the street, feeling on top of the world. Back in the Green, everyone's been asleep for the past few hours—with the exception of Grammy, who's probably still entertaining. Since we've been in Foods, the street has emptied, and I get a brief chill despite the warmth of the night . . . until I hear chatter wafting from down the block and realize that almost every Other Sider must be at The Corner. It's so close that we decide to leave our bikes at Foods and, hands in pockets, we do as the lady with the pinwheels suggested and follow the noise.

It's a short walk, but long enough to let the excitement of being alone on the Other Side in the middle of the night sink in. I look at Conor to see if he feels it too. The nervous smile plastered across his face lets me know that he does, and it just gets wider as we near the crowd milling around the front yard of a shotgun-style house where the street dead-ends. The moon's high in the sky now, and it's probably nearing midnight. Not that the Other Siders care—a trumpet trills through a clumsy scale as we approach, and there's a nice drum beat accompanying it—a wild, tribal rhythm contrasting against the trumpet's soaring melody.

The house itself, like most other surfaces on the Other Side, is plastered with flyers and posters. The door—propped open with a shaggy block of cement and only partly visible over the tangle of people socializing in front of it—has been painted over so many times that it's easier to make out the texture than it is the lettering. But I think it says "The Corner."

I check the ragtag crowd of Other Siders for Rachel or Tom, but don't see anyone I recognize, so we squeeze and jostle our way inside. Like Tom and Rachel's house, there are no interior walls in the building, making it a sort of miniature dance hall. And it's loud inside, louder than I would've expected. There must be at least a hundred people in here, all of them are laughing and talking and jerking to the music, which is emanating from one very noisy duo at the far corner of the room.

The space itself is a lot like the inside of Food Eats—undecorated except for the stamped tin ceilings overhead. The walls are plain white and unflyered; the floors have been painted white as well, but scuffed back into a sort of grimy grey, and the only piece of furniture is a small bar made of thick, roughly hewn planks of wood. It occurs to me that, except for Tom and Rachel's place, the Other Siders tend to decorate the outside of their houses and just let the insides be.

What The Corner lacks in architectural ornamentation, it makes up for in characters. I'm glad again that I brought Conor with me instead of Scott—he's wearing one of his jerseys, a bright yellow and green shirt, so we're not totally twins. A guy in a backwards hat and no shirt dances across our path with a woman in a green velvet romper, and Conor looks at me with wide eyes.

"I . . . see why you snipped 'em," he says, pointing at my sleeves.

"Yeah," I nod, but at that moment I catch Tom's eye across the room and feel myself going a little red. I'll be matching someone tonight, just not Conor: Tom's still wearing his sleeveless DMBRVR smasher. I look down, hoping that maybe he didn't recognize me, but it's a ridiculous trick to pull. The whole reason I came down here was to steel my resolve with sludgy coffee and then find Tom and Rachel, and here Tom is, squeezing through the crowd toward me and Conor, who looks over at me and shouts, "Do you know *that* guy too?"

"Shhhh," I shout back. "Yeah." Tom's almost next to us now, and is holding out his hand for a shake . . . until he hesitates and wipes it across his chest. I don't blame him—being zapped once is bad enough.

"Hey, Hank," he says, all warmth and welcome. "Where've you been all my life?"

I introduce Tom and Conor, and Tom asks where Dad is. He must've made some impression here; first Greg, now this. It occurs to me that maybe they don't want kids running around the Other Side, and I try to choose my answer carefully . . . but I feel myself taking too long. The song ends, and the room goes relatively silent before I answer.

"Hey, boys' night out—no biggie. Rachel'll be happy to know you're here," he says, scanning the crowd. "I'm gonna go find her. Help yourself to the bar." Conor raises his eyebrows at me, and Tom catches it. "Just apple cider. Non-alcoholic. We were too impatient to let it ferment. Tastes better this way, anyway."

"Rock and roll," says Conor, making to high-five Tom. Tom, remembering his last shock, squints at us skeptically. "It's cool, it's just me," I say, and Tom slaps Conor five before backing into the crowd. The drums start back up, slowly at first, and then getting faster and faster. The room starts swirling to the beat, spinning and laughing and spilling apple cider. Tom spins into it, and then it's just Conor and me again.

We make our way along the walls to the bar on the far side of the room. It's lined with brimming mugs, and we take two. I know it's basically worthless here, but I throw some scrip down as a tip, and we go back to watching the room. It really is another world here; it's hard to believe the Green Zone and the Other Side exist in the same universe. The Green's so hard-scrabble, so utilitarian— and the Other Side . . .

It's like a wonderfully dirty whirlwind of color and sound.

I take a sip of the cider and look over at Conor to see if he loves it as much as I do—it's super sweet, and more cinnamon than apple—but he's staring at the dance floor, transfixed. I take another sip, and have settled into a head-nodding half-dance when I'm startled by the bartender tapping me on the shoulder.

I turn tentatively, wondering if I've done something wrong . . . if—and the thought freezes me with irrational fear—Tom pranked us into drinking alcoholic cider. But it's Rachel, still in her tuxedo shirt dress that's belted thickly in the middle. Still just a little grubby. A little paint-spattered, too.

"Like it?"

"I . . . I *love* it!"

My voice sounds high-pitched in my head, and I wonder why I suddenly feel so nervous. Like, sweaty-palmed nervous. I wipe my hands dry on my shorts and tell myself that I definitely, definitely don't have a crush on Rachel. I just . . . I guess I'm not used to much attention. Meanwhile, Conor and Rachel are staring at me, waiting for me to come back from my space journey.

"Nice shirt," Rachel says, looking me up and down. I swallow hard and think of Freckles.

"You too," I say, wincing as soon as the words leave my mouth. "So hey." I poke Conor's side. "This is my friend Conor. Conor, this is Rachel."

"Nice ta meetcha, Rach," Conor says, not sweaty or nervous.

Rachel and Conor exchange pleasantries, and then the conversation sort of wilts as we watch the dancers and sip our cider. Before I know it, Rachel's on the other side of the bar, dragging Conor and me by the wrists onto the dance floor. Her grip is strong, her hand cold and unexpectedly rough. Conor's loving it, and immediately starts shrugging his shoulders in exaggerated rolls, integrating into the crowd. I'm not sure exactly what to do, though—it's more awkward to stand still, like I'm doing, than to dance . . . but I don't know *how* to dance.

I look around and decide to copy the first person who looks like they have moves. Rachel's reaching her outstretched hands toward the ceiling and shakes them like she's found religion, and I do that for a while until my arms get tired. Then I do a sort of modified stomp dance, courtesy of the shirtless guy in the backwards hat, letting my arms hang free. Conor's doing a neck-swaying monkey thing with his eyes closed, and I can't stop myself from laughing. Rachel catches my eye and laughs too, but then she breaks away, moving through the crowd to the far side of the room.

We keep dancing, even though Rachel's gone. The drums are frenzied, and the floorboards bend and creak to the rhythm, bouncing us up, keeping everyone moving. The room's pulsing like it's alive. And then, in counterpoint to the drums: a lugubrious, throbbing bass line. Everyone's head turns: in the corner of The Corner, in a dirty tuxedo shirt dress with paint flecked up and down her arms . . . is Rachel. She smiles at the room and thumbs the thickest string of her heavily stickered and similarly paint-flecked guitar.

The room reverberates, the walls literally shaking, and then explodes in cheers. I'm cheering too, yelling my head off. So is Conor. The drums keeps pounding, and the bass keeps throbbing, working through a raucous crescendo. The people and the dancing and the music, the cinnamon sting of cold cider at the back of my throat—it's overwhelming, and I squeeze my eyes shut for a moment of solace, to center myself, but am confronted with shocks of colored light playing against the inside of my eyelids; a dancing retinal noise.

And then, from the corner of the room, an electric squeal—

Tom, plugging in his guitar with maximum feedback. The room explodes again, louder than before, as Big Dumb River launches into what I recognize as the first song from their record—Rachel screaming, mostly incomprehensibly, alongside Tom's shrieking guitar:

Do it! Do it! Do it!

I look over at Conor—he's sweat-soaked and bouncing along with the rest of the Other Side, riding the warped wooden floor beneath us. I shiver and hug myself, wiping the sweat from my arms and checking for a tell-tale buzz. But I'm fine—goosebumped, but not outside of myself, not like before. I just feel . . . older, alive in the world.

I keep hugging myself well into the set, happily shivering despite the heat.

10

The sun shines impatiently through my bedroom windows, and I squint, trying to remember how I got here. Someone knocks on the door, also impatient, and I roll out of bed. Conor's tangled in a pile of sheets on the floor, drooling, and I step over him as nimbly as I can and make my way downstairs. My feet feel heavy on the steps, and for once I don't have the energy to take them three at a time.

I'm halfway down when there's another insistent knock at the door.

"Coming," I yell through a bubble at the back of my mouth. Clearing my throat, I try again, "*I'm coming!*"

More knocks in response. Continuous knocking, in fact, until I open the door and catch Grammy off guard, mid-knock.

"Henry," she says, shrilly. "Why aren't you at School?"

I'm so tired that by the time I can formulate a coherent response it's too late.

Grammy inhales sharply, shaking her head. "I went by the School to give you *this*." She gestures accusatorily at me with a loosely wrapped plate of melon cubes, likely leftovers from her get-together the night before. "And Mr. Moonie had *no* idea where you were. *No* idea."

"Time?" I ask, scratching my head and trying not to yawn. I realize as I'm asking that it's too bright and hot and noisy to be anything but noon, and immediately run upstairs to wake up Conor, yelling "One second, Gram!" over my shoulder.

Upstairs I nudge Conor with my foot, catching a glimpse of myself in the mirror while he rolls over. I slept in my clothes again, and my hair has decided to wake up in right angles. I try to smooth it down, but it won't take.

"Conor," I say, and he covers his head with the sheet. "Conor!" He grudgingly opens his eyes. "Conor, we overslept."

"What?" he says, sitting up and shielding his face from the sun. "Overslept?"

"Yeah, I think it's probably twelve or something."

He sits for a second, taking it in, and then—genuinely confused—asks, "So what?"

It's a good question, and it stops me in my tracks. Why does Grammy care whether or not I'm at School? It's not like anyone's been on time since the Powerdown, and there's not much reason to even be at School for the time being. I leave Conor to wake up at his own pace and make my way back downstairs.

Grammy's standing in the foyer next to my and Conor's bikes, still holding the melon plate.

"Gram," I start cautiously, "why're you so upset about me not being at School?"

"Your parents," she says dramatically, and then stops and recomposes herself. "Henry, if I'm looking after you, I *have* to know where you are."

It doesn't seem quite right. If Grammy was that concerned about me being alone, she would've insisted that I stay at her house. I'm thirteen, though, and—like she told my parents before they left—old enough to be looking after myself for a few days.

Grammy walks over to where I'm standing on the stairs and gives me a long and tight hug. "Henry, until your parents get back . . ." she whispers, her body shaking with silent sobs. "Until your parents get back, you have to promise me that you'll be where I can find you."

"Okay, Grammy," I say, feeling a little remorseful. "It's going to be okay."

She pats her cheeks dry with her fingertips and looks me in the eye. "I have so, *so* many meetings, Henry—so much business . . ." Her body shudders as if she's about to start crying again, but she holds it in. "But I'll be by, I'll be checking in on you." She kisses me loudly on my ear.

"Okay, Grammy," I say again, wondering what could be bothering her. It couldn't be me, not really. Or my parents, who are safely in the City by now, probably halfway through finalizing the Charter, if not done with it already and on their way back. And Grammy's usually the strong one in our family—the one Mom and Dad go to when *they* have problems. It doesn't make sense, her being so upset, and that worries me.

"What's . . . what's wrong, Gram?"

She puts the melon plate on the hall table and walks toward the door as if to leave. "Growing pains," she says over her shoulder, as she disappears into the sunshine.

Conor walks up behind me and slaps my shoulder. "Everything okay, Hank?"

"Yeah," I say, not really knowing whether everything is all right or not. I shake myself of the uneasy feeling Grammy brought over and grab a handful of cantaloupe. Popping a slimy cube in my mouth, I twirl an invisible mustache and say with my best super-villain accent: "I *could* use a *buh-scuit*, though."

Conor laughs, and we wheel our bikes out into the day. Outside, the sky is a brilliant, all-encompassing Mayan blue, and any doubts I'd been having about the rightness of the world immediately evaporate. Walking our bikes to school, we recount our adventure in checklist form: *Last night we rode our bikes* (forefinger). *Alone* (middle finger). *Through the Grey Zone* (ring finger). *To get the coffee* (pinky). *That kept us dancing until morning* (thumb).

And the ride home was nothing. We were too tired and happy to be scared, and the route was familiar enough—at least to me—that it went quickly, like it was less an adventure than a daily routine.

"Hey, man," Conor says, interrupting our recollections with a flash of furtive sincerity. "That thing . . ."

"Yeah?"

"The, um. The Mouse thing?"

"Hey," I say, feeling magnanimous. "Not even a thing."

"So it's okay if we bring them next time?"

"Maybe let's play it by ear," I say, my stomach falling at the thought of having to babysit a bunch of kids on the Other Side. I'm happy I brought Conor, but I want it to be just ours for just a little longer.

"Sure," Conor says, and then looks toward the School and sighs. We're almost there, less than a block away. "Don't really see the point of this anymore, though." I start to agree with him, but feel suddenly too exhausted to carry on the conversation. I wonder how many hours of sleep we got, and figure that if we got home before dawn and woke up around noon, it would have to have been about eight full hours—certainly enough to function.

I look over at Conor, blinking the sleep out of my eyes, and then rubbing them for extra effect. Outside of his sweat-stained shirt, he seems fine. Better than fine—he has a bounce in his step.

It's been a rough couple of days, I think. *Of course you're tired.*

It's funny how much everything can change in less than a week. I go through the list again, counting on my fingers like before: *Other Side, almost died, kissed a girl, night bike ride* . . . I try to think of a change for my thumb, dirty and curled in my palm, and it comes to me as we walk through the gates into the front yard of the school: *quit School* . . .

It takes me by surprise, saying that—even just to myself. But Conor's right: I guess I don't really see the point of it anymore. Before it was all there was, and after the Charter, it'll be an actual school again—an "institution of higher thought" and everything, but right now it's just a place we go to keep out of trouble and grow a few crunchy vegetables. It's actually kind of painful to imagine wasting time here hiding in attics and talking about nothing when there's the Other Side, color-drenched and waiting for us. We could be . . . we could be starting a band, or learning how to paint, or doing *anything*.

Eating *buh-scuits* and drinking coffee.

I catch sight of Mr. Moonie in his baggy suit and dull red tie waving at us from the steps and feel a twinge of guilt. Some things, I think, don't change.

"Hey there, Mr. Moonie," Conor calls out, and I manage a half-hearted wave.

Mr. Moonie takes that as a cue to stop waving. "Ho, boys!" he calls out, tucking his chin into his many-folded neck and pursing his lips, waiting.

"How's the . . . um . . ." My mind's not working too quickly today. "How's the Prince?"

He doesn't smile, but his eyes light up as he canes his way down the stairs. "Oh, him," he says with a voice so deflated it matches his neck. "His grandmama came by with a fruit plate." Conor laughs, and I sort of shrug into myself. "S'alright, Hank," Mr. Moonie says, allowing himself a crinkly smile. "Whatta you boys been up to, now?"

"Oh, you know . . ." Conor says.

"Nope."

I pull myself together. If I'm going to be an adult, I guess I have to act like one. "We had a late night on the Other Side, sir."

"Hey, now!" says Mr. Moonie, "*L'autre côté!*"

"G'bless you, sir," Conor says, knowing full well that Mr. Moonie hadn't sneezed.

"You know," Mr. Moonie continues, unfolding a white pocket square and patting down his forehead. "I heard about that place, s'posed t'be a real nice time."

"Oh, yeah, sir," Conor says, sounding relieved at the unexpected direction our conversation has taken. "The best."

Mr. Moonie squints at both of us and then scans the horizon. "Better'n here, anyway." We look at him, just a little shocked. "Oh, y'all know—same old, day in, day out." He leans on his cane. "Once we get ourselves fixed up it'll be good again, but . . . it's the waiting that'll getcha."

Conor says, "Yessir," and I nod along.

Mr. Moonie gives us one last appraising look, touching his chin almost to his chest. "Well, you boys have fun, but you tell your Grandma next time, y'hear?" We both nod again, and he taps his cane and turns back to the School, waving behind him.

That's when I see them, leaning over the wrought-iron railing of a second-floor balcony, looking at us. Scott's in the center, scratching his chest and laughing—and the girls are on either side of him. I shade my eyes to get a better look.

The girl on the left is somehow familiar, and I only just recognize her as Alice, my supposed next-door neighbor. Mouse—balancing on her tip-toes, long blonde bangs perfectly framing her sharp, anxious face—is holding her shoulder for support. Then there's Scott, pointing at us and saying something I can't make out. Next to him, haloed in light auburn hair and meeting my gaze: Freckles.

I instinctively look down, and then—embarrassed about acting so totally embarrassed—look back up at her. Freckles is still staring at me, smiling.

"Hey," I say. "Conor." And then, whispering out of the corner of my mouth, "What's that girl's name again?"

"Huh. Alice? Again? She lives—Conor grabs me by my shoulders and shakes—"Right. Next. Door. To. You. Are you for real?"

"Oh, I know Alice," I say. "I mean the other one. The girl with the . . . freckles."

Conor throws his head back and lets out a short bark of a laugh. "That's the girl you kissed."

"Well," I say. "Just a peck."

"You're amazing," he says, letting go of my shoulders to wave to the balcony crowd. "You know that?"

I look at Freckles one last time before we head inside and shake my head clear.

Upstairs, on the balcony, everything's a little weird. Scott, in a wrinkled, water-stretched shirt, looks exactly the same as usual, but the girls are all flirtatiously angled behind him, which would make him look tough if he wasn't fighting a blush and losing. Conor notices it, too, the red creeping around Scott's ears and down into the stretched-out neck of his hard-luck shirt. The weirdness.

"*So*," Conor says, hesitantly drawing it out. "What's . . . um, what're you guys up . . ."

"Hey," Scott bursts out, awkwardly cutting Conor off.

" . . . to?" Conor finishes.

Alice and Freckles smile at each other, and I smile as well. Until I make accidental eye contact with Mouse, who's smiling too . . . but differently. Like she's going to bite me. I look away, jerking my gaze toward the city, which also seems strange. It's like an overexposed photograph; there's too much light.

"So," says Alice, breaking the silence. "Where have you guys been?" I squint, refocusing on my shadowy friends in the foreground, trying to find something distinctive about Alice to latch onto.

"Us?" I ask, shading my eyes with both of my hands, trying to shut the light out and play it cool. "We were . . . up late."

"On the Other Side!" Conor pronounces dramatically, like someone selling cars on the radio. I cringe. It's not just Conor giving up on our secret so easily, although that is irritating. It's his exuberance, the sudden volume of his voice reverberating inside my skull. That and the light.

The brightness.

I massage my temples with my thumbs and try to blink my eyes back into some semblance of normality while Conor brags about the Other Side to Alice, Freckles, Mouse, and Scott. I wish I could join in and not seem like such a spoilsport . . . but it's too much. Every little sound is suddenly an earthquake; shivers follow my stiffening spine down to locking knees and into helplessly flexing toes.

Looking down, eyes squeezed almost completely closed, I start shuffling toward the open balcony door to darkness and quiet. It's easier to sneak back in than to try to explain, I think, cringing again at the thought of having to actually speak.

But I'm walking on pins and needles, and then—reaching unsuccessfully for something to hold onto—falling. "Hey!" shouts Scott, catching me under the arm and getting shocked for his efforts. "Stop!"

I wish, I think, suddenly on the ground, surrounded by tittering silhouettes, my pulsing head tilted toward the sun I tried so clumsily to escape.

Buzzing.

"Inside," Conor's take-charge voice says. "We need to get him inside." I let myself exhale, feeling secure on the warm concrete of the balcony and in Conor's capable hands. But Scott, who's obviously shaken, stops him before he saves me. "Careful," he whines. "He . . . he *burned* me!" An urgent voice I don't quite recognize—it must belong to Alice—says, "Come on, come on!" and someone grabs me under my shoulders, dragging me the few feet inside. Shielded from the searing light of the sun, I gingerly open my eyes.

A very concerned-looking Conor is the first person I see, flanked by two wide sets of eyes: Freckles and Alice. I can hear Scott whimpering behind them, nursing his hand on the balcony. "Th-thanks," I manage, trembling. Conor shakes his head and points behind me, but I can't make myself turn around. "Julia . . ." he says.

Mouse.

I try to picture her picking me up, skinny arms straining, pulling me into the cool darkness of the Library with a few quick tugs. I want to turn around, to reconcile the Mouse I thought I knew with the Mouse who saved me from the sun. But I can't turn, my body's still stiff, locked from the neck to the knees . . . so I strain to hear.

And turn instantly cold.

It's Mouse, sobbing quietly.

"Hey," I say, looking at Conor and the girls but projecting backward with all my heart. "Julia . . ."

She doesn't answer.

"Julia, *please*," I call out, but her sobbing just gets louder. "*Mouse!*"

"Don't call me that!" she shouts, squeaky voice breaking, as she runs past me and out the door, cradling her electrocuted hands. There's a moment of shameful quiet before Scott walks slowly into the room, still shaking the shock from his own hand. It's only then—after Mouse is gone—that my body starts to unlock. "You okay?" Scott asks, and I nod with my chin like Mr. Moonie.

"I'm okay."

"Well," Conor jokes after a minute. "Now that everything's completely back to normal . . ."

Alice looks at him and laughs. Scott and Freckles join in, and everything would feel back to normal if I wasn't sprawled out on the floor.

If it wasn't for poor Mouse.

"We should get Moonie, we need to get your *parents*," Freckles says, the severity and the strangeness of the situation catching up with her. "We should . . ."

"Don't," I say, testing my legs. "Lemme . . . explain."

It's funny, telling everyone about my condition after trying to hide it for so many years. Not freeing, because I never felt trapped, but funny. I almost don't believe myself, hearing it out loud:

Henry Long doesn't have a heart.

"It's really, um . . . it's usually not a problem," I hear myself saying, realizing as I stumble through my explanations that this conversation is comically overdue. Fittingly, a copper plate on the bookshelf behind Scott reads: "Biography, 921-928."

"It's not strange to be electric. Everyone has a charge—" I realize I'm directly quoting Dad and feel a creeping sheepishness, but carry on regardless—it's just a hundredth of the charge it takes to power

120

something like a remote control. The spikes are game-changers, though. I can be sitting quietly at the kitchen table, listening to fuzzy jazz on the radio, when a solar flare ninety-three million miles away will send me momentarily haywire, flipping the radio into white noise or shutting it down completely, leaving me sitting alone in shocked silence.

So I have my alarm clock and record player in an aluminum-lined closet, but ninety-five percent of the time I'm basically a hundred percent normal. Dr. Singh always downplays my condition by pretending I'm like an electric eel, which shock their prey into dinner with six hundred searing volts—a good five-hundred and eighty-eight more volts than I have running through my hands on a good day. "Oh, killer," she'll say, shaking a thermometer near my lips with feigned fear, "Please don't . . . *don't* . . ." Then she'll roll her eyes back into her head and convulse like I've fried her up.

She hasn't noticed any adverse effects on my health, though, and I see her pretty regularly, so I can't complain. And the few times I've felt like complaining, Mom's always been there to remind me that not being able to have a phone to text my friends is a pretty small discomfort compared to the discomfort of not being alive. One time I said that if I wasn't alive, I wouldn't feel anything, much less discomfort—but after seeing her face I decided not to ever point that out again.

"Wait," Scott interrupts, his face stern with concentration. "When were you last in the Hospital?"

"Yeah," I say, taking a deep breath and trying to tally everything up. "Technically . . . um, two days ago? And again—a day before that?"

"And your parents just left?" Freckles is outraged, her normally eggshell skin so red you can barely see her freckles. She's shouting now: "They just *left* you here? Passing out? *Alone*?" Conor puts his hand on her shoulder to calm her down, but she shrugs him off and stares at me, expecting an answer.

"Well," I say, wondering how to even start explaining the dam and its blown capacitors. I start making one of Dad's illustrative hand gestures, trying to remember which way my fingers should bend, wishing I hadn't tuned him out so completely. That's when I realize that if I'm passing out, the problem must be not be fixed after all.

The spillway must still be open.

I look at Freckles, tired and scared, my hands limp at my sides. "I don't know," I say, and try to blink back the tears that surprise me by showing up in the blurry corners of my eyes.

"Hey!" Scott says. "Hey, hey, hey!"

Freckles, hugging herself, shoots him a withering look. "Really helpful, Scott."

"I have to go," I say weakly, forcing myself up on even weaker legs.

"Where to?" asks Conor, obviously unsure about whether he should help me or wait for some kind of adult supervision.

"Where the river meets the lake," I say, steadying myself on the banister as I slowly make my way down the Library's heavily worn wooden staircase. For some reason, this support, my hand sliding purposefully down the rail, makes my situation seem even more impossible than it did when I was upstairs on the floor. Mom must not have done enough to stop the dam since it's running again so soon, I think, and I'm just a kid.

A broken kid.

I stop mid-step, picturing Mouse, shocked and flying down these stairs so fast she's barely touching the threadbare carpet runners. Hurt and alone.

"Hey," Scott says, startling me. He's right behind me, alongside Freckles, Alice, and Conor. "Before we go to the lake . . . do we have time for me to get my swimsuit?"

Everyone smiles, me included.

"Going to get Mouse first," I say, and we walk together out of the Library. I half expect to have another attack, but—to my relief—that doesn't happen. It's still bright outside, but the trees aren't glowing anymore, and everything looks basically as it should, in the realm of the real.

Just very, very bright.

$$\text{⚡ ⚡ ⚡}$$

I shield my eyes again and take a look around. It's the same beautiful day it was when I woke up, clear blue skies stretching without break in every direction. A big yellow crane trundles down the Avenue, clattering metal parts mixing with the excited mid-afternoon birdsong.

Nothing's changed, but it all seems so strangely sinister now. Like even a day this perfect can't be trusted. I turn around to my friends, still bunched up behind me, and thickly realize that they probably think I'm going to fall down again. "I'm—I'm okay guys," I say. Freckles and Conor still look skeptical, so I continue. "Seriously, you don't. . . . Thank you, but you don't *have* to come with me."

"That's where you're wrong, *dude*," Conor says, theatrically confident, punching me softly in the shoulder. It doesn't hurt, but I'm knocked off balance anyway and—to everyone's horror—I teeter precariously on the steps

"Sorry!" Conor says, less confident. "So, where are we going again?"

It's a good question. I want to find Mouse, to see if she's all right. But I'm going to have to get to the dam, too, and tell Guv there's still a problem. It's too far to bike, though, and I'm definitely not feeling steady enough to try. And then, what if the problems get worse as we get closer . . .

I take a big breath and scan the grounds for inspiration. A handful of kids are gardening, pinching dead brown leaves off of otherwise healthy plants and making quiet small talk amongst themselves, but other than that, not much is going on. Slouched up against the book drop, surveying the Avenue over a sheaf of notebook paper, is Mr. Moonie. I consider telling him about my . . . problem, but now that we have a plan, it doesn't seem necessary.

"Hey," he calls out. "If y'all are leaving, you gotta go tell your Gramama!"

I wave in acknowledgment, too tired to get into it, and Mr. Moonie nods back. "You know I love her, Hank, but she's a *lotta* lady." He holds out a spotted, quivering hand and continues. "Bad for the nerves." Scott and Conor stifle laughs behind me, and I can almost hear Freckles glowering at them to stop. I wave again at Mr. Moonie, who says, "All right then," cracks his papers by way of goodbye, and gets back to not really reading them.

"That's actually a good idea," Alice says. In all of the excitement, I'd forgotten she was with us—it's like she's a total blind spot.

"What's a good idea?"

"We need to tell Mrs. Long about this," Alice says, and Freckles and Scott look like they agree with her. Conor, who's walking both of our bikes, says he'll do whatever I want, and I appreciate the solidarity—but Alice is right: of course I should see Grammy. She'll be able to take care of the dam. She'll be able to take care of everything.

And just like that, the black curtain of hopelessness ascends and the day seems full of opportunity again. *Grammy.* I take a deep breath, quietly giving thanks to the hot summer air for filling my lungs, tickling my capillaries and buoying me back up into the afternoon. "Alice," I say, full of affection for my alleged next door neighbor, "I love . . ."

Freckles, brows arched, catches my eye, stopping me midsentence.

" . . . that idea."

On the way to Grammy's, I fill everyone in on the whole Powerdown situation, why it's aggravating my condition; why my parents *had* to go. They're all aware of Zone politics in a vague sort of way, the way you know that other countries have presidents, but you don't know their names. I'd be like that, too, if it wasn't for Mom.

Mom, I think, *please. Hurry home.*

Living with the acting Mayor, or whatever she is, I hear about almost everything that happens behind the scenes; the compromises that are made and the deals that are cut. Not secrets, really, but not common knowledge either; boring stuff about the "unsustainability of monocultures" and more exciting stuff like the Other Side. The downside of being an insider, though, is that Mom's helping salvage the Zone now when *I* need her.

And she'd be here if it wasn't for the Charter, I tell Freckles. They're protective of me, my parents, and definitely wouldn't be gone if they didn't have to be. It's just . . .

An opposite kind of protectiveness. Like they're protective of any experiences I might miss out on if they decided to be overprotective. Or, at least, that's what I heard them telling Grammy one night. Which is why Dad didn't mind riding through the Grey with me, to the Other Side, when we got so depressed listening to records from Before.

It's not their fault they're not here. It's no one's fault. It's just a thing that happened: I was born with a heart that didn't work, and they need to sign the Charter.

Still, I wish they were here.

I t's a long walk to Grammy's house.

We keep to the middle of the freshly paved street, kicking the occasional chunk of sweating black asphalt, but otherwise keeping our heads down. I'm still moving at three-quarter speed, recovering from fainting and inclined to be sluggish anyway because of the suffocating heat. Freckles, Alice, Conor, and Scott are also feeling the sun, at unhappy equilibrium with the syrupy midday air.

Our conversation tapered off into a thoughtful silence a long time ago. And after a few blocks, that thoughtful silence had turned into a thoughtless, plodding silence—a quiet discomfort that left us slow-witted and heavy-lidded.

Ready for a nap.

That is, until we reach Grammy's house.

From a block away, a colloquy of slamming doors perk us up. I jerk my head up and see a glossy black jeep peeling out of Grammy's driveway into a too-wide arc, screeching over the sidewalk, veering wildly in our direction. Someone yells, "*Car!*" and I'm instantly awake, thrumming with adrenalin as the jeep continues to swerve down the street, straightening out but not slowing down. I look around, getting my bearings: Conor and Alice are running toward the sidewalk, and Scott is tugging my arm almost out of its socket.

"Come on," he's yelling. "Come *on!*"

I look at Freckles and freeze. "Henry," she yells, pulling my other arm so hard my elbow pops. "Come *on!*"

But I can't. I know I should, I know I *have to*, but my legs feel rooted to the street. Freckles tries to pull me one more time and then scampers out of the road with Scott, who looks at me like I've completely lost my mind. I turn my attention back to the street and the accelerating black jeep. To my horror, it doesn't seem like the driver's lost control at all.

In fact . . . she seems to be aiming for me.

I close my eyes, willing my legs into action, but everything's happening so fast, and the continued shouts of Conor and Freckles have the opposite effect on me as I stare down the bug-eyed headlights of the approaching jeep, paralyzed with fear.

Waiting for my life to pass before my eyes.

At the last moment, the jeep slows—just barely—and veers back onto the curb. I feel it pass me, its hot wake ruffling my hair as the driver holds down the horn. Jump-starting me back into the world of the living. She's skinny with blonde hair and a black suit, wearing tortoiseshell sunglasses. I only see her for a split second as she passes, but I try to imprint her face into my memory—her cruel smile and angular chin. I try to scan the faces of her passengers, too, but they don't even bother to look at me as I stand helpless in the middle of the street, less than a foot away from death at their hands. From what I can see of them, though, it seems like they're carbon copies of the driver.

Anonymous suits; escaping silhouettes.

Between them, though—

In between the two suits in the backseat is a very unhappy-looking Mouse, sweaty blonde hair hanging limply, sticking to her frowning, red-splotched face as she stares disconsolately out the wide rearview window.

"Mouse!" I shout, sprinting after her on my newfound legs as the jeep swerves back onto the road. "*Mouse!*" It's no use, though. Even though I can still hear them screeching and revving through the Zone, they're long gone.

And Mouse with them.

I stand rooted again in the street, shocked, until Conor catches my attention by nodding toward Grammy's still open door. We look at each other tautly, our summer malaise replaced with adrenalin and apprehension. And I run, for the second time in as many days, toward Grammy's house with a cringing fear in my chest.

The blue hydrangeas are still brightly blooming in her front yard, softly catching the light as if there was nothing to worry about. As if the door to Grammy's wasn't fully open, letting a sickly light into the shadows of her well-kept house.

I stop at the door, holding Conor back with an arm across his chest.

"Grammy," I yell, hoping for—but not expecting—an answer. "Grammy!"

Conor pushes through my arm just as Freckles catches up with us on the doorstep. "Let me," he says, looking me in the eye and stepping sideways across the threshold.

Thirty long seconds later, Conor calls my name from the back of the house, and, expecting the worst, I walk slowly toward the kitchen. Stopping in the airy front room, I'm suddenly overtaken with a desperate urge to run back out into the sunshine and track down the jeep. To rescue Mouse. To do anything but follow Conor back into the dreaded kitchen.

But he calls again, and Freckles squeezes my hand hard . . . and continues to squeeze as we make our way back, her cold fingers wrapped strongly around my hot ones. It's funny, I think, distracted by her touch. I'm not buzzing her now—after playing chicken with Mouse's kidnappers—when all it took was a late night and a nice walk to school to zap Mouse.

And the dam, I grimly remind myself.

Meanwhile, Conor is at the kitchen table with Grammy, who's staring out the window above the sink with blank eyes, not registering us or anything else around her. On the ornately detailed tablecloth in front of her is an unmarked manila envelope, which stands out against the white lace.

"Grammy," I say, voice shaking. "What . . . what happened?"

She doesn't look up, and it's not clear that she even heard me. I rush over to her, shaking my hand free from Freckles. "Grammy," I whisper, squeezing her arm. "*Grammy!*"

I feel tears start to leak out of my eyes, and seeing Freckles and Conor walk back toward the living room, wipe them off with the back of my hand. "*Grammy,*" I say again, shaking her. "What happened?" My voice must be especially keening, because she finally notices me, annoyed—and then her face softens.

"Your parents," she says. "There's been a problem."

"What?" I go cold. "Who were those people?"

Grammy sighs, looking older than usual, and goes back to staring out of the kitchen window. I follow her gaze. The world looks pretty, framed by the glossy white woodwork; there are more blue hydrangeas out there, and beyond them, two sparrows chasing each other around a stunted avocado tree. I squeeze Grammy's shoulder, massaging her back into conversation.

"Your parents are being held for treason against the federale government," she says, loudly and in a matter-of-fact monotone.

And then she looks at me, her eyes watering, and sweetens her voice. "Things are . . . bad on the Outside, Henry."

"Treason?" I ask, flinching a little at my voice's rising pitch. I feel completely smashed, as if the jeep had run me over instead of swerving, and all I can think about is my parents wedged between two suits, like Mouse. Heading for trouble as I lay broken on the ground.

"Secession," Grammy says, holding eye contact.

"*What?*"

"They knew what the Charter meant . . ." she says, looking away, her voice low and tired. "And they took your parents."

They took my parents.

I run the phrase through my head a few times until I can't stand to hear it anymore. I want to feel my stomach go cold, to cry and beat my fists on the floor. But I just feel hollow, disassociated from myself.

"And Julia?" I hear myself ask in a too-level voice.

"The girl?" Grammy says, holding up her hands helplessly. "She came while they were here."

There's a sharp intake of breath from the doorway behind me, and I turn around to see Freckles biting her pale lips white. "Where are they taking her?" she asks, voice shaking. Grammy just looks back out the window, and Freckles turns to me imploringly. But there's nothing I can do. They took my parents, and they took Mouse. I sit down next to Grammy and gently pry her clenched fist open so I can hold her hand.

After a moment, she turns to me again. Muted voices in urgent conversation carry over from the other room: Freckles and Conor and Scott. I try to block them out and focus on Grammy. I'm still not buzzing any more than usual, but her rings vibrate slightly in my hands.

"I fainted again today," I say, and feel her start to sob. She hugs me tightly and whispers, "I'm so sorry, Henry. I am *so* sorry." Her accent is thicker than she usually allows it to be, syllables pulling out like clover honey. Sitting in the kitchen of her meticulously decorated house, surrounded by scavenged heirlooms and salvaged finery, it occurs to me how terrible all this must be for her.

She didn't ask for any of it—for treasonous children and a grandson without a heart, for hard knocks and Powerdowns. You could find Grammy in the society page of the newspaper almost every Sunday Before, dripping in pearls with a pageant smile. I squeeze her tighter.

"*I'm* so sorry, Grammy."

She holds my head to her neck and runs her fingers through my hair. "It's okay, baby," she says. And then, "They're taking back the Zone."

"The men in the black cars?"

I feel her nod. "They know about the dam, about everything." She's talking quickly now, the floodgates finally open. "I woke up to a threatening letter. I looked for you at School, and then at the house . . . they were waiting for me when I got back."

I squeeze her tighter, feel her flinch.

Oh, no . . .

"Did they . . . ?"

"They made sure I told them everything I know," she says, not meeting my eyes. They hurt her, is what she's saying. Right before they stole Mouse and tried to run me over. Spasms of anger course through my body and I tense, looking toward the fruitless avocado tree in the backyard and trying to keep my emotions in check. Grammy holds my chin firmly in her hand and turns my head so I'm facing her again.

Now it's my turn to look away.

"We all knew something was coming, Henry." I shake my head—I didn't know anything was coming. "Your mom knew it too, we just hoped for the best. The threat . . ." She gestures limply toward the manila envelope in front of her, hand-delivered by the enemy. "That was here, on the kitchen table, when I woke up. I knew it was over then."

Seething, I finally meet her crinkled eyes.

"The country's gone wrong, Henry. It's everyone for themselves . . . the federale government is doing everything they can to stop another Civil War."

"Are they?" I ask, still angry. "Are they stopping another Civil War?"

Grammy searches my face. "No, Hank." Her voice is soft and warm again, caring. "You know we just want to live. The way things were . . . *Before*."

In the living room, the conversation has fermented into a fully-fledged argument, with Freckles pushing to rush out and find Mouse right away, and Conor wanting to wait it out and see what we can learn about the kidnappers.

"Besides," Conor says, on the ragged edge of shouting. "Hank needs us here!" Freckles says something I can't make out; after that it's just angry whispers. Grammy glances at me with a pained look, squeezes my arm, and gets up with just a little difficulty.

"*Children*," she intones, suddenly an attention-demanding *grande dame* again. As she heads for the living room, I catch a glimpse of the darkening bruises beneath the sleeves of her blouse and cringe, unable to imagine the kind of monster that would be capable of hurting Grammy.

And now those monsters have Mouse.

I follow Grammy to the other room, where she's pacing before an anxious but quiet audience. "The agents who took your friend," she begins, "consider everyone in the Zone a traitor to the federale government, and are prepared to treat us all accordingly."

That shuts everyone down, except for Alice, who starts to sob quietly. "They have my parents," I say, breaking the unbearable silence with a crack in my voice. "They're prisoners, in the City."

"Furthermore," Grammy says, slowly, looking us each in the eye. "*We're* also prisoners. Those people you saw, the ones who took your friend . . . they're just the beginning." The air in the room is stifling as this sinks in—the idea that we're all in danger, that everything we know is about to end. Grammy holds up the manila envelope from the kitchen table and waves it at us. "These," she says, "are our walking papers. They want us out, and they're sending their *thugs* to get us." Alice, still crying, calls wetly for her mom and runs for the front door, which she leaves slapping on rusty hinges in her wake.

Grammy nods seriously at the rest of us. "But," she says, "We don't have to take it."

"You're saying that that jeep is just the start," says Conor, a little dubious. "But how do we know that?" Construction noises in the distance support Conor's doubt—outside, it's business as usual. Streets are still being restored, houses being rebuilt.

Grammy opens the envelope and hands it to Conor, who hesitantly pulls out a handful of eight by ten photographs. I can't see what they're pictures of, but Scott and Conor's face turn ashen looking at them, and after a minute or so Conor drops the photographs on the worn Persian rug.

"What can we do?"

"Get out," she says, her voice brittle as ice and just as chilling. "We have to get out."

I pick the photographs off the floor.

They don't make sense at first—they're just shot after shot of abstract shapes. I flip through with a creeping familiarity until I recognize that they're aerial views of the Zone, schematics with our major occupations—the Library, the dam, the Avenue . . . even my house—marked with bold red Xs. Which would be sickening enough if it weren't for the last photo, which shows the whole Zone underwater, the same Xs superimposed over an aerial photo of the Zone during the Tragedies; totally flooded.

"Library, nightfall," I say, looking at Conor and Scott with as much bravery as I can muster. "Get everyone."

Freckles gives me a sideways glance; I was laid out on the ground, incapacitated, a little more than an hour ago, and she clearly hasn't forgotten it. "What about your heart?" I pat my chest, looking blankly around the room, then rush with purpose to Grammy's spotless kitchen. In the cabinet above the sink, next to a jumble of cords and bright white appliances, is what I'm looking for: a roll of aluminum foil, charred brown in places and crumpled from reuse. I realize the ridiculousness of what I'm about to do, but it can't be helped. Even if it doesn't work, it's the best I have. I unroll the foil and give it an exploratory sniff, silently thanking Grammy for keeping such a fastidious house. Despite how it looks, it's been washed clean of cooking grease and smells faintly of lemon soap.

That settled, I go about wrapping my chest.

It's not perfect: the foil is loose and crinkly over my shirt, cold on my bare arms. But it doesn't take long, and I'm skinny enough that I'm able to wrap myself a few times for extra protection. Feeling a little bit like a dollar-store Tin Man, I take a deep breath and walk hesitantly back into the living room, which is quiet as the Grey, everyone lost in their own dark thoughts.

"Hey," I say, eight eyes instantly on my aluminum wrap. I don't know what I expected, but it wasn't the emotionless scrutiny I'm getting. I squeeze my arms into my sides, pushing myself into the cold and scratchy foil. After an uneasy moment, Conor asks, "Is that really going to work?"

I shrug, and he breaks out into a smile. Which catches, working its way around the decreasingly depressing living room until even Grammy has a reluctant twitch at the corners of her pursed mouth. I'd want to let this moment stretch out forever, if it weren't for Mouse and my parents. But that's the whole problem: Mouse and my parents.

"So . . ."

Everyone looks at me expectantly and I bite my cheeks, trying to hide my nervousness. "The most important thing," I start, voice cracking at the memory of the photos from the manila envelope, "is the dam." I look at Freckles, and she meets my eyes and nods encouragingly. "The people who have Mouse and—" I clench my teeth for a moment and Grammy cringes sympathetically. I start over. "The people who have Mouse and my parents are there."

Conor looks at me questioningly and opens his mouth to object, but I answer him without even having to hear his question. "If they're planning on messing with the river, that's the place to do it."

"Then why do we want to go there?" Conor yelps, his cheeks flushing with frustration.

Scott nods in agreement. "No point in ending up like Mouse." Freckles shoots a fierce look at Scott and then at me, waiting to hear how I'll respond. It's true that I'm not excited about going into the thick of things, but I don't see any other option. I sigh, and the expansion of my chest rips the aluminum foil down my side.

"And what about your heart," Conor says, pointing at the obvious. "The dam's making you sick; you can't go there."

I have to concede that he has a point.

The room settles back into a muffled anxiety while I try to think of what we can possibly do to fix the situation, to get Mouse and my parents back. But it's so much to process, and I get stuck on thinking about how overwhelming everything suddenly is instead of coming up with actual solutions.

"Then it's settled," Freckles says, looking determinedly around the room, her entire aspect brimming with the confidence I was trying to embody earlier. Everyone looks at her, surprised into silence. After a beat or so, I hesitantly take the bait.

"What's settled?"

"You're going to go to the Library and gather the kids inside. I'll check to see if you're right about the dam. If the federales are already there, we should evacuate the Zone. And if they're not, we could maybe . . . do *something* to stop them. Everyone else can either come with me or help round up people in the Green." Grammy nods approvingly while Conor and Scott stare at Freckles, agape.

"Okay," Conor finally says. "If you're going, I'm going with you."

"Me too." Scott shuffles to stand behind Freckles as if we're choosing teams for kickball. Grammy, smiling tautly, follows him.

"What?" I say. "Everyone's going but me?"

I want to fight them, but I'm feeling ill again. It's not my heart, though—it's a weakness in my knees, an overarching exhaustion weighing me down into acceptance. Limp, my arms flop against my sides, rubbing noisily against the foil. "Who's going to . . . ?"

I trail off and Grammy finishes my sentence for me: "Round up the troops?"

I nod, exhaling shakily.

"I'll take care of that, Henry. You just get some—" A sudden hot breeze gusts against the windows, rattling them in their panes. The front door, open since Alice ran away in a panic, bangs against the front of the house. We all shiver despite the heat, thinking about Mouse and my parents, about Alice running home, alone on ominous streets.

We make our way outside with hesitation, checking for black cars. Remembering the aerial photos, I jerk my neck back and scan the skies for helicopters. But there's nothing, no activity except for the buzz of distant construction and fat and happy bumble bees lazing around Grammy's hydrangeas. And beneath that, faintly, the steady beating of my artificial heart.

I close my eyes for a moment and focus on the sounds, noises that I've heard every day since I can remember. I tell myself to wake up, that this is all just a stupid dream. *Dad's back at home, crushing walnuts for nutraloaf and trying to remember the lyrics to old jazz numbers. Mom's out fixing the city, but she'll be home soon too, and we'll all . . .*

A car door opens and I snap to, eyes cracking open with a sudden terror. But it's just Scott getting into Grammy's old sedan. I watch as he and Conor and Freckles file solemnly in, letting the severity of the situation slowly sink in again.

This is really happening, I think, forcing myself out of my daydreams as Grammy pulls me into a tight hug. My aluminum wrap crinkles between us, and I'm suddenly enveloped in her liberally applied perfume. It's a floral scent I've always associated with special occasions.

"I was wrong, Hank," she whispers sweetly, her lips mashed up against my forehead. "This isn't growing pains." I sigh, letting myself be comforted by her closeness, thinking that everything's going to be all right after all. And then she whispers again, louder, almost savagely:

"*This is war.*"

She squeezes me one last time and walks with purpose to the car, which she pulls unceremoniously out into the street, not looking back once. Scott and Conor and Freckles, on the other hand, crane their necks until Grammy sharply turns the corner, leaving a rattling hubcap in her wake. They're not the most inconspicuous group of spies, I realize, shivering at the thought. If the government really has taken control of the dam, she's driving them all straight into danger.

Feeling acutely alone, I scan the street a second time and start making my way back to School.

12

The days are long now, and there aren't many shadows to hide in, but I manage to slink back to School on the shady sides of back streets, checking behind me so often I get a crick in my neck. Every once in a while a truck trundles by and I make myself as small as possible. But I don't see any more slick strangers. In fact, I don't see anything other than the occasional contractor.

Despite everything—or maybe because of it—my mind wanders. One moment I'm flattened against a garden wall, terrified; the next, I'm distracted by a handful of green-striped dragonflies, imagining myself in their armored bodies while they flit in and out of the same overflowing garden. To their bulging bug eyes, I'm just splashes of light, segmented and prehistoric.

Like them.

It's a comforting thought, to be somehow not Henry Long, and—dragonfly-like—I slip into it, my long tail quivering in the heat of the sun. But as soon as I let down my guard, rusty brakes screech in the distance, piercing my foggy insect consciousness. Freezing, I remembering myself and my situation.

That I can't afford to daydream anymore.

Especially since I keep repeating Grammy's parting words to myself, mostly in my head, but sometimes out loud like a crazy person. "This is war," she said. Scott and Conor and Freckles and Gram aren't going to be storming the dam or anything . . . and it's not like anyone else in the Zone is a Navy Seal, either. If this is war, it's not one we have any chance of winning.

A terrible vision stops me cold: Mouse and Grammy and Freckles and the rest of them trussed up in a rust-stained puddle in that burnt-out corner of the warehouse by the dam, Conor straining at restraints that only bite tighter and tighter into his dirty, bloodied wrists.

And then there's me.

I might as well be with them, considering how much good my body is doing me lately. The more I try to ignore it, the more I obsess about it, hands balled into bony fists; the only constant over the last three days is my spastic heart. And now that the federale government has decided to take over the dam, *to drown the city*. . . . It was bad enough when it happened naturally, but to do it on purpose? After everything the Zone's been through; after all the rebuilding?

My fists shake weakly at my sides as I imagine worst-case scenarios: *I could die, my parents could die, Grammy could die, everyone could die. The power could spike again and my heart could explode. Everyone could drown. The Other Side could drown. There would be no one left to care.*

A dragonfly alights on an azalea bush flowering out over the sidewalk, its tail and wings quivering in the bright afternoon sun.

Except for you, I think. *You'll remember me, right?*

A truck rumbles by, trailing construction dust, and I automatically track it with fearful eyes. When I look back, the dragonfly is gone. I'll have to pick up the pace, especially since I've relegated myself to back streets. As I approach the Library from the rear, I hope Grammy's doing the same—being careful. The Library looks different now—somehow shabbier and smaller. And quiet, more so than usual. Inching around the garden toward the front of the building, on edge, I notice that no one's milling around in the front yard; there are no dirty-kneed kids squishing bugs. A car door slams and I stop dead in my tracks, breathing loudly despite my best efforts at silence. After a few tortured seconds, my heart pounding dully in my head, I hear what I've been praying for: car wheels spinning out on gravel—leaving. With a deep, steeling breath, I peer around the chipped stucco corner of the Library and see a black jeep peeling out down the Avenue, its heavily mirrored windows reflecting the Library in reverse . . . and my own distorted face.

My first instinct is relief, and the tenseness in my chest loosens as I quietly exhale. Crisis averted, I'm just about to step out into the front yard when I see them, out of the corner of my eye: two more black jeeps, parked haphazardly on the streetcar tracks in front of the Library. And leaning against them, three more well-dressed strangers, all in black.

I slump back against the wall.

"Hank!"

The disembodied whisper repeats, and—unable to place it—I scan the garden. A few dragonflies flit around stalks of summer okra, already crowned with delicate yellow flowers. The voice whispers my name again, impatient, and I arch my eyebrows at them disbelievingly

It couldn't be . . .

"Henry!" The voice isn't a whisper anymore, it's an urgent half-shout, short and sharp like a bark, and I realize with a half-embarrassed start that it's coming not from the garden at all, but from a window over my shoulder. Looking up, I see a nondescript girl draped halfway out the windowsill, her face red from hanging upside down.

"Alice!" I shout, wincing almost immediately at her upside-down cringe. Still, I smile to see her. It seems funny to recognize her, unassisted, for the first time when she's mostly upside down, her sun-bleached hair covering three-quarters of her face. I point to the back of the Library, and she nods, pressing a finger tightly against flushed lips and gesturing toward the Avenue. I quickly retrace my steps, sneaking between the corroded metal book drop and the roughly stuccoed wall to keep out of view and then tip-toeing toward the heavy storm door at the back of the Library. It's slightly ajar, and so little used that I can't remember ever having seen it open before. To my surprise, a flash of hands beckon urgently from the darkness within. I look over my shoulder, then make a run for it, only stopping after I'm gripped and pulled into the Library by what feels like a hundred grasping hands.

The darkness inside is sudden and complete.

I have to blink past the fireworks playing against the insides of my eyelids until I see well enough to blame the drapes drawn tightly across the Library's many windows, which had been thrown open since the Powerdown for circulation and light. Thick and decadent, these have always seemed like one of the last vestiges of Before . . . but now, seeing them through the Zone's grey veil, I notice that the stately red velvet is balding in spots. The afternoon sun strains against these thinning sections, giving the room a hazy, candlelit feel.

Standing in a semi-circle around me are most of the children from School, with a gaggle of adults standing protectively behind them. Some I recognize and some I don't. At a desk in the corner, scratching something into a leather-bound ledger by actual candlelight, is Mr. Moonie. Still tugging at my arm, red-faced, is Alice. Standing behind her is Mary, the honey-skinned girl from spin the bottle. Seeing them together again, I'm distracted by a fractured memory of soda buzzing in my veins and Freckles' thin lips pressed against my cheek. That was just upstairs, less than two days ago. Now, looking at Mary and Alice, ashen-faced in the moldering study, it's hard to imagine a world where two days ago even existed. "*Everyone's here?*" I whisper, not wanting to break the quiet of the room. The last time I'd seen Alice, she was running—wailing—from Grammy's house. Something must've happened between then and now, something that got everyone in the Zone to cram into the darkness. And I have a sinking feeling that it wasn't Alice spreading the news, door-to-sobbing-door. She nods in affirmation, Mary somberly repeating the nod behind her.

"Almost everyone's here," Mary says over Alice's shoulder. Her voice, loud against the quiet, seems to galvanize the room, which breaks out into hushed whispers. Mr. Moonie finally looks up from his work and seems genuinely surprised to see us, as if he hadn't noticed us come in. "Half the Green's here," she continues. "The jeeps—"

"Half'a the Zone's here, all right," Moonie interrupts in a tired voice, rising from his cracked leather chair and shuffling toward us, brandishing his cane at a trio of adults who'd started raising their voices in argument. "First time most of 'em have visited a library." We laugh out of courtesy, but it's obvious that beneath his codgerly exterior he's genuinely upset to have the place overrun.

"Hey, Mr. Moonie," I say, rubbing my suddenly sweaty hands dry on my shirt, which crinkles uncomfortably beneath my wet palms. He raises an eyebrow at the aluminum foil I'd forgotten about and then gloomily pats me on the back, ignoring my flimsy armor.

"How's . . ." I try to dredge up some historical personage, a sadsack writer or warrior queen. The generously mustachioed captain of a despite-all-odds flotilla. But everything pales in comparison to this moment; to everyone packed in the library, hiding in the musty darkness.

My parents . . .

"How's everything?" I manage, lamely.

"World-wracked." Moonie orates, as if drawing from some dark recess of his memory, and he seems to inflate as he continues, voice deepening. "Gut sacked. Attacked." He gestures toward the Avenue beyond the drapes with outstretched cane and closes his eyes, looking thirty years younger despite his quivering, chinless neck: "*To-night I smell the battle; miles away / Gun-thunder leaps and thuds along the ridge; The spouting shells dig pits in fields of death, / And wounded men, are moaning in the woods.*"

The room gets momentarily darker, probably from a passing cloud—but I take it as sign. Grammy had seen it, and now Moonie smells it: war. The closest I've come to anything like it is with the Tragedies, and those always came tinged with excitement—swirling green skies and air crackling with static, the preparatory rush and the tight-lipped evacuations. Moonie taps his cane back onto the floor and deflates, an old man in a wrinkled linen suit again.

This feels nothing like the storms.

"Sigfried Sassoon," Moonie says with a thoughtful sigh, making his way back to his desk, where he flips back through his ledger. An expectant thrill courses through my tensing muscles—an urgency that Moonie doesn't show any signs of sharing. "No clear ties to the City, none that I knowah. Except, of course, in that . . ." He reaches for a word, looking me searchingly in the eye. His eyebrows are enormous, great white waves cresting up his wrinkled brow. "In that sort of . . . interconnected humanity, shared oversoul . . ." He taps his ledger. "In the Emersonian sense!"

"No clear ties to the city, either, Emerson," Moonie says, settling back into his chair with a sigh. "But worth knowing anyway. Worth knowing anyway."

Unable to contain my nervous excitement any longer, I interrupt Mr. Moonie's historical reveries. "How'd everyone know to come here?" I ask, looking first at Moonie and then back around the room. Only Alice and Mary have stayed in the study—after the excitement of my arrival had dissipated, everyone else moved on to other, less poetic wings of the Library.

"What's that?" Moonie asks, nose already back in some great and dusty reference book from Before. "I've no idea, Mr. Henry Long, why the Zone feels the need to condense into this dead end of a house when any rabbit worth its teeth would be running for the brush."

Mary, Alice, and I share a nervous glance. "They were driving up and down the Zone, the strangers," Mary says, the color draining from her face at the memory. "*Snatching people.*"

"When I realized . . . I started running to my house from your grandmother's," Alice cuts in as Mary starts shivering uncontrollably. Her voice is level, but only just. "I had to get my parents. I ran into them on the Avenue. They were racing here, to get me."

"None of which explains," Mr. Moonie pipes up from behind his book, the folds of his neck quivering with theatrical indignation, "why all of y'all came to *me*."

I catch Alice and Mary's eyes again. They're unfocused, with the exhausted looseness of waning adrenalin. No explanation is necessary, and Moonie knows it. Everyone knows it, because everyone feels it: a negative energy. Parents felt it creeping into their consciousnesses and instinctively came to the Library to find their kids. Kids came to the Library because they didn't know where else to go. Even unattached adults found themselves drawn inextricably here. The Library's the beating heart of the Green, the de facto town hall. Plus, I think—remembering how fast I went the first time I skateboarded down the sloped driveway—it's on high ground.

Moonie, its reluctant custodian, knows it. Even cloaked as he is in the past, he smells the coming battle, too. It's one thing to smell battle, though, and another thing entirely to be a comfortably old historian dropped into the middle of the fray without a musket.

I rub my bare shoulders, suddenly cold. The room has darkened again, and not just because of a passing cloud. It'll be fully dark in an hour or so, and it's with a squirming uneasiness that I realize I'm the only person here who knows there's a possibility that tomorrow we'll all wake up fifteen feet underwater. My face flushes with shame for having forgotten the only other people who know about the plot against the City.

"Grammy's coming, too," I say. "And Conor and Scott. They went to the . . ." I pause, feeling Moonie and Alice and Mary's eyes on me. "She had to check on some things. We're supposed to meet here at nightfall."

Moonie checks the dimness of the light slipping in through the threadbare drapes and then considers me for a long moment. "They got some time then, and the nights're blacker now. Should be easy enough to slip in a little later."

I nod, turning to leave, and then stop myself. Moonie's looking at me strangely, his eyes wrinkling up beneath his glasses like he has something he thinks he wants to say, but he's not quite sure what it is yet.

"Your Gramama . . ."

"Yessir?"

"She got ev'rything she wanted yesterday?"

"Yessir, Mr. Moonie."

His squint eclipses his eyes completely, and he settles back into his chair with a creak. I wait for a follow-up, but Moonie's already back in his ledger, more comfortable in Zone history than the actual Zone.

Mary pokes me in the side, loudly crinkling my aluminum corset.

"Okay, Mr. Moonie. I'm gonna go have a look . . ."

"All right, then, Hank," Moonie interrupts, not looking up. With that, Mary and Alice and I slowly back out of the room and into the Library proper, leaving Mr. Moonie with his books. We're greeted with the dull roar of what must be the entire Zone condensed into the central hall of the Library, where the old oak circulation desk still stands, corners worn round and slightly worse for wear, beneath a tarnished brass plaque exhorting "SILENCE."

"What I don't need," a red-faced man in an orange vest shouts above the noise, his neck straining with the effort. "Is some slick federale telling me what I can and can't do!" He wipes the spittle from his bottom lip while his audience, two other men in reflective work vests and a woman I vaguely recognize as one of my mother's friends, seem to agree.

He starts up again and I linger, wanting to hear what exactly the "feder-*rallys*" are up to, but Mary and Alice tug me through the crowd. I try to pick up what people are saying, but it's white noise, individual conversations indistinguishable from each other in the roiling chatter of the hall. Even so, bits and pieces surface, filtering their way through the tumult. It's all shock and worry and indignation, a few rough curses and long sighs.

Mary and Alice finally stop at the far corner of the hallway, leaning against the curved banister of the Library's great spiral staircase. Behind us is an ancient corkboard that I'd never really looked at in any detail. Now, turning my back to the crush of humanity we just worked our way through, I take a look. Tacked to the board are disintegrating flyers from Before, advertisements for "Free First Yoga Lessons" and "Read the Classics! Book Club"—the kind of stuff people concerned themselves with twenty years ago.

I stare at the board for a moment longer, letting the shouts of the room settle into a rumbling hum, a vibration I can feel resonating through my core. It won't be long before I have another attack—I can feel that, too: a building thickness, like static gauze. I think back to the dragonfly, to Mouse. To my parents. To the cattle egrets guarding the dam. To Rachel and Tom and Food Eats. To old Mr. Moonie in his study, trying his very best to pretend that everything that's happening is already all ancient history. I think back to all of them and try to modulate my breathing, to dissipate the gathering electrical haze through sheer force of will.

Fully engrossed, I jump when someone squeezes my shoulder from behind, flailing spastically against Mary and Alice beside me. It's the last straw for my aluminum wrap, which wafts anticlimactically to the floor. I bend down to pick it up, but the hand is back on my shoulder.

"Henry?"

It takes a moment to focus, and when I do it's to a tear-streaked face set on top of the fluffiest dress I've ever seen, in the Zone or anywhere.

"Hi, Mrs. Wallace," I say, scrunching my nose as a nervous-looking couple, their arms comfortingly around each other's waists, and an angry-looking man with a furrowed brow join her.

"Henry, Henry, *Henry*," Mrs. Wallace keens, cupping my face in her hands. "It's *so* good to see you, honey."

"Okay," I say, distracted by the anxiously staring couple and the angry man, who's starting to pace behind them. Mrs. Wallace's outfit isn't helping either—the more I look at it, the more I'm sure it has to be a wedding dress. "It's, um . . . it's good to see you, too, Mrs. Wallace."

She turns her head, smiling wetly at her friends, who nod encouragingly—or, in the case of the angry man, exasperatedly. "The thing is, Henry," she says, clasping my hands meaningfully. "We were wondering if you'd seen my Conor. Or Scott. The Staltons can't find Julia, either."

She gestures back to the apprehensively quivering couple behind her.

Mouse's parents.

They have to be. They even look like her; small and sharp. Rodential. I'm suddenly paralyzed with the impossibility of telling them about Mouse's abduction: *I'm so sorry, Mr. and Mrs. Stalton? They have her . . .* Mrs. Wallace, seeing the dread in my eyes, gives my hands another squeeze and holds it reassuringly. "I hope you don't mind that I *told* them . . ." I exhale with queasy relief and give Mrs. Wallace a grateful smile. She returns it, showing lipstick marks on her otherwise white teeth.

"I know it's a secret, but . . ." Mrs. Wallace trails off, her smile retreating into the worry lines creasing her otherwise very pretty face. And then, whispering: "I thought that since you're her *boyfriend,* she'd be with you."

I grimace, shaking my head and silently cursing Conor. I can feel Mary and Alice arching their eyebrows on either side of me, and start going red right as Mr. and Mrs. Stalton break out into sobs. Mrs. Wallace turns to embrace them both.

"We'll find her, don't worry," she coos.

"And what about Scott?" asks the angry man, seemingly unconcerned with the tearful scene taking place two feet from him.

In all my years of being friends with Scott, I'd never met his family or slept over at his house. Scott was either with us, goofing off, or he wasn't—I never thought to dig any deeper than that. And if I was Scott, I wouldn't encourage any digging. His dad—Mr. Malgré—is a lumbering, red-faced man with breath like rotten spinach, and I feel my face collecting into a defensive sneer despite my best efforts.

"He's with my Gram," I say in a small voice, wedging myself against the side of the staircase, between Mary and Alice, who're also plastering themselves to the wall. "He and Conor and Freckles should be here any minute . . . when it gets dark."

Mr. Malgré takes a step forward and puts his face directly in front of mine, scrutinizing, while I try to disappear into the wall. "Conor and *who*?"

"Conor and our friend Evelyn," Mary answers forcefully, stepping forward to my rescue. "Mr. Malgré, we've all had a rough day. If you could just give us a little . . . *space*, Scott should be here shortly."

Mr. Malgré squints appraisingly at Mary for a long moment, and then at me and Alice. Finally, raising his bushy red brows, he turns around to the emotional puddle that is Mrs. Wallace and Mouse's parents. "Conor's gonna be here soon, with Scott and 'em," he says, gruffly, and starts to make his way toward a group of construction workers at the far side of the hallway.

Mrs. Wallace clasps her hands together and yelps, gathering Mr. Malgré into a weepy, thankful hug—which he tries unsuccessfully to shake—and then, almost as an afterthought, she looks around the room, searching.

"And where are you parents, sweetheart? Everyone keeps asking where Mayor Long is!"

I slump against the wall, suddenly sick to my stomach. Alice and Mary squeeze my hands almost simultaneously, and we all watch Mr. Malgré as he stalks over to his friends, shaking off Mrs. Wallace's hug. No one here knows anything about the treason, about what's really happening. Not Mr. Malgré, not anyone . . .

Except for me.

And Alice.

It makes it seem almost unreal, like make-believe.

Mrs. Wallace looks at me questioningly, then scans the room again, double-checking. By the time she looks back at me, I'm eclipsed by Mr. and Mrs. Stalton, who don't seem to notice Alice and Mary at my side. A sideways glance at Alice and Mary confirms that they're more than happy to be ignored.

"It's so good to meet you, Henry," Mouse's dad enthuses, gripping my hand in a frantic shake. I can feel myself shocking him, but he doesn't seem to notice. Mouse's mom, a thin, furtive woman, like her daughter, embraces me. "What a kind boy," she says, half-whispering. "What a kind boy."

And then it occurs to me that not only do they think I'm Mouse's boyfriend, but stupid Mr. Malgré made it sound like Mouse was coming with Grammy, too. A soursplash works its way up the back of my throat and into my mouth, like I'm going to vomit. I swallow it with a cringe and take a deep breath.

"I'm sorry, Mr. and Mrs. Stalton, but . . ." I say, the words coming out sounding strangled. I can't bring myself to tell them that Mouse was taken, and I definitely can't bring myself to tell them that I'm not Mouse's boyfriend. I can't even look at them—their earnest, thankful faces. " . . . but I have to go. Right now."

I guiltily break free of Mrs. Stalton's hug, peeling her hand from my arm when she tries to hold me back, and leap blindly up the stairs, tugging Mary's and Alice's shirts as I go. Mrs. Wallace sees my exit from halfway across the room and calls out, jogging over to the Staltons to see what's happened. I turn, surveying the hallway one last time—the entire Green in one room. A grim version of the entire Other Side packed, dancing, into The Corner.

Out of the corner of my eyes, amid the tumult of the hallway, I catch the hope draining out of the Staltons' faces, Mr. Stalton cradling his wife's head in his arms, not looking worried or angry, just broken. He looks up at me blankly, making eye contact, and I turn away, unable to bear his gaze.

The second floor is crowded too, albeit a little less than the ground floor, but the third floor is empty, and I make a snap decision to slip out of my secret window, to hide in the attic one last time. It's almost muscle memory, like I could do it with my eyes closed. It's twilight now, out on the balcony, almost fully dark, and I spot at least ten jeeps driving slowly up and down the Avenue. Overhead, a helicopter cuts menacingly across the Green, chunky blades chopping purposefully toward—I imagine, darkly—the dam.

I shuffle up the brackets as quickly as possible, not daring to check that Mary and Alice followed. I feel, them, though, shaking the drainpipe behind me, and in a few breathless seconds we're on the roof, then back in the dark and dusty heart of the Library. I've never been here so late in the day, without the magic of the sun beating through stained glass windows, and it's actually pretty creepy. *Appropriately* creepy. I pull one of the broken chairs away from a pile and collapse into it, resting my hot cheek against the cool, lacquered wood of its attached desk.

"You're really a mess," says Mary, not unkindly. "You know that?"

I do know that, I think, wishing I could be in bed listening to my parents goof off in the kitchen downstairs instead of flinching at the sound of approaching engines on the Avenue. There are no other possibilities in the attic, though, not anymore, and I wearily look into Mary's expectant face; she's staring through the shadows as if waiting for an explanation.

"Well?" she says, hands on her hips.

"I know," I say with a grudging smile, trying to wipe the grime from my face with my grimy hands. "I know I'm a total mess."

"I didn't know the woman in the wedding dress was Conor's mom," Alice says, wistfully, kicking her heels against the wall. "She's so sad."

"What do you mean?"

"I heard her telling Mrs. Stalton that she wore it because it's the nicest thing she owns, and even if she loses everything again, she can't bear to lose it."

I sit with that thought for a moment, trying to figure out whether or not I should feel sad for Mrs. Wallace. I don't think I should, though, because Conor's coming back, and Mrs. Wallace has everything. It's the Staltons Alice should feel sad for, and for me. I look toward our muddy reflections in the stained glass windows, thinking about Mouse and hoping—for her parent's sake—that she's okay.

Out of nowhere, a ridiculous coincidence occurs to me. "Isn't Stalton a kind of cheese?" I blurt out, before I can stop myself.

"Oh-my-God," says Alice, sighing dramatically. "You are *so* obsessed."

"With your girlfriend," laughs Mary, making sarcastic finger quotes. "Mouse."

As if on cue, rain starts pattering against the black windows and the roof above our heads. All three of us shiver instinctively, both because of and despite the looming threats outside.

"And *Evelyn*?" I ask, cavalierly changing the topic. "Are her parents here, too?"

Mary and Alice both laugh again, rubbing their hands over their skinny arms as if they were cold despite the heat of the attic. "She lives with her aunt," Alice says teasingly. "And no one calls her that."

I could've sworn that Mary called Freckles that earlier, but now I'm second-guessing myself. I look down at my feet, avoiding the girls. "What do we call her then?" I ask, not looking up.

"You tell me, *loverboy!*"

Mary and Alice break out in a peal of good-natured laughter just as thunder strikes, a resonant boom that sustains for a few long seconds, rattling the windowpanes and stripping us of our feeling of temporary security. We stand quietly as the rain picks up, pounding against the attic with seeming purpose. A flash of lightning fills the room, throwing long, imposing shadows on the walls and ceilings, and is followed shortly by another rumbling clap of thunder. I wedge myself into a corner and clutch my chest apprehensively.

Curiously, though, the attic air seems fresher, cleaner—and the asphyxiating thickness I'm expecting doesn't come; just more rain. Alice walks over to the window overlooking the Avenue and traces angry rivulets with an idle finger, and Mary—still waiting for her parents to arrive—joins her. Even from the far corner of the room, I can tell it's really coming down. The scratch of wind-slashed branches creaking against each other punctuates the rain, and beneath that, a car door slamming. I prick my ears and hold my breath, expecting more: a helicopter, military orders shouted over the weather.

"I think," says Mary, peering through colored glass. "I think I see Conor . . ."

I exhale, relieved. "Anyone else?"

"Yeah," she says, and my heart catches, fearing the worst again. "But no people in black."

"It's like a clown car," Mary says, crowding Alice at the one clear triangle of stained glass. "They keep coming out."

Grammy is already holding court in the main hallway of the Library by the time we make it down from the attic, soaking wet from our slippery descent. It's even more crowded than before, and oppressively musty, heavy with the agitated breathing of the crowd. I attempt, unsuccessfully, to rub my arms dry, noticing that a good third of the people assembled are similarly bedraggled—nervous latecomers who waited until nightfall to leave their houses. Grammy's dripping, too, wet cardigan hanging limply on her frame as she calls everyone to attention.

Standing soggily behind her are Conor and Scott. I search the crowd for Freckles, but she's nowhere to be seen, so I try to make eye contact with one of the guys, standing on my toes, even coughing . . . but Conor's staring reverently at his shoes, avoiding his mom—Mrs. Wallace—who's also trying desperately to get his attention. Scott glances at Mrs. Wallace a few times, eyes widening at her wedding dress, and nudges Conor, but Conor's steadfast in his inattention.

I finally give up and scan the rest of the room, scrunching my nose and holding my breath to keep from gagging on the growing smell of mildew. It's funny, and a little troubling, how many people I don't recognize in the room. It's almost easier to count the people I do know: There's Guv, from the dam, holding his hardhat deferentially at his side, and with him a few others dressed just the same who must've come with him. One of them looks particularly shaky, and I figure he's the one who almost drowned the other day.

"Friends," Grammy begins in a loud, clear voice, "We're all here for news." The hallway erupts in assent, and she waits until the hubbub dies down before continuing. "I'm here to tell you that there's some good news . . . but there's definitely some bad news."

"Where's Mayor Long?" shouts Mr. Malgré, and a few of his new construction worker friends echo the sentiment, egging him on even though Mom's not *really* the mayor. "Shouldn't she be here telling us the news, not hiding behind her *mama*!"

The hall erupts again, angry shouting exacerbating the smell and the uncomfortably wet heat. I try to make a mental note of who's on Mr. Malgré's side, but have trouble keeping track since most of the hall is only vaguely familiar; almost everyone's a stranger, and, whether or not they agree with Mr. Malgré, everyone's upset. Even Scott, who I can't remember ever seeing without a smile. For a split second, I catch him glaring at his father, fists clenched at his sides. It even looks like he might shout something, until, out of nowhere, a splitting crack silences the hallway.

And then another, and another.

Heads turn toward Moonie's oak-paneled study. In the doorway, Moonie stands, cane raised aloft . . . ready to crack against the wood-paneled walls a fourth time. After a few quietly apprehensive moments, Moonie gestures to Grammy as if to say, "Go on, then, honey."

"The bad news," Grammy shouts, her voice raggedly accusatory, "Is that we're all traitors."

Silence.

In control of the room once more, Grammy lowers her voice. "The Government *thinks* we're all traitors, anyway. They told *Mayor* Long they were going to approve the Charter; they dangled that in front of her nose and they lured her out of the Zone she helped rebuild. Three times. And then they arrested her for treason, and they're holding her prisoner. They arrested Mayor Long, my daughter, and at least two other citizens under that charge."

I look at Mr. Malgré and his friends, whose chins are all jutted at the same defiant angle, then look away, scanning for more reactions. I wish I was back on the Other Side—I barely feel like I know these Green Zoners anymore. Grammy continues, "They've taken control of the dam, and you've all seen that they're patrolling the Zone. I don't know exactly what they're looking for, but you should all know that they'll use force to get it."

She pauses, inhaling dramatically.

"You should also know that they have the *worst* plans for us," she says, an incongruous sparkle in her eyes letting me know that she has some plans of her own. "Guv?"

Guv shuffles toward the circulation desk where Grammy is standing. "Hey," he says in his soft, gruffly sweet voice. "I, uh . . ." Someone yells for him to speak up. "I'm an engineer at the dam," Guv continues, too loudly. "Ms. Long showed me some pictures the Government tried to use to scare her, pictures of the Zone . . . permanently flooded."

The crowd in the Library gasps, Mr. Malgré and his friends included. Anticipating disorder, Grammy quickly cuts in. "We tried to do right by everyone with the Charter. But we're doing too good apart from them, and they don't like it. They don't *want* the

Charter. They'd rather the Zone be uninhabitable than for us to be free of them and their taxes. They want everyone to have to move north, or west, or anywhere else where we'll know better than to try to get *fool* ideas like self-sustainability in our heads. They'd rather this be a swamp than for us to be able to stand on our own two feet." She nods at Guv encouragingly.

"But they can't do that," Guv says, and the Library erupts in cheers. One of Mr. Malgré's friends yells, "*Right on!*" and I decide to go a little easier on them.

"No, I mean, they took control of the dam earlier this afternoon thinking they could open the spillway and flood the city, but . . ." Guv smiles, unable to contain his amusement at just how wrong the Government's plan is. " . . . opening the spillway won't flood the city, just the wetlands out by the ol' airport. In a few years, the river might think about changin' course, but we've been planning on that all along. There's nothing left to flood out there if that happens."

I shake my head in laughing disbelief, along with everyone else in the room. I should've picked up on it earlier, when Grammy first showed me the pictures—Dad certainly spent long enough explaining the dam to me—but all I could think of was the nightmare of the Tragedies, of Mouse in the backseat of a black jeep and my parents under arrest in the City . . . political prisoners. It's no wonder we don't want to depend on them anymore—they didn't help after the Tragedies, and they didn't even get *this* right.

"Long and short of it," Guv says, "is that old river systems like this one, they won't just *do* what you want 'em to. They may be in control of the dam right now, but they got no idea what exactly it is they're controlling."

Grammy cuts in, steely voiced but smiling toothily. "Which is gonna be the key to getting those lying federales out of our business once and for all. They had a chance to sign the Charter, to have us on their side, and they decided they wanted to destroy the Zone instead. To keep my daughter, to keep Pete and Sue Stalton's daughter, barely a teenager, rotting in some rat-infested prison until the day they die."

Mrs. Stalton punctuates Grammy's speech with a bone-chilling wail, and I gasp along with the rest of the room, hoping, praying that Grammy's exaggerating to make her point. I'd literally worried myself sick, but until now had only envisioned Mouse and my parents in, like, a locked hospital waiting room. Reading magazines, bored, with an armed guard outside of the door. I hadn't let myself even begin to think about the . . . *d-word*.

Meanwhile, Grammy reaches into her voluminous purse and pulls out a handful of glossy eight by ten photos, the government's projections of the permanently flooded Zone. Red-faced, tendons standing out from her wiry neck, she waves them. "We tried to do for ourselves what they refused to do. We gave them a chance. And now they're trying to terrorize us; they're trying to erase us completely."

She catches her breath, letting this sink in. Conor and Scott stand behind her uncomfortably, looking younger than usual. I can't catch Conor's eye, but I manage to get Scott's attention and mouth, "*Freckles?*" Nudging Conor, he holds up a finger, like there's more he wants to tell me—but when Grammy starts talking again, he just shrugs, then nods reassuringly. "For a minute there I thought they were going to get away with it, too. But this"—Grammy gestures to the hallway, everyone standing stock still—"this is just growing pains." I flash back to the first time she'd mentioned growing pains; the inchworm circling down her gleaming kitchen sink.

"What d'you suggest we do, then, Mrs. Long?" Mr. Moonie asks with his trademark drawl, casually breaking what had grown into a very taut silence. "They're still patrolling in those . . . *jeeps*," he spits it out reluctantly, as if the concept of a jeep was just as bad as the people driving them. "Taking people. Taking *kids*." The parents in the room all instinctively wrap their arms around their children. Mrs. Wallace looks manically at Conor, who's still staring down at his shoes.

"They can't scare us with a flood, we know they can't do that." Grammy looks at Guv for verification, and he nods first to her and then, authoritatively, to the crowd. "But we can let them think they've scared us away, at least until they've gone back up north. We'll hunker down in our houses, we'll hide out in the Grey, we'll sneak over to the Other Side."

The thought of the Other Side is cold comfort when people are dying . . . but my stomach growls at the thought of a biscuit from Food Eats. I can't remember the last time I ate.

"We'll let them think they've won, that we've cleared out. And when they're gone, we'll regroup. We'll fortify, we'll arm ourselves, and we'll *secede*. We'll commit the treason those bastards are accusing us of." Grammy's face shakes indignantly, her eyes staring through the Library into a vengeful future.

"All right then, Mrs. Long," Mr. Moonie says with finality, tucking his chin into his neck. "Just so long as everyone has a plan." He faces the crowd—the Green Zone—and shakes his head. "You don't have to go home. Fact, sounds like you probably shouldn't . . . butcha sure as heck can't stay here."

A few nervous laughs pepper the crowd, but nobody moves. Mr. Moonie looks over us and then pointedly at Grammy, to whom he says, "Seriously, now, y'all have *got* to go," before he shuffles back into his study, closing the door definitively behind him. I can't say I blame him—the only thing he'd ever asked for was peace and quiet to do his work, and now *this*. With Moonie gone, the room has erupted into pandemonium, everyone talking loudly, over talking, shouting, trying to figure out where to go next.

"Hey," Mr. Malgré yells over the din. "Hey, hey, hey!" The room reluctantly quiets down. "Y'all heard Mrs. Long, here. We got to get *gone*." A murmur of assent, followed by a few unhappy grumblings that I can't quite make out from my perch by the stairs. "I'll tell you where," Mr. Malgré says, positioning his wide red face right up against a nervous-looking man, one of the unhappy grumblers who had dared to speak up against him. "We're gonna get out into that night while we still can."

"What about . . . fighting back?" someone shouts from the depths of the crowd.

Mr. Malgré steps back from the man, who quickly disappears into the safety of the crowd, and answers only by looking disappointedly around the room and biting his cheek. Still primed from her recent rally cries, Grammy raises her voice once again to fill the silence.

"We'll fight back, and we'll win," she says, looking determined. "But look around you. We're not exactly battle-ready." She nods toward all the parents with their children, to Mrs. Wallace in her dirty wedding dress, to the soggy latecomers. "We're gonna need to regroup, to get some outside help. Right now. Literally, *right now*." She pokes the air imperiously for emphasis. "We need to scatter. It might be days, it might be weeks, but we'll meet back here when those black cars are gone." She laughs grimly. "Whether Moonie wants us to or not."

Again, a few nervous laughs. "*Oh*," says Mrs. Wallace, gathering the long lace train of her dress in her hands as if to leave. "And where *exactly* are you going again, Milly?"

Wincing, Grammy touches her upper arm, where I saw the bruise, and then quickly drops her hands to her sides. "I'm not hiding out at home, that's for sure," she says steelily. "I'll head to the

Other Side, lie low for a few days. We checked it out on our way back from the dam, and it looks like it's deep enough in the Grey that federales won't bother looking for signs of life there; if we're smart and stay indoors, we should be fine. I hear they have some good eats, too," she adds with a half-smile.

I know it shouldn't, because she's always made it her business to know everything, but it surprises me to hear Grammy mention the Other Side. I'd been thinking of it as secret, like the attic before it. But I guess everything's thrown open now: the attic, the Other Side, even the Green. I slump against the wall and sigh, remembering Mom's cool, soft hands feeling my forehead for a fever; her suggesting that Dad and I ride over to the Other Side for something "new."

We found something new, all right, I think, watching everyone separate into twos and threes, in anxious discussion. *If Mom and Dad were here* . . . But I can't think like that. I try to plan my next move, too, while Grammy visits each of the groups, making note of their plans and offering sober, whispered advice. Of course I'll go to the Other Side, too, and warn Tom and Rachel and the rest of them. That is, if they don't already know about the federales . . .

I walk through the Library, looking for someone to talk to about what happens next, after the black jeeps leave, but everyone's preoccupied. Conor's finally reunited with Mrs. Wallace, who's holding his head to hers like he might slip away at any minute, and he seems to have let down his guard and is holding her back. Mary and Alice are with their respective parents, who I don't recognize, not even Alice's parents, who can't actually live right next door to me—I'm sure I've never seen them before. Grammy's busy advising everybody but me. The only people who look like they want to talk are the Staltons, who're making a desperate beeline toward me.

Panicking, I duck into Mr. Moonie's office, trying to look as if I'd been heading there to begin with, and slam the door behind me, shrinking at the sound, but happy to have made my getaway. Moonie looks up from the book he'd already lost himself in, steepling his fingers and arching his brow.

"Oh," I say, not quite sure what to say. "Everyone looks like they're leaving soon?" I don't know why I made it into a question, but Moonie smiles encouragingly and the rolls beneath his chin smile, too, so I carry on. "I'm going to the Other Side, looks like we're gonna stay there until it all . . . blows over."

Creaking, Moonie stands and throws open the drapes. I flinch toward the floor in anticipation of a hundred lurking federale eyes, angrily hovering helicopters; waiting handcuffs and government restraints. But it's really storming now, rain beating down against the glass in broad sheets that hide us from the outside world almost as effectively as the heavy velvet drapes. Incongruously, Moonie intones: *"The sunlight falls, low-ruddy from the west, / Upon their heads. Last week they might have died / And now they stretch their limbs in tired content."*

"You're coming too, right?" I ask, nervous from the open drapes. And from Moonie's poetry.

"That's Sigfried again," Moonie says distractedly. "Ziggy. *The rank stench of those bodies haunts me still.*"

"What?" I ask, recoiling.

"The name of the poem. The same one from earlier. I looked it up while everyone was   " He waves his hands dismissively and pulls the drapes closed, hiding the rain. "I won't be accompanying you to the Other Side, Mr. Long," Moonie says, gesturing toward his cluttered desk. "Too many loose ends to tie up around here. Especially now."

Of course, I think. Mr. Moonie's whole life's work has been trying to solve History, like it's one enormous, sprawling jigsaw puzzle without corners or sides. Everything that's happened up until this very moment, these crazy last few days, is now officially another piece for him to place. Me, standing in his dark, mildewy office, making plans for the future . . . I'm history to him, too. Like Mom, the mayor, and our centuries-dead relative, the former governor.

I roll my shoulders and shake my arms, getting rid of the phantom cobwebs I suddenly feel sticking to my wet and dirty skin. "But what if they look here?" I ask, agitated at his lack of concern. "The federales?"

Moonie laughs dryly and then coughs, chest rattling like the panes in the windows. "Nobody's gonna bother an old man, an academic," he says, wiping the moist corners of his mouth with a faded red pocket square. "And I don't have anything they want . . . unless they're lookin' for book t'read."

"I saw 'em, Mr. Moonie," I say, not laughing. "They're dangerous."

Moonie arches a brow and purses his lips, holding back a smile. "In that case," he says, unscrewing the tarnished brass top of his cane and pulling out a thin sword, like a fencing saber. "They can have at it!" He waves the sword theatrically, cutting the heavy air with an awkward flourish, and then re-sheathes it, turning it back into a walking cane.

For a moment I'm at a loss for words. I point at the cane and hesitantly say, "I never knew . . ."

"That's the point, Henry," he says, affecting an air of mystery and puffing out his chest. "Not knowing. That's *exactly* the point."

"Okay," I say.

"School's out, Henry," Moonie says, tapping his cane decisively on the floor and sitting back down to his work. "Not that this was ever much of a School, of course. But I'd like to think you learned *something* here."

"Sure I did, Mr. Moonie," I say, nodding in affirmation, more confused than ever.

"Good luck then, son. Surprise the hell out of 'em." With that, Moonie turns back to his book. I start to say goodbye, and Mr. Moonie waves without looking up, so I open the door as if to leave.

"One more thing, Henry," Moonie says, nose still in his book. I wait in the doorway, hoping for clarification or guidance; some words of wisdom to get me through the next few hours at the very least. "Do tell your gramama that she's gonna need to pick somewhere else to hold her meetings next time."

I sigh, rolling my eyes. "Okay Mr. Moonie," I say. "Bye, then." I look back over my shoulder before I close the door behind me; he's already scribbling madly in his leather-bound journal, making notes and marking dates. I push the heavy oak door closed, leaving Moonie to his dusty histories, and walk into the emptying main hall, which is still buzzing with activity. Up until I'd closed the door, I felt fine—upset, but in control. Walking out of Moonie's study into the tumult of the Library, I rub my eyes with my fists, wishing I could push them hard enough to reset everything I'm seeing, to make all of this go away.

"*Henry!*" A familiar, high-pitched voice caws as a hand catches my arm. I look up. It's a small woman with a glowing, hopeful face and the whitest smile I've ever seen. I almost don't recognize her without her white coat and clipboard . . . and when I do recognize her, I inadvertently flinch.

"I was hoping I'd see you," she says, rooting around in her purse. "How's the heart? Still feeling faint?"

"H-hi Dr. Singh," I stutter, not knowing where exactly to start. I touch my chest, self-consciously feeling for the flimsy aluminum wrap and remembering that I'd lost it earlier. "I'd been wearing . . . foil, to keep it safe, but it . . ." Dr. Singh is nodding seriously, still rooting around in her bag.

"It fell off."

Dr. Singh smiles sweetly. "Good thinking," she says. "There's really no telling how non . . . *anatomical* organs are going to react to these kinds of anomalies." She gestures vaguely to the room. "The best you can really do is monitor and react."

"That's, um . . ."

"I know," she says, still smiling. "Not very reassuring. But I can promise you, whatever's happening with your . . ." She pauses, rustling through a deep crevice in her purse.

"My non-anatomical heart," I prompt.

"Right, whatever's happening with your heart, it's better than having no heart at all, right?" She smiles triumphantly, finally extracting a thermometer. My gag reflex starts up just seeing it, and it gets immediately worse when she carefully unravels a long black strand of hair from its casing.

Dr. Singh sees me pulling a face and wipes the thermometer on her shirt. "Not quite up to Hospital standard, but then"—She gestures vaguely for the second time—"we're in the wild now. Anything goes, right?" I shiver. "Now, let's see how you're doing." Without thinking, I open my mouth, and in an instant the thermometer is wedged painfully into the soft underside of my tongue. "No moving then, keep it in there," Dr. Singh admonishes. "Don't think I've forgotten your fondness for theater." She pushes the thermometer into my tongue again to make sure it's secure, then grabs my wrist and quickly checks my pulse.

"What I've been wanting to tell you, Henry," she says, surveying the room, "is that I do think, given your symptoms, that it's probably a good idea for you to get away from here for a while. Take a vacation, go to the beach or something." Dr. Singh laughs at this. She has a lovely, musical laugh that makes me want to join in, but this feeling quickly evaporates when she drops my hand and adjusts the thermometer again, poking it sharply back into my tongue's soft tissue.

"You can't change the ticker, is the thinking," she says while I wince, choking down an urge to spit out the cold thermometer. "At least not yet, not here. But you *can* change its context."

"Mgoim do da obber sibe," I say, wondering if that's going to be far enough away.

"Oh, don't talk, sweetheart, or I'll have to leave it in for another minute." She taps her watch, checking the time, and stares at it for a long stretch. "That should be good." She takes the thermometer out of my mouth and holds it up to the light. "Ninety-eight point six, and pulse is completely normal. You're fine."

"But what about the fainting?" I ask. "How far away should I go for that to stop?"

Dr. Singh wipes the thermometer on her shirt and tosses it back into her purse. "Between you and me," she says, frowning for the first time since I've seen her. "I'd get as far away from this place as possible." Someone opens the back door to leave, giving a burst of cold wind the run of the hallway. I shiver, holding my bare arms to little effect. "*I* would," she says matter-of-factly, "if it wasn't for the Hospital."

I thank Dr. Singh, giving her a quick, tight hug, and silently forgiving her for all the pain she's inflicted on me over the course of the past thirteen years. Just as I pull away, someone pinches my arm.

"There you are!" Grammy chirps, strangely upbeat. "Dr. Singh, good to see you."

"You too, Mrs. Long," answers Dr. Singh, her voice steely. "Your speech . . . was very interesting." Grammy inclines her head in thanks, and Dr. Singh sharply adds: "Please remember that our Hospital has a limited number of beds."

A look passes between Dr. Singh and Grammy that worries me more than anything I've seen today. It's not hatred or aggression, but a cool, almost clinical, understanding of the shape of things to come. I take a jagged breath, consumed with a sudden fear for my parents, and for Mouse, as the bloody reality of fighting for the Zone sinks in.

"Take care of that heart, Henry," Dr. Singh says, clapping me on my shoulder, and I look blankly after her as she strides purposefully through the thinning crowd.

⚡ ⚡ ⚡

It's a packed car on the way to the Other Side. Grammy's driving, tapping the gas pedal with a nervous rhythm I can't quite place, and Conor and the skinny engineer are sharing the passenger seat, hands pressed protectively against the dash. I'm in the back with Mrs. Wallace, Guv, and another, fatter engineer from the dam. The fat engineer, who's actually not fat so much as he is husky, is obviously interested in Mrs. Wallace. I can tell by the way he focuses on the lace of her dress instead of meeting her eyes, and by the way he chivalrously gives her as much space as possible. Which would be fine, except he's scootched over so far that he's half-sitting on my leg.

Not only is it still raining—all of us are dripping from the crazed run to the car—but Grammy has her headlights off so as not to draw any unwanted attention. The darkness, coupled with the pounding rain, makes it almost impossible to see, and even though Grammy's driving painfully slowly, we keep running over deceptively deep troughs where the road's been ripped up but not yet repaved. The first time this happened, I was trying to get the story about their trip to the dam, about Freckles, from Conor, and Grammy—cursing—shushed me, saying she needed complete silence to concentrate on the road.

I cross my fingers, praying that the tires on Grammy's old sedan hold up at least until we get to the Other Side and imagining worst-case scenarios regardless: the car turned over in a muddy ditch, wheels spinning against the rain, while a fleet of black jeeps surround it. My parents, dead. Mouse, dead. Myself, alive in a federale jail, in a full-body cast from the car crash.

Waiting for the end.

The storm makes it easy to feel hopeless, to give myself to it. I stare sadly out the window of the car—which is silent except for the rain's white noise and Grammy's occasional muffled curse—and let the engineer sit on my leg, because nothing seems to matter anymore. Even the Other Side, when we finally reach it, seems depressed. The flags are tangled and mottled with dirt. The million multicolored flyers are peeling off walls, collecting into unrecognizable piles of soggy pulp when they hit the ground.

It feels uncomfortably like the Grey, to be honest. Quiet and creepy. Grammy idles the car, and we all wait in silence, unsure whether to stay or make a run for it. I bounce my knee, feeling trapped by the crush of the crowded back seat and by the emptiness outside. All my life, I'd been raised to believe that—no matter what—it was possible to carve out a life here, to grow something new and vibrant out of the silt-rich dirt. But now even the Other Side is covered in mud and darkness; in a mute, collective fear . . . and it feels like no matter what, the Zone always ends up buried in a dingy, heartless Grey.

The white noise of the storm envelops the car, and we marinate in our increasingly black thoughts until we can't bear them anymore. Grammy, snapping first, slams the car into drive.

"No use waiting for the rain to stop," she mutters, as if to herself, jerking the car into the middle of the road. We inch down the main stretch, drawn to a wavering beacon calling out to us through the rain: a lone light, flickering orange, behind the drawn blinds of Food Eats. As hopeful as I feel about this single sign of life—and we *all* feel hopeful, if Mrs. Wallace's gasp is anything to go by—the contrast of the one flickering window against an entire unlit street is troubling in a way I try not to think too deeply about. Grammy pulls up to the curb in front of Food Eats, and then slightly over it, scraping the undercarriage of the car against unyielding cement with an otherworldly screech. The restaurant's blinds shake hesitantly in response, dirty fingers propping open dusty plastic slats just enough for nervous eyes to peek out into the wet, black night.

Lightning strikes, spotlighting the monsters on the mural next to Food Eats—the happy, grilling Frankenstein and the toothy vampire having trouble drinking out of a straw—as the rain pelts down with a renewed sense of purpose. Without stopping to think, I pop open my door and run out into it, forsaking the relative safety of the car for the promise of a warm *buhscuit* and some less downtrodden company. It's terrible outside, but as bad as it is, the air is thick with the scent of wet flowers, and I'm happy to be pounding on the door, shouting my name with an excitement I'd thought I'd lost forever.

"*It's me*," I yell, rain pouring down my face, into my eyes and mouth. "*It's Henry Long.*"

A bolt slides open and the door's thrown wide, nearly knocking me off balance and into the mud. Standing dryly in the doorframe is a very haggard Tom, who pulls me into the restaurant by the shoulder of my shirt while waving everyone else inside.

"Hank," he says, face gaunt. "Your friend told me you'd probably be coming back tonight."

I shake the wet off of me as best as I can while I let my eyes adjust to the light. It's weak, just a single naked bulb with a thick amber filament, but compared to our blind drive over, it's like being in the center of the sun. In any case, my blinking eyes finally adjust and settle on the only other occupant of Food Eats.

Freckles.

She's leaning against the back wall, a plate with a half-eaten biscuit beside her, looking both happy to see me and sorry that we've had to come.

"Hey," Tom says, nervously ushering Grammy and the rest of our comically large party into the Food Eats. "Quickly, please." He scans the street behind them, which is empty to the naked eye, and rushes the engineers, who are similarly scanning the street. And then, with a snap, the door closes, and Tom slides the bolt back into place.

"Hello again, *Thomas*," Grammy says, as if she's been here before.

Like she owns the place.

"Milly," Tom says, walking toward Grammy with his hand outstretched. "Hey." Grammy proffers her wrinkled paw for Tom to hold in greeting, which he does, relieved to see her.

"*What?*" I say, the word out of my mouth like a screech from a hawk—sharp and high-pitched. "You two *know* each other?"

"This is ruined," Grammy says matter-of-factly, unbuttoning her wet sweater and spreading it out on the counter. Ignoring me. "That was cashmere," she sighs wistfully, and then shakes her head back into the present. "Status?"

"She told us you'd be back tonight," Tom says, gesturing toward Freckles. "Told us everything . . . about the federales and the cars, the kidnapping, the photos." He takes a deep breath, momentarily overwhelmed. "Everyone who stayed after hearing about that is at The Corner, making plans and—"

A big trumpeting sneeze cuts Tom off, and Mrs. Wallace finds herself suddenly, sheepishly, at the center of attention. The rest of our group has gravitated toward Freckles, and is huddled wetly in the corner. "Sorry," Mrs. Wallace says in a strangled voice, holding back another sneeze.

"Oh, right," Tom says, just as Mrs. Wallace sneezes again. "Bless you! Carel left, but I think . . ." He continues, clumsily banging his way back into Food Eat's kitchen. "Good, they're still warm."

Meanwhile, the skinny engineer, to the bigger engineer's chagrin, thinks to offer Mrs. Wallace a handkerchief from his back pocket. She instinctively accepts it with a nod of thanks, the big engineer pouting theatrically behind her back. Seeing the handkerchief more closely, though, Mrs. Wallace changes her mind.

"Actually," she sniffles, delicately holding the greasy rag between her thumb and forefinger, "that's very sweet of you, but I think I'm okay." The big engineer smiles widely and reaches for the plate of sticky buns Tom's placed on the counter while Mrs. Wallace surreptitiously wipes her nose on her dress.

The smell of sweet, baked bread and gooey cinnamon expands from the tiny platter to fill even the darkest, most wet corners of the restaurant. It's almost like Tom went into the kitchen and came back a magician: everyone perks up and reaches for the plate. Tearing apart the soft, spongy bread of the bun—taking time only to lick the melted sugar from my fingers—I start to feel a spreading warmth. It's a small comfort compared to the looming darkness and threat of war, but *this sticky bun*, I think, eating around an unexpected raisin, *is symbolic of* . . .

Thunder rolls again outside, rain lashing against the rattling windows. Inside Food Eats, though, everyone's smiling. *Symbolic of this*, I think. *The anti-Grey.* I quietly thank the fireplug of a cook with the thickly waxed mustache and the tattoos ringing his neck, hoping he's okay, wherever he is.

"Carol . . ." Guv says, appreciatively ripping into the last of his bun. "This is her restaurant?" For a split second, I get a visual of

Carel in one of Mrs. Wallace's frilly aprons. He looks like a bear in people clothes, and I almost choke on my bun trying not to laugh.

"*Kah-rell,*" Tom says, still chewing. "He's originally from Belgium, but we met him in Baltimore. Worked as a dishwasher back then, if you can believe it, 'cause he couldn't speak any English." Everyone shakes their heads in disbelief. "If you like those," Tom continues, pointing at the empty tray, "you should try his waffles." The room falls into a thoughtful silence, a sense of wellbeing shrouding us from the storm outside. "Food Eats is actually Milly's, though."

I look to Grammy so quickly that my neck almost snaps. "Technically," Tom adds by way of explanation. I notice that Conor's wide eyes mirror my own, and feel justified in my astonishment.

"Oh, don't be so surprised," Grammy says dismissively. "We needed construction workers, the Other Side popped up, your mother needed some loans to finance the whole thing . . ." she makes a loose motion with her hands that I take to mean *and one thing lead to another.*

"So, wait," I say. "You own this place?"

"Not own, just an investor," Grammy says, patting her wet sweater down, distracted. "The Zone just needed a little help to tide everything over until the Charter. We were gonna get everything back then . . ." She rolls her eyes, miming annoyance. "But since that went south, it looks like the buns are on me."

"Thank ya, ma'am," Guy says, rubbing his stomach demonstratively. "Delicious." Grammy inclines her head in theatrical recognition and returns to worrying her sweater, which seems to have doubled in size since she hung it up.

"First time I met Milly face-to-face was when she dropped her off," Tom says apologetically, open hand stretched toward Freckles. I didn't mean to sound accusatory, but I know I did. The Grammy/ Tom thing was a surprise, and now I'm sensing the good feeling in the room slipping back into anxiety with a growing sickness. "Before Milly it was just . . ." He searches for the words. " . . . *scrip* for weekly supplies, everyone scrambling to live from meal to meal."

"Well," Conor says, always happy to break an awkward silence. "D'you have any more buns back there, Ms. Long?" Everyone laughs, but it's obvious that the darkness has crept back into the corners of Food Eats. Our warm and cinnamony moment is already a memory. After the room settles back into quiet contemplation, Freckles brings up the others.

"Once I started telling people about the cars, about Julia, everyone freaked."

"It's true," Tom says, his lips tightening. "Most of these people, they came here because they had to. Some of them, like Carel . . . they can't afford to have any more problems with the federales."

The revelation startles me almost as much as Grammy's involvement with Tom and the restaurant. I knew the Other Side was different, but I didn't realize the Other Siders were on the *run*. I shiver, despite the gooey warmth in my stomach. Carel must've been terrified when he heard about the federale kidnappings, but he still took the time to put the sweet buns in the oven so they'd stay hot for us.

"I know it's still wet," Tom says, ambling toward the door. "But now that everyone's settled, we should probably go see everyone who stayed. They're gonna want to hear what y'all have to say."

14

After a quick talk, Freckles and Conor and I decide not to go to The Corner with the adults. I'm curious to see how it goes—especially now that I know about the Other Siders' questionable pasts—but we had enough town meetings for a lifetime at the Library, and everyone agrees that it's not like we'd have a lot to add to the discussion anyway. Staying at Food Eats isn't an option either, though. The restaurant feels fully creepy now, the seeping darkness having colonized the last remaining vestiges of light.

Even the flickering bulb overhead seems to be losing heart.

Instead, Tom offers to drop us off at his house, where we can dry off and keep Rachel company. It seems strange to me that Rachel wouldn't be at the meeting, but Tom shrugs his shoulders and says she's in the middle of something. "We wouldn't be interrupting, would we?" I ask, irrationally nervous about being in the same room with Rachel and Freckles, but Tom just smiles wanly and shakes his head. "I don't think you could interrupt her if you tried."

When we get to Tom and Rachel's place, soaked again from the two-block run from Foods, I understand why he said that.

The rest of the Other Side might as well be washed away for all the signs of life we're seeing, but Rachel has their generator working overtime. It seems dangerous, considering that everyone's trying to hide from the federales; every window is aglow, light shooting out of crooked windows into the soggy night like she's somehow found space for a pulsing star in their dusty, cluttered cavern of a living room. The rickety, gold-painted exterior catches and reflects the light, magnifying the effect.

And the music . . .

It's more a feeling I get than an actual resemblance, but silhouetted against the dull night sky, rumbling and shaking with vintage rock and roll, Tom and Rachel's hunchbacked house looks and sounds like a massive, grumbling, cosmic cat about to pounce. It's strange—funny in a way I can't quite explain without sounding crazy—so I let the rain wash down my face, soaking into dirty clothes I've decided will probably never be dry again, and laugh my way past the mannequins on the porch and into the belly of the beast.

Rachel is sprawled on the hardwood floor among the stacks of books and records and memorabilia, painting. She's still in her black tuxedo shirt dress, but it's no longer spattered with paint; it's streaked with it—crisscrossed lines in varying shades of yellow and pink and turquoise and red. She doesn't hear us come in—the music is too loud—and we stand vibrating in the doorway. The fuzzed-out amplifiers are cranked up so loud it sounds like they might not make it through the song.

It's only when Rachel stands up, wiping a brush clean across her already paint-encrusted side, that she notices me, Tom, Conor, and Freckles dripping in the doorway. She says something, smiling. Only I can't hear her. None of us can. Tom walks over to the amps and turns down the volume.

"Hey," Rachel shouts into the still-loud living room, wiping a paint-wet hand across her now-yellow forehead and wrinkling her nose. "What are you guys doing here?"

I look at Tom questioningly, wondering how much she knows. He just shrugs anxiously and heads for the door. "I gotta get back to The Corner, Rach. Mind taking care of our friends, here?" He gestures at us like we're a box of abandoned kittens, and Rachel nods her head in maternal affirmation. They blow kisses at each other, and Tom's gone by the time we look up from our cold and pruning feet.

"Towels," Rachel says, shaking a turquoise finger in the air like this is the best idea she's ever had. She dives into the maze of crates—stacked boxes of porcelain and books and records—making her way to a towering ziggurat of fabric. There must be some system to the mess, because in no time Conor and I catch two oversized beach towels, scratchy from overuse. "More coming soon," Rachel promises Freckles. "Shoulda thrown one to you first . . ."

"It's okay," Freckles says, trying to mean it.

I rub my face red with the rough towel, drying off as quickly as I possibly can, and then move onto my hair, happy in my decision not to go to another soggy meeting. Out of the corner of my eye, I catch a fingerprint-smudged reflection of Conor patting himself dry and notice that something's . . . *off.*

"Conor?" I ask, draping my towel over my shoulder. He looks up questioningly, his strong, wide-set nose streaked with turquoise. "You have something on your face," he says, gesturing to his cheeks. "And . . ." He scrunches his painted nose and ruffles his hair.

Freckles, still waiting on her towel, looks at us and laughs. We're both striped with paint from the towels. Rachel looks down at her paint-streaked hands and grimaces. "Well," she jokes, "good to see some color in your cheeks, anyway."

After we've all dried off, Rachel—hands washed—offers us dry clothes to sleep in from the pile. They're too big, but it doesn't matter . . . it feels so good to finally be dry. Watching Rachel wipe her brushes clean, I curl my toes into mismatched woolen socks and yawn. It's been a long day, and, letting my eyes wander haphazardly around the room, I realize that for a room that has everything, there doesn't seem to be a couch or an extra bed.

"I meant to ask," Rachel calls over her shoulder, scrubbing the paint from her arms with repurposed beach towels. "How's the guitar?"

The gui . . . tar?

For a confused half-second, the word is as meaningless as any random sounds haphazardly struck together. And then, with a corrective shake of the head, it comes back to me. Of course. Tom's guitar: glossy black and just a little chipped on the head where the body meets the neck. It's probably still wedged in the corner next to the closet, collecting dust.

Lonely.

"Oh," I say, a little ashamed—despite everything that's happened—that I haven't yet spent any time with Tom and Rachel's gift. "It's awesome." Rachel looks up at me encouragingly. "I, um, haven't had much time to actually . . ."

Consolidating her painting supplies into a splattered crate, Rachel says, "You gotta practice if you wanna wail!"

She's right, of course. But I'm a little startled by how cavalier she is about everything the Zone's been through the last couple of days. Between the Hospital and the dam; the hiding and the fear and the water-logged flight, I can't think of a free minute I've had in the last three days. And I start to tell her that, but it seems like so much to explain, and I'm so very tired.

I yawn loudly instead, not meaning to but unable to stop myself, and Freckles and Conor unconsciously follow my lead. "My manners!" Rachel exclaims, looking shocked. Breaking out of the yawn, I snap to attention. Rachel's started digging through the pile of clothes that the beach towels came from, and I wonder what she's going to pull out of it next.

It turns out that she's not pulling anything out of the pile, she's flattening it.

"Guys, sorry, but girls get the bed." She gestures toward the thin, grey mattress on the floor in the corner, without sheets and abutting a person-sized tangle of electrical cords. I can sense Freckles cringing behind me. "You can camp out on the pile. Should be pretty comfortable, but if you feel anything . . . sharp, or whatever, just move it around."

Rachel flops down on the grimy-looking mattress, arms and legs spread like she's making a snow angel. I make my way to the pile of clothes and cautiously sit down, feeling for hidden scissors or whatever else might be buried down there. It's really a lot of clothes, though, and I sink happily into them, leaving ample room for Conor, who's still standing—uncertain— with Freckles.

"Where's your dad, again?" Rachel asks, staring thoughtfully at the ceiling. The record that was playing when we came in has finished, and the sound of the storm raging against the corrugated aluminum roof joins the scratch of the needle on empty vinyl to fill the room. If the rain keeps up, we might get flooded out of the Zone without any help from the federales.

"He's . . . my parents. They're political prisoners."

"Right," Rachel sighs theatrically, turning over onto her propped elbows. "I know *that*. But where?"

It's a good question. Somewhere in the City. The capital of the decreasingly United States. Past that, not a clue. I want to tell her as much, that I'm worried they're being mistreated; *tortured*. Laying, bloody, on cold wet stones in a basement, electricity sparking from the greasy, whirring machines the federales are using to break them.

But I can't.

I can feel my face contorting instead, hot and angry tears welling up behind my eyes.

"Nah, that's not what jail's like," Rachel says, sensing my fears. "They're probably in some classy compound eating smoked salmon with plastic sporks, watching the news on loop." Conor settles in next to me, making a nest out of jeans and sweaters. I'm still not sure I can talk without losing it, but he speaks up for me.

"How d'you know that?"

The wind howls outside while Rachel thinks about how she's going to phrase her answer. Freckles, tired of standing, sits tentatively on the corner of the mattress. For a split second our eyes lock, and I jerk mine upward as if suddenly distracted by a crack of thunder.

"Almost everyone here's had problems with the government," Rachel says, taking time to choose her words. "Not because we're bad people or anything. We're just . . . like *you*. Sometimes you just want to make your own rules and not be flooded out for living on your own terms."

I try to imagine what rules the Other Siders might have made that would have landed them in federale jail, but Rachel goes on. "Like, Carel. He's from Belgium and came here for school, for a degree in philosophy, if you can believe it. He ended up finding philosophy in food instead of books, so he dropped out of college; his visa ran out, and he just stayed."

"And he went to jail for *that*?" Freckles asks, finally comfortable— or tired—enough to curl up on the mattress next to Rachel. She's wearing an enormous green sweatshirt and black basketball shorts with bright red trim, an outfit I wouldn't wish on my worst enemy. But, somehow, the ridiculousness of the borrowed clothes just enhances her prettiness. An artfully bent wrist peeks out from a ragged sleeve; her neck gleams white amidst voluminous green folds.

Against my better judgment, I try to remember what our kiss felt like. But it was so quick, and all I can remember with any clarity is stumbling out of the attic, my heart beating double-time. I look at her lips for inspiration: pink, chapped, pursed with worry.

Perfect.

And then they twitch.

Looking up, I meet her eyes and realize with horror that it's because she's noticed me staring.

"Oh, not at all," Rachel says. "They tried to get him to leave a few times, but he always got back somehow. Carel went to jail because he hooked up with a bunch of eco-warriors and took over a mountain."

We all stare at her, agape.

"Totally trumped-up charges," she says dismissively, rolling onto her back. "Government-funded company was going to blow it up so they could strip mine for coal. Ecological nightmare. I mean, can you imagine thinking it's okay to blow up a mountain?"

I find Carel's portrait on the wall, green-skinned with a lilac mustache pointed imperiously upward, and try to imagine him baking high-altitude biscuits with a rifle strapped to his back. "Anyway, Carel and his buddies had the top on lockdown for half a year before they finally got taken. He was only in prison for a month or so before they tried to deport him again."

"And you?"

Rachel looks at Conor with an arched brow. "Now, that would be telling!" She laughs warmly, brightening the room. "Kidding, kidding. I haven't actually been arrested. They don't have to arrest you to make you feel like you're in jail, though. Everything you do on the Outside is tracked, they're always watching. Jail is just a place they watch you more obviously, so you don't have a chance to make any trouble for 'em."

I try to take in what Rachel's saying, but get distracted by Freckles again. It's hard not to look at her because she's sitting right in front of me, but I don't want her to think I'm creepy, so I try to look around her instead. But not looking at her—looking over her shoulder or at the flaking walls or ceiling—feels just as obvious as staring right at her twitching lips.

I'm trapped.

"Your mom understood that," Rachel continues, her voice soft and serious, and I decide that the only way to escape my Freckles problem is to close my eyes. "It was nice to live in a place where people got it."

⚡⚡⚡

When I next open my eyes it's morning, and I'm stretching awake to sunshine and the amplified whispers of the still-spinning record. Carefully, trying not to wake up Conor, I extricate myself from the nest of clothes and tip-toe over to the window. The street outside is muddy and littered with branches—leafy victims of the storm—but otherwise, you couldn't ask for a more beautiful day.

I open a few blinds and check the walls for power switches. We'd fallen asleep with the lights on, and a lifetime of Green Zone conditioning has left me very uncomfortable around wasted energy. All the lights seem to lead directly back to the tangle of wires at the foot of the mattress, though, and just as I think there's no way I'm going anywhere near that, Freckles stirs. Her face is creased with red indentations from a hard night mashed up against a makeshift pillow, and her cheek is glistening with what looks like drool. But in the morning sun, she looks prettier than ever.

"Where is she?" she yawns.

"Huh?"

Freckles points at the other—empty—half of the mattress. Rachel is gone. I shrug and look around the room, searching for clues. Drying on an otherwise cleared space on the floor is the painting she'd been working on when we dropped in yesterday. I was too distracted by the tumult of the storm to take a closer look then, but now I can see that it's a self-portrait.

"Paint's still wet," I notice, wondering how long she'd been awake; if she'd painted through the night.

Freckles rolls out of bed and pads over to the clearing, yawning. "It's not like the other ones," she says, scanning the rows of cartoonish portraits on the walls and wrinkling her nose. I hadn't made that connection, but she's right. Rachel's coffee-colored skin is a glowing, earthy brown, not a pink or green. Her eyes are still almond, her hair a sun-kissed copper. Her face takes up the majority of the canvas, too, bleeding out onto the ragged edges.

I lean in, careful not to touch the still-tacky acrylics, and see that the apparently uniform color of Rachel's face is actually composed of thousands of tiny strokes of pink and blue and green and yellow—her usual color palette. From a few feet away, she looks alive in a way that I can't quite explain, except that it makes my soul feel too big for my body.

"Whoa," Conor says, stretching his arms and looking over my shoulder. "*Art!*"

We contemplate Rachel's self-portrait for another minute or so in the increasingly bright room, until, stomachs grumbling, we decide to venture out of the house and find the rest of the Other Side. It's stifling hot inside, and—despite the federale threat—the sunshine and the painting have left me feeling so empowered, so full of good will, that I don't think twice about throwing open the creaking front door and walking to Food Eats in broad daylight, in the middle of the street. Conor and Freckles must feel the same way, because we joke all the way there, laughing loudly, invincibly.

The shades are tightly drawn, so you wouldn't know by looking at it, but Food Eats is completely packed. And it's obvious when we squeeze our way inside that we're the only ones who got any sleep last night. Every face that greets us is tired, and there's at least one person blowing their nose at any given moment. No one seems to be smiling, and I can feel my morning sense of wellbeing start to evaporate.

I don't recognize a lot of faces here, either, so I make my way to the back of the restaurant, dragging Freckles and Conor behind me. It takes us a while to navigate our way through the breakfasting crowd and up to the counter, but I'm determined. Already at the counter, waiting patiently for breakfast, are the two engineers we rode here with. Like most everyone else at Foods, they're looking ragged, but I tell myself that if anything can rejuvenate the Zone, it's Carel's hot and delicious breakfast.

Only, Carel isn't behind the counter.

The kitchen is filled with thick, grey smoke from burnt butter, making it difficult to tell who exactly is cooking. It's only when he curses and steps—coughing—out from the smoke that I recognize Tom. He's sweating heavily, wearing a dirty apron loosely around his neck and holding a plate of crunchy, black pancakes. Seeing us, he hands the plate to Conor and then sneezes repeatedly into the crook of his arm. The husky engineer looks longingly at the plate, but seems resigned to waiting.

Conor nibbles contemplatively on the charred corner of one of the pancakes. "Long night last night?" I ask Tom, holding my hands out to awkwardly receive three slopping mugs of coffee. He sneezes one more time and then rubs his bleary red eyes with the heel of his hand.

"Meeting just ended, just now. How'd ya guess?"

Conor shrugs and takes another crunchy bite of pancake. I don't know how he can do it. As hungry as I am, the hundred running noses in the room have momentarily put me off of my appetite, and the pancakes look like something you'd line your driveway with. I notice that Freckles isn't reaching for a bite, either.

"So," she says, covering her coffee with a delicate hand as Tom erupts into another violent sneeze. "What's the plan?"

"Welp," he yawns, stretching the itch out of his face. "It looks like we're just gonna see how things go." Freckles raises an eyebrow incredulously, as if to say "all night for *that*?"

"I know," Tom says, absentmindedly picking at Conor's burnt pancakes with one hand and rubbing his temple with the other. "*I know*. It's ridiculous. Of course, there was . . . debate. A lot of people left, couldn't stand the thought of just chancing it."

"And you?"

"Good question." Takes off the apron and hands it to the husky engineer, who's still waiting patiently for his breakfast. "Help yourself, man."

While the engineer fumbles with the apron strings, Tom squeezes my shoulder with a cold and dirty hand, guiding me conspiratorially to the far corner of the restaurant, Freckles and Conor in tow. "Truth is," he whispers, eyes flickering nervously around the crowded room. "We can hide, but the federales won't stop until we're accounted for. Been through this before, and waiting *ain't* the answer."

"So . . ." prompts Freckles, quizzically sustaining the *oh*.

"So once they realize there are stayers, that opening the spillway isn't gonna flood everyone out, they'll think of something else. It might take a while, but they're not just gonna walk away."

Tom is leaning against the wall as if he'd be on the ground without it, completely downtrodden, but his cynicism doesn't get me down. On the contrary, the muscles in my legs and arms go instinctively taut, flexing, and my heartbeat quickens. I've been worried about the same things he has, the seeming impossibility of getting things back to the way they were before . . . and honestly, it's a relief to hear someone else voice them.

It means waiting and hiding isn't an option.

It means we *have* to do something.

I'm about to tell Tom as much when his eyes momentarily narrow, and then, with effort, he forces himself to stand without aid of the wall, his face plastered with a good-natured smile.

"There you are!"

I turn around, knowing before I do that it's Grammy. I briefly wonder what could have happened last night to make Tom react the way he did, but before I draw any conclusions I'm wrapped up in a tight, sickly sweet-smelling hug.

"It's so good to see you, Panky!" Grammy says, overflowing with an uncharacteristic positivity and rose-scented perfume, pinching my cheeks. I see Conor and Freckles smirking out of the corner of my eye, but am too nervous to feel embarrassed. "What's going on?" I blurt out, just as Grammy coos, "You look like you got a good night's rest!"

Tom, still stiffly smiling, shrinks against the wall, but Grammy doesn't seem to mind my outburst. "Oh, nothing much," she laughs. "And thank you again, Thomas, for sparing your cook this morning. I simply had to get one of his . . . *recipes*." Behind her, Mrs. Wallace, red-nosed from sneezing, digs into a big, fluffy stack of the engineer's pancakes, and—stomach growling—I make a mental note to get some for myself, now that Tom's not at the griddle.

"The plan, you've heard it?" Grammy asks, turning her attention back to us. "We're going to hide out for a while, aren't we?" she says, looking meaningfully at Tom. "Until those jackals realize they're actually *helping* us with the dam . . ."

"And then we're gonna fight 'em?"

"Oh, Lord, no," Grammy says, looking at me like I'm crazy. "An eye for an eye makes the whole world blind, Henry. And we're lovers, not fighters, aren't we?"

I shrug while Tom shivers visibly behind her. It's a total departure from her rabble-rousing speech last night, and I wonder again what went down at the meeting . . . what could've happened between Grammy and Tom, who seemed so friendly last night.

But more importantly . . .

"What about Mom and Dad?"

Grammy gestures dismissively, the fat antique rings on her wiry fingers clanking dully. "This is business, Hank. All of this." She looks around Food Eats appraisingly. "The Other Side only exists because we needed workers to rebuild the Green. The Green only exists because we're all so invested in the Zone. We don't want, and can't afford, to live anywhere else. Henry," she continues, gripping my shoulders and pulling me into a tight hug. "The government is business, baby."

"But Mom and . . ."

"Your father. I know, I know. The federales have something we want. They're trying to send a message. We have something they want, too. Fidelity, loyalty. Access to ports, to the river. Power. As long as they respect our *business*, and mind their own, we can work this out."

It makes a superficial sort of sense, but the glimpse I got last night of the bruise on Grammy's arm worries its way into my brain, giving me doubts . . . and the kidnapping, the attempted flooding— none of that was what anyone could call *business*, not even Grammy.

"I thought this was *war*," I say, uncertain. "Last night you said . . ."

Grammy shrugs. "Last night I didn't have the whole story."

"Well, what's the whole story?" I whine. "That Mom's less important to you than this restaurant? Than some *recipe*?"

"Some wars are fought with weapons," Grammy says, choosing not to acknowledge my petulance. "And some wars are fought with . . ."

"Wits?" a voice pipes up from behind me.

Grammy looks at Freckles as if she hadn't noticed her standing with us this whole time. To her credit, Freckles holds her ground, not flinching under Grammy's hawk-like evaluation.

"Wallets," Grammy mutters, after a long pause. "Most wars are fought with wallets." She runs her jewel-encrusted fingers through Freckle's hair, rolling the sun-blonde tips contemplatively. Freckles bugs her eyes as if she wants to disagree, but bites her tongue instead. "Where are your parents, honey?"

"My aunt," Freckles mumbles. "She . . . she's staying in the Green."

"I plan on staying in the Green myself," Grammy purrs, then laughs enigmatically, heavily-shadowed eyes widening larger than I've ever seen them before. "We've rebuilt too many times for anyone to kick us out over something as stupid as treason. But first," she says, letting go of Freckle's hair. "Some coffee. I should be able to get a cup in my own restaurant, right?"

The room explodes into a nervous cacophony as Grammy bustles purposefully toward the husky engineer, who's red-faced and smiling now, flipping golden pancakes with proud flourishes for a growing crowd. "These are just growing pains, Henry," she calls out reassuringly, without a backward glance.

My stomach doubles up on itself as sweet steam from the engineer's pancakes rises up in hypnotic curls that catch the yellow morning light. And the smell: thick slabs of white butter and golden syrup that glows as if it's lit up from the inside . . .

Tom sighs with annoyance, loud enough for us to hear over the din.

"I'm sure his cooking isn't that much better than yours," Conor says distractedly, eyes still hungrily locked on the promise of another, better breakfast. Tom scowls with exasperation, but it's lost on Conor, who's already pushing himself to the front of the line. I make to follow, but Tom wraps his arm around my shoulder and surreptitiously leads me to the door.

I look longingly backward as Tom toes open the chipped green screen and nudges me outside, briefly locking eyes with Freckles, who shrugs apologetically and hurries after Conor. We're out before anyone else realizes we're gone, Tom gingerly shutting the door behind us and gesturing for me to follow as he slides into a tiny passageway between Food Eats and a tall, overgrown fence.

We work our way down the side of the building without a word, grime from the soft wooden siding rubbing off on our fronts while claws from the vine that's claimed the fence rake our arms and pull our shirts. I can hear everyone inside, but indistinctly, and the further back we go, the quieter it gets. It's a tough squeeze, and because the narrow alley is littered with half-bricks and broken glass, I have to concentrate on each careful step.

Combined with tentative birdsong and the reassuring smell of wet soil, it's strangely calming—meditative, even. I focus on a patch of moss sprinkled with tiny white flowers; a fat snail stuck resolutely to the wall. If it wasn't for the scent of frying butter seeping cruelly through exhaust panels mounted high on the side of Food Eats, it'd almost be like we were completely alone.

Tom must feel the same way, because he suddenly stops, leaning his back against the fence and wedging his right knee up against Food Eats. We contemplate our dirty, scratched arms for a moment before Tom sighs again, then half-heartedly punches the wall. It's more of a resigned knock, really, but it must have hurt, because he shakes his fist with a wince almost as soon as he connects.

"What's up?" I ask, my voice hushed to match our surroundings. "What happened?"

Tom lets himself slide down the fence an inch or so before he turns to face me. He looks tired, like he doesn't really want to tell me what he brought me out here to tell me. But he does, with effort.

"How well do you know your grandmother?" he asks, not whispering. The question sounds overly loud, and it hangs in the air for a moment before it fully registers.

"Uh," I stammer, not knowing what to say. "She's my *grandmother*." Tom winces again. "What's going on, Tom?"

"The meeting last night . . . it was terrible. No solutions. We talked about fortifying, about fighting. But it's obvious we don't have an army or anything like that."

It feels ridiculous to be hearing words like *army* while we're wedged in a dirty alley, alone. For the first time since I've known him, Tom looks young and scared . . . dwarfed by the towering strangeness of our predicament. It makes me wonder how young and scared I must look; suddenly anxious, I clutch my chest in anticipation of a spike.

Tom, oblivious, goes on. "It was pathetic. She wanted to fight, but most of us . . . We're all here because we're running away from something. I can't afford to get in trouble with the government, Hank. No one can. I think she realized that and . . ." He turns to me and points at my chest. "You okay?"

I nod, half lying. My heart isn't doing anything weird, but I feel like it should be—and that worries me. It's hard to put my finger on, but there's a disconnect. Like I'm *watching* myself not having a problem in this quiet, non-threatening alleyway . . . and I definitely should be having a problem. Honestly, I should be freaking out. The fact that I'm not makes me feel like I should be freaking out even more.

"Hank," Tom says, his voice lowering to a conspiratorial whisper. "I think she's going to try to turn everyone in."

Normally, this would have tipped me over the edge, but—staring past Tom into the jungle of the backyard—I lose my train of thought. The morning cool has given way to the dead heat of the day, but it's comfortable where we are, enveloped by woody vines and shaded from the unforgiving sun. Still, the silence is oppressive, and I know I should say something, so I do my best to pull myself back into the moment.

"She wants to fight," I say, knowing as I say it that while Grammy may have wanted us to fight last night, she doesn't now. Last night she was cornered, but today she seems to have collateral. It sounds awful, but Grammy's always been a business lady, a mover and a shaker. If it means trading a few outcasts for my parents and for the Green, I know Grammy is fully capable of turning in the Other Siders.

She could probably even do it with a smile.

"She knows they'll take the deal, too," Tom says, ignoring my admittedly hollow protest. "*She knows it.* The feds don't want wilderness, not really. They want order." He's whispering, talking more to himself than to me, but after a moment of reflection he lets loose a bitter, barking laugh.

"They don't want to wipe us out. They want to lock us up."

I'd like to say the sun was eclipsed by gathering clouds that cast the eerily quiet Other Side in a grim pallor; that, confronted with Tom's suspicions about Grammy, I lost my appetite.

But, of course, I can't.

The alley is thick with the smell of buttermilk and barley flour, and the sun is just as bright as it was before.

Before . . .

My stomach growls, a long, unhappy meow that carries surprisingly well in the stifling heat of the alley. I feel flat, deflated by what Tom said, but he literally shakes the concern from his head and claps me on the shoulder with a smile.

"Breakfast?"

I check his face for remnants of worry: frown lines around an otherwise ever-present smile, or sweaty creases in his grease-streaked brow. But there's nothing; only kind, tired eyes. Two dancing bees alight on a vine behind him, and I suddenly, guiltily, crave honey.

Grammy, I think, stomach growling again despite my clenching gut. *How could you sell these people out?*

We trudge back to the front of the restaurant, picking our way around fallen branches and stubborn puddles, reminders of the storm. Food Eats is still in full swing, so boisterous compared to the quiet alley outside that my first instinct is to cover my ears. The scent of fresh pancakes hits me just as hard as the noise, though, and a syrupy wave of wellbeing washes through me, smoothing out the cacophony of the room.

Everyone's here.

Mrs. Wallace is nodding intently at the skinnier engineer, smiling; Conor's assiduously working on what must be his third plate of pancakes; and Freckles, bugging her eyes at me, is trying to catch my attention.

I pretend not to notice.

Instead, it's a throaty, sarcastic laugh that I'm drawn to. I only half recognize it at first. When I finally spot Grammy—shaking her head appreciatively, reddish-brown lipstick lining her white mug of coffee—everything seems to fall away from her.

Or, I *wish* it would—but Food Eats continues to bustle despite my sudden, unexpected need to be alone with her. Freckles is still staring intently at me, sending all caps communiqués via eyebrows; Conor is still shoveling butter-drowned pancakes into his mouth. And Grammy, finally caffeinated, breaks out into another fit of laughter in the corner. She laughs the same way Mom does, loud and unselfconsciously, with her whole body. I want to run to her, to hug her around the stomach and feel the warmth from her arm as it drapes protectively over me.

It would be so easy to just let her fix everything, to believe that she could get Mom back.

I take a tentative step forward, restrained only by a half-memory of the helpless inchworm she sent down the drain; by *growing pains* and what they might mean for the Green Zone and everyone on the

Other Side. For Mouse. I can't even *imagine* what growing pains might mean for her. An errant shiver runs up my spine to the base of my skull, where it ends in an unconscious gag. Grammy owns this place; she made that pretty clear last night. She owns this place, and she's acting like she owns these people. She owns the food they're eating, and she owns . . .

Grammy notices me, frozen in the doorway, and waves me over, spans of hammered gold bracelets catching the light as she smiles encouragingly before turning back to her conversation, graceful hand still lingering in the air. My heart sinks as I realize, without a doubt, that Tom is right about her. She's too calm and too self-assured for someone under siege. For someone bruised, with a daughter under federale lock and key.

Why won't you fight? I want to yell, to shake her. To convince Grammy that there must be another way to win back the Green. But that's not her style . . . and I have to grudgingly admit, unclenching my fists, that it's not my style, either. Instead, I ignore my growling stomach and burst back out into the sunlight, tripping over my still-hesitant feet at first and then picking up my legs and sprinting down the street.

Leaving everyone behind.

My heart's beating double time in my ears, filling my head, and I don't want to look over my shoulder to check if anyone's following me. I take a deep breath, feel my lungs fill and expand, and count halfway to ten before my nerves win out and I sneak a peek behind me.

There's nothing except blue skies and a dusty, uncomfortable calm. I exhale a grateful, ragged breath. No one is following me. There's also nobody in front of me; the entire Zone is either holed up at Foods or hiding behind shuttered windows and hastily barricaded doors. Either that, or they've escaped the Zone entirely, like Dr. Singh said she wished she could do back at the Library.

Last night. That was just last night . . .

Remembering the terror and tumult of yesterday, I make a quick, nervous turn toward Tom and Rachel's rickety house, saying a silent thanks for streets devoid of black federale sedans. Wishing hopelessly that I could just hide out in the Library attic until this whole situation just took care of itself. *Until it's over*, I think, not wanting to think about what "over" might mean. Better to wait for Tom and Rachel at their house . . . they'll have a plan. And if they don't, Mom and Dad will. All we have to do is get them out and they'll take everything back to the way it was.

Everything will be fine.

I jump up their porch stairs and, breathless, pull open the peeling front door. *Unless something happens, something terrible, and Tom and Rachel don't come home.* I shake my head, trying to physically shake off the doubt and negativity that's set in.

It doesn't work.

I just feel my brain sloshing from side to side, hear my heartbeat amplified inside my skull, as I shut the door behind me. It's slightly warped and doesn't fit the frame, so I jiggle and force it closed. The door remains stubbornly ajar, and I try shaking my head again to calm my nerves.

"Hello?" a female voice calls.

Mid-shake, I don't hear the voice well enough to recognize it. Flattening myself against their atypically white wall, I quietly curse Tom and Rachel for not having a door that locks.

"*Hank?*"

It can't be, but it sounds like . . .

"Mom?" I croak.

The shades are drawn and the hallway is mostly shadows, and I whisper out of deference to the darkness. My voice, small and hopeful, barely makes it through my dry lips. When it does, it sounds as if it's coming from a distance, like it belongs to someone else. Someone tired and hungry.

Someone alone.

Hot tears roll down my hot cheeks without bidding, and I call out again, louder, but I can barely hear myself over the fuzz that's filling my head. Frustrated, I call again, even louder. But it's no use, I realize, collapsing.

It's happening again.

⚡⚡⚡

I wake up disoriented, blinking cool water out of my eyes—registering first a jagged pulsing between my temples and then, uncomfortably, the warmth of a lap beneath my throbbing head. I push down on my eyes with the heels of my palms and, seeing stars, wipe them dry.

Staring down at me, smiling and holding a dripping hand towel, is Rachel. Her hair is pulled back into small, wet fist of a ponytail, and she smells faintly of green tea. I scrunch my nose, squinting, and prop myself up on my elbows.

"You changed," I say, wincing at the cracks in my voice. Rachel stands up, laughing, and tosses the wet hand towel at me. Instead of the paint-flecked tuxedo dress she'd been living in for the past few days, she's wearing jeans and a crisp V neck.

"Yeah," she says, pointing dismissively to something behind me. "I finished."

Propped against an unstable pyramid of over-stuffed milk crates is her self-portrait. It's glossier than it was this morning, and seems to be radiating out beyond the canvas and illuminating the dusty room. If I didn't already know it was made of a million little dots I never would've—

"It's so different from the others," I say after a moment, my voice steadier than before. The rest of her paintings look like cartoons next to the new one, afterthoughts. Rachel looks around the room with me, eyes moving from pink-skinned portrait to green-skinned portrait, all bright, unmixed palettes and bugging eyes.

"Last one for a while," she mumbles, dropping a plate of stiff-looking pita and white cheese in front of me and wiping her hands on her jeans. "We usually eat at Foods," she shrugs, apologetic. "This is all we got." The pita is crunchy and the cheese is hard, but it will do. I chew a hunk of it into mush and swallow, then reach for more. After a few helpings, I feel less shaky, and the buzz behind my eyes seems to have receded.

"Mind if I have some?" Rachel asks, reaching for a slice of cheese and popping it into her mouth.

"You don't change clothes until you finish?"

She smiles, still chewing on the rubbery cheese. After a few long seconds, she spits it into her hand instead of swallowing. "I didn't realize how bad this was," she laughs, rubbing her tongue with her shirt sleeve to get the taste out. Unfazed, I reach for another piece. It feels good to finally be eating. I could chew harder bread and more rubbery cheese. Rachel gags and laughs, looking for somewhere to put the cheese she wasn't able to swallow. She folds it into a page ripped from an old magazine and wipes her hands on her jeans.

"Doesn't usually take me that long," she says, nodding back at the painting. "But I wanted to make this one count, you know?"

"Because it's the last one?"

Rachel shrugs, then heads back into the dusty piles of yellowed books and records from before, clearly looking for something. I reach for another chunk of cheese and cringe as one of the stacks crashes around her legs.

"It's safe out there," she says, rooting haphazardly through a mountain of clothes. "You know that, right? All the federales are off at the dam. I rode out there this morning. They have that thing on full blast, just watching it go."

That explains it, the fainting.

"Everyone's still holed up," I say. "Scared."

"Think fast."

Rachel tosses something from a clothes pile at me, and a zipper hits me in the side of the head. Laughing, my hands still full of pita and cheese, I let it slide to the floor, where it joins the rest of the clutter.

"If they're really trying to flood us out, they're going to figure out that they're wasting their time pretty soon. Then they'll be back."

I inspect the heavy black canvas between my feet, not smiling anymore. It's a duffel bag, a big one.

"I know," she says, her voice soft and sympathetic. "I don't think we have much time."

Just then the front door blasts open and we both flinch, Rachel dropping to the floor. I'm frozen, my heart plummeting to my ankles. *Too late.* The sun is behind whoever's in the doorway, so I can't make them out. It looks like two, maybe three shadows rimmed in sunlight, inching their way into the room.

Military.

A floorboard creaks, but otherwise the room is silent.

"Hey . . . guys?"

I recognize the voice, but—still stunned by the initial terror at being found—can't make myself answer.

"You here?" one of the shadows shouts as another shadow slams the creaky door shut behind them. It bounces back open an inch or two, still too warped to fit the frame, but blocks the sun anyway. Standing nervously in the hallway are Conor and Freckles. Before I've had a chance to find my voice, Rachel jumps up from the floor as if nothing happened, wiping the dust from her hands on increasingly dirty jeans.

"Definitely could've been them," she says, even though she just finished telling me that all the federales were down at the dam. That there was nothing to worry about. "Wouldn't have been surprised."

"Could've been who?" Conor asks as he falls next to me on a pile of clothes, instantly relaxed. Freckles, still standing, helps herself to a hunk of cheese.

"Been looking for you," she says, slowly chewing and then making a face. "Tom said you might be here."

Conor, burping, nods toward the duffel. "What's with that?"

I shrug and look toward Rachel; he and Freckles follow suit. But Rachel, unaware, is back to ripping through piles of clothes, looking for something.

"You guys didn't see any federale cars or anything on the way over here, did you?" I ask, almost hoping that they had, that they could disprove Rachel's theory about the dam. But Conor just shakes his head as Freckles squints at me inquisitively.

"Yeah," I sigh. "Me neither."

Rachel, having found what she was looking for, frantically starts making new piles of clothes. The ordered chaos of the house seems less ordered than before; most of the previously precarious stacks of books and records have collapsed, and she looks like a salvage worker in a disaster area.

"She says they're all at the dam, the federales, trying to flood the Zone . . . but they're actually doing the opposite. The engineers bought us some time," I say, silently thanking Guv while fingering the zipper on the black duffel. "I have a feeling the idea is to get out of here before they get back?"

"*Exactly*," Rachel sings, tossing handfuls of clothes at me, Freckles, and Conor, and then wiping her sweaty brow with the back of her dirt-streaked hand. "Out of sight, out of the Other Side. Outta the Zone. Out."

This time I make the catch.

"It's a last-minute thing," Rachel explains. "All I know is, a friend came back this morning, and if anyone can help get your parents back, it's him." She puts her hand on my shoulder, squeezes, and wraps her other arm around Freckles. "Do you have someone you need to be with?"

Freckles shrugs.

Nodding, Rachel pulls Freckles into a quick hug. "Good," she says, turning to Conor. "Tom'll explain everything when he gets here."

"My mom," Conor stammers, sitting up as Freckles inspects an oversized black hoodie with orange bleach stains, wrinkling her nose. "I can't . . ."

While Conor stutters objections, my knees start bouncing with nervous energy . . . with excitement. Even if I didn't want to leave, the federales have the spillway completely open—if I don't want to keep passing out, I have to go. Besides, there's nothing to do here but wait, anyway. Grammy can scheme all she wants. She can make deals and plot to betray the Other Siders, and it won't matter, because we'll get help from the Outside.

We'll get my parents back.

Rachel's started taking her paintings off the wall and stacking them on the sunken, sheetless mattress in the far corner of the room, leaving bright squares of show-flyer wall paper where they once hung.

Taking a quick inventory of the outfit she tossed me, I'm happy to see that it's more "Other Side" than the dry clothes she gave us yesterday. Like Freckles and Conor, I got a black hooded sweatshirt; they must've brought these down from Baltimore, because it never gets cold enough for a jacket in the Zone. Also, a pair of black jeans with holes in the knees. I glance over to my pleated khaki shorts, still wet from last night, and smile.

"Should probably get changed," Rachel says, checking her watchless wrist and then shaking her head. "I don't think we're going to have much time."

"What about all your stuff?" I ask. Rachel's paintings are stacked on the bed and there are records everywhere—the reason Dad and I came to the Other Side in the first place. Tom was supposed to start a radio station . . .

Freckles arches her brows at me like I'm insane and says, pointedly, "What about everyone else?"

Rachel looks at me first, and then at Freckles. For the first time since I've known her, there's no trace of a smile on her face. No laughing eyes, no knowing smirk. Just a tired face, like the ones all the grown-ups end up having sooner or later. I can't stop myself from turning my head toward her self-portrait for a comparison, but it's already stacked with all the other paintings.

"You're not gonna be able to help anyone in the Zone," she says. "Not if you're here. And you can't look like that out there." She gestures at the mildewing pile of the clothes we came in. "Like you're boarding school runaways."

Conor stands up and looks from me to Freckles. "I'm sorry," he says. "I have to . . . I can't leave her." I want him to come with us—he's the most athletic, the most able. The one most likely to help us pull off whatever our plan ends up being. But I understand. Conor's all his mom has left—Mrs. Wallace in her rain-spattered wedding dress—and he knows it.

Freckles puts her hand on his shoulder. "Conor . . ." Her voice is sweeter than usual, empathetic, and then—when Conor shrugs her hand off—she gets a steely look in her eyes. "Tell my aunt.

If you see her, tell her . . ." Freckles looks at me, annoyed, and continues, "Tell her Evelyn went to get Julia back. And tell Mary and Alice. And Scott. Let them all know."

Conor nods and then, with one last apologetic look, runs out of the room, throwing open the door, casting the room in a warm yellow light. Freckles squints into the sun as I break the ensuing silence.

"*Evelyn?*"

"Evelyn," she admits dismissively. "But nobody calls me that."

16

For the second time, Freckles goes over the list of people we're missing, running their names over her fingers like beads on a rosary: Scott's with his dad, mean old Mr. Malgré, in the Green. And Mary and Alice both left the Library with their parents last night. We didn't see them at The Corner, so they're probably hiding out back home, too.

"Everything's going to be fine," I say, cuffing my too-long black jeans and rolling up the sleeves of my borrowed sweatshirt. The outfits Rachel lent us are too hot for the Zone, but she promised that we'll thank her when we get to the City—federale central. Freckles looks at me searchingly, worried.

"How can you know that?"

Rachel and Tom's clothes are too big on her, too, but her face looks cool framed by the black hood. An amber curl streaked with blonde falls from behind her ear while I'm thinking about how to justify my optimism, and I fight a terrible urge to stroke it back into place. Instead, I take a deep breath and try to remember the poem

Mr. Moonie recited; I know there must have been at least one easy line in there I could quote right now.

But I can't.

I can't even focus on Mr. Moonie, let alone some old poem.

All I can think is that I really *don't* know that everything's going to be okay. Mouse was kidnapped. My parents were kidnapped. The Green Zone is crawling with government agents hell-bent on re-enacting the Tragedies. Grammy's got something weird up her pastel sleeves. And it's not like there's any easy solution to anything, anyway. In my gut, I know that everything is going to have to get a lot worse before it gets better.

If it ever gets better . . .

The poem completely forgotten, I force myself to at least picture Mr. Moonie. His rusty red tie holding up twenty skinny chins, his immaculately pressed seer-sucker suits. He's never leaving his Library. And I haven't seen any of the other kids who go to School there on the Other Side, so I'm assuming they're all holed up in their houses, too. Hiding, huddled in the Zone.

The federales want to flood all of them out . . .

"Everything's going to be fine," I say, slowly, making sure I sound like I believe myself. "Because . . . it just has to be fine."

Freckles looks like she wants to argue, but visibly bites the inside of her cheek and nods once in agreement instead. We're sitting on Tom and Rachel's narrow back steps while they pack up all their records and paintings, wedged next to each other so our legs are just barely touching. Tom had come sneaking back from Food Eats about an hour after Conor left to rejoin his mother. Apparently they'd crossed paths, because Tom handed me a freshly penned note from Conor as soon as he walked in the door. There was nothing on it—except for Conor's older brother Ben's address.

In the City.

I'd slipped the scrap of paper into the front pocket of my hoodie and keep touching it every few minutes to reassure myself this is really happening. I'm terrified that if I keep fooling with it, it's going to fall out and we'll make it to the City and have nowhere to go, but I can't help myself.

"That should do it," Tom had said confidently, as if everything was settled now that we had a place to go once we got up north. As much as I wanted to believe him, Tom's optimism seemed about as baseless as mine. Freckles and I still don't even know how we're getting out of the Other Side, except that some "friend" is coming for us, and so far he hasn't showed. It's not a stretch to think that this entire operation is just as precariously planned—but we wouldn't know. Tom's been too busy packing to fill us in.

Daydreaming on Tom and Rachel's back stairs, I secretly hope that their friend has rough, capable hands and a history of bloodshed. That he's the kind of friend who can take out twenty federales, if it comes to that. I feel a little guilty about hoping for violence, but . . . he'll have to be tough if we have any hope of getting out. Black jeeps might not be policing the Other Side anymore, but I have a hard time believing they don't at least have a net set up around the Zone with the helicopters from last night at the ready.

Just thinking about it, my leg starts shaking. My knee bobbles against Freckles, our loose black jeans rubbing together erratically as I finger the address in my pocket.

Escape.

I turn to Freckles, wanting to share my excitement, but stop myself when I see that she's already looking at me with searching green eyes, her pale, chapped lips partly open. All of a sudden, I'm hyper-aware of our touching legs, and try to stop mine from bouncing by gripping my knee with a trembling hand, which Freckles squeezes with slender, cool fingers.

I stop shaking, instantly calm, and—exhaling—drift toward her.

Our mouths are warm together, dry lips framing awkwardly-touching tongues. I'm not sure what to do with mine, but Freckles moves hers in a slow, wide circle and I just keep still so I don't get in the way. My knee starts bouncing again, uncontrollable, as I realize that I'm breathing her breath, and Freckles tightens her grip.

It's different than it was with spin the bottle, in the attic. Softer, and less terrifying.

I feel my heart beating in my temples and wonder if she can feel it, too. Either way, we don't hear Tom until he's almost on top of us, jangling the handle of the rear door that's pushing insistently against our backs.

"Hey," Tom calls through the door as Freckles pulls slowly away from our kiss, locking eyes. "Ride's here."

My face breaks out in a lopsided grin, and I try to fight it—to stay cool—but the smile wins out. Freckles wipes her mouth with a baggy sleeve, wrinkling her nose. "No buzz," she murmurs, and I can't tell if she's disappointed or relieved.

Back inside, Rachel slouches languorously amid the wreckage. The apartment is turned upside down, the carefully curated maze of their belongings flattened on the floor. Leaning against the front wall is a small stack of milk crates and an overstuffed duffel bag. "No telling how long we have," Tom says, grease-streaked and sweating. The overstuffed crate of books he's straining to drag out the front door litters yellowed paperbacks in his wake as he calls over his shoulder: "Truck's out front. Gotta get a move on."

I follow his lead, grabbing the fraying fabric handles of a deceptively heavy duffel and staggering after him. Parked on the front lawn is the front cab of a rusted out semi-truck. It's enormous—the balding wheels are easily as tall as me—but without the trailer, it looks stubby and sad; more trash than truck. The passenger side door is open, and Tom's fitting his crate into an already crowded back seat with some difficulty.

I drop the duffle and pick absentmindedly at the peeling metallic paint on the dented hood as he wedges everything in, wondering how we're all going to fit. A sliver of once-glittery red catches beneath my thumbnail. After a minute of concerted chewing, I manage to get it out, but Tom's still rearranging.

"I don't think we're all gonna fit," I say, trying to make it sound like a question. The rear of the cab is almost all boxes already. "Unless there's a trailer or something."

Tom sighs, more out of agreement than frustration. "It's just you two who are going," he says. "The rest of this stuff—I'm not trying to save everything, just the basics for now."

I try not to let any panic creep into my voice as Tom shoves his duffle into the truck. "You're not coming with us?"

"Just y'all and the dog," he says. "Everyone else is just gonna have to hold tight, for now."

"*Dog?*"

"She's getting a last walk in," Tom says, jumping down from his elevated perch. The cab of the truck is so stuffed that I really don't see how even just Freckles and I are going to fit—much less with a dog— but I keep that observation to myself. "Should only be a few minutes."

We all stand awkwardly on the front lawn, waiting for the driver and his dog. It doesn't help that Tom and Rachel aren't coming, and I wonder with a growing fear if maybe we should stay with Grammy and the rest of the Other Side after all.

If it's crazy for me and Freckles to be striking out on our own.

If it is, no one admits it.

It's Rachel who breaks the silence. "We've done this sort of thing before," she says, unable to hide the stress that sounds so unfamiliar in her voice. "So don't worry too much."

"I'm not worried about *me*," I lie. "It's you guys I'm worried about. When Gram finds out I left . . ."

Tom winces, but quickly shrugs it off. "Listen, we have a plan. For Conor and anyone else who stays. For your Gram, too . . . if she wants."

"I don't think she'll want," I say, and Tom nods in sad agreement. "And if there's a plan . . . shouldn't we stay, too?"

Rachel and Tom shake their heads simultaneously as Rachel pokes Tom in the ribs, an unsubtle prompt. "The plan works best if you're . . ." Tom starts, then hesitates.

"The plan works best if you can get your parents back down here," Rachel interjects, her voice strained and overly sweet.

Freckles doesn't look convinced, but she holds her tongue, choosing to glare pointedly at me instead of pressing them for more details. Shrinking under Freckles' stare, I'm about to ask for specifics when a squat, muscular dog with a square head bounds into the yard and, panting, stares at each of us in turn.

"Oh, good," Tom says, visibly relieved as he scratches the dog behind the ears. "Go time."

Jogging after the dog is a red-faced, fire plug of a man—also panting—with rough-hewn tattoos circling his neck. He's looks vaguely familiar, except . . .

"*Carel!*" I shout, recognizing him despite the smoothly shaved space where his heavy handlebar mustache used to hang. He stops jogging and rests his hands on his knees, breathing deeply.

"How . . . you . . . know . . . ?" he manages, spitting and coughing between words. Tongue lolling, the dog looks back at him as if she's laughing. Carel raises his heavy head just long enough to shoot her a dirty look and curse gutturally in a language I don't recognize. I do manage to catch her name, though.

It's Julia.

"It sounded like you were going say that your plan works best if we're gone," Freckles finally says, her voice quavering with determination as Tom and Rachel share an uncertain look.

I kneel, introducing myself to the dog, letting her sniff and lick my hand and then scratching her behind the ear. She's brindled—black and brown and white all mixed together—with stiff, dirt-caked fur. She turns to look at me as I scratch her, white froths of saliva dripping from loose red lips as I work my way down her back, massaging. Behind me, Tom and Rachel reluctantly explain their plan to Freckles, who listens critically with her hands on her hips. I pretend not to listen as the dog thumps her tail in the grass and rolls onto her back.

"It's gonna sound bad," Tom says, "but it's all we have right now. We think Hank's gramma is planning on double dealing with the federales, right? She thinks they'll barter for Mayor Long; that she'll get her daughter back if she gives the rest of us up." Freckles nods skeptically while I keep scratching the dog, trying to find the sweet spot that'll make her legs kick. "So," Tom continues, picking up steam. "While Carel helps you guys bring Henry's parents back, *we're* gonna make Milly think we have Henry. That way, we can be sure that Milly won't make any deals while we're trying to get Mayor Long back. We'll have a . . ."

Tom rolls his hands, searching for the words. "A united front against the federales, no double dealing, nobody turning anyone in," Freckles says matter-of-factly. Tom and Rachel nod, obviously embarrassed by the implications of their plan.

Freckles looks at me, mock-amused.

"Do you *mind* being a hostage, Henry?"

It wouldn't be a bad idea if it worked . . . but I know it won't. No one's going to believe the artsy Other Siders are the hostage-taking types, especially not Grammy. And even if she does, Grammy isn't so easily manipulated. She'll still make the trade with the federales and chalk it up to growing pains . . . she just might feel worse about doing it.

And yet, even though we're talking about holding *me* hostage, I feel bad for Grammy.

For everyone.

But I need to go—and as soon as possible, if the federales have the spillway open like Rachel says. Otherwise, I might as well just check myself into the Hospital now. Besides, if there's a chance we can save Mom and Dad, Grammy and the Other Siders' plans won't matter, anyway.

I should feel scared, or something, but I don't. I don't feel scared, and I don't feel the buzz I've come to expect from my overworked heart. It's strange. I know I should be grieving for the Green Zone and crippled with fear; frightened for Mouse, my parents, and myself. But, despite everything, I'm just . . .

Not.

I hadn't believed it when I'd told Freckles, not totally, but now it really does seem like everything's going to be okay. Like it *has* to be. It's just suddenly so obvious that we're fated to be together: the electric kid and his freckled girlfriend, the foodie eco-bomber, the Other Siders. And Julia-the-dog . . . a living, drooling sign that even if we don't know what we're doing, we're on the right track.

The realization makes me so unexpectedly happy that I touch two fingers to my neck and, finding a pulse, check to make sure I'm not having another episode. My pulse seems normal, though; better than normal, even. It makes me wonder if Dr. Singh was wrong back in the Library . . . if the best thing for my heart is for me to be living in the chaos, not protected from it.

"I wanna go," I finally say, more to myself than to anyone else. Freckles, hearing me, looks up from a smiling, panting Julia and nods in agreement. We lock eyes for a second. Her face is dwarfed by the hood of her borrowed black sweatshirt, so her serious expression looks more cute than stern. I blush and turn away suddenly, bumping into Rachel.

Rachel must have heard me, too, because she squeezes my arm reassuringly. "You'll eat better there than here," she says, gesturing toward Carel, who's ready to get the show on the road. Her voice is bright and cheerful, but there's a sadness beneath it. I drape an arm around her shoulder in a one-armed hug while she jokes that she's going to miss Carel . . . but she's going to miss his biscuits more.

"Okay!" Tom calls. "We're doing this thing, right?"

Rachel and I both nod enthusiastically, feeding off of Tom's energy as he gives us a double thumbs up, but when we start walking to the truck, I notice that she's blinking back tears.

"It's . . . it's a ghost town," Rachel whispers, her voice soft and hollow, like she's been running from these ghosts for so long she's almost one of them. I turn to look at her, to make sure she's okay, but her reddening face is already wet with tears. Like that, the mood of the morning tilts again, jarring me into full-fledged anxiety.

"Hey," I say, my voice high-pitched and conciliatory. "*Hey* . . ." Rachel's tears cut paths of golden brown through her dirt-streaked cheeks as she stares blankly into the Other Side. Following her gaze, I see a thousand drying flags hanging limply throughout the mostly deserted zone; the flyers and posters lining the street pulped and unreadable from last night's rain. In Tom and Rachel's front yard, a handful of pinwheels spin lackadaisically in a sluggish breeze. When we leave—Carel and Freckles and I—it's just going to be Tom and Rachel in this puddle of a town. Tom, Rachel, Grammy, and a bunch of Green Zone castaways hiding from the federales.

I drape my arm around Rachel's shoulders and pull her into a tight squeeze.

"I just . . . we . . ." Rachel whispers, talking more to herself than to me. "We tried so hard to make this work." I squeeze her again, so tight that she laughs despite herself. "I guess it still could. Maybe I'm just being cynical."

It *is* a ghost town, though—like the Grey. Rachel slumps against my arm. We both know it's not just pessimism; the Other Side is dead. "Come with us," I say, smiling hopefully and wondering why it hadn't occurred to me earlier. "There's room in the truck, we'll just squeeze togeth—"

Rachel shakes her head no, but she's smiling again, wiping the tears from her big almond eyes with paint-flecked thumbs. "We have to try," she says, shaky but determined. "Even if it . . . we have to fight against it—otherwise it's just going to follow us everywhere we go."

I think of Mouse and my parents, of how vibrant and happy the Other Side was before the federales showed up, and know that she's right. If Tom and Rachel can trick Grammy into joining forces by getting me out of the picture, and if Carel can somehow help free my parents and Mouse . . .

"Just, come back, okay?" Rachel says, knuckling my chin up and kissing me dryly on the cheek. Freckles's eyes narrow, and I pretend to need to tie my shoe so I can gracefully extricate myself from Rachel's grasp. As I kneel down, a black jeep cruises in front of us, slowly enough for me to make uncomfortable eye contact with the blonde driver. Her face is startlingly expressionless except for her full, pale pink lips, which are twisted in a nasty sneer. Time seems to stop as we stare at each other, surprised, until she raises a two-way radio.

"Go! Go, *go!*" Tom shouts, picking Freckles up beneath her arms and tossing her unceremoniously into the truck. "Rach, run!"

Even though the blonde federale has cruised right past us and is almost a block away, we break apart like an exploding bomb. I pull myself into the cab as quickly as possible, wedging in next to Freckles on the wide front seat while Tom and Rachel sprint toward the main strip. Carel struggles with Julia-the-dog, whose massive neck flexes terrifyingly in anticipation of a chase, but he finally wrestles her into the truck as well. She scrambles across our laps until she's crammed, drooling, against the window.

As expected, it's a tight fit. And Carel is a bear of a man, so when he heaves himself into the front seat—which is just one big bench upholstered in a ripped, hot plastic—we all squish that much closer together . . . except for Julia, who stretches across our laps.

"Everyone buckled?" Carel asks, slowly—infuriatingly—strapping himself in. Freckles wrests her hands free from beneath Julia and yanks her seat belt down across her chest, but has trouble finding the matching catch in the tangle of the front seat. I feel so panicked that I don't even try. "No driving without belt," Carel says, snapping his own across his chest as the black jeep rounds the corner again.

"Go!" I whisper, nudging him with my shoulder, eyes locked on the jeep and the two black cars now trailing it. "Please, go!" Carel shrugs and turns the key in the ignition . . . but nothing happens. "Old truck," he explains, gesturing with his chin at the sun-blistered dashboard and the panel of antique dials and gauges below it. The needle for the speedometer has fallen off its pin and settled in a pile of dust, and the other indicators are similarly blasted. Carel cranks the engine again, and when it turns and then chugs to life he thumps the steering wheel and shouts, "But good!"

As we reverse, skidding into the street, we're confronted with three more federale jeeps idling halfway down the block in an ominous V-formation. I stop breathing for a long second, then the adrenaline kicks in. Julia, barking viciously into the window, feels it too—but Carel's oblivious. For a big man, Carel's short, and

215

he has to scoot forward in the seat to see over the steering wheel. While my eyes are locked on the federales, my heart pounding in my ears, Carel takes his time getting situated, double checking his seatbelt and then casually cracking his knuckles. "Oak-ay," he finally mumbles, shuffling his bottom forward one last inch and stomping on the gas. "*Allons-y!*"

We jolt backward into a cloud of grey smoke, our heads dully thumping Tom's boxes behind us. I look over at Freckles, who's grinning anxiously, and wonder what face I'm making. The truck doesn't have rearview or side mirrors, but we're surrounded by so much oily smoke that I can clearly see my reflection in the slobber-streaked window.

I look terrified.

Carel, completely calm, makes some adjustments and stomps on the gas again, propelling us forward through the exhaust. Despite everything, the truck seems to have some power behind it, and I cross my fingers that it's going to be enough for us to outrun the federales. I crane my neck, trying to glimpse them through the smoke—and see that they're still idling in position, which makes me nervous for some reason. More nervous than if they had immediately given chase.

I almost say something, but the truck is loud—rattling with exertion—and it doesn't seem like Carel even cares that we're being followed. Instead, I look anxiously at Freckles, who stares back at me with wide, expectant eyes. We're both shaking with the effort of the truck while Julia continues to attack the window.

"What is it, girl?" I ask, scratching her bristling haunches, careful to keep my hand well away from her slavering jaws. She either doesn't hear me above the racket or she chooses to ignore me, because she just keeps barking, pausing occasionally to reposition her face against the glass. We're out of the smoke now, and picking up speed—but the labored hacking of the engine is getting louder, and I peer nervously at the dashboard to see if everything's okay . . . remembering, too late, that most of the gauges are broken.

"Hank," Freckles yells, grasping my hand mid-stroke and yanking me over her lap so I'm squished up against Julia, my cheek pressed wetly against the drool-streaked window. "*Look!*"

Past the sparkling red hood of the truck, there are six or seven federales in black suits just milling around their cars, which are still idling in V-formation in the middle of the road. They're all staring at us, transfixed by the stuttering truck. Carel spins the wheel and my forehead strikes the glass as the truck executes a fumbling U-turn, my eyes locking on the blonde woman from before. She sees me make note of her and waves choppily before disappearing behind our swerve. It's a short and sinister salute—like she's just letting me know that she knows where I am, and where I'm going.

That she doesn't even have to chase us.

I fumble for the window crank on the inside of the door, but have trouble turning it with Freckles and Julia mashed against me. After some uncomfortable twisting, I'm finally able to get it open, and, craning my head out into the wind, look behind us at the shrinking *federeles*. Most of them have already dispersed into the remains of the Other Side, but the blonde woman hasn't moved.

"They're not going to chase us," I say, slumping back down into the overcrowded cab. I'm basically sitting on Freckles' lap, so she hears me over the engine and the wind, but Carel inclines his red, freshly shaved face toward me inquisitively. "They're not following us," I yell as Carel nods encouragingly. "They're . . . they're going after the ones who stayed!" Not waiting to hear his response, I lean back over Freckles and Julia and stick my head out the window again.

As we putter away amidst Julia's manic barks and occasional clouds of oily exhaust, more black cars screech onto Tom and

Rachel's front lawn, skidding purposefully in the wet grass as federales on foot surround the house. Despite the noise inside the truck and the rush of federales, the Other Side seems quiet—almost devoid of life. Even Tom and Rachel's house looks dead, its wood sun-bleached and warped by rain.

The road ahead of us is flat and straight, but I train my eyes on their house until it shrinks into the distance. First it blends into the Other Side, and then the Other Side blends into the Grey Zone. I tell myself that I'd see if the federales got anyone, that I'd at least know—but after a few minutes the entire Zone is just an ashy smudge on the horizon, and I haven't seen anything.

As quickly as that, we're on our own in the middle of nowhere, jangling down an empty two-lane highway lined with tall grass and stunted pines. Every so often, a quicksilver burst catches my eye, the noonday sun reflecting off the river through the trees. I count quietly to myself between these sightings, trying to discern a rhythm, but there's none—only the occasional heron taking harassed flight at our noisy approach and a sky so blue you'd think nothing was wrong.

Maybe the last sky Tom and Rachel will see for a while.

And Conor and his mom, Mrs. Wallace. Even mean Mr. Malgré, and Scott. Everyone on the Other Side—the pinwheel lady, and Greg the drummer. There were so many people packed into the party, dancing, at The Corner the other night . . . it's hard to imagine them all hiding in hot, dusty attics, waiting for the federales to drag them to some cold northern jail.

And all the families still hunkered down in the Green Zone, living off of stale nutraloaf behind barricaded doors and shuttered windows.

Something tells me the construction workers are a hundred miles away by now, leaving the Zone to sink in on itself like before, beneath the river and all the unmixed concrete they left behind, with only Mr. Moonie—with his poems and secret sword—to guard it.

Why can't they leave us alone?

The fresh bruise on Grammy's arm flashes hotly through my head, and I shiver before I even realize what it is I'm seeing. No matter what she was planning, she was . . . she *is* my family, and my not choosing her over the Other Siders seems suddenly . . .

Unforgivable.

The truck abruptly stops rattling and lurches forward, picking up speed, and I feel Carel's thick hand on my shoulder, pulling me protectively back into my seat by the nape of my hooded neck. Julia, thankfully, has stopped barking, either because the truck has quieted down or because Freckles is rubbing her thumb methodically between her big, wide-set eyes. Freckles—looking noticeably less content than Julia-the-dog—squints questioningly.

"No one's following us," I say, squeezing Julia out of my seat. "They're all . . ."

I let the sentence hang, not wanting to think about the federales closing in on the Other Siders anymore.

On Tom and Rachel.

On Grammy.

"We were wrong gear," Carel says, breaking the silence again and smiling broadly at a shift stick hiding behind the oversized steering wheel. "Also, emergency brake!"

He thumps the dashboard with his short, thick palms, his broad chest shaking with silent laughter. "Friends will be all right, I think. Always, our friends are all right. But now," Carel pulls his shoulder strap away from his body and then lets it slap resoundingly against his generous stomach. "Buckles."

I settle back into my narrow wedge of seat and fasten my belt.

"No belt for dog," Carel says with noticeable regret.

Feeling my legs start to sweat beneath all my borrowed clothes—the oversized black hoodie and the matching black jeans—I finger the address in my pocket, wondering how we're going to make it all the way to the City like this. Outside, the river stretches ahead of us, wild and muddy and free, running unrelentingly toward the dam—the dam that was supposed to save us but brought federales instead. I hope the river crushes it, destroys it like everything else it's destroyed in the Green Zone. It was bad enough when the dam was just messing with my heart, but now . . .

The adrenalin rush from the escape has run out, replaced by a full-body ache and a dull apprehension of the days to come. It's just me and Carel and Freckles from here on out—I know that. I look over my left shoulder at Carel, who's rubbing the stubble on his upper lip where his mustache used to live, and then at Freckles, who's wrapped around Julia, who's sleeping heavily in her lap.

If my parents are going to escape, it's going to have to be us who get them out.

There's no one else left.

17

It's still light when I wake up, but barely; the sun's hovering non-committally in a way that could mean either dusk or dawn. Rubbing a crick out of my neck, I try to piece together how long I've been out, if I slept through a night of driving or just for a few minutes. The scenery doesn't hold any clues; it's just more wet pines, more glimpses of the river.

One thing's certain: I slept with my head mashed awkwardly against my own bony shoulder, and now the left side of my neck is so sore that I can barely turn to look at Freckles.

The fading light and shade of tree branches overhead play across her face so quickly that it almost makes me dizzy to look at her, anyway. It's funny—I'm so used to being around Freckles now that I don't even really notice her freckles. I have to refocus my eyes to see them: a light dusting of cinnamon across her nose and glistening, heat-pink cheeks.

The air is warm and stale in the car, and despite the passenger window being open, I find it suddenly difficult to breathe. After a few stifling moments I reach a breaking point and—whispering, so as not to wake Freckles—ask Carel if he'd mind rolling down his side as well. I shouldn't have bothered with whispering: if the high-pitched squeal of his ancient window crank miraculously didn't wake her, the hot and ripping cross-breeze from both sides of the truck would.

Julia-the-dog twitches in Freckles's black-sweatshirted arms, her muscular legs kicking sleepily against my thighs as Freckles reluctantly stretches awake. She yawns widely, her eyes still squeezed shut, as I instinctively scratch Julia's taut white belly.

"Where are we?"

"What?" Carel shouts, unable to hear her over the wind. I start to repeat the question, but the squeal of the crank drowns me out as Freckles rolls her window almost all the way up. I feel Carel looking inquisitively at me, but my neck spasms when I turn my head to meet his gaze, so I just keep my eyes forward, on the road, and wish he'd do the same.

"Good," Carel says, noisily rolling up his window again. The cab of the truck is instantly sweltering. "Everyone awake, everything quiet. Time for to talk." A bead of hot sweat rolls down my neck into my shirt. The black asphalt road stretches hotly in front of us, oil-slick mirages melting into the quickly darkening sky.

It's going to be an uncomfortable night.

Carel shifts beside me, and I brace myself as the truck slows down and swerves, bumping carelessly onto the shoulder of the highway and back. Freckles stares past me with an expression of mute horror: Carel's twisting on his seat, rifling through the boxes in the back of the cab.

"First," he says, falling heavily back into the driver's seat and taking control of the drifting truck. "Dinner."

Carel rustles around in what sounds like a paper sack, and my mouth waters in anticipation, hunger from the missed pancake breakfast trumping my fear of his hands-free driving. Even as the truck changes lanes of its own accord—driverless again—I fantasize about what he's going to pull out: thick slices of white cheese on hunks of freshly baked bread, spicy mustard and heirloom tomatoes. Or, even better . . . fist-sized, flaking biscuits slathered in apple butter, warm black coffee in a thermos to wash them down.

I wipe the sweat from my brow with the back of my hand as my stomach turns on itself, thanking fate for giving me Carel instead of Mr. Malgré, or Guv, or anyone else from the Zone. He might not be the hero I had hoped for—he's barely keeping the truck on this empty road—but if this had to happen, I think, looking at Freckle's expectant face, I'm glad I'm with someone who can cook, and someone . . .

Someone I kissed.

With everything moving so fast, I haven't had time to really think about what happened with Freckles on the back porch of Tom and Rachel's house before the federales came. She's staring at me like she's been thinking about it, though—like she's been waiting to catch my eye. When she does, she squeezes my knee and smiles. My heart starts beating double time and my face goes red, but it suddenly feels like everything's all right again; like everyone's going to make it out of this, after all.

"Radish," Carel says gruffly, saving me from any possible awkwardness with Freckles by smacking my chest with a heavy bunch of wet greens. They fall into my lap—leafy stems connected to oversized red radishes still muddy from the ground they grew in. "You three share," he adds. "No time to cook, but Julia prefers raw."

I squint at Freckles, too shocked by our unexpectedly meager supper to be disappointed, but she's still in middle of the moment I thought Carel had wrecked, and we resume staring at each other. Her waving hair parts perfectly, despite the sweat and the heat, as her surprisingly long, delicate fingers scratch dust out of Julia-the-dog's bristly chest. Transfixed, I can't believe that someone as graceful as Freckles would want to kiss someone like me. That she might want to again.

I look up from her hands and notice that she's still staring at me, lips parted. Inhaling, I slowly—very slowly—position my hand next to hers on Julia-the-dog's stomach. Holding my breath, never breaking eye contact, I inch my fingers through Julia's fur, toward Freckles' long white hands. When I finally reach her fingers, they're strangely cold to the touch, and I exhale sharply as she grips my hand with them, letting the radishes slip from my lap to the floor of the cab.

In a flash of fur and muscle, Julia flips against the cracking plastic dashboard and wiggles to the floor, barking sharply at the radishes rolling between my legs before taking one in her jaws and crunching wetly. Freckles laughs, reaching for the rest of the radishes— brushing briefly against my knees on her way down—as Julia growls territorially, settling her muscle-bound torso on top of them.

"Julia," Carel reprimands from the side of his mouth, eyes finally on the road ahead. "Julia, sharing!"

Julia barks twice in protest, but—after a sharp look from Carel—retreats beneath the dash where she resentfully gnaws on her bitter, half-eaten dinner. Meanwhile, Freckles picks one of the recovered radishes from the floor for herself and hands the rest to me, her fingers lingering coolly on mine.

The moment ebbs away as Julia growls and slobbers at our feet. Freckles pulls away, rubbing her radish halfway clean on her jeans and then taking a crisp bite, wiping the soil from her lips with the back of her hand.

We kissed, I think. *She kissed me, and I . . .*

"Is good raw," Carel says, interrupting. "Usually, I cook into pie. Goat cheese, walnuts. Flake crust." He takes another generous bite, and then, through a mouthful of radish: "Is nice this way, too. Healthy."

The first thing I notice when I take my first bite is the dirt, grits of minerals and sand catching in my gums and crunching between my teeth. Then the spiciness kicks in, so strong that my tongue swells. Coughing uncontrollably—the spice tickling the back of my constricting throat—it's all I can do not to spit the radish out half-chewed. Carel claps me on the back, laughing so heartily the seat shakes.

"Is maybe better cooked," he admits, as I blink the redness from my eyes and cough my throat clear. Freckles doesn't seem to mind the spice, though, because she picks another radish from my lap and takes a bite.

Julia-the-dog doesn't seem to mind either, so I toss the rest of mine between her paws.

"How many days are we going to be on the road, do you think?" I ask. He looks at me, expressionless, and for the first time since I got into the cab of the truck, I remember that I'm sharing it with an incredibly thick-necked and intimidatingly tattooed man. Shrinking uneasily back into the hot plastic seat, I turn my attention back to the road ahead. We're still following the river, which is increasingly visible through the thinning pines: a strip of silvery black winding next to the highway, escorting us out of the Zone. Only, it's flowing in the opposite direction, back down toward the dam. "A few days, we'd be in Canada," Carel finally says, mouth full of radish. "The City: before morning."

My empty stomach tightens. "That soon?"

Carel swallows and nods. "Maybe before," he says, gesturing at the black road ahead. In the twenty minutes since we woke up, night has started falling in earnest, and the highway's truly desolate. Carel hasn't turned on the headlights yet, if they even work, so we're careening north by the remnant light of a sun that's already set and the ghostly glow of early stars. "Not much traffic."

Freckles shifts beside me, in my blind spot, and I turn instinctively, flinching at the sharp pain running down my neck. "I slept weird," I say, over my shoulder, by way of explanation.

"What's it like?" Freckles asks Carel, casually kneading my shoulder blades with the palms of her hands. I flinch again, this time not with pain, but surprise at how casual she is about rubbing my back. I wonder if this means she thinks we're boyfriend and girlfriend now or if we *are* boyfriend and girlfriend. She works a knuckle down my spine, and *that* hurts—but I don't want to stop her. Instead, I clench my teeth and lean back into the pain. "The City, I mean . . . have you been?"

"Is the same everywhere," Carel answers, not looking away from the darkening road. "Worse there."

I finger the worn scrap of paper in my pocket; Conor's brother's address. He was so much older than us, and left when we were so young, that I only really half-remember him—he looked a lot like Conor, but skinnier, with a wry twist to his smile. I wonder if we'll recognize each other . . . if Conor's gotten word to him somehow; if he'll even want to see us.

"Everywhere is bad," Carel continues, "except Other Side and Green Zone, a few other places. Too many people. Too many problems. *Fait comme des rats*," he mutters, his head shaking sadly. "Trapped."

This is the most I've heard from Carel since I met him, and hearing him talk reminds me for the second time since we left the Other Side of what Rachel told us about his time in jail. It's hard to make out his expression in the dark, but he looks strangely more sinister without his super-villain mustache. The indecipherable web of tattoos wrapping around his neck—and down into the thick

226

curls of chest hair spilling out of his shirt—don't make him seem any less scary.

"Did you . . ." I ask hesitantly. "Did you really blow up a mountain?"

Carel whips his head away from the road, toward me, and I cringe back into Freckles' terrible massage. The truck starts to slow, decelerating until we're stopped in the center of the highway. Carel maintains heavy-lidded eye contact with me the entire time. His face is mainly hidden in shadow, but I can tell he's not happy.

"Who told you I blow up the mountain?" he says, turning off the truck.

His voice is gruff, and—as Freckles stops rubbing my back—it occurs to me that I've just gotten on the wrong side of a very dangerous man; an ex-convict, even.

Maybe an escaped *convict . . .*

Like Freckles, I freeze.

Carel is obviously waiting for an answer, but I can't make myself give him one. My heart's in my throat, buzzing faintly with a fear I don't want to acknowledge. Admitting it makes it real: we're in the middle of nowhere with a stranger. And I . . .

I agreed to be his *hostage.*

It's just Carel.

I try to visualize him making us breakfast at Food Eats, joking with Tom and Rachel, insisting on seat belts. *They wouldn't put us in a truck with a crazy person*, I tell myself, but—as hard as I try to believe it—I'm not convinced. Carel's heavy frame is tense in the driver's seat, as still as the tall grasses lining the highway. It's a windless night, and now that we're not driving, the air outside the truck feels as hot and stale as the air inside. The ratcheted drone of dwindling late-summer cicadas whirs in a never-ending crescendo, making the heat even more unbearable.

As the silence stretches on, the cicadas fill the night until their hypnotic chirping seems to be all there is to the world. Mom showed me one once—not the cicada itself, but the empty shell it left behind when it molted. It didn't look like any bug I'd ever seen . . . it was too big, too unbelievable. I scan the trees on either side of us, but it's too dark to make anything out, and there doesn't seem to be any movement. No herons or sparrows or bats; no fireflies. *It's too hot for them*, I think. *It's just us out here. Me, Freckles, Crazy Carel, and the terrible, throbbing song of a thousand overgrown crickets.*

I take a deep, centering breath as Freckles surreptitiously knuckles my side, nudging me out of my reveries and back into the front seat of the parked truck. I know she wants me to speak up—to break the silence—but I hold my own, gripping the plastic seat beneath my sweating knees as she continues to poke with increasing intensity.

"I never blew mountain up," Carel finally says, contemplating the night through the driver's-side window. "I stopped mountain blowing up. Big difference between."

"Oh," Freckles says, with apparent relief, as she starts massaging my shoulder again. "That's good, right?"

"Well, we maybe blew up *some* things," Carel says, turning back to us. "But not mountain."

Freckles stops massaging me again. "*Blew up* some things?" Her voice is so shrill that Julia-the-dog jerks up from her dozing and growls.

"Listen," I say, finally finding my shaky voice. "It doesn't matter about the mountain thing. Whoever blew up whatever, it just . . . doesn't matter. We'll get to the City, get Mouse and my parents back, and get back to the Green. That's the plan, right?"

Carel sighs deeply and flips the key in the ignition. We start rolling down the center of the highway again, hovering over the faded yellow lines. Almost as an afterthought, he switches on the headlights. Only one of them works, but there's not much to see anyway; just the road ahead and the menacing shadows of crooked pines. Tracking their broken, black silhouettes against the slightly-less-black sky, I try to convince myself that whatever Carel did doesn't really matter, that we're all here now and there's nothing we can do to change that. Julia's back to snoring on the floor; Freckles is gently pinching my side again, and I'm—

I'm terrified.

"*Does* matter," Carel says loudly, shaking his head and slapping the heel of his hand on the steering wheel for emphasis. "*Government* wants to blow up mountain for coal, for gas." He holds two beefy fingers up to my face and, shaking, smacks them back onto the drifting wheel. "They want *power*. That's why they shut down Other Side. That's why they take girl and parents." The truck slows, then lurches forward as Carel bounces his foot on the gas pedal.

I hold my breath and shrink as far as I can into my suffocating hoodie, but Freckles—more curious than concerned—leans over me so she's face-to-face with Carel.

No . . . no, no, no, no . . . I furrow my brows, projecting wordlessly. *Sit down, sit down.*

But Freckles doesn't share my concerns about being trapped in a truck in the middle of nowhere with an angry ex-con. "So the federales were going to blow up your mountain," she asks softly, her elbows distractingly propped against my legs, which are slick with sweat beneath Tom's baggy black jeans. It's strange how she touches me, like it's no big deal. I wonder what would happen if I reached out and pulled gently on one of the golden brown waves that's fallen from behind her ear. Of course, I can't—my arms are pinned again. But even if I could, I don't really think I *could*.

"So they could get coal," Carel explains, spitting out the word as if he's been sucking on ashes. "Everything else is gone, no more fuel . . . just coal. Dirty coal." He shakes his head, genuinely angry. The shaved spot where his mustache once lived is stark white against his flushed pink cheeks, which would be funny at any other time. Right now, though, it just seems like a joke at our expense. A reminder that the fun part of Carel is no longer with us, if it ever really was.

"Dirty water, dirty air, sick people, ruined mountains," he says with a raspy finality, his voice more sad than angry. Freckles sighs and collapses back into her seat, resting her head on my shoulder and snuggling sadly in. Except for the ratcheting chassis of the truck and Julia's continued snoring, we continue driving through the darkness in silence. The pines continue to thin, exposing the black wetness of the river to our right and empty expanses of grassland to our left.

Carel rolls down his window, letting the hot night air rip through the cab, and Freckles hunkers down further into my shoulder.

18

Julia snores dryly at my feet, kicking her paws against my legs every once in a while as if she's dreaming about running, while Freckles breathes heavily, her arm settled comfortably across my empty stomach. I'm exhausted, but so wired by hunger that I feel like I have a better chance of fainting than falling asleep. I want to move, to stretch my aching neck and forage in Tom's boxes for something—*anything*—to eat.

Even radishes.

It's almost unbearably hot with Freckles wedged against me, and I've been sweating so much beneath my hoodie that my mouth feels chalky and cracked, but her hand is nested like a porcelain bird on my overheated chest, and the last thing I want to do is disturb it. One wrong move and she might lift her arm and turn toward the window—so I hold my breath and keep my eyes on the road, scanning the horizon for some sign of relief.

There's nothing out there, though.

We've finally veered away from the river and the trees, and—outside of an ambiguous blue glow in the distance—there don't seem to be any other landmarks. Just broken asphalt, weakly lit by our one working headlight and the waning quarter moon. I close my eyes and try to sleep, telling myself that if I can just make it until morning, we'll have breakfast and everything will be okay again.

I still can't sleep, though.

It's too hot and loud, too impossible to relax. Instead, I concentrate on the weight of Freckles' hand on my chest, how it rises and falls with my every breath. When she finally shifts after what feels like hours, I open my eyes, hoping to see the first pink tendrils of tomorrow on the horizon, but it's still night, and will be for a while. Freckles buries herself deeper into my side, sleeping so deeply that I'm racked with a desperate, exhausted jealousy.

Something *has* changed, though.

Nose wrinkling into a pre-sneeze, I inexplicably start choking. I can't place the smell, but all of a sudden it's filled the truck completely: a sharp, chemical stench I taste in the back of my mouth, in the roots of my molars. I look to Carel for explanation, horrified, but he just grits his teeth and steps on the gas.

Freckles, coughing, stirs groggily awake. Our eyes meet for a brief moment—mine watering in advance of another sneeze, hers bewildered—before she heaves toward the passenger side window and frantically rolls it down.

"It's just as bad out here," she shouts, hanging her head out the window. I can hear her ragged gagging over the foul, roaring crosswind and say a quiet thanks to Carel for not making us a real dinner tonight. As hungry as I've been, there's no way I'd be able to hold it down. Julia, wakened by the excitement, joins Freckles at the window and snaps unhappily at the noxious night air.

Outside, sterile blue floodlights shine across seemingly endless concrete fields. It's the most electricity I've seen in one place since before the Powerdown . . . and it doesn't even look like there's anyone around to use it. I squint past the glow of the lights, nervously checking for the federales that must be there somewhere, hiding.

Waiting for us.

But it's just highlighted emptiness.

Carel nods toward a line of pulsating blue in the distance. "Refinery," he says, as if that was all the explanation we needed for the sickening smell. "Not in Kansas anymore."

Freckles drops back into her seat and, looking whiter than usual, wipes her mouth with the back of her hand. "I hope the City isn't this bad," she groans, slouching down next to Julia-the-dog, who's still hanging out of the window, nose pointed querulously toward the refinery. "I don't think I can take much more of this."

"Is worse," Carel says, eyes still on the road. "Smells better, though," he adds, looking at us and smiling for the first time I can remember since our narrow escape from the federales. I'd just assumed his default expression was a scowl, that the mustache hid it. Now that I see him smile, I realize that he's just been glowering this entire trip.

"You . . . were happy there," I say, nervous about making him angry again, but encouraged by his smile. "On the Other Side. You always seemed so happy."

Carel locks his small brown eyes with mine as he guns the accelerator, shooting us blindly through the toxic cement wasteland. "Of course," he says, his smile fading into a gentler version of the scowl we've grown used to. "No cities, no people, no violence."

"There's nothing *here* either," Freckles mumbles petulantly. She's doubled over against the door, hiding her face in her hood and sounding completely miserable. Julia, unable to place the stench, starts whining inconsolably, echoing Freckles' sentiment.

"City is *here* and violence is *here*," Carel says, raising his voice over the ripping wind and keening dog as he points with heavy emphasis at the concrete on either side of the roadway. "And *here*," he says, pointing at the road itself. "No more trees, and the river . . . dirty from *this* refinery. And others, many others. Bad to drink, even in the Green."

Carel's shouted indignation mixes with Julia's whimpers and the cross-wind until all three jumble incoherently together. Light-headed, I drop my face between my knees to stop the world from swimming. The awful chemical smell is still strong, and my chest heaves reflexively against it. "Poisoning land—biggest violence," Carel yells over the tumult. "Hurts everyone."

Unable to anchor myself against the sick, I scramble over Freckles toward the window, where I hang my head next to Julia's. Carel keeps talking inside the truck, but I can barely hear him out here. The wind whips across my face and through my hair, and I try to spit the sickness out through chapped lips, but my mouth is completely dry. I inhale deeply instead, watching the ground rush darkly beneath me as Julia whines nervously at my side.

Finally, mostly sure that I'm not going to puke out of the window, I drop back next to Freckles, who looks like I feel. "The dam," Carel is saying. "Also no good. Wanted to blow up, but— is okay, for making Green Zone and Other Side . . ." He gestures vaguely with his thick, hairy hands for a moment, tapping the steering wheel in frustration.

"Self-reliant," Freckles says. She doesn't sound so good, like she's about to lose her radishes. As if on cue, the incessant buzzing of the cicadas seems to have stopped. "We were supposed to be self-reliant."

"Clean power from dirty river, get rid of federales . . . was good idea. Should have known they would want to steal."

I slouch down into my seat and, ignoring the crick in my neck, pull off my hoodie, stuffing it down by my feet, beneath the dash.

It's still stifling—even with the windows open, the air is so heavy I feel as if I'm drowning—but my arms are glistening with a cooling sweat and the breeze is a relief. I nudge Freckles with my elbow to suggest she do the same, but she just curls further into herself.

I poke her again. Now that I've finally taken my sweatshirt off, it seems ridiculous that we were ever wearing them—it must be close to a hundred degrees and the sun's not even out. But she groans quietly, still sick from the smell, and I decide not to push it.

"People tell you *end of world is coming,*" Carel says, talking more to himself than to me or Freckles. "End of world is *here.*" He thumps himself on the chest. "*I* am apocalypse, *you* are apocalypse, all people are apocalypse. We are sickly bugs with smoke and poisons."

"Sickly bugs," I repeat unthinkingly, snapping Carel out of his monologue.

He shakes his head in frustration, indecipherable tattoos writhing on his neck. "Outside," he says, and then mimics the deafening song of the cicadas with a throaty flourish. "Terrible singing." I want to point out the absence of cicadas—*the sickly bugs*—as we drive through this industrial wasteland, but it just seems to prove his point.

"No one is in belts," he says, looking over at me and Freckles. "Stay safe in belts."

Belted up again, we drive without talking. Julia stays perched at the window, tongue lolling in the chemical breeze, Freckles slouches back down into herself, groaning occasionally; and I sit quietly, watching the landscape change. At first it's all the same: eerily lit concrete as far as the eye can see, fenced in with chain link and barbed wire. Every so often, a jagged series of smokestacks punctuate the still-dark horizon.

After a while, the endless sea of concrete gives way to rows of modest, mostly unlit houses. I lean forward expectantly, but the yards are strewn with trash and most of the windows seem to be broken. The houses are mostly squat and built from a strangely yellow brick, but otherwise, it's exactly like the Grey Zone: torn curtains waving in blank windows like shredded ghosts, rusting memories strewn across grass so overgrown it waves and bends in our wake.

Ruins.

I didn't know what to expect from the City, but it wasn't this. Not more of the same old Grey. "Time to close windows," Carel says, rolling his up and double-checking that the driver's-side door is locked. Freckles just moans and curls tighter into herself. Slowing, Carel reaches over us and secures the passenger side. It's instantly claustrophobic in the cab. Freckles unfolds herself unhappily and, sitting up, dryly whispers something about needing air. Julia-the-dog whimpers in agreement, but nobody makes a move to open the windows again.

Outside, illuminated only by the pale light of the moon, are creeping shadows. I gasp as we're suddenly surrounded . . . too startled to exhale. There are *hundreds* of them: gaunt, loosely-clothed specters stalking from house to house, shouldering bags full of what looks to be trash. As we drive past them, they're so intent on rummaging through their landfill of a neighborhood that they barely look up in recognition of our passage.

Only after the third ghoulish block does one of the pickers take notice of us, a woman roughly my mother's age dragging a tattered suitcase across the street. Her face is dirty and tight, as if she barely has enough skin to cover it, and—as she's caught in the soft glow of our one working headlight—we lock eyes. Hers seem to glow white, refracting the light from the truck, and I shiver despite the heat. She just smiles, though, standing stock-still in the middle of the street. It quickly becomes apparent that she's not going to move, so Carel slows and veers the truck around her, continuing on into the night.

"*Civilization*," he spits bitterly, whistling through his teeth. "Is bad out here, yes?"

"What was wrong with that lady?" Freckles asks, snapping out of her misery. "It was like she was—"

She swallows the word, but I'm thinking it too.

It's like she was a zombie; the way her eyes glowed and her skin didn't fit on her body. Her ghastly smile. The hair on the back of my neck is still standing on end, and my heart's buzzing with a mixture of fear and otherworldly anticipation.

"She's just people," Carel says dismissively, sensing our adrenalin rising. "All are just people. Poor people. Her, she was blind— cataracts from pollution. Not so strange here."

Without warning, Carel spins the wheel into an aggressive U-turn and curses to himself so quietly that I barely hear him over our squealing tires. My back tightens as we screech back into the crowd of Pickers. "Food bag," Carel says gruffly, gesturing to us as he quickly rolls down his window. Freckles is quicker than I am and hands him the brown paper sack of radishes and other vegetables he'd packed for dinner.

Carel rolls the top of the bag and drops it unceremoniously onto the street. None of the Pickers seem to notice, so he blasts the truck's deafening horn twice and a hundred glowing eyes fix on us. "Just people," he repeats, but we all exhale when he shifts into reverse, shooting backward into the darkness as the Pickers converge on our meager bag of food.

We make our getaway in a silence that's only broken after the Pickers are well behind us. "Suburbs," Carel says, obviously sickened by the thought of them. "They live here, off trash. Sick people," he repeats to himself, settling back into the road, and I admit to myself that it's easier to feel sorry for them now that they're safely behind us. I'm glad we helped them, though, even if it was just with those terrible radishes . . . but I can't shake the blind woman's terrifying smile out of my mind.

We've rolled the windows back down, now that we're alone again, but there's no ambient noise from the outside world. No construction, no other cars. No cicadas—not even the *bugs* live here. It makes the Grey Zone look like paradise, I think, still shivering. Here, with all the Pickers, it feels lonelier . . . sadder. Freckles, so excited a few minutes ago, bites her bottom lip so hard it's almost the same pale pink of her color-drained cheeks, and even Julia-the-dog seems downcast.

"What do they do with the trash?" I ask, not really wanting to know but unable to sit through another prolonged silence. Carel shrugs his bear-like shoulders and shakes his head.

"Burn it. Trade, with each other for more trash, or with the City, maybe, for food if they find something good. But . . . *look*," he says, gesturing at the waste outside with outstretched palms. "Nothing here but trash and poison."

Freckles bursts into tears beside me, and I wrap my arm around her trembling shoulders. I try to imagine the Green Zone like this, a skeletal Mr. Moonie and Mrs. Wallace picking through broken scraps of the past as the City funnels the electricity from our dam back north, to the families of the men and women who stole the other Julia. And my parents.

It doesn't seem possible. We'd fight back . . . we *are* fighting back.

Only now it just feels like we're driving, and I remember how hungry I am, now that Carel's dropped all our food for the trip out the window. I can't blame him, but my stomach growls so loudly that it startles Freckles out of her tears and makes Carel jerk his head.

"More food in back," he says. "Best to eat before City."

Saying a silent prayer of thanks, I get on my knees and start rearranging the over-packed backseat. For the first time since we've left the Other Side, I let myself really worry about Tom and Rachel—Tom must have been nervous-to-breaking about the federales to ask Carel to carry so much of their stuff away from the Other Side and into the unknown.

"There's a cooler in the back," Carel says from the front seat. "Red one."

I don't see any red coolers, though . . . only dusty boxes bursting with records. I have a feeling the food is buried at the bottom of the pile, so I start rearranging. The first box I try to slide toward me is heavier than I thought it would be, though, and its worn cardboard flaps rip as other boxes collapse on top of it.

"*Careful,*" Carel shouts from the front seat, peering back into the shadows as Freckles shifts, accommodating my kicking legs. "Red cooler, not white cooler."

Both coolers are wedged in the very back, behind the mess I've accidentally created and beneath a square something, covered with a dirty pink sheet. My relief at finding the food fades as I lift a corner of the sheet, revealing the painting beneath. It's Rachel's self-portrait, the one she finished right before we left, and it's still glowing . . . even here in the dusty backseat of a too-hot truck, surrounded by empty-eyed Pickers and industrial poison. Her smile cuts through the darkness, and I swell with a sense of confidence I haven't felt since I convinced Conor to night-bike with me to Food Eats.

"Should be toward back," Carel says. "Red cooler. Sandwiches inside. And coffee."

I crawl, sighing, toward the back and drag the red cooler toward me, careful not to disturb the dirty white cooler beside it, which Carel seems uncharacteristically anxious about. Inside, as Carel promised, is a tall green thermos and a stack of sandwiches wrapped loosely in wax paper. I unfold the topmost sandwich, pulling the paper down low enough to see a full cross-section.

It's even better than what I could have hoped for: an entire creamy-green half of an avocado sitting precariously on a generous chunk of cheese, balanced between chunks of golden brown bread at least an inch thick, with yellow sprouts spilling out the sides.

I refold the wax paper and take stock of the cooler: there must be about ten of these in there, enough to feed us four times over. "Why," I ask, slipping back into the front seat with a handful of sandwiches, the thermos of coffee wedged under my arm, "didn't we have *these* for dinner?"

Carel just shrugs and grabs a sandwich from my lap. "Was hungry for radish."

We eat our breakfasts in silence, taking turns slurping lukewarm coffee from Carel's thermos as we drive through what's left of the suburbs. I wonder what time it is; it feels like we've been driving through the darkness forever, but it must still be the middle of the night. There's still no sign of dawn on the horizon, only an ethereal blue shimmering in the distance, much brighter than the fluorescent lighting of the industrial sector we passed earlier.

Even though I've never been outside of the Zone, I know what it is. I can feel it in the accelerated beating of my mechanical heart.

The City.

It's pulsing with electricity, waves of power radiating off its jagged skyline, funneling the life from the impoverished surrounding suburbs just to shoot it out into the empty night sky. The darkness surrounding us seems more black in comparison, and I can't tell if it's the muddy coffee, the anticipation of the City, or the rippling electrical charge in the air that's making my chest buzz.

I kind of like it, the excitement. We'd spent so many hours and days just hiding out, waiting and running. It's like the universe is letting us know that we're getting close to something big.

That it's time to finally stand up for ourselves.

After being so hungry for so long, Carel's exploding avocado sandwiches taste almost unreal—it's only when I'm halfway through my second one that I'm convinced I haven't hallucinated them. With each bite, I feel stronger. With each slopping sip of coffee, I feel more resolved to take on the City. To keep the Green Zoners from becoming like the Pickers. Freckles squeezes my knee meaningfully between bites, so I know she feels it, too. The anticipation . . . the jitters.

Even though we still don't have any plans, and it's just us against an entire throbbing city of federales.

"Might be close enough now," Carel announces through a wet mouthful of coffee and bread as he fiddles with the chipped knobs of the antique dashboard radio. It takes a few seconds to warm up, slowly lighting from within with a soft orange glow, the speakers crackling with white noise. Carel tweaks the knob so quickly that the channels run together in an incomprehensible blur until he settles on a wavelength at the far left of the dial. There's still some static in the signal, and he unsuccessfully attempts to twist it into perfection as a squeaky-voiced DJ stutters through the empty night.

"Still too far," he says, slumping back into his seat, frustrated by the fuzz. It could be that we're too far away, but more likely it's my heart. I decide not to say anything—so far I've been lucky, and bringing up my aluminum foil-wrapped life seems like it would just jinx everything. Besides, incredibly, I recognize the song the DJ just introduced as *"a brutal demo by everyone's favorite friends in the underground, Big Dumb River . . ."*

I mean, I don't actually recognize the song, but the screeching voice is definitely Rachel's, and I can almost see Tom playing his angular, shrieking guitar like the first time I saw them . . . with Dad, on our first trip to the Other Side. Just as the drums and bass kick in, Carel twists the volume up so it's loud enough to overpower the jangling truck and the ripping wind.

It's funny how it hits me.

Like I'm back at The Corner with Conor, the dance-scuffed floor bouncing beneath our feet to the frenzied rhythm of the entire Other Side jumping along to Tom and Rachel's squealing feedback. I get goosebumps remembering the sound—the way it moved *through* me, vibrating into my bones, down into my blood and back.

It's almost better in the truck, because we're moving, too, hurtling away from entire weeks spent hiding out in the dusty Library attic, surveying the construction and the slugs in the garden below. Away from nutraloaf and doing nothing; from the still-moldy wreckage of Before.

Even with everything so messed up, it's better to be on the road.

Carel hangs his arm outside of the truck and beats a heavy hand against the metal of the door in clanging, off-beat time with the music while Freckles feeds Julia-the-dog her crust, laughing as her broad pink tongue searches for crumbs. I move to finger the creased slip of paper with Conor's brother's information on it, but it's in the sweatshirt I took off, on the floor.

I tell myself to get it later, then squeeze my eyes shut and let Tom and Rachel's driving music wash over and through me. It's almost like I'm outside of my body again, like I'm having an episode.

But different.

I've never felt so much like myself, I think, deeply inhaling the hot cross-breeze and reaching for a victorious swig of cold coffee. *Never felt so much a part of the world.*

"Friends run station," Carel shouts by way of explanation. "Is part of school."

Both Freckles's and my heads snap toward Carel.

"School?"

After the brutality of the federales and the inhumanity of the Pickers in the suburbs, it hadn't occurred to us that the City would be anything other than a totally militarized zone—that it might harbor a place like the Library, or anyone like Mr. Moonie, slightly rumpled and intoning war-ravaged poetry and historical anecdotes to the children.

That there would even be kids in there.

"**W**ell, *college*," Carel explains as he turns down the radio, insinuating finger quotes with the shrug in his voice. "City has some good things, too. But mostly bad."

"And the federales just let them do whatever they want?" Freckles asks, incredulous. It seems amazing that the black-suited men and women who bruised Grammy and shut down the Zone would tolerate Other Sider rock and roll. Especially broadcast from within the City limits.

"Is not much of a resistance," Carel says dismissively. "Federales too busy, not worrying about students or music."

We slow as we near the City, which looms large and bright before us. High-rises—hulking shadows stretching implausibly skyward from the ambient glow of the city—seem to pierce the starless sky, and it's not until Freckles tugs at my arm a couple of times that I'm able to pry my attention away from them.

"What?" I whisper, my eyes flickering back to the towering skyline, each building buzzing with more power than the Green

Zone could use in a lifetime. Freckles yanks on my hand again and nods toward the road ahead, a pained look on her unnaturally illuminated face. Four black jeeps are parked on either side of the road, a few hundred yards down the highway. The drivers, dressed in black military uniforms—not suits—stand at attention in the center of the street, thrown into dramatic contrast by the blinding floodlights they've set up at intervals around their roadblock.

"Backseat," Carel says, a tremor in his husky voice. "Dog too."

I let Freckles crawl into the back of the cab first, then whistle to Julia-the-dog. She's curled up beneath the dashboard, resolute. I try to drag her up onto the seat by her studded collar, but she just rolls away, thick neck straining against my feeble tugs.

"Come on, girl," Freckles whispers, patting her thighs. Julia's ears perk, and she launches up onto the frayed plastic bench and over the top of the seat, into Tom's packing catastrophe and Freckles' arms. There's not much room back there, but I carefully follow, wedging myself up against Freckles and Julia as Carel pulls a thick curtain closed in front of us.

Except for the floodlights, visible even through the knobby curtain, it's completely dark in the backseat. And cramped. I'm perched on a stack of loose records from the box I ripped earlier, and the sharp corner of another box pokes me right between my shoulder blades as Julia-the-dog rearranges herself so she's half-sitting on my lap and half-sitting on Freckles. I wouldn't have thought it was possible, but it's even hotter behind the curtain, and soon the stale air in the back of the cab smells almost completely of Julia's panting, radish breath—erasing any daring thoughts I may have had of one last kiss before our capture. There's nothing to do but sweat and watch the floodlights grow through the curtain as we approach the roadblock.

"Checkpoint," a metallic voice calls out, a federale amplified by a loudspeaker. Freckles trembles against my sweat-slick arm as

Carel slows the truck, and I wish there was something I could do to reassure her . . . but all we can do is hide. "Please bring your vehicle to a complete stop and turn off the engine, sir."

Footsteps approach our truck, federales inspecting from every angle, tapping sharply on the wheels and the doors—the side of the cab, inches from my stock-still head.

"Purpose of your visit?" a federale asks Carel, his tone authoritative but bored. Even Julia-the-dog picks up on the tenseness of the situation, and we all three hold our breath.

"Pickup," Carel answers, although . . . strangely, it doesn't sound quite like Carel. Freckles cocks her head, and I lean closer to the curtain.

"*Pick . . . up*," the federale slowly repeats to himself, as if he's writing it down. "And," he continues, falling back into his clipped military speech, "what are you picking up in the city this morning?"

"You know how it is, man," not-Carel says. All trace of the gruff Belgian eco-warrior is gone—like his curling waxed mustache—replaced with a slick and comfortable local trucker. "Boss tells me to drive in for a pickup, doesn't bother telling me what for. Could be milk and kittens, but it's probably just more trash for the Pickers."

"No food leaves the city," the federale says sternly, tapping his pen against his clipboard. "No edible export."

"Y'all are eating kittens now? Naw man, you know it's trash for the Pickers. It's always just more trash."

"*Trash . . . run*," the federale says, audibly relieved, as he scratches Carel's revised answer into his checkpoint form. "Quick trip, then. I'll sign you out in a few hours. Good to go?" he calls to the federales who've been checking the undercarriage of our truck with mirrors on poles.

"Good to go," one of them shouts in affirmation, slapping the door with the heel of his hand to send us on our way.

"Alright, see you fellas in a few hours, okay?" not-Carel calls affably out the window, slapping the outside of driver's-side door and twisting the key in the ignition. "Don't miss me too bad!"

The engine turns over sluggishly a few times, but doesn't catch. That's when Belgian Carel comes back, cursing under his breath as he tries again, revving the tired engine until—finally—it catches, the truck jangling heavily back to life. Freckles and I exhale at the same time, slumping back against the boxes as we lurch past the checkpoint and into the City.

Julia-the-dog—scrambling, scattering records in her wake—is the first into the front seat, and Freckles and I follow her lead. Now that we're on the inside, there's no sign of the monolithic superstructures that dominated the skyline a few minutes ago. I crane my still-stiff neck in search of them, but the streets are too narrow to see past the roofs of the five- and six-story apartment buildings that line them.

They're not skyscrapers, but these are impressive, too—solid brick cliffs with limestone facades and curling iron-worked balconies; each one as fancy as the Library, each one a million-dollar townhouse before the Crash. But, *now* . . . every balcony has a working garden, enormous squash and cucumbers hanging heavily from their orna-mented railings. Lines of rugged black irrigation hoses run down the facades, funneling rainwater from the sagging gutters above to the crops below. These converted townhouses may still have looked stately and sophisticated if it wasn't for the overburdened laundry lines stretched between balconies, spanning the street in every direction. Looking up, it's a constellation of yellowed shirts and threadbare jeans, punctuated with the occasional billowing skirt.

Even though it must be almost three in the morning, most windows are illuminated from within with flickering yellow lights so bright they make the street below feel desolately black in compar-ison. It's impossible to see more than suggestions of people behind them—they're all shadows shrouded in patchworked curtains and overgrown foliage—but every so often, just beyond the corner of my eye, I feel someone looking back down at me.

As we rumble through the City, our one working headlight casting a wobbly beam into the sticky night, I notice that Carel is also paying more attention to the living room lights than to the street ahead. Like we're at sea and they're the stars he's navigating by.

It's a comforting thought.

Until Freckles, Julia, and I jolt forward in a bony pile against the dashboard, the truck's rusty brakes shrieking into action. "Be more careful," Carel shouts out of the window, and then turns to us as he rolls slowly past an indignant cyclist. "You all weren't wearing seat belt?"

I shake my head clear, eyes locked with the cyclist we'd almost hit. He's yelling at us, spitting curses at our grimy windshield as he steadies himself on his pedals. No one's hurt, but the fuzzy bubble of rock and roll radio we'd been floating through the City on has given way to an explosion of noise: the unrelenting jangle of the City outside. It's almost like the cicadas on the way here, but with more depth and rhythm.

More fury.

Working my jaw from side to side, I try to pop my ears back to normal, but it's no use. The City's almost deafening. Driving in, the radio had only been turned up halfway, and it's hard to believe I'd been too distracted by the sights to register the sounds, the *loudness*.

I notice that Carel's glaring at me, so I rub my ears one last time and fasten my seat belt. It *had* been a close one— if we'd been going any faster, we would've all been thrown, bloody, through the bug-plastered window.

And yet, here we are. Driving as if nothing's happened. Despite the shock and the angry protestations following us down the street, it's not long before I lose myself in the swirl of the City:

the sing-song sales pitches of the cross-legged traders who line the sidewalks; ratty-looking punks with their hard-worn wares spread out on colorful scarves; heavily tattooed older men selling incense and fruit and batteries from the front baskets of their beaten-up bicycles, weaving through pedestrians and rusty pedicabs as they call out their merchandise.

Freckles and I stare wide-eyed at the sheer mass of people milling about in the streets in the middle of the night. Every block we pass is more of the same; the crowding never seems to lessen. It's like the entire Green Zone packed into the Library, times a thousand. Except no one's wearing khaki shorts and white-collared shirts. In fact . . .

They all look sort of like Tom and Rachel.

"I didn't know that . . . we thought . . ." I stumble, rubbing my elbow where it had hit the dashboard, and feeling a telltale buzz instead of a bruise.

"It's like the Other Side!" Freckles shouts, face plastered to the window. I follow her gaze, noticing for the first time the graffiti blanketing the bottom ten or so feet of every available wall, a mess of shaky bubble letters and jagged political slogans obscured in places by large paper drawings that look like they've been literally pasted onto the brick, like wallpaper. Amazingly, there's no sign of any federales; no black jeeps or suits, just a city full of dirty Other Siders sitting on overcrowded stoops, bartering fruit for batteries and weaving their bicycles through crowded streets toward even more crowded streets.

In fact, we're in the only car on the road, which is why Carel is having such a hard time pushing through the congestion—and why we're getting so many open-faced stares. The streets don't seem to be meant for cars here.

Carel snorts derisively in response to Freckles' excitement. "Is nothing like Other Side. Look, too many people. Nobody doing nothing, just walking around." He raps on the glass of the front windshield, drawing the attention of the City-dwellers ahead. "Living off trash, one meal away from *Pickers*."

Freckles slumps down next to me and sighs, theatrically annoyed. "Can I ask you something?" she says, a shrill edge to her voice. "*Why* do you talk like you can't speak English? We heard you talking to the federales, you sounded totally normal."

My face tightens.

I'd wondered the same thing at the checkpoint, but—not wanting to say anything that would make Carel shout again—I'd let myself get distracted by the City, by the chaos of it all. Carel doesn't seem that bothered, though; he just shrugs his shoulder and clears his throat as if in disgust. "Hate to talk like . . . *them*," he spits. "If federales are normal, no thanks. Prefer French, but no one speaks here." Julia's nails skitter across the floor of the truck as she scrambles into Freckles' lap, and Freckles instinctively pets her, despite her frustration with Carel, who has admittedly been dragging a cartoon storm cloud behind him ever since we left the Other Side. It's gotten so I barely trust my memory of him serving biscuits with a smile.

But I guess everything's different now.

I never would've guessed that the City would be so fun and familiar. I'd expected it to be sterile and clean, full of steel and glass and stern-eyed federales with strong jaws and crisp black suits. Never in a million years would I have predicted rock and roll radio and thousands of Other Siders packing the streets. That Carel can speak perfect English and chooses not to—that almost doesn't seem so strange in comparison.

"Why are these people all out here in the middle of the night, anyway?"

Carel ignores the question, grumbling a response to what Freckles said earlier instead, about the City being like the Other

Side. "Anyway, being Other Sider means getting out, living for yourself . . . not living off others. Not living like this, in big federale prison."

Scanning the streets from the privileged vantage of the truck, which is tall, if lumbering, I try to recast the City as Carel imagines it: nefarious and doomed. But all I see are laundry lines and glowing windows and thousands of Toms and Rachels. The apartments *do* seem to be rippling, though, their lights doubling, then tripling, then doubling again. I shake my suddenly groggy head, but my vision doesn't clear. Instead, the pandemonium of the city goes unexpectedly quiet. Carel's still complaining to Freckles, but I have to strain to hear—it's like they're underwater.

"Have to be out in two hours," he says, as I ball my shaking hands into nervous fists and try to will my vision and hearing back to normal. Unsuccessfully. "Told guards I'm just picking up, can't afford to stay and be arrested. Could go away forever."

The City continues to swim in front of me as I shiver and pop my jaw, forcing myself to hear. *To stay conscious.* "Have trailer to pick up from school friends. No time to go anywhere else. You can find the way, yes?"

"I . . . I think so," Freckles stammers, not sounding so sure. "Hank knows where we're going, right, Hank?"

I want to respond, but I can't—it's taking all my energy just to keep myself from fainting. Lights flicker and fade into white as my eyes strain back into my pounding head, the rumbling of the City obscured almost entirely by the cloud of an attack. *Not now,* I think, gritting my teeth. But it's too late; I'm already slipping away.

"*Earth to Hank,*" Freckles teases through the haze as she elbows me in the side. "You still have the address, right . . ."

The buzz jolts me back into the front seat of the truck for just a split second, although the clarity of everything makes it seem longer:

Freckles' face, heart-shaped and pink from the heat, wreathed in messy brown curls, mouth hanging open in shock. Julia-the-dog perched on Freckles' lap, legs tucked, rabbit-like, beneath her taut, square frame, bright red tongue lolling out onto the plastic seat. Carel scowling into the traffic enveloping us, fidgeting with the grimy knobs of the dashboard radio, which seems to have lost its signal completely.

Falling heavily back against the headrest, I let the crashing thunder of the City rush in as Freckles squeezes my hand, electricity jumping jaggedly from myself to her as I slip out of consciousness. "*You're* . . . doing it again!" she whispers, her voice wavering somewhere between concern and wonder.

The last thing I remember before I pass out is my hand resting in hers as Carel jerks his head toward me, cursing loud enough for me to hear him through the fog.

And then I'm gone.

⚡ ⚡ ⚡

If he doesn't wake up in the next fifteen minutes, we need to take him to a hospital, someone says to a murmur of agreement, their voice high-pitched and agitated. I try to force my eyes open, to let them know I don't need to see a doctor . . . that this has happened a lot recently and Dr. Singh said I should just roll with it. That I should get as far away from the Green as possible, I want to joke. But as much as I strain, I can't seem to move. It's as if someone's stolen my bones and left me draped helplessly across the back of a chair.

We don't have time.

How long's he been like this?

An unpleasant realization needles through my exhaustion. *I don't know how long I've been out; I could be anywhere, with anyone.* I try to force my eyes open again, fighting against the boneless sleep and losing. As helpless as I am, it wouldn't be so terrible if I could just know that everything's okay. The crick in my neck is finally gone, replaced with a warm emptiness. I sigh contently despite the danger, my chest rising and falling without a care in the world; as if, despite all signs to the contrary, everything is going to be all right after all.

That's when I realize the room's gone silent.

Even without seeing, I can feel everyone's attention focus on me with an almost audible snap. Holding my breath, I will myself back to sleep . . . but a tickle at the back of my throat spreads and intensifies, and I sputter, racked back into consciousness with ragged coughs.

That's a good sign, right? someone asks, sounding a little unsure of themselves. It's a voice I don't recognize, and I curse my body for not keeping quiet. It's too late for that, though, so I just keep my eyes squeezed shut instead, afraid of what I might see if I open them. Carel could have been recognized and arrested after I passed out. It's not like a shaved mustache is a fool-proof disguise—he has a tan shadow outlining the white skin where it used to be, and a million tattoos as well. If he's as wanted as everyone says he is, there's no way the federales can miss him.

Chewing on my tongue, I walk through the entire scenario in my head, step by increasingly panicked step.

The biker incident would have drawn attention to us and earned us a federale tail. I didn't see anything else with a motor, and as the only car on the road, we'd have been easy to track and bust. The federales would have surrounded us as we waded through the crowds, rapping on the windows to get our attention and then ripping the doors open, throwing Carel to the ground before cuffing him and dragging him off to some bottomless federale jail, the truck left idling on the streets to be scavenged and stolen.

If they were lucky, Freckles and Julia may have gotten away, melting into the tumult of the sweltering midnight crowd. But we haven't been particularly lucky so far . . . not really. Just on the run. And now the only sign of us ever having been in the City would be Rachel's self-portrait propped against a graffitied wall somewhere, between jars of incense and rows of grimy silverware.

We'll rot here.

But probably not, I try to convince myself, still playing dead.

The voices sound too jumpy to belong to federales. And—now that I'm more awake—I recognize the smell of Julia-the-dog's radish breath, feel the weight and warmth of her dusty nub of a tail wagging against my feet.

Maybe one hour. I recognize Carel's husky voice and purposefully foreign accent. *Only twenty block, but so much traffic.* It's good to hear Carel, to know that he's here and okay, not rotting in solitary somewhere, or worse. Just as I'm about to finally open my eyes, the room explodes into whispered argument. I can't make out much, just scuffles and resentful sighs, so I lie still and decide to wait it out.

After a few taut moments, the argument seems to have moved elsewhere, leaving only receding footsteps in its wake . . . and then quiet.

I count to five and peer through my eyelashes, holding my breath with the hope that I'm not trapped in some godforsaken federale holding cell. Instead of bars, though, I see Julia's slightly crossed eyes an inch from mine, staring back expectantly. As soon as she notices I'm awake, she jumps onto my chest and paints my face and neck with slobbery kisses and breath so bad I can't keep pretending to be unconscious.

"*Henry!*"

I turn my head, slowly, as the warm emptiness of semi-consciousness gives way to an aching fullness. Even though I'm happy to hear Freckles' voice—sweet and concerned, relieved, but also a little angry around the edges—my brain is throbbing so hard against the inside of my skull that I feel like it might actually pop.

And the soreness.

I must have been flexing with all my strength while I was out, because my calves and hamstrings and even my stomach, where I've never seen a muscle in my life, aren't just burning—they're ablaze.

"Hank," Freckles cries again. She's sitting beneath me, on an overstuffed sofa, my head resting awkwardly on her angular thighs. I blink up at her, but can't make out her face. She's silhouetted against a series of bluish fluorescent lights overhead, but somehow her green eyes still seem to sparkle through the shadows. *Cat eyes.* I shiver beneath my hoodie, which is spread, blanket-like, across my chest, remembering the Library attic after she'd kissed me the first time. "We showed Carel's friends the address you had in your sweatshirt, Hank. For Conor's brother . . ."

Without warning, she's cradling my head in her bony arms, clumsily hugging her face against mine. Her cheeks are wet with tears. I hadn't realized she was crying. "They recognized his name," she whispers, her voice ragged with frustration. "He's a stupid federale. There's no way he would've helped us."

I go cold despite the warmth of Freckles's hug.

I'd tried so hard not to think about it, to focus on getting to the City instead of being crippled by impossible logistics. But all my fragile hope was on everything just *working* once we got here. On Carel knowing what to do, and—for some reason I can't quite place—on the dumb, crumpled piece of paper Conor gave me.

And now it's useless.

I try not to think about Mom and Dad, but that's . . . impossible.

The federales have them, and they have Julia-the-girl. I wouldn't be surprised if they have Grammy, too, by now. I try not to think about what the federales are doing to them, but it's not easy. Dark thoughts about bloodied lips and dirty cells are like a red, rising tide, threatening to drown out all rational thought. Like a thick, white fist, dragging me into the backseat of a black jeep, stealing me from my home and family.

It's not fear that grips me, though.

It's a sudden, physical anger.

I take a deep, centering breath, trying to control myself . . . but my muscles are already so taut with rage that I actually feel fiery tendons pulling on cold, aching bones, yanking my exhausted body into reluctant action. *They can pull my bones until they snap*, I think, hating my body for fighting against itself at a time like this. *I couldn't get up if I wanted to, much less walk. Much less save anyone . . .*

Instead, I lay tensely seething in Freckles lap, gritting my teeth and riding out the pain until I'm mobile enough to do something about it. Freckles sweeps my hair across my sweating forehead with the tips of her smooth, cool fingers, and I hold onto the feeling, focusing on it with all my shuddering concentration. It's just me and Freckles now, me and . . .

"Ev . . . Evelyn," I manage to say, whispering through hot, cracking lips.

"No one calls me that," Freckles laughs, pulling her hand away from my forehead in mock irritation and then, thankfully, returning it

"You really don't even know my name, do you?" she says.

20

"Ava," Freckles whispers, stroking my hair across my forehead one last time before extricating herself from beneath me. "Everyone except you and my mother calls me Ava."

Her name rasps out of my chalky mouth, startling me into a rattling cough. She's already somewhere behind me, though, shuffling around, so I'm not sure if she heard me or not. Propping myself up on my elbows, I take stock. The sofa I'm lying on is balding green velvet, soft and worn from use.

"Like, what if I was still calling you *Girl Shirt*," she says. Even though the sofa was once plush, the floor tiles are cheap linoleum; swirls of institutional grey and brownish purple designed to hide a thousand stains. Before they can hypnotize me into a depressive spiral, I look away, head pounding, and sit upright, sinking a few inches into the battered old cushions.

"Glad . . . you're not," I croak, my bare shoulders tingling unpleasantly at the memory of matching all the girls with their rolled up sleeves . . . and the inevitable game of spin the bottle that followed. *The soda that brought us together came from here,* I think.

From Conor's traitor brother.

But I'm too tired to be angry about Conor and the worthless scrap of paper I'd put so much stupid hope into. Better to focus on recovering from the attack; on coming up with a new plan of action. Or even just on how good the air feels in here, so clean and cool. Colder than I've felt in ages.

Air-conditioned.

"Maybe I *am* still calling you that," she teases. "But stop talking, okay? You sound terrible." Somewhere behind me I hear running water, and I swallow dryly in anticipation, ignoring the coppery taste of blood at the back of my throat.

"I can keep calling you Freckles, though, right?" I call over my shoulder, trying to sound fully recovered, but breaking out into a hacking cough instead. Julia-the-dog joins in, barking enthusiastically from her perch on the far end of the sofa. It'd be funny if I wasn't doubled over, red-faced, unable to stop coughing.

"I *told* you to stop talking," Ava calls over my hacking and Julia's angry, cough-like barks. When I lift my head from my hands, her face softens. "Here, water," she says, handing me a paper cone she must have found and filled at a water cooler in this room. I instinctively swivel my head, looking for it; I could drink a hundred of these, but all I see are racks of magazines and newspapers, some recent, some yellowing. Meanwhile, Ava collapses onto the sofa next to me, taking Julia's head into her lap and stroking it like she'd stroked mine earlier.

"There, girl," she whispers, scratching behind Julia's ears as her tongue lolls onto the ancient velvet upholstery. "Hank'll stop bothering you now. He just needed something to drink."

I need more water. The paper cone was barely a trickle, and I might need something else, too. Like painkillers. A do-over. I shake my head, trying to clear it, and catch my smudged reflection in a wall of windows. I look tired and small.

I get up on wobbly legs and wind my way past the periodicals, toward where I think the bathrooms probably are; away from my pathetic reflection, from the still-dark world outside. The parts of my legs that aren't numb are on pins and needles, so I drag my sneakers on the swirling purple linoleum, not wanting to raise a foot and risk losing my balance. By the time I start getting my land legs back, I'm adrift in a sea of bookshelves.

Back in a library, I think, smiling despite myself.

It's all beige metal shelves and elaborately labeled science texts—not at all like Mr. Moonie's polished wood and heavily-thumbed classics. But still, it feels good to be surrounded by books again—comforting, like Freckles and I were destined to end up here.

Ava, I mean.

Freckles is Evelyn is Ava.

It's a lot of names for one person, and I realize that I don't even know her middle or last names.

After I find and half-empty the water cooler, I start feeling a little bit more like myself. The library, on the other hand, seems increasingly strange. The fluorescent lights lining the ceiling are bright and cold, like the arctic air-conditioning, and there's an overpowering smell of floral-scented disinfectant. The sweating, crowded city just outside the windows might as well be a fever-dream.

By the time I shuffle back to the couch, Ava has one of the City newspapers snapped open in front of her face. "So," I ask the paper, "where's Carel?"

"I dunno. They argued a little, him and his friends, when we got here, and then they left," she answers, flipping to another section. "He told us to stay here until he got back, no matter what."

"That doesn't sound good," I say, falling back into the couch. "The *no matter what*."

It's funny . . . it feels like we've been with Carel *forever*, and before that, with Tom and Rachel, and even Grammy, and always in crisis. Except for the back steps of Tom and Rachel's house, this is the first time Ava and I have really been alone. Even with everything, though—his radishes and his glowering, the long silences and the outbursts—I wish Carel was back here with us.

It just feels empty without him.

"There's something *else*," she says, folding the newspaper in half and trailing off. "I thought I'd see if there was anything about the Green or the Other Side in any of these papers."

"Is there?"

Ava hands today's halved paper to me in answer, nodding at a bold headline: "Final Survivors Relocated: Life Goes On In Spite of Looming Threats." Beneath the headline is a grainy picture of at least fifty people standing in front of a nondescript black bus. They all seem to be happy—grateful, even—but I feel my face start to go numb as I scan the accompanying article.

It was bad enough that they'd been living in the ruins of a disaster area for the past fifteen years, abandoned by an increasingly threatened national government, it reads. *But even worse: recent meteorological surveys indicate that the disaster area they called home is going to be hit again, and harder than it ever has before.*

Swallowing a rising bile, I flash back to Grammy's house in the Zone—the brightly blooming hydrangeas spilling over her sun-warmed porch and the manila envelope that she showed us, arthritic hands trembling with genuine anger. She said the federales left it with her as a warning, that the aerial photos of the Zone with red Xs superimposed over every place worth caring about were threats. That the accompanying projection of the Zone underwater, the same red Xs drowning in a river gone wild, was a call to war.

I believed her, I think, my throat stinging with a sickeningly sharp acidity. *Without thinking, I believed her.*

"No," I say, my voice shaking with disbelief. "This isn't real. The federales were the ones who wanted to flood us out." Ava doesn't agree or disagree, she just sits quietly next to me, stroking Julia, while I flip manically through the rest of the paper, ripping the sections apart for more information. "They thought we were going to secede, so they broke in. They *took* my parents and Julia."

There's nothing else in the paper about the Green Zone, but there are plenty of pictures of tanks and war atrocities; headlines about last-minute actions in terrible global conflicts. Ava's article isn't even on the front page, or in the first section—it was buried almost on the very last page of a very troubled paper. Dropping it on the floor, I nervously rifle through the surrounding racks of magazines and newspapers, looking for answers, but it's all more of the same: wars, riots.

Starvation.

Clammy-handed, my fingers smudge illegible streaks into the newsprint of pages and pages of disasters. All those years at School, bored in the attic, and I had no idea any of this was happening. That if anyone needed saving it was the *rest* of the world, not the Zone.

"Henry." Ava taps on the first, slightly ripped newspaper article I'd abandoned—the one about how the federales *saved* us. "Did you see her here?"

I stop what I'm doing, let the newspaper fall in a crumpled pile at my feet. "See who?" I ask, barely whispering. I'd been more focused on the article than the photo, which was underexposed and hard to make out, but now, scanning it more closely, I spot Mrs. Wallace— no longer in her dirty wedding dress—and the husky engineer, his arm draped around her shoulder; next to them is Conor, looking stoically into the camera, and Scott, who looks slightly less stoic. Guv's there, too, and even a scowling Mr. Moonie, a little more wrinkled than usual. He never wanted to leave the Zone, didn't even want to leave the Library. And now, here he is, unhappily sitting in a federale newspaper: an old and unwilling participant in the history he only ever wanted to study from the comfort of his cracked leather chair. He doesn't seem to be leaning on his secret-sword cane, so I can only hope he lost it after putting up a fight.

Tearing my eyes away from Mr. Moonie, I take a deep breath, trying to pull myself together. That's when I see her, huddled in the far right of the picture. Her parents, the Staltons, hovering protectively around her, shrouding her in shadows . . . but there's no mistaking her. Julia.

"Are you okay?" Ava asks, her voice soft and high. "You're . . . you're *clutching* your chest."

"Huh?"

I look down, and only after a moment do I recognize the bone-white hand clenching at my shirt as mine. I want to let go, and try to, but . . . I don't seem to be able to. Everything's off; I don't recognize half of the people in the photo, and I don't see any Other Siders.

Or Grammy.

I run a finger across the grainy photo with my non-clenching hand, smudging it as I search for something I can't quite place.

A clue.

My parents.

Quickly scanning the faces, I desperately check and double-check each row of "survivors." It was easy to miss Julia-the-girl—she's wedged in the corner of the frame, hidden between her long-suffering parents and folded in on herself—and I'm hoping Mom and Dad will similarly materialize, heads bobbing up from behind some too-tall-engineer's shoulder. The more I look, though, the more it's just lines of blurred eyes staring inscrutably back at me. Feeling smudged myself, I'm not sure who or what to believe anymore.

"Hank!" Ava shouts, her hands on my shoulders, shaking me, as the newspaper falls onto the floor for the second time. *They're dead,* I think darkly. *There's no way they're not.* Ava's still shouting, and I wish we lived in a world where I could snap to attention—to fight, to find my parents alive despite all odds and triumphantly save the Green. But I'm struggling just to keep my eyes focused, and I can barely hear Ava over the engulfing emptiness. *How am I supposed to save anyone when I can't even save myself?* I think, six desperate words echoing at the back of my pounding head.

Henry Long doesn't have a heart.

That's when the shaking starts.

⚡ ⚡ ⚡

It's an all-encompassing shiver—metal and wood creaking ominously, as if the building itself is straining at its federale foundations. Escaping.

I feel it in my legs—which seem to be falling out from beneath me again—before the blast registers, and start angling for a wall to prop against. It's only when the books start falling off their shelves that the splintering explosion outside finally resonates into the hush of the library. Julia-the-dog is gone at the first sign of trouble, disappearing into the heart of the building, her stub of a tail quivering behind her. When the lights go out, they quit without any ceremony no pop ping bulbs or blackened filaments, just an instant blackness and the accompanying clunk of the central air-conditioning giving up on itself.

Sightless, I grab for Freckles's hand and, gripping it, feel less afraid.

Strangely, as the building dies around us, I feel suddenly hyperaware—my skin taut with pins and needles, a crackling power surging through my legs and arms and back inwards again, charging into my chest like a million roaring volts. I want to shout, to jump up and punch holes in the ceiling. To grab Ava by the shoulders and just *make out with her.*

Instead, I take a deep breath, remembering—as the adrenaline ebbs—the precariousness of our situation. Ava's stopped yelling, and now that the lights and air-conditioning have given out, it's eerily quiet . . . It's not yet dawn, but since it's dark both inside and out, the windows are no longer mirrored; instead of our own wobbling reflections, we're faced with a cityscape illuminated only in patches by federale floodlights and the lanterns of first responders: sinister polka dots of briefly-illuminated smoke and gleaming military boots.

Completely powered down. Still holding hands, our vision slowly adapting to the night, we try to survey the damage. It's hard to get our bearings at first, but it seems like we're on at least the sixth floor—higher than the roof of the Library back home and most of the other buildings here. As federales start to converge on the streets below, we can see that the City's frenzied in the aftermath of the explosion, shadows roiling in the red glow of flashing emergency lights. It's impossible to tell what happened, though; the shaking only lasted a couple of seconds, and I can't spot any source for the panic on the ground outside of the blackout.

"*Holy* . . ." Ava whispers next to me, trailing off. We can't hear them or see their faces, but I can tell that people are yelling on the ground; I can feel it in the pulsing of the crowds. I rest my nose and forehead more fully against the soundproof glass, look-ing down. It's almost peaceful, watching the chaos from above—I could almost lose myself in it if it weren't for the finger poking insistently in my side.

"Henry," Ava whispers, almost reverently. "Look to your right."

Mesmerized, I don't want to tear myself away from the mad-ness below, but down the block, just barely in view, is the scorched crater of a building—smoking grey teeth thrown into terrible relief by the federales' flashing reds. It's surrounded by what look to be soldiers in full military regalia. They don't seem to be doing much more than holding a line, although some are firing what I hope are warning shots with their oversized rifles.

It sounds like terrible, muted applause through the triple-ply glass.

⚡⚡⚡

We stand slumped against the windows, watching the curling, charred smoke disappear into the greasy, predawn light. We watch for so long, in fact, that I lose track of time almost completely. I don't remember wrapping my arm around Ava's shoulders, but it's there, and my cheeks are cold from where hot tears have streaked them. Ava's cheeks are wet, too. Glistening, even. I lean toward her, tightening my grip on her shoulder in what I hope is a reassuring way. The scene outside blurs as our faces draw together.

"I feel like I'm going to puke," Ava says, jerking her head to the side and spitting dryly. "I'm going to puke."

"Okay," I say, quickly letting go of her shoulder and slouching slightly backward against the window. "Do you want to . . . go to the bathroom or something?"

Ava shakes her head *no*. "I'm not actually going to, I don't think. I just . . ." she gestures at the still-churning mass of people below. "What are we going to do now?"

"Carel said . . ." I start, wondering if the obvious plan is still to wait for him to get back. Even though the City's in turmoil, we seem to be safe here—and anyway, I can't think of anywhere else we would go. Even with the lights out, I can tell that Ava's defiantly arching her brow, as if she's two steps ahead of me.

"He said to wait, not to leave under any circumstances," I say, holding my ground. The current that started coursing through my body after the explosion is still cycling through twitching muscles. Interestingly, the aching soreness from earlier is completely gone. For the first time I can remember, I feel like I can do anything. Still, even though I haven't heard any guns for a while, I'm not anxious to abandon the cool and quiet of the library for the terrified crush of humanity outside. "Don't you think this is, like, the best circumstance *not* to leave under?"

Leaning forward against the window, I peer down at the street below again. It's barely dark anymore, but there's a search light scanning the streets from a helicopter circling above, and some of the armed federales are still carrying their industrial-strength flashlights.

There's no way I'm going down there, I think, wiping the fogging view clear with the heel of my hand. *It's insane to even think about.*

"Henry," Ava says, jabbing a finger emphatically at the glass outside. "You do know that *Carel* did this, right?" My chest twinges as Ava's accusation registers, and it takes me a second to realize it's not my heart this time.

It's dread.

"Did *what*?" I ask, knowing as the words escape my lips that she's right. The dirty white cooler he was so worried about. The argument I only half heard. The mountain he said he didn't blow up. I immediately regret the disbelief in my voice as Ava slides her back down the window, turning away from the City and sprawling on the cold tile floor with a discouraged sigh. I slide down next to her.

Now it's my turn to feel like I'm going to puke.

Instead, I stare into the dark library alongside Ava, waiting for her to elaborate. My eyes had adjusted to the slight light outside, but the inside of the library is still blacked out, and the surge I've been feeling since the explosion is knotting in my chest. I try to massage it down through my shirt, deeply kneading my pulsing muscles and ribs, but can't quite get to the charges that have started coursing through my core.

It doesn't make sense, I think, clenching my jaws to keep from freaking out. *The City's powered down; there's nothing to mess up my heart anymore.* But something *is* happening. I can't deny that when I can actually *feel* energy surging through my body, giving me all-over goosebumps. But I'm not slipping away like before. Something new is happening. Something growing, *spasming*. I trace small circles against the tips of my forefingers with my thumbs and feel the charge building in my shuddering hands . . . not quite crackling, but buzzing slightly, painlessly, as the pressure in my chest lessens.

I hold and release, testing, then hold again, letting the current through.

After a few long moments, Ava hesitantly breaks the silence. "Did you think it was weird that Tom and Rachel chose Carel to drive us here?" she asks, her question echoing out into the encompassing quiet.

"I . . . dunno," I mumble, distracted. My fingers are pressed together like batteries to wires, their tips itching with excess charge. Everything's weird, is what I meant to say. The Green Zone was weird; the Other Side was *definitely* weird; my whole stupid heart thing is weird, and the worst; and being here—holed up in the City, waiting out a riot with *something growing in my chest*. "There's no way Tom and Rachel are behind this," I say, tapping the back of my head against the glass to indicate the frenzy outside, not wanting to pry my steepled, throbbing hands apart. "If that's what you're saying."

"I don't really think they are," she says. "It's just—it feels *complicated*."

Somewhere in the blackness, Julia barks, accompanied by plodding, scraping footsteps. Paralyzed with sudden fear, Ava seizes up beside me. I'd join her, but I'm too hypnotized by my fingers to be concerned about company. They're stiff, cramped with current and . . . *glowing*, slightly. I'd have missed it if I wasn't paying attention, or if it wasn't quite as dark in the library. But, after staring at them for almost a full minute now, it's inescapable. My fingers are tingling; almost imperceptibly emanating a cold, white light.

The uneven steps grow louder, along with increasingly excited yips and barks. Even if I wanted to, I wouldn't have to look up from my pulsing fingers to know that Julia-the-dog found Carel; I know he's in the room with us when the footsteps abruptly stop and Freckles takes a break from her paralysis to recoil, flattening herself silently against the window behind us.

"Good," Carel says as he plops onto the velvet sofa. "You're awake." His voice is jagged and dry, and he seems to have dropped his thick Belgian accent again. Julia jumps up next to him and, whining, sniffs at something on his thigh. I'm still too hypnotized by the pulsing current cycling through my peaked fingers—through my entire galvanizing body—to tear my eyes away. Now that my eyes have adjusted, I'm starting to see that the soft glow is actually a hundred thin strands of white-hot light coiling between my trembling hands.

"It got ugly," Carel is saying, stroking Julia's thick head as she licks his leg. "Pickers jumped the roadblocks when lights went out. Looting for food. We didn't—" he coughs violently, irritably hacking soot from the explosion onto the library floor. "Didn't expect."

Ava's voice, impossibly small in the enveloping blackness, breaks the ensuing silence. "The guns," she says, almost whispering, still flat against the window. "The explosion . . . All those people, it . . . *they were like us.*"

Carel seems to ignore her. "Got back fast as I could," he says, coughing again, out of breath. "I felt bad to leave you here like a dead person."

·21·

I finally break out of my trance and look at Carel. Even veiled in the library's shadows, I can tell that his whitening face is streaked with blood and ash; the fading sofa slowly darkening beneath him.

"You're *hurt*," I shout, shocked into loudness. I start to jump up, to run over to him, but Ava grips the legs of my jeans tightly and pulls me down next to her trembling body. Only Julia-the-dog seems to acknowledge me, looking up from Carel's lap with a lolling, bloody tongue. *She's cleaning his wounds*, I think, swallowing the rising, sour bile before I actually vomit. *Carel was shot.*

"Everyone else . . . the students. My friends. They leave after," he says thickly between coughs, slipping back into broken English. He's delirious, his eyes closed, but darting beneath purpling eyelids. "Your gramama only pay them for first half, anyway."

"My . . ." *Grammy*, I think, trailing off. I try to pull away from Ava, but her hand remains clenched on my jeans so tightly that I can barely move. "He's *shot*," I whisper, my voice quavering with a sudden anger. "He needs *help*!"

"Shot after he blew up that building," Ava answers matter-of-factly, barely audible but resolute. I'm not sure what to make of her calmness, and it momentarily startles me into inaction. Meanwhile, Carel continues to talk on the couch, his voice ratcheting weakly like a sugar-drowned engine.

"Is war," he says, so softly I can barely hear him despite the quiet of the library. "They take out power, we take out power. They steal your parents, we . . ."

We steal your parents back.

But Carel doesn't say that.

In fact, he doesn't say anything.

Instead, I feel Ava's grasp loosen as he slumps limply into the blood-soaked couch cushions . . . and just like that, I don't want to run to Carel anymore. Julia, sensing a change, wimpers inquisitively, mirroring my own pathetic impulse. Before long, the library is echoing with her sharp and mournful keening.

"He's not dead," Ava says stiffly. "He can't be." I refuse to even think about it, not with Julia's increasingly agitated barks and the City in chaos behind me. Not with Grammy behind all of this, and my parents still out there. Waiting for the second half of a plan that's never going to happen—that can't happen—with Carel motionless on the sofa.

"He's not dead," I agree, slowly backing against the window. "Just . . ."

"Henry," Ava says, tugging on my shirt as Carel's arm falls heavily against the cold, tiled floor. "I think he might be, though. Right?"

We're both pressed against the window again, shivering against the glass—as far away from Carel as possible—when, somewhere beneath us, a door slams with a heavy metallic *thunk*. My breath catches in my throat and holds. Our best-case scenario is that it's Carel's returning friends, and *they* just helped him blow up the City.

Our worst-case scenario . . .

"No more waiting," Ava says, stepping purposefully away from the window, her head cocked. Listening. Muffled footsteps reverberate between the floor and ceiling tiles, but they're impossible to place. Except that they're getting closer. "Let's go!"

Ava breaks into a run before me, her slapping footfalls resounding like shotgun blasts in the marbled emptiness. Somewhere beneath us—or above, it's difficult to tell—I can hear the phantom footsteps gaining momentum.

I take off after her, slipping on the newspapers we'd left strewn on the floor as I pull on my sweatshirt; falling over my own legs as the phantom footsteps grow closer. Trying not to think about Carel. By the time I catch up with Ava in the library's pitch-black elevator bay, I'm panting and soaked in cold sweat. And still, she's ahead of me—kicking open the emergency door and rocketing down the maintenance stairs.

It's pitch black in the windowless stairwell, and hot—sweltering compared to the periodicals wing we'd been hiding out in. I almost can't hear Ava's noisy descent over my own heavy panting. I hold my hands in front of me, hoping they'll shed some light, but they're glowing so subtly I start to doubt what I'd seen earlier: the coiling, jumping sparks. We're leaping down steps four and five at a time now, landing in blind, crashing squats.

Finally, I catch up with Ava on the ground floor. She's leaning with her ear against a heavily stickered door, starkly illuminated by a lonely red exit sign which must be plugged into some sort of emergency system. I prick my ears too, but don't hear any trace of the phantom footsteps . . . just the fading echoes of our own escape. Even in the near-total dark, I can tell from the crunching underfoot that it's dirtier down here than in the rest of the library, littered with empty chip bags and soda cans and crumpled-up notices for long-past symposiums.

"No use," she says, shouldering the door open. "Too thick to hear through."

The stairwell, instantly humid, fills with greasy light and ash from the explosion, propelled inside by the deafening blades of a handful of low-flying helicopters. Ava pulls the door shut, cocooning us in darkness again, just as the now-familiar sound of gunfire makes its way into the stairwell, where it softly pops and hangs uncomfortably between us. I have no idea what they're firing at out there, and my first wild hope is that it's the military getting everything under control.

Until I remember we're against the military.

Probably.

"H-hey, Ava," I say, my stomach in my throat. "Do you still have that address?"

"Conor's brother is a federale, Hank," she answers into the door. "He won't help us."

That's when I hear them again: the phantom footsteps. They're in the stairwell now, up a few flights and walking—not jumping, but growing louder with each passing second. There are voices as well, but I can't make out what they're saying. I just know they're getting closer. Ava must hear them, too, but she doesn't show it; she just leans her forehead against the door, not moving.

"Hey," I say, crinkling over the candy-wrapped floor as I walk toward her. "Who says he won't help us?"

The footsteps are louder now, the voices almost distinguishable. One of them sounds like it's laughing, but not. It takes me a moment to realize it's just someone saying *Ha-Ha-Ha*. I can't imagine anyone laughing or even pretending to laugh with everything that's happened, and a shiver runs down to the base of my spine, then shoots back up.

"*Them?*" I ask. Ava's still not really moving, just rolling her forehead listlessly against the door. "Listen," I say. "Conor's our friend, and I trust him. I trust our friends."

"Like Carel," Ava says, the sarcasm in her voice breaking under the overwhelming futility of the situation. She sounds like she's starting to cry, and I want to comfort her, but the footsteps are growing louder. There's just not enough time . . .

"Yeah," I say. "Like Carel. I still trust Carel."

Ava laughs into the door, one sharp bark that sounds uncomfortably like the fake laugh of our pursuer. "Listen," I say, forcing myself to remember the happy, mustachioed man at Food Eats and not the lifeless shadow upstairs. "He was . . . Carel *is* our friend. Whatever he did out here, he did it for us. For the Green. He wanted to help us."

She hesitates, and the phantom footsteps—still slowly descending—punctuate the silence. Doors open and slam shut at every floor, as if our pursuers don't realize we went all the way down; they're thoroughly casing the building.

Everything just keeps getting more complicated.

It could just be Carel's friends, looking for us, wanting to help us now that Carel's . . .

Or it could be federales, looking for Carel's friends.

And even if they are Carel's friends, neither Ava nor I are anxious to meet the people who blew up the city.

And if they're federales, well . . . Conor's brother is apparently a federale, and with Grammy and Carel behind the bombing, it looks like Ava and I are the bad guys.

There are too many possibilities and not enough information, just grainy newspaper photographs and Carel's last words: " *They steal your parents . . .* "

"You're right," Ava finally says, still talking into the door, but slowly pulling the crinkled address out of her hoodie pocket. "If this really *is* war, we have to be able to trust our friends." I nod into the darkness, reaching out my hand for the slip of paper.

My pulsing white hand.

Ava's eyes widen as the address flutters to the ground. "Henry," she says, her voice barely audible, her mouth opening and shutting a few times before she finds her voice again. "You're . . . *g-glowing*!"

I'm doing more than glowing, though.

My outstretched fingers are suspended in a thrumming sphere of the whitest, clearest light I've ever seen. My hand looks almost translucent inside of it, the atoms of my palm and fingers jumping around like the writhing core of some otherworldly sun. In slack-mouthed shock, I look to Ava for reassurance, noticing the long shadows I'm casting on the stairwell walls, and the strangely familiar graffiti beneath them.

Colorful monsters with cartoon faces, like on the Other Side.

Rachel.

"These floors are all clear," someone barks above us, breaking the trance. "Some action on the ground floor—gonna check it out."

"Quick," Ava whispers, her eyes suddenly focused with purpose as she backs against the door. "Turn it off."

Turn it off?

I flex my hand into a loose fist, testing to see if I have any control over the pulsing orb of light, but it just constricts and expands to twice its original size. My other hand twitches at my side, and, looking down, I notice with panic that it's glowing as well. The leg it's resting against is shockingly translucent, like my hand within the orb—atoms swirling and realigning. Hypnotic, like running water . . .

Meanwhile, the phantom steps continue their methodical approach.

Ava looks panicked, her face white with refracting light, but also strangely giddy. Her shadow, towering shakily behind her, grows taller as she steps toward my outstretched fist.

"You *have* to turn them off, Hank," she says, mesmerized. "We can't go outside with you like this . . ."

And we can't stay in here, I think, painfully aware of every scraping footstep in the stairwell. Closing my eyes for concentration, I rub my thumbs in circles against my fingers like I did on the floor upstairs. When Carel was still alive. *If this turned it on, it should turn it off,* I hope, willing the crackling light out of my hands. It doesn't seem to be working, though.

Even with my eyes closed, I know I'm engulfed in a sea of white.

"*Hank,*" Ava shrieks, and my eyes snap open to another color altogether. I've set the thick layer of trash covering the floor on fire, soda cans and chip bags blackening in licks of orange flames, flecked with chemical greens and blues. Ava's backed against the exit door, her feet inches from the fire, but I seem to be standing in the middle of it, my hands still radiating with a blindingly white light. Less than a foot away from me is the crisping pile where Ava had dropped Conor's brother's crumpled address.

Our last, best hope.

"Hey," someone yells, snapping me back into the moment. "*You guys gotta get out of here!*" My head jerks toward the voice, but my eyes refuse to focus on anything but Rachel's graffiti, which is peeling off the sweating cinderblock walls in big, bubbling flakes. It's strange, watching the paint melt. We should be melting, too, but the light—*my* light—is cool to the touch; I barely feel any heat from the flames licking at our heels. "Hey," he shouts again, his voice ragged with smoke. "We're here to help."

I can see people crowding the first-floor landing now; I count about six of them looking down at us, their cheeks red from the fire. Our phantom footsteppers. Most of them look like Other Siders, patched jeans and threadbare shirts. The one who's trying to get me and Ava to go with them, though, is in federale military fatigues—creased black pants and shining boots, a holstered gun at his hips.

Complicating everything.

"Hank," Ava calls out, her voice sharply inquisitive, but muffled by her hand. Although we may be safe from the heat, the smoke is thickening, and—coughing—I realize that we really do need to get out while we're still able. Ava's shoulder is pressed against the door, waiting for my signal to make a break for it.

"Not that way," the federale pleads from the landing as Ava tentatively cracks the door open, feeding the hungrily reaching fire with a rush of crisp air, the chaos of the city joining the growing flames of the stairwell as Ava and I flatten against the still-cracked door. The federale strains to be heard over the sirens and helicopters and megaphones. *"Not that way, they're shooting . . ."*

The federale's right. They're shooting out there. Carel's already . . . Carel's proof of that. And with the address gone, there's nowhere to go. We'd just be running blind, with me as a helpfully glowing target.

"Please," the federale yells again, shielding his face from the flames. "We don't have much time."

"Time for what," I shout back, my voice higher and shakier than I would have liked. I sound unhinged, like a crazy person. But we're out of options, and that tends to make people crazy. The wrong choice could mean death, and not just for me, but for Ava and everyone. It's too much, too complicated. It doesn't help that we're standing so close to my fire and I can smell the melting soles of our pursuers' shoes, can hear them sticking to the floor . . .

And I don't know who the good guys and the bad guys are anymore.

"Henry," the federale yells again, urgency straining his voice. "We can get Mayor Long, but we need to act fast."

That gets my attention, and Ava's, too. I feel her next to me, pulling the door completely shut, as I inch forward, finding a path through the flames. As I get closer to the federale, I get the strangest feeling that—against all odds—I know him from somewhere, know his face. It's strong and square, like you'd expect from a soldier, but somehow familiar.

It's hard to tell through the smoke and shimmering heat . . .

It's been so long since I've seen him, more than five years since he moved to the City. But even older and in the uniform, he looks like his brother. "Ben?" I ask, my voice softening as Ava relaxes next to me, the scared stiffness leaving her body. "*This* is the guy," she exhales. "*This* is Conor's brother. Oh, thank you, thank you, thank you . . ."

"I know where they're keeping 'em, Hank," Ben shouts, nodding in confirmation. "But we don't have much time. The generators should be up and running soon."

Of course. Mrs. Wallace was in the grainy photo of survivors, too, nestled into the protective embrace of one of the river engineers, a forced smile on her ashen face. *His mom.*

I'd been so focused on the revelation that Ben was a federale that I'd forgotten where he'd come from. That even if he was military, we had a friend on the inside.

As suddenly as the hallway erupted into fire, we have options again. I turn to Ava, bursting with a happy, nervous energy for the first time since . . . since Conor and I night-biked to the Other Side. A million years ago. She wraps her hand in mine, and only as I feel the soft warmth of her fingers on mine do I remember my pulsing charges and look down in horror at our intertwined hands, both now ensconced in my thrumming orb of light. They're doing the thing. The fluid, translucent thing. But it doesn't seem to hurt her. In fact, when I look up from our hands in mute horror, she's leaning toward me, the fire crackling happily around us, as a pulse of cool, white light fills the stairwell.

My heart hasn't bothered me since the explosion, but I feel it ratcheting tightly in my chest as I lean in to meet her.

"*Are you serious?*" Ben barks through the flames. "Let's *go*! Up the stairs and to the back, there's a better exit."

I jerk toward him, annoyed. And Ben seems to notice my hands for the first time.

"Whoa," he says, backing up against the railing. "Whoa, whoa, *whoa*." Ava laughs behind me as the rest of the renegades trip backward up the stairs, their mouths agape.

"Yeah," I say, leaping over the last blackening pile of trash and onto the stairs. "I think you guys did this, actually. When you . . . blew up the power plant?"

Ben cringes noticeably, then nods in acceptance despite my threadbare explanation. "Yeah?" he says, visibly upset. "That was stupid. I told her that was stupid."

"Told *who*?" Ava asks as we bound up the stairs to join them, her hand still in mine.

"Not much time," he says, evading the question. "Think you can turn those things off? We don't want any attention when we're out there . . ."

I point toward the fire, my hands casting the dwindling orange flames in an unnatural white light.

"That's what happened last time I tried."

22

Most of the clotheslines crisscrossing the City's skyline have been taken in, so the kaleidoscope of windows lining the narrow streets reflect only the thick grey haze that's passing for morning. Having escaped the library through a service exit leading into an alley piled high with reeking dumpsters of wet, composting garbage, we're running, pushing through the sweating masses toward where Ben says my parents are being held.

Despite the insanity of a few hours ago, the streets are packed. The first federale responders had tried to corral rubberneckers away from the ruins of the power plant, Ben says, but an influx of Pickers diverted their efforts. With resources as limited as they are, the City can't afford to have their boundaries breached.

They can't afford any more mouths.

Especially now.

I don't get too much more out of him, distracted as he is by keeping us on the run and undercover, both of which would have been easier if the morning hadn't turned so uncooperatively overcast. By the time we'd escaped the stairwell, my fists were on the verge of supernova. While the renegades formed a nervously protective circle around us, Ava had wrapped them in our sweatshirts, tying the sleeves and hoods in massive knots, praying the sun would cut through the fog, camouflaging any light that got through.

So much for that.

It's not easy slipping through the crowds after Ben with shaggy, glowing paws. Besides the stares, I keep having to stop and pull Ava's loosening knots tighter with my teeth.

Still, it's better than nothing.

Now that it's no longer wreathed in a million soft yellow lights, the City seems less like the Other Side and more like the Grey Zone. The people seem grey, too. Nobody's hawking their wares on the sidewalks; there's no music or resonating laughter. Just a thin layer of soot covering everything in sight and grim, worried faces as far as the eye can see.

At least the Grey was empty.

Here, armed federales stand like sentinels in the middle of the streets, tracking us with suspicious eyes as we try to unobtrusively push through the crowds. Luckily, Ben's in uniform and is quick to bark a few authoritative words at any federale who tries to stop us. The federales all back down when they recognize him, and I wonder what he's giving up to help us.

To help the Green.

And we're not just under the watchful eyes of federales—it feels like *everyone's* staring. I try to concentrate on my feet, to avoid eye contact, no matter what. To distract myself from the reality of the City; from the chilling memory of Carel, limp in the library, Julia-the-dog curled forlornly at his side.

"*En route* to Central," Ben growls at an inquiring federale ahead of us. "At ease."

We speed up to pass the chastened federale, but soon enough we're trudging through the unnervingly quiet crush of the City again

"*Hank*," Ava whispers, her quiet urgency exploding through the muted streets like another bomb. "*Are you okay?*"

Startled, I look up to flickering streetlights throwing a thousand widening eyes into and out of shadow. I follow their gaze downward, to my wrapped hands, which are engulfed in a radiant light that's blinding even in groggy daylight. One of the sweatshirts, I notice—casually, as if it's not connected to my body—is sparking with blue flames, like it's trying to prove a point.

"*Off,*" I whisper angrily to the torches at the end of my arms. "*Turn. Off!*"

Ava arches her brow and takes a few cautionary steps back into the shocked, but still silent and unmoving crowd. Remembering the stairwell, I take the hint, but the sweatshirts flare around my fists anyway, then melt away, the remaining bits flaking off in crispy sheets that reveal the two seething orbs of my fists.

They're bigger than before, and angrier, with ropes of electricity whipping wildly between them.

⚡ ⚡ ⚡

The crowd shifts around me, torn between backing away into safety and stepping forward to make room for rushing federales. I hear them, shouting, guns drawn. But I can't seem to tear myself away from my hands, flexing fluidly within balls of light like glassy minnows in a stream—too quick and changing to get a good look at.

"I've got this," Ben shouts desperately, not breaking the spell. "Guns down! *Guns down!*" The federales, drawn inexorably forward, keep their weapons trained on us, and I feel Ben's thick hand on my shoulder, pushing, as he whispers, "Hank . . . *run*," out of the side of his mouth. "*Keep straight—you'll know where to go when you see it.*"

I start off slowly, not sure if the closing sea of people will part for me before I hit them. Ben's still shouting behind me, ordering the federales to back down. When he sees me looking over my shoulder, he nods encouragingly—then tackles the nearest federale in a rolling dive. "*Run, Hank,*" he barks as he pins the soldier to the ground with a rippling arm, his unholstered gun trained on the remaining federales, who've finally slowed their approach. "I have this."

I tell myself that I would've stayed around to help if it wasn't for all the firearms, but . . . cradling my still-flaming hands against my chest like an infant, I break into a full-on run, Ava trailing closely behind me. Ben's voice follows us, rising above the shouts of the other converging federales. "Follow the jeeps!"

It's overwhelming at first, everyone staring at the two of us as we sprint through an unfamiliar City, which parts instinctively at the sight of the sparking electrical bombs I have for hands. Overwhelming to know that the burden of rescuing my parents—and the Green—falls squarely on me. Despite everything, though, it feels so unbelievably *good* just to run again, without losing my breath or passing out, that I smile as I pick up speed.

With each footfall, my calves flex, generating what feels like muscle. With each surprisingly cool breath, my chest expands, my lungs filtering oxygen from the dusty City air through rushing blood to pounding legs and arms. For the first time in my life, I feel what it must be like to be truly strong.

And *fast*.

The long strands of Christmas lights the locals have strung across the streets crackle on and off as I pass beneath them, strobing alongside the streetlights and flashing windows in my wake.

In the eerie quiet of the narrow streets, the white noise of radios and televisions snapping quickly on and off as I pass sounds almost like a standing ovation.

"*Hank*," Ava yells from somewhere behind me, muffled by a growing distance. "*Wait!*"

Jogging in place to give Ava time to catch up, I look back over my shoulder and can barely believe the ground I've covered. Ben's federale scuffle is nowhere in sight, and neither is the library. Even Ava's just a smudge in the distance, leaving me alone, surrounded by ashen-faced locals, all backed against walls and crowded on stoops, giving me a wide berth.

"No exit without permits," someone calls to me matter-of-factly from a second-floor window, emboldened by distance. Overhead, a street lamp burns so brightly, its straining filament breaks apart with a pop.

"What?"

"No one gets in, no one gets out," he says, the rest of the crowd nodding in solemn agreement. "Not without permit. Roadblock goes both ways, and you'll never get out with *those*." He points to my hands with his chin, and—feeling conspicuous with fifty sets of eyes on me—I look away, craning my neck for Ava. She's still a ways off, though. Frustrated, I turn back to the man, stretching my arms behind my head to hide them from his wide-eyed ogling.

The effect is . . . *not intended.*

Jagged ropes of white light arc angrily upward from my hands in the direction of the stretch, crackling through the broken street light above, leaving the lamp hanging by a molten thread from its anchoring pole. After a long second filled only with the sound of angrily sparking wires, there's an *en masse* clearing of the road. As the locals push and shove each other back onto side streets and into powered-down apartment buildings, Ava finally catches up.

"They saw me coming?" Ava asks, breathing heavily. I nod, laughing nervously, then point to the smoking lamp as the guilt sets in. *Henry Long, Destroyer.* "Huh," she pants, nodding a few times in the affirmative while catching her ragged breath. "Okay, just go a little slower, yeah?"

I'm careful to cradle my hands in front of my chest when we start off again. One wrong flick of the wrist and Ava could end up in the Hospital. Or worse. It crosses my mind more than once that I should probably be scorched by my writhing white hands as I press them protectively against my chest.

But I'm not.

I try not to over-think it.

There are a million things that could go wrong; it's just chance protecting us from chance at this point. Behind us, the lamp finally falls free of the pole, landing with a dull, wet thud against the asphalt, still too melted from the pulse to shatter. As freaked out as I am, Ava does have a point—it's not so bad. And there's no way anyone's going to keep us anywhere we don't want to be, permit or not. I want to sprint away as fast as I can—to feel my revitalized body crank into impossible gear, the hot wind whipping through my hair—but I have to concentrate on keeping pace with Ava, otherwise I'll lose her.

And I can't lose her, too.

"This *was* like the Other Side," she says, having caught her breath. "Now it's like everyone's already dead."

I cringe, remembering Carel. But she's right. Even more unsettling than the quiet are the zombie-like locals. Yesterday it was block after block of Tom and Rachels, artists and rock and rollers partying in the streets until daybreak, all light and music. Even the graffiti was the same as on the Other Side. Today, it's like we're running through shadows.

"They're not dead," I say, shrugging the thought off like a too-hot sweatshirt. "Just stuck here." Even as I say it, I know it's more than that. There were a lot of horrible things in the newspapers I flipped through in the library, but they were all just headlines: print on grainy paper. The federales shield their cities from the realities of stuff like that. From people like the Pickers, who live—if you can call it living—right on the other side of their roadblocks, full of cataracts and cancers from chemicals and toxic wastes.

After last night, though, all these people know what it's like to be a headline.

To be scared, like us.

Like the Pickers.

The thought chills the blood in my veins, and I pick up the pace, slowing down only when I feel Ava pull pleadingly at the hem of my shirt. But even jogging, my mind's still sprinting forward, connecting dots: the federales are able to protect their cities from the truth because they have power. The power to make everyone pretend like nothing's really wrong, even if they know otherwise . . . even if they're pretending at the expense of the Pickers and the Green Zone.

And Carel literally exploded that power last night.

Grammy did, too.

Most of these blank-faces were still outside when the federale power plant exploded, disoriented in the dark; noses twitching at the acrid, singed air as their illusion of safety abruptly faded. And then, punctuating the darkness: deafening rotors of low-flying helicopters and constellations of sparking federale guns. Those that weren't injured in the aftermath were herded, shaking and scared, like chattel through the narrow streets—away from the encroaching Pickers and the smoking remnants of federale power. This morning, most of them are just waking up to the hazy light of the City-as-it-really-is for the first time—unable to leave, even if they wanted to.

More prisoners than citizens.

"Carel was right. They're not like the Other Siders," I whisper to myself, a spasm of guilt working its way down my neck and back. After everything they'd already been through, I'd used my own newfound powers to scare them out of my way. Like they weren't even people.

They're not like the Other Siders yet, I correct myself with resolve.

It's impossible to miss the federale base where Ben says my parents are being held—and not just because Ben told us to *follow the jeeps*. Standing solidly in the middle of a smooth stone plaza is a column-lined bunker of limestone topped with a gleaming gold cupola. City Hall. Not the kind of place the federales would have built for themselves, given their predilection for black, but infinitely more impregnable than the glass skyscrapers dotting the skyline.

An armada of sedans and jeeps are haphazardly parked across the plaza, boulders in the river of suited federales flooding the block. Some are talking surreptitiously into the sleeves of their blazers, others are conferring over maps unfolded on hot metal hoods. The door of a helicopter slams shut as its rotor starts whirring, drawing my attention to a bank of helipads at the far end of the plaza. The suits arguing over the map, used to this distraction, anchor it to the hood with the heels of their hands and raise their voices, not missing a beat.

"Okay," Ava says, her voice drowning beneath the rising helicopter, which blows her already wavy brown hair across her sweating, soot-streaked face. "What now?"

It's a good question.

The federales are too preoccupied to have noticed us standing at the perimeter of their operations, and I instinctively step back, trying to melt further into the surrounding mass of locals; compensating for my hands, which I squeeze furtively behind my back. We've been running from federales for so long that it feels strange to be on the offensive. Impossible, even—like we're wrong to even consider it. Watching the flurry of activity on the plaza, I wonder again if there's any truth to the newspapers . . . if the federales really were just trying to save the Green Zone, despite us.

If that's just what they're trying to do now.

Save their city.

Despite us.

No matter what Grammy or Carel says, this whole thing *has* to be more complicated than just us being good and them being bad. And even if it *is* that simple, there are so many other federale cities just like this one. A country full of them. If the federales are really as bad as Carel says they are, there's almost no reason to try.

Except for my parents, who are being held on the top floor of *this* building.

In *this* city.

Quit stalling, Henry, I whisper, trying to work up a plan and coming up with nothing except a sinking despair. Shivering despite the heat, I look down at my hands—still ensconced in shimmering balls of cold, white light—and the weight of the past week descends on me all at once. There are so many federales just in the plaza and on the front steps—at least a hundred   and I can't imagine making it through them without getting shot at, let alone up the seven-or-so stories to my parents.

How did we even get here?

My hands crackle sympathetically as I fight back the tears welling up behind my eyes. A month ago I was hiding out in Mr. Moonie's attic, reading dusty adventure novels from Before in soft, mottled light to the hopeful sounds of construction on the Avenue. And now . . .

How did I turn into this?

"Good," Ben whispers roughly into my ear, very nearly clamping his scraped and bloodied hand on my shoulder and then, eyeing my hands, reconsidering. "You found it." Where there should be a palpable relief, I feel only shock. Ben's shirt is ripped, and his face is swelling from a few well-placed kicks, but otherwise, he seems to have escaped the pile-up intact.

Alive.

"The actual military's still at what's left of the plant," he continues, gesturing with what looks to be a broken finger. "These are just the suits. Not so bad. Have to get in there before the power's back up if we want to get through the security, though."

Without warning, Ben breaks away in a crouching run toward the nearest car, where he hugs the ground, enthusiastically gesturing for us to follow. Ava looks at me and then shrugs, following his lead. I take off after her, landing in a dusty squat next to the car's muddy rear wheel. Almost immediately, the sedan's engine turns quietly over, lights flashing on as my newfound electric field coaxes it into neutral.

Ben, who had been leaning against a front wheel—casing the plaza for our next jump—feels the car purr to life and turns to me incredulously. "You've *got* to be kidding me," he says, and then repeats himself as he sprints to the next car for cover. With our hiding place possibly comprised, Ava and I have no choice but to follow, hoping that no one will notice our chain of self-starting sedans.

Unfortunately, whoever parked Ben's next choice left the radio on, and as I slide next to him on the smooth granite of the plaza, the car fires noisily to life, an asinine talk-radio show blasting at full volume. "Seriously," Ben repeats, pulling his handgun from its holster and standing up to face the federales who've started to converge on us. As he aims the gun in a protective circle, he nods anxiously down at my throbbing hands. "If you're gonna use . . . *those*," he says, "now would be a good time."

Taking a deep breath, I remember the reflection of the melting lamppost in the fearful faces of the people I once thought were like Tom and Rachel. I look up at Ben, still in a standoff against the federales he was sided with until last night—when *I* came on the scene—and wonder how many of them are like him. Just waiting for a chance to do the right thing. How many of them have grainy photos of their mothers in federale newspapers.

"*No violence*," I whisper, stretching my arms up toward the overcast sky. The rippling blaze in my hands is a beacon in the plaza—drawing both federales and storm clouds. "The boy," one of them shouts into the mounting wind, plastic bags and fallen leaves gusting across the ominously darkening plaza. "It's the boy!"

"This is not exactly what I had in mind, Hank," Ben calls over his shoulders, his pistol still trained on the growing crowd of federales. "I don't think I can hold all of them . . ."

I don't answer him . . . or the federales, who now have a new prime suspect in the power plant explosion, and, accordingly, have all switched their targets from Ben to me. "*Put the bomb down, son,*" a grey-haired federale shouts. "*Nobody has to get hurt.*"

It's too late for that, I think, remembering Carel and, for the first time—instead of trying to turn it off—willing the writhing light from my hands. Almost immediately, it's like night again, wind and rain whipping our faces red as the federales inch forward, taking the first few shots. Their guns are louder than when we were behind the soundproof glass of the library, almost deafening, but they don't faze me. My only concern is Ava, trembling beside me, clutching my waist. And the *power*.

My back arches, quivering, the electricity shooting from my fingers as if it's being drawn from my body by the roiling black sky itself, inch by excruciating inch. Past the pain, I'm vaguely aware of a cacophony of radios and lights, the black federale fleet switching on as the electricity builds, volumes rising until their tinny car speakers blow from the current, popping and melting along with their headlights in a collective hiss.

There's yelling, too.

Ben, holding his ground despite the jumping electric column I've created between myself and the heavens, calls wordlessly into the hurricane wind. The federales, not sure whether to advance or retreat, shout predictable but impossible instructions for me to "drop the bomb."

And me? I'm screaming from the sharp, pulling agony of electricity, like nails yanked roughly and continually out of my aching fingers; yelling from the frustration and weirdness of the last few days, from homelessness and loneliness and betrayal. Yelling—eyes squeezed shut—for Carel and Grammy and Ava, who's crouched defensively behind me. I don't hear any of it above the swirling vortex of the plaza, but I feel the primal screams rushing from my throat into the rolling thunder and lightning, into the rain that's mixing with tears on my twisted face, echoing throughout the City's narrow streets.

⚡⚡⚡

And then, as abruptly as it started, the sky lets loose my pulsing hands, which fall limply to my side.

They're full of pins and needles where before there was fire, and—falling finally silent—I try to rub them out as Ben runs across the empty plaza and through the federales' wide-open front doors. The storm remains, black clouds swirling swiftly overhead as lightning repeatedly strikes the charred weathervane topping City Hall's golden dome.

"All clear," he shouts, soaking wet and clutching his arm; giddy, despite himself. "I don't know how you did that, Hank, but you scared 'em *out!*"

"You okay?" I ask Ava, my throat raw from screaming. She nods mutely and stands, surveying the empty plaza. The heavy rain turns to hail, which ricochets against the idling cars and melts on the plaza's warm marble tiles.

"*It's a ghost town,*" she whispers, more to herself than me, and the awe in her voice makes me blush. Taking a step forward, ignoring the increasingly large flecks of ice raining down on us, she reaches for my tingling hand. "Are . . . are *you* okay, Henry?"

She squeezes my fingers reassuringly, and I look down at our hands—the fire is gone from mine, leaving a sort of dull white glow. I'm not sure whether or not I miss it, the power, but I think I'm okay. I haven't felt this relaxed in years, and there's something about standing here with Ava, staring into her searching green eyes . . . Before I know it, her rain-wet arms are wrapped tightly around my shoulders as my nose nestles warmly in the crook of her neck.

"*Seriously?*" Ben calls from the open doorway, thin lines of blood mixing with the weather and trickling down his arm. "We have maybe five minutes, ten if we're lucky." I pull back, staring into Ava's eyes until she smiles back at me and nods. Ben yells again, more out of amazement than frustration. "Let's *go*, people!"

The inside of City Hall is as deserted as the outside, and Ben confidently leads the way through the emptiness, jumping over the detritus of the quick federale exit—strewn papers and capsized chairs—as he escorts us through the various vestibules and offices with the self-assurance of someone who had spent a lot of time there.

Like the university library before it, the elevators aren't working, so we start our ascent to the top floor in an industrial stairwell filled with broken chairs and trash bins. Unlike before, Ben leaves a trail of blood behind him as he takes the stairs four at a time, leaving me and Ava to follow in his leaking footsteps.

"Actually," Ava says, grabbing my wrist and guiding me back out into the elevator bay. "I just thought of something."

"Hey," I say, jerking uncertainly back toward the stairwell. "My parents . . ."

"Just push the button, Hank," she sighs, pressing my hand against the up arrow, which lights up instantaneously, the mirrored elevator doors sliding smoothly open. Ava hits the button for the top floor once we're inside, and we check our incongruously filthy reflections in the seamless aluminum door as we glide swiftly upward, the tiny elevator lights flickering above us as we drip sootgrey puddles on the high-gloss floor.

We're both pale, and shivering from the wet. Ava wipes her dripping hair out of her face with the heel of her hand, and— unthinking—I do the same to mine, streaking dirt across my brow. The floors ding as we pass them, moving ever closer to my parents. For a horrible second, I convince myself that the federales took them when they fled, that they could be anywhere. Ava sees the flash of panic across my face and squeezes my hand. "They're *going* to be here," she whispers, the steel edge of surety in her voice.

And, as the doors slide noiselessly, magically open onto the eighth floor . . . *they are.*

"Henry!" Mom shrieks, shaking Dad awake as we walk into the room, the elevator going dead behind us and dropping heavily to the lobby as the overhead light flickers on. They're disheveled, wearing the same clothes I remember them wearing as they boarded their plane, and sitting on a large, unmade bed placed haphazardly in the center of some sort of executive office, judging from the portraits on the walls. It's still hailing outside, rice-sized grains of ice clacking lightly against barred windows.

"Hank, it's Hank, baby!"

Dad shakes immediately awake, kicking the blankets off of his feet as he feels blindly for his glasses. Putting them on, he stares, astonished, as I run toward them, jumping into their outstretched arms. *"How?"* he whispers incredulously, eyes crinkling with questions as he and Mom pull me into a tight, weepy hug.

"It's complicated," I say, tears hot on my cheeks. "I'll tell you when we get home."

Home.

Their hug only loosens at the sound of pounding footsteps growing louder in the adjacent stairwell. I'm so happily distracted by the reunion that I'd forgotten to tell my parents about Ben, and their fear of returning federales spreads irrationally to me . . . until, out of the corner of my eye, I catch Ava biting back a smile.

And I smile, too, despite myself.

"Let's go, guys," Ben yells down the stairwell, as if we're still lagging behind him. *"We can get outta here, but we gotta hurry."* The hallway door slams open as he stumbles breathlessly into the room, the echoes of his noisy approach reverberating through the stale, wet air.

"You have got to . . ." he exhales, spotting us as he leans his bleeding shoulder against the dark wood paneling, sliding into an exhausted squat. " . . . be kidding me."

23

"So, wait," Dr. Singh says, shaking the disinfectant from the thermometer and positioning it against the soft underside of my already-bruised tongue. "You're worried because you feel *fine?*"

I know better than to try to talk. I've already dislodged the thermometer twice, the last time spitting it onto the floor in a fit of gagging—so I've promised myself that the third time is going to have to be the charm, even if it kills me. "Because frankly, Mr. Long, this is the *best* I've ever seen you. No fainting, no fatigue," she continues, needling the thermometer snugly beneath my tongue as I cringe, fluorescent lights flickering sympathetically overhead.

Thermometer secured, Dr. Singh taps her clipboard with her ballpoint pen and jots a quick note.

"*Power*-ing electron-*ics* instead of . . . dis-*rupt*-ing," she intones, drawing out the syllables to match the scratching of her pen. "Strange," she says, looking me squarely in the eyes again. "But that's better than before, at least."

I shrug, but she's right. I've only been back in the Green for a few days, and already everything is easier than before. I feel that especially now, sitting in the warm, gleaming Hospital, shelves of bandages and disinfectant lining the walls. It wasn't that long ago that Ben was bleeding into the pilot seat of a stolen federale helicopter as he angled us upward into the blackening clouds, inexplicable ice hailing against the windshield so hard I was sure it would crack.

And, as the shuddering hull creaked ominously, buffeted by the storm I'd somehow created, it *did*: glass and ice shattering around us, the cabin instantly filling with gusts of cold, wet wind as Ben struggled to maintain control of the veering aircraft with his one good arm. As my stomach dropped in terror, so did the helicopter. One moment of nauseating weightlessness followed by an anxious, hopeful second . . . and then another.

"*Hang tight*," Ben had yelled over the deafening squall as we listed precariously to one side. Through the rain, I could see him bracing his wounded shoulder against the pilot-side door, twisting the throttle for all it was worth as we continued our ragged ascent. It had been a miracle when we'd broken through the clouds into the cool, endless blue of the sky above—all of us exhaling at once despite the wind whistling sharply through the shattered windshield, chilling us to our quivering bones.

As if we were in the clear.

"It's just a quick jump," Ben had said, bravely, betrayed by his bloodless white face as Mom and Dad exchanged glances. "Should be there in half an hour if we can avoid the weather." He'd shot a cautionary look back at me.

No more storms, got it.

I remember thinking how funny it was that I'd sweltered in my hoodie for the entire trip to the City, waiting for it to get cold, like everyone'd said it would . . . and now that we'd left and

I finally needed it, it was a pile of ash. Even funnier was that, as the cold set in, it turned out that I didn't actually need it after all. The wetness steamed from my skin, sizzling as if from tremendous internal heat.

⚡⚡⚡

"Ninety-eight point six degrees." Dr. Singh nonchalantly tosses the thermometer back into an electric blue vial of disinfectant, snapping me back to the present. "Normal."

I arch an eyebrow, skeptical.

"So you *glow*," she says, sighing dismissively into another patient's chart, not even bothering to look at my pulsing hands for confirmation. "Believe me, the others are worse off."

⚡⚡⚡

We'd barely recovered from our short but frostbitten flight back to an eerily abandoned Green Zone when news reached us that we were being followed. Strangely, it had come in the form of Mr. Malgré, Scott's mean old dad, who creeped up on our borrowed federale helicopter before the blades had even stopped spinning. "Ten-four," he'd shouted into a squealing walkie-talkie while his construction worker friends emerged as if from nowhere to surround the battered helicopter. "It's them."

He'd thumped twice on the helicopter door and then unceremoniously yanked it open while the rest of us were still exchanging uneasy looks. "So happy you could join us, Mayor Long," he'd shouted over the still-spinning rotors, his wide red face breaking out into a smile as the vegetal stench of rotting greens filled the cabin. "I got someone who wants to see you."

"Mr. Malgré," Mom had said softly, in cool acknowledgment, as the open helicopter door darkened with his dubiously welcoming crew. Dad straightened next to her, readying himself for a possible confrontation, while Ava and I shrank back into the cargo hold. Mr Malgré kept smiling, despite our obvious discomfort—or maybe because of it—his thin, chapped lips stretched tightly across the vast expanse of his face as if strained from lack of use. If Ben, weak from blood loss, hadn't finally passed out, the awkward tension of that moment might never have passed.

"We've got an injured pilot," Mom had said matter-of-factly as Ben's limp hand fell heavily onto the floor. "Linda Wallace's oldest." Mr. Malgré let his ill-fitting smile drop and nodded gravely over his shoulder.

"Pilot's gonna need a medic, boys. Looks like a *fed*, but he's one of ours."

It was only after Malgré's men pulled Ben out of the cabin and into a waiting car that we finally stepped out of the helicopter. The heavy air, thick with the scent of magnolias, felt the same as it always had, and I was thankful to have the familiar Avenue, where we'd unceremoniously landed, beneath my feet. To be within spitting distance of Mr. Moonie's Library, which was still sitting regally atop a gently sloping hill, looking the same as always.

But somehow different.

Empty.

Ava must have felt it, too, because she shivered beside me as Mr. Malgré reached his hand to me as if to shake. "Henry," he'd said, the walkie-talkie in his other hand going haywire as he stepped toward me and then stopped, fiddling with the dials on his shrieking receiver to no avail.

"*Okay, boss?*" the driver of the car had called, leaning out of the window of what finally registered as a black federale sedan.

Mr. Malgré nodded absentmindedly and it squealed off into the desolate morning with Ben propped insensibly against the passenger-side window. It was only when Mr. Malgré finally looked up, frowning, from his walkie-talkie that he noticed my glowing hands.

"We heard you did good over there, son," he'd said, stepping cautiously back with his own stubby hands safely by his side. The receiver stopped shrieking, and he nodded appreciatively at me, his terrible smile returning. "Now *that*," he'd said, gears turning. "We could use—"

"*Mis-ter Mal-grey*," Mom interrupted, stepping in front of me with her arms crossed across her chest. "Status update. How'd you know to expect us, and . . ." she'd said, furrowing her brows as Mr. Malgré chuckled under his terrible breath. "And what's going on here, anyway?"

"May-or Long," he'd said, mimicking Mom as Dad and I held our breath, shocked. "You're gonna have to get those answers from someone else. There were some *changes* while you were gone."

"Is this your way of telling me, *Mister Malgré*, that this is one of those 'out of the frying pan' situations?" Mom said, keeping her cool as I became increasingly concerned about the federale car that had carted Ben off. Even though Scott Malgré is one of my best friends, Mr. Malgré was never a likeable man, and he seemed to be taking an inordinate amount of pleasure in keeping us in the dark. I didn't have to try very hard to imagine him saving his skin by throwing in with the federales.

My fists flexed just thinking about it, and Malgré's walkie-talkie shrieked in response.

"Let's just say the Green's a fire you can warm your hands by," Mr. Malgré had said, not waiting for us to follow as he started walking down the abandoned Avenue, leaving us standing—confounded—beneath the still-spinning blades of our stolen helicopter. "Coming?"

he'd called over his shoulder, and then chuckled quietly to himself, his generous frame shaking with the effort.

Despite our misgivings, we followed. Ava jumped ahead, almost keeping pace with Mr. Malgré, but I held back with Mom and Dad, too nervous to leave their side after . . .

After having lost them.

I didn't want to think about that, though. And I didn't want to think about that federale car, either, or the head of Mr. Malgré's square shadow, which was cast ominously onto our feet by a rising sun. The oak trees lining the Avenue shivered in a hot breeze, their leaves whispering in anticipation of the carefree calls of early birds. Unthinkingly, I wrapped my hands into Mom and Dad's, squeezing thankfully. They'd looked at me with wide eyes, startled for a moment by my buzzing fingers—then squeezing back. Soon we fell into the quiet rhythm of the Green, punctuated occasionally by derelict cars and streetlights fuzzing on as we approached them and fading out again in our wake.

"*Hank*," Ava had shouted after a few minutes of walking, beckoning me forward with an exaggerated wave. "C'mere a sec!"

I was hesitant to leave my parents so soon after having been reunited, but Dad nudged me forward with an encouraging pat. It felt good to be in the Zone again, jogging past the construction equipment on the springy black asphalt of the freshly paved Avenue. Closing my eyes, it was almost possible to pretend nothing had happened.

Except . . .

I could feel the difference in how effortlessly I ran, carving through the humid morning like a knife through water, eyes closed as if I was dreaming. When I opened them, exhilarated but not winded, I was met with the shadowed specter of Mr. Malgré, leading us through the Zone as if we'd been gone for decades instead of days.

"What do you think?" Ava whispered as I sidled up next to her. I could hear my parents arguing indistinctly behind us; when I turned around, Dad smiled and waved, but Mom still looked upset . . . until he squeezed her hand and, looking up, she saw me and smiled. "You don't think this is, like, a trap or anything, do you?"

My parents raised their voices again, and then lowered them sheepishly when I looked back a second time. More than the federale car or Mr. Malgré's general untrustworthiness, that made me wonder if Ava's hunch was right. A steamroller parked on the side of the road turned quietly on and then off as we passed it. If it was a trap, I could do my thing again; bring down the sky and escape. The problem was, we didn't really have any place to escape to . . .

Aware of our limited options, I eyed Mr. Malgré as if for the first time. "I dunno," I finally said. "What do you think?"

"I don't trust him," she'd whispered, conspiratorial despite the distance between us and Malgré. "Let's go back to the Library, or the Other Side. Anywhere but after him."

"*What about Ben?*" I'd mouthed back, the words barely leaving my lips. "*My parents?*"

"Listen," Ava had said. "I'll just make a run for it, then. If anyone's there, I'll let them know you're with Malgré."

I nodded, distracted by my parents, who were lost in a distant, heated conversation. No matter how hard I focused, I couldn't make out what they were saying. It was all lost in the rustling leaves and singing birds I'd found so comforting just a few minutes before.

"If anything happens," she'd said, squeezing my wrist. "I'll find you, okay?"

I nodded again, turning toward Ava, whose face was suddenly so close to mine that my eyes wouldn't focus. About halfway through our kiss, which was quick and hard, my parents finally stopped arguing. I pulled reflexively away to check if they'd seen us, and she was gone, sprinting nimbly across the street and disappearing into an overgrown garden hedge.

A warm blush spread up my neck and across my face from my buzzing chest as I considered jumping after her into the bushes to avoid Mom and Dad's smirks. But the moment passed before I could take it, and instead of following Ava out of Mr. Malgré's trap, I was facing my mother, whose mouth was agape, and my father, whose ear-to-ear grin was just as bad.

"She, uh," I said, backtracking bashfully toward my parents. "She had to go."

"Yeah," said Dad, unsuccessfully stifling a laugh, Mom still speechless at his side. "Should we wait for her?"

"Wait for who?" Mr. Malgré asked, casually spitting onto a cracked cement curb of the old university campus where Dad taught. "We moved headquarters from the Library to here," he said, waving at the grey stone walls with one hand by way of explanation and wiping spittle from his lip with the back of the other. "After Moonie got took."

My stomach sank as the grin disappeared from Dad's face. Malgré didn't seem to care, though—about Freckles or Moonie—as he hitched up his filthy khakis and led us through an imposing stone archway. "We'll talk about this later," Mom whispered, squeezing my shoulder and nodding sharply back at where Ava had made her escape. "About *that*."

"More defensible here," Mr. Malgré said as we entered the grassy quad, smiling terribly. I'd expected to see something like the City on the other side of the arch—a sea of refugees packed safely within the thick, strong walls of the university. But instead, there was nothing. Just a row of carelessly parked cars on the far side of the quad, most of which seemed to be federale sedans. "Prisoners," said Mr. Malgré, sensing the sudden tension rippling through our party.

"*What?*" Mom, glowering, stopped in her tracks. "Federale prisoners?"

But Mr. Malgré had already moved on, disappearing under another stone archway on the far side of the quad, leaving me and Mom and Dad to jog after him. While I scanned the rows of tall windows staring blankly down at us, looking for peeking eyes and flashes of movement that never came, Mom and Dad lost themselves in quiet argument about the very idea of *prisoners* in the Green. I tried to eavesdrop, without much success, until Mr. Malgré stopped unexpectedly, surprising Mom in the middle of a whispered screed. All three of us looked around, as if dreaming, at a tidy, familiar front porch rimmed with intricate gingerbread woodwork and clusters of blue hydrangeas still glistening with dew from the night before.

"You got a problem with the prisoners," Mr. Malgré said to Mom, his face stretched into another sinister smile. "You can take it up with *her.*" Mom didn't wait for his permission, pushing by him so quickly that he lost his balance and teetered heavily at the top of the stairs, the door slamming open behind him.

"*Mill-y,*" she yelled, angrily prolonging the *y* as she stomped through every room of the house, looking for Grammy with me and Dad in her wake. "*Mildred Lo-ong.*"

It didn't take long for Mom to find her, sitting quietly at the kitchen table like the last time I'd come looking for her, hands crossed contemplatively in her lap. Low-watt bulbs flickered dully to life as I walked into the room, while a walkie-talkie crackled and spat in front of her, its black metal worn silver in places from use. Far from looking chastened, a coy smile flashed across her powdered face—in fact, she seemed delighted by the electronics buzzing awkwardly to life around her.

"Sarah Long," Grammy said, her voice kind and . . . *normal.* Like nothing had changed in the Green Zone. "You may be *acting* mayor, but I am *not* Mildred to you. You just call me Mama." With that, she got up and hugged Mom tightly, and then Dad.

And then me.

"Our little rebel," she'd said, as her trademark pearl earrings grazed my ear, cold to the touch. When she pulled away, her eyes locked with mine. "I won't say I wasn't mad you left, and mad at Tom, too. I heard what you did, though," she'd whispered, pointing back at the sputtering walkie-talkie on the table with a heavily ringed hand and then pinching my cheeks. "It's good you went."

"They got the helicopter," Mr. Malgré interrupted from the doorway, his sneer noticeably absent. "Ben Wallace'll move it to the quad when he's patched."

Grammy looked quickly up from me to Mr. Malgré, her pale face darkened with long shadows as she released my cheeks. "You're dismissed, Malgré," she'd snapped, the strained goodwill of our reunion draining out of the room as the walkie-talkie crackled to life.

zcht—No reason to—zcht—Stop them, Cap'n—zcht—Better out than—

Jerking back toward the kitchen table, Grammy clutched the walkie-talkie in her bejeweled hands; fiddling with its dials as if her life depended on it. "It *was* coming in clearer . . ." she'd hissed, slamming the sputtering radio back down on the table in frustration while shooting me an unmistakably accusatory look. " . . . *before.*"

I backed out into the hallway, behind Dad.

"What's going on?" Mom asked, fully recovered from the shock of seeing Grammy like this. "What do you know? We saw the cars. Malgré said you have . . ."

She could barely bring herself to say it.

"*Guests?*" Grammy looked up from the walkie-talkie, smiling sweetly again. "They were making us nervous, Sarah, those federales. After they took you and the others, and then Henry disappeared, too . . ." She jangled her wrists in my direction by way of coy explanation. "Well, some of our bigger boys were nice enough to return the favor."

"But," Mom said, backing nervously out into the hallway with me and Dad. "*Prisoners?*"

"Oh, Sarah, don't be such a prude," Grammy spat, her sweetness instantly gone. "We took some radios and a few cars. We leveled the playing field one tiny bit." *You leveled their power plant*, I thought, but I didn't say anything as the walkie-talkie crackled to life again, its reception clearer with me huddled safely in the hallway.

Repeat—zcht—evacuation in progress—zcht—evacuation in progress—

"Besides," Grammy said, smiling again, "you started something bigger than us. The City's been emptying out since you left so . . . *dramatically*. It sounds like we're gonna have a lot more guests soon, so you better get used to 'em."

⚡ ⚡ ⚡

The Pickers started showing up a few days afterward, true to Grammy's prediction, sun-bleached from their travels and telling stories of freak blizzards and scrambling federales. I was stuck at home, so didn't see them, but I heard news in bits and pieces— as murmurs floating up through the creaking floorboards of my bedroom, my ears pressed against the cool, dark wood. They were flooding into the Grey Zone, more every day.

And not just Pickers, either.

Evacuees from the City proper, and even—if the living room reports could be believed—some federales, like Ben, who I hadn't seen since Mr. Malgré's men carted him off. To be fair, I hadn't seen *anyone* except my parents since we'd left Grammy's house. Instead, I stayed in my room and peeled the protective aluminum covering off of all my old stuff, crumpling it up into an enormous ball that I tossed from hand to glowing hand. Dad came up when he could, trying to piece together everything that happened while he and Mom were federale prisoners. But no matter how many times I told the story, he just couldn't seem to wrap his rational mind around it.

"So, one more time," he'd say, shaking his head in disbelief while counting the impossibilities on his hairy fingers. "Carel the *chef* blew up *their* power plant, and you think he was hired by *Grammy*. And, when the power plant blew up, *you* . . . think you got *its power*?"

I'd just shrug and steeple my fingers. My new game was to touch my fingertips together, building up a charge, and then pull them slowly apart until the connection finally broke, jagged white wires of electricity snapping back into my hands like popped rubber bands. By the fourth or fifth time I tried to explain everything to Dad, I could get my hands about two feet apart before the connection snapped.

Without fail, Mom would call Dad back downstairs before we were done talking. There was always something happening, something she needed consultation on. Most of the time they argued about when the federales were going to recover from Carel's attack and storm the Green Zone, taking us by force. Dwarfing Malgré's impromptu defenses and exacting revenge for our federale prisoners. From what I could hear through the floorboards, they weren't fun conversations . . . but whenever he was called into one, Dad would get up with creaking knees and, pausing in the doorway, say something apologetic like, "We'll get this sorted, kiddo."

I didn't need anybody's apologies, though, and I didn't need sorting.

I was just . . .

I don't know, *restless*.

My entire body was on pins and needles, my muscles flexing and ready to go . . . only, there was nothing to do. Mom had her secret meetings downstairs, and both she and Dad had made it clear that they didn't want me out of the house, not after everything that had happened. I didn't *want* to be separated from them, either . . . but after a few days in my bedroom, I couldn't take it anymore.

Just for something to do, I unplugged every power cord in my room—lights, record player, alarm clock—and watched in quiet wonder as nothing changed. The previously aluminum-wrapped lamps continued to cast tall shadows on the wall; the flickering red time stamp on the alarm clock advanced a minute, and then another. I watched in quiet wonder for a while, and then—bored—picked up Tom's guitar, wrapping buzzing fingers around its dusty neck, and strummed experimentally.

Even unplugged, it shrieked with feedback, and—startled—I tossed it onto my unmade bed.

Mostly, though, I laid on the cool wood floor and eavesdropped while idly spinning an increasingly hot light bulb between my thumb and forefinger, its filament whitening and then melting, leaving the sizzling bulb suddenly dark. Downstairs, the front door slammed shut as one of my parents' "little spies"—Dad's words—was ushered out, then quickly opened again as Mom's voice carried up to the second floor. "He's fine," she'd said. "Still recovering. I'll tell him you came, sweetheart."

I ran to the window, leaving the dying light bulb spinning on the floor as Ava walked dejectedly away, Conor and Ben at her side. Ben's entire shoulder and right arm was wrapped in thick white plaster, but his left was draped around his younger brother's shoulder. I was happy to see them reunited, and wondered how long it had been since they'd last seen each other. Ten years, probably. Maybe even more.

I hadn't seen Ava since she'd run off into the Green, and thought maybe—

But that didn't matter.

She'd come.

I took the stairs five at a time, slipping dangerously in my worn socks and banging against the already battered wall at every landing. "Hank, baby," Mom said, blocking the doorway with a wooden frame stretched with rough canvas. "Do you know what this is?" She'd angled the painting toward me, and it was all I could do to stop myself from barreling through it. Sliding to a stop across the slick wood floors, an excited smile stretched across my cheeks— my first since being home. It was Rachel, her face comprised of a thousand shimmering strokes of color—acrylic smile radiating through darkness of the foyer as if the painting itself was alive.

As if she was trying to tell me something.

"Ava brought this?"

I was so surprised I could barely get the words out. As impossible as it seemed, there was only one place I could think of where she could have gotten it. The foyer lights flickered overhead as the ghost of that morning on the Other Side—when Conor and Ava and I had seen the painting for the first time—came back and shook me by the shoulders, sending goosebumps down my arms.

"*Hank*," Mom said, exasperated, as I made to angle past her toward the door. "I just don't think you're ready to be out there. It's like the Wild West, and you're . . ."

I was in my pajamas still, had been in them for days: a pair of fading flannel boxers and socks that hung loosely around my ankles, the elastic stretched far past the point of no return. As Mom stood in the foyer crinkling her nose at my buzzing chest, I felt self-conscious about my shirtlessness for the first time in days. There was no way to tell her that I liked the way the wood felt against my stomach when I lay pressed against the floor; cold, at first, but somehow connective. Like I could feel the house sighing heavily beneath me as it inhaled my parents' guests and then exhaled them out again, full from their company.

Instead, I just crossed my arms, covering myself as best as I could.

"*You know?*" Mom said in conclusion, never having finished her thought. "We're opening the dam again. Your grandmother *started a war*. Who knows what could happen . . ." As she continued through a list of possible catastrophes, I tried to pin down the last time I'd seen that painting.

We'd left it in Carel's truck!

By all rights, it should still be there, where Carel left it. But instead, it's in front of me, propped casually between Mom's hands as she recounts in grisly detail how the engineer had fallen from the dam that time, totally unexpected, and how those kind of accidents happen all the time. That you can't plan for them, and that's why we call them—

" . . . accidents," Mom said, her voice raising. "Henry Long, are you even listening to me?"

"I love you . . ." I'd said, running back up the stairs as quickly as I'd jumped down them. "But I have to go."

"We're powering up, baby," she'd shouted after me as I flung myself into my bedroom from two well-worn banister knobs. "Anything could happen." I smiled as I pulled a shirt over my head, thrusting my white-hot hands through the holes where my sleeves used to be.

That was exactly what I was counting on.

24

The Hospital had been my idea.

Truthfully, it had been my only way out. All those hours lying in my room, bored—I just thought I was depressed. That the shock of everything that had happened in the City was catching up with me. I hadn't realized I was a prisoner in my own house until I'd gotten back downstairs and Mom was still blocking the door.

"Baby," she'd said, her voice ominously soft. "You can't leave— there are prisoners, strangers. People are *missing*. It's just . . . it's too dangerous."

I met her eye and raised my glowing hand, casting a weak light across the dim foyer, illuminating Rachel's painting, which leaned face-down against the wall behind her. "But," I'd said, the light intensifying alongside my racing pulse. "I can help; I can . . ."

"You can't leave. You're as sick as *they* are," she shouted, startling me into silence. "You're *glowing*, Henry." Her face crumpled up as she backed against the front door and slid slowly down to the floor, collapsing into a pile of tears. "Honey, you're a *battery*," she spat, her strangely shrill words almost lost in her heaving sobs.

The air in the room hung stale between us.

It was the first time I could remember her snapping at me like that; the first time I'd seen her like this. As Dad ran into the foyer and cradled Mom in an all-encompassing hug, I realized that everything had shocked her more than it had me—the City, the explosion, the escape, Grammy and Mr. Malgré.

Me.

And the truth was, she was right.

I am a battery.

Dad shot me an apologetic look as he stroked Mom's head, wiping away her tears. "Stress," he mouthed, and I nodded blankly while slowly inching backward toward the stairs and then—sensing a way out—advancing.

"Hey, Mom," I said, my voice high and conciliatory as I knelt down next to them. "Maybe you're right." She nodded, still sobbing softly in Dad's arms. "Maybe I should go to the doctor, get checked out."

"Dr. Singh can come here; we'll get her," Dad said, shooing me away with a nod toward the stairs. "Henry, buddy, maybe you could give us a minute?"

I was on the second-floor landing, hopeless and dragging my feet, when Mom spoke up. "*No*," she wailed, her voice raw from crying. "Dr. Singh's too busy to make house calls. And Hanky *should* see her, make sure he's okay. Come here, baby," she'd called out, her wide-open arms limp but inviting. I ran back down the stairs and threw myself into her hug, casting all three of our faces in my throbbing white glow. "Be safe, Panky," she'd whispered, her cheek wet against mine.

⚡⚡⚡

I left quickly, squinting my way into the blinding sunlight before they could change their minds. As I was crossing the threshold, Dad offered to bike with me, but Mom caught his wrist, pulling him back into a tight-armed hug. I hadn't realized how rattled she'd been; how fearful she was of being left alone.

"Bye, guys," I'd said shakily, one foot in the dark foyer and one on the front steps outside. "I'll see you soon, okay?"

Dad nodded, smiling tensely with a strong, locked jaw, and turned back to Mom. The last I saw of them before the door slammed behind me was Dad gently stroking her tear-wet hair out of her face and behind her ears.

My bike was still where I'd left it, leaning unlocked against the side of our house, the padding on its ripped seat still wet from the last time it rained. As I mounted it, I felt the wetness spread across the seat of my pants and instantly stood on the pedals, the bike swaying back and forth beneath me as I shredded out across the muddy front lawn toward the Avenue and the Hospital beyond. As I pedaled, I tried not to think about leaving my parents so soon after I'd found them; about Mom crying on the dusty floor of the foyer, and Dad, helpless but still trying so hard to help her.

To bring everything back to the way it was.

And yet, the Green Zone had already changed so much since we'd gotten back just a few short days before. Our house was far enough from the Avenue that I hadn't seen or heard much of it from my dirty bedroom window, but as I pedaled toward the Hospital, it seemed impossible that I'd been so bored just a few minutes before. The streets—which had been desolate upon our return and more or less empty for *years* before that—were streaming with the evacuees I'd heard bits and pieces about through the floorboards.

My eyes darted across the crowd, scanning for familiar faces—Mr. Moonie, leaning casually on his cane, or Mouse's bobbing blonde ponytail. But everyone was focused on a sort of makeshift stage in the distance, their backs toward me. And even with so little to go on, I quickly lost hope of finding anyone I knew. It was obvious that this was a sea of haggard but hopeful strangers—construction workers and Pickers; no khaki shorts in sight. Which meant, I realized, my stomach protesting from a sudden emptiness, that the Green Zoners from the federale newspaper might still be missing.

Still captives.

We got my parents back and lost everyone else, I thought, clenching my handlebars with whitening knuckles.

My gut turned again as silence rippled across the murmuring crowd, drawing my attention toward the source of the shushing. Standing on the raised orange platform of an orange crane, lording above the crowd with a blaring megaphone, was Mr. Malgré. I tried to ignore his grating voice as it reverberated down the tree-lined Avenue, but it was too loud, too all-encompassing to tune out.

"You're poor and you're hungry," he yelled, his jowls quivering with the effort. "But it don't have to be that way." The crowd cheered, shouts of assent rippling down the Avenue like firecrackers. "They stepped on you, and they told you what to do and how to do it. They did the same to us, too." Mr. Malgré chuckled into the megaphone. "Isn't that right, boys?"

The crowd laughed along with Mr. Malgré as I craned my neck to see who he was talking to. Standing behind him on the cherry picker were two of his goons, and wedged between them were three heavily-restrained federales, their ragged suits hanging loosely from their bodies. The gags on their mouths ensured they couldn't respond.

"Mayor Long don't take too kindly to these sorts," Mr. Malgré sermonized to the rapt crowd, obviously swayed by his own rhetoric, and I felt my gorge rising as I remembered Mom weeping on the floor. Despite her own internment in the City, those tears were for the federales Mr. Malgré had taken prisoner as much as they were for me—and I would've shouted to that effect if Grammy hadn't stepped forward from behind the wide-eyed federales and reached for Mr. Malgré's megaphone. "Mayor Long, everybody," Mr Malgré shouted to thunderous applause as he handed it to her, the clicking of her rings against its hard plastic handle magnified ten thousand times across the Green.

Shocked, I turned quickly off of the Avenue and onto a side street, not wanting to hear Grammy betray her own daughter. *So much for the Charter*, I thought cynically, settling onto the bike seat as my hands flared hotly on the handlebars at the thought of Grammy stealing Mom's title. *So much for family*.

I don't know how long it took for the crashing waves of anger to subside; for me to remember what I was supposed to be doing. *Growing pains*, Grammy had said so many times; I'd even heard her say it just now—despite my best efforts to out-pedal her resounding voice—to the gathered crowd, and wondered bitterly how much the Green would have to *grow* to turn into exactly what we were supposed to hate.

Into federales.

The sky was its impossible Mayan blue again, and the trees above were filled with the carefree songs of migratory birds, but there was nothing I wanted to do more than lay down on the recently paved asphalt and wait for the bloodcurdling cheers from the Avenue to pass. For everything to pass. Reacting against my sudden exhaustion, the electricity continued to course through my body, energizing despite my instincts. As another burst of cheers erupted, I stood on the pedals again, a hot wind drying my tear-streaked face.

I could have doubled back to the Avenue and started another storm, washed the Green—*my Green*—of Malgré and his screaming fans. The thought crossed my mind . . . but that's not what I did, as much I wanted to.

The people weren't the problem.

Grammy was.

So I let them have their hateful rally and continued to the Hospital, pedaling so hard and fast that my bike's frame shook beneath me. Not for a checkup, like I'd told my parents, but to follow up on a hunch. Even though Grammy and the federales had killed the Charter with their underhanded machinations, that didn't mean we had to become federales to be free. If Carel was alive like I hoped he was—if it was him who brought back Rachel's painting—he'd understand, and he'd help us take the power back here, too.

Like he did in the City.

He had to. He owed us.

Anxious, adrenalin pumping, I tried to cut through the university quad, where all the reclaimed federale cars had been parked. But in the few days since I'd been there, someone had erected a rough blockade—charred black cars, burnt down to their frames and stacked menacingly across the entrance: all that remained of Malgré's federale spoils, burnt for spite and showmanship.

I knew, as I tried to avoid crashing into the blocked entrance, that I was going too fast.

That, with my newfound strength, I was going faster than humanly possible.

That I wouldn't make it.

As the skinny wheels wobbled under the pressure, then slid out of my control, artlessly tossing me into what would soon be a quivering mass of nasty scraps and fractured bones, I realized I had jinxed myself.

I never should have said I was going to the Hospital for a checkup.

⚡ ⚡ ⚡

The pain was instant and sharp, and I heard myself moaning— as if from a distance—as another megaphone squealed from inside the compound, a voice I didn't recognize running through military-sounding drills.

"*Mount*," it screeched. "*Aim. Hold it.*"

I breathed in deeply, steeling myself for whatever might come next, then cringed in agony as something *tore* in my chest; a fractured rib, I hoped, and nothing worse. Even if it was worse, I couldn't lay there, splayed out on the asphalt, waiting for Malgré to find me. Pulling myself agonizingly up onto loosened fists and bloodied knees, I wiped the gravel out of my hands, one of which hung limply by a swelling wrist. The military drills continued inside the quad, nails on the chalkboard of my throbbing head, and—despite the pain—my hands blazed furiously in response to the braying orders.

Despite the pain, but also . . .

Healing it.

As the power coursed through my broken body, pulsing, I flexed my limp hand, surprised that it was no longer limp, then took a deep, painless breath. Almost imperceptibly, the rest of my wounds closed, leaving fresh pink skin where moments before there had only been dirt and blood. And even *that* had been burned away by the light, leaving almost no evidence of the crash except for a ripped shirt and mangled handlebars.

"Hey," someone shouted roughly from atop the charred barricade as I made my way back to my bike, which had skid a good twenty feet beyond the quad. "You. *Stop!*"

I didn't stop, though.

Without looking back, I sprinted the rest of the distance to my bike and quickly mounted it, shaking my head in amazement as I stood in the pedals and took off toward Dr. Singh, who I realized—screaming triumphantly into the wind—I wouldn't need to be seeing anymore. The wheels, slightly bent from the fall, wobbled unsteadily beneath me . . . but I kept screaming, reveling in my newfound powers for the first time since the explosion, until I was in sight of the Hospital.

The parking lot in front of the Hospital was packed with Pickers, who'd set up a sort of makeshift camp—and it was immediately obvious why Mom said Dr. Singh was too busy to make house calls. Unlike the crowd on the Avenue, these evacuees weren't cheering. Instead, the air was thick with the sound of labored breathing, an almost suffocating colloquy of sickness. Everywhere I looked, sallow faces stared blankly back at me, their skin almost translucent from spending so many years living off of federale waste.

Squeezing through them—apologizing in whispers as I brushed against their brittle bodies—I headed for the lobby, which was also packed. In deference to the sickness, I tiptoed through the Pickers, holding my breath until I made it through two double doors marked "Hospital Staff Only" and into an empty hallway. Exhaling, I gave quiet thanks for my good health—something I'd never done before, especially not in the Hospital—and started searching for Carel.

The first room I checked had four cots, all occupied by cadaverous Pickers. And the second. And the third. Slowly jogging down the hallway, my footsteps resonating against the dirty white tiles, I checked every room; they were all the same, with no sign of Carel anywhere. *He's dead, of course he's dead*, I'd thought, the hopelessness of the Hospital weighing down on me so heavily that I felt short of breath. With so many sick people and Grammy starting wars, it was no wonder Mom was crying on the floor.

You should have stayed with her.

You shouldn't have come.

That's when I started running, quickly checking the rooms as I passed them, even though I was increasingly sure that Carel wouldn't be there; that I was stupid to think he might be. I picked up speed, careening around corners in search of an exit that I just couldn't seem to find. And still, even after I'd given up, Rachel's self-portrait nagged at the back of my mind. We'd definitely left it behind in our hasty exit from the City, and there was no other way it would have gotten back to the Green Zone.

To my house . . .

"*Oh,*" Dr. Singh exclaimed in surprise, looking up from her charts just in time for me to literally run right into her. "Henry!"

25

"D r. S-Singh," I stutter, startled back into the present. "I was, um . . . looking for you?"

She nods, staring clinically at my hands. "Yes, I'd heard you were back," she says, flipping a page on her charts. "Interesting development, Mr. Long." She licks the tip of her ballpoint pen, then starts writing. I'd gotten so used to it that I barely pay it any mind now, but as the scratches of her pen echo through the empty hallway, I notice the fluorescent lights flickering overhead.

"Fascinating," Dr. Singh says, tapping her pen against her teeth, coolly professional in the face of my strangeness. "And how do you feel, Henry?"

"Hold that thought," she says, cutting me off just as I start to answer; pointing with her pen to the flickering overheads, she quickly walks away. "Probably best," she calls over her shoulder, already halfway to down the hallway, "to do this in the x-ray room. Don't want to finish anyone off, do you?"

Jogging after her, I'm sheepishly aware of the haywire buzzing following me to the lead-lined room, where Dr. Singh waits for me, a thermometer ready in her hand. I'm tempted to tell her that I'm not here for a checkup, that I'm probably invincible now, but she looks like she hasn't slept in days and I don't have the heart. Instead, I start to tell her that I'm fine—that she should focus on the Pickers—but as soon as I open my mouth to dissuade her, she shoves the thermometer beneath my tongue.

"So," Dr. Singh says, gesturing toward my hands with her pen. "How'd this happen?"

"Actually, I'm okay," I say, the thermometer slipping out of my mouth and onto the floor. Pursing her lips in disbelief, she drops the contaminated thermometer into one of her lab coat's voluminous pockets. On the counter behind her is a glass jar filled with more thermometers and neon blue disinfectant; she takes a new one out of the jar and shakes it dry before I have a chance to explain.

"So, wait," she says, positioning the new thermometer against the soft underside of my tongue. "You came to the Hospital because you feel *fine?*"

⚡ ⚡ ⚡

Twenty minutes later, Dr. Singh walks me back to the waiting room with a clean bill of health. "A good diagnosis, Dr. Long," she says by way of goodbye. "You *do* seem fine. *Good*, even . . . Maybe don't come back too soon, though," she whispers conspiratorially. "We only have one generator—can't have you blowing it up."

I laugh nervously, not sure if she's referring to the flickering lights or if she thinks I had something to do with the explosion in the City; that I'm responsible for these legions of sickly Pickers. I leave without finding out, tiptoeing quickly back to my bike through the wan-faced crowd; wondering what my next move should be.

Now that everything's changed, though, the real question is whether my next move is going to be what I think it *should* be, or if it's going to be what I *want* it to be. Because I *should* go home to my parents before they start to worry and let them know that Dr. Singh said I'm okay; tell them everything I saw on the Avenue: Mr. Malgré taunting the prisoners, Grammy stepping in as Mayor.

But they already know all that.

Mom almost said as much when she was blocking the door, trying to make me understand how important it was to stay inside.

Still, it *should* be easy to just go home. Dr. Singh said she hadn't seen anyone fitting Carel's description, and that's why I left my house in the first place. She'd squeezed my wrist when I described how I'd left him, but the last bullet wound she treated was Ben's, she'd said—pointing to an x-ray of his shattered shoulder on the wall—and before that, the last one had been Before.

And yet . . .

I start pedaling to Conor's house, guessing that he and Ben are still with Ava—that they can put me back in the loop, that we can find Carel together. But there's no way they're still in the Green Zone, I realize, not now that it's turned into what I saw this afternoon. Changing direction, I find myself following the bend in the river; coasting in smooth, wide arcs through the bigger estates of the Green and into the more spottily paved Grey, the fading orange machinery of abandoned construction sites becoming less and less frequent as my resolve grows. Just because we left the Other Side with the federales doesn't mean they still have it, and if Carel's alive, of course he'll already be there with Conor and Ben, and maybe—hopefully—Ava.

With *everyone*.

I try not to get my hopes up, but I can't help but think that if Mr. Moonie and the rest of them made it back, they'll have headed for the Other Side, too. Especially if they'd caught wind of

Mr. Malgré's power grab in the Green . . . and with Malgré giving amplified speeches in the middle of the Avenue, I don't see how they could miss it.

My stomach growls with a sudden anticipation. I haven't eaten much of anything for days. Even if he's feeling better, Carel probably won't be behind the counter of Food Eats . . . but it'll be open all the same, with a few familiar Other Siders, haggard but alive, propping up the elbow-worn Formica counters, eating mounds of steaming biscuits smothered in salted butter and drinking coffee so black it stains your tongue. That is, if Grammy hasn't shut it down.

It has to be open, I reassure myself, mouth watering hungrily at the thought. *People have to eat.*

My bike glides so smoothly that it feels like it's pedaling itself, like I'm being pulled—effortlessly—by the prospect of a hot meal and familiar faces. I just wish Mom and Dad were here to see the Grey. While there were a lot of strangers on the Avenue kowtowing to Mr. Malgré and . . . *her*, there are scores more here—Pickers who weren't so sick after all, and federale refugees, all setting up camp on overgrown front lawns while they clear out the ruins. It's what my parents have always wanted, ever since the Tragedies: Greening the Grey, like Before. It's still early days, but if Dr. Singh can help those Pickers crowding the Hospital, it's not hard to imagine the Grey Zone filling out like an actual neighborhood again, full of families and—

I wave at a rag-tag group of evacuees as I pass them, the glow from my hand streaking beside me like a low-flying comet, and their happy shouts follow me as I turn onto the far end of the main drag, where hundreds of flags and banners flap lethargically from dormant telephone poles and riotously-painted houses, unfazed by the federales. A dog barks faintly in the distance, heralding my approach, and I smile.

It's Julia.

After that terrible night in the truck, I'd recognize her bark anywhere.

Unlikely as it seems, a crowd of people are grouped together at the far end of the street like some sort of welcoming committee, and I realize that either those cheering evacuees recognized me from the City, or I was expected, with news of my approach somehow preceding my arrival.

It makes sense, I think. If my parents have "little spies," why wouldn't the Other Siders? It could have been Dr. Singh—she knew I was looking for Carel, although . . . if she was an anti-Malgré operative, she could have just told me where he was rather than play dumb.

Still . . . like everyone else in the Zone, I'm sure she had her reasons.

As I shield my eyes with the hand I may or may not have temporarily broken earlier in the day, a warm glow of wellbeing spreads across my already buzzing body. They're hard to make out, but I spot Tom, and I think I see Rachel as well. Ben's white plaster cast stands out amidst the crowd, and it looks like Ava and Conor on either side of him. Behind them, as red and rusty as the day I first saw it, is Carel's truck. They're all waving and shouting, and I'm grinning so hard I feel it in my ears. As I get nearer, I start waving back, prompting more cheers to break out for the returning hero.

"*I made it,*" I shout.

It's only when Julia's barking turns manic and then—reaching a crescendo alongside the whooping and hollering of Tom and Rachel and the rest of the group—stops abruptly as she scampers, whimpering, to hide beneath Carel's truck, that I realize they're not cheering for me.

They're white-faced and screaming.

Terrified.

Judging from the collective tilt of their necks, whatever they're warning me about is behind me, and it's big. I take my feet off the pedals, dragging the rubber soles of my shoes across the broken pavement until I come to a skidding stop about thirty feet from my welcoming committee. Pausing before I turn to face the terror, I let the bike clatter to the ground and take a deep breath as a flock of S-necked egrets take off into the distance from the banks of the darkening river beyond the Other Side.

For one long moment, I wish I was one of them.

That's when the pressure drops, leaving me cold despite my sizzling heat. Shivering, I take one last look at my friends. They're all there, like before the federales came: Tom and Rachel and even Moonie. Ben, still staring skyward, mouths, "*You have* got *to be kidding me*," as I catch Ava's widening eyes.

"Henry!" she shouts, her voice swallowed by a sudden gust of wind as the sky churns ominously above us. "*Run!*"

My calves spasm instinctively, ready to sprint for cover—but, squinting at Ava through the first slashing drops of rain, I stand my ground. Listening. In the distance, barely audible above the rain and wind, is a familiar whirring. Helicopters cutting through the storm. The muscles in my legs flex again, the tension rippling up my back and neck.

Federales.

All at once, the rain starts in earnest, the sky opening up as if on cue to blasts of crashing thunder. Still, nobody moves—not me, and not my "welcoming committee." They're immediately drenched, so wet they're not even bothering to shield themselves, and stock-still . . . staring as the rain evaporates three feet above my head, unable to penetrate the waves of heat radiating from my pulsing core.

Flexing my fingers, I feel the power surge, cords of white hot electricity crackling across my palms and up my goosebumped arms. We've been through too much to run, all of us—my parents, the Other Siders . . . the entire Zone. We've come too far to give everything up, to the federales or Malgré or *anyone*.

I've come too far.

Whatever happens, I think, watching Moonie unsheathe his sword before I turn slowly around, clenching my fists into wildly pulsing orbs of cold white light; smiling. *We're all in this together.*

THE END